Praise for Haywood Smith

"Liberal doses of humor!"   —*Booklist* on *Ladies of the Lake*

"Smith's fizzy exploration of enduring friendship and family signals more changes ahead for Georgia, her family, and the red hat matrons. Fans of the series will enjoy and look forward to the next."
—*Publishers Weekly* on *Wedding Belles*

"This is a wonderful story filled with love, laughter, and a family. . . . This book is a winner."   —*Night Owl Romance Reviews* on *Ladies of the Lake*

"Haywood Smith's brilliant new novel *Wedding Belles* hits all the right notes because of its authentic Southern voice but will satisfy readers everywhere because of its heartfelt message for mothers, daughters, and yes, even mothers-in-law. Smith is hilarious and wise. It's perfect for book clubs."
—Dorothea Benton Frank, author of *Lowcountry Summer*, on *Wedding Belles*

"A joyous, joyful ode."   —*Booklist* on *The Red Hat Club*

"I absolutely loved this book and can't wait to share it."
—Cassandra King, author of *Queen of Broken Hearts*, on *Wedding Belles*

"Haywood Smith knows what the readers want, and doesn't hold back."
—*A Romance Review* on *Ladies of the Lake*

"A tribute to women who emerged victorious through divorce, menopause, spreading waistlines, and other tribulations."
—*Chicago Tribune* on *The Red Hat Club*

"It's hard to keep good women down, as *The Red Hat Club*'s bestseller status proves."   —*Publishers Weekly* on *The Red Hat Club Rides Again*

Ladies of the Lake

Ladies of the Lake

· · · · · · ·

HAYWOOD SMITH

ST. MARTIN'S GRIFFIN ❦ NEW YORK

LADIES OF THE LAKE. Copyright © 2009 by Haywood Smith. All rights reserved. Printed in the United States of America. For information, address St. Martin's Press, 175 Fifth Avenue, New York, N.Y. 10010.

www.stmartins.com

The Library of Congress has cataloged the hardcover edition as follows:

Smith, Haywood, 1949–
    Ladies of the lake / Haywood Smith. — 1st ed.
        p. cm.
    ISBN 978-0-312-31695-2
    1. Sisters—Fiction. 2. Georgia—Fiction. 3. Domestic fiction. I. Title.
    PS3569.M53728L33 2009
    813'.54—dc22

                                                        2009016205

            ISBN 978-0-312-99078-7 (trade paperback)

            10 9 8 7 6 5 4 3 2

For my precious sisters, Betsy, Elise, and

precious Susan, who are all far too kind and

well adjusted to provide food for fiction

· Acknowledgments ·

THIS BOOK IS for all the sisters in the world, good, bad, and indifferent.

The Good Lord has blessed me with many things, most of all, a wonderful family. Among them are my three precious sisters and brother, all of whom are far too normal and well adjusted to provide sufficient conflict for a novel, so the sisters in this book are cobbled together from my imagination and recollections of others I've observed in my long life, with only a few amusing quirks borrowed from my own. Both my grandmothers were wonderful people—again, too kind and genteel to provide material for the colorful character of Cissy, who was inspired by all those daring flappers of the Lost Generation.

The five of us Pritchett kids spent many precious summers at "Lakemont," and though I am no dancer and never have been, I did borrow liberally from my wonderful memories of my maternal great-grandmother and her house at Lake Rabun.

Another great blessing in my life have been my loyal and patient editor and publishers at St. Martin's Press, Jennifer Enderlin, Matthew

Shear, and Sally Richardson, and my wonderful agent, Mel Berger. Thanks to you all for believing in me and making my dreams a reality, one book at a time.

Special thanks, too, go to the people who've helped make it possible for me to keep writing: my wonderful assistant and friend, Ambar, whose spreadsheets, prayers, and shared devotionals help keep me sane and out of trouble with the IRS; Dr. Susan Tanner of Spherios in Roswell, Georgia, my holistic internist who referred me to Dr. Donald Dennis, ENT, in Atlanta, who diagnosed my immune problems and fungal arthritis. Mold-proofing my house and adjusting my diet hasn't been easy (I'm allergic to everything but lobster and rhubarb), but words aren't adequate to express my gratitude for Dr. Dennis's generosity and wisdom that have finally, finally freed me from pain after all these years. It's a miracle. I don't even have to take Advil anymore.

Thanks, too, to endocrinologist Judson Black in Atlanta for helping sort out my squirrely pituitary issues.

A huge thank-you goes to my wonderful friend Debbie McGeorge for always "getting it," and being game to drop everything and go play every once in a while. I prayed for a friend, and you're God's answer, clear evidence that He has great taste. Thanks, too, for your sharp, smiley eyes, encouragement, and support for my books.

Thanks, too, to my friend Doug Jackson, whose avid reading, intelligent conversation, and book reviews keep me up on what's good, bad, and indifferent in the book market and the world in general. Thanks for the breakfasts at the diner and the lunches at Golden Corral, Doug. And thanks for being my friend.

To my wonderful friend Roslyn Carlyle, I love ya, girl, and I hope I'm half as amusing as you are when I get to be twenty-eight like you. You are so brave.

As always, thanks go to Georgia Romance Writers for putting up with a scatterbrain like me. As I tell my son, I'm so busy keeping up with what's not real that I don't do so well with what is, but my fellow writers love me anyway.

Thanks, too, to Deborah Smith, Sandra Chastain, and Debra Dixon of Belle Books for publishing my fun little handbook, *The Twelve Sacred Traditions of Magnificent Mothers-in-Law*.

My life is never boring, and God keeps giving me new experiences to share. When I got bitten by a rabid raccoon in my driveway last April, I was able to see the humor in the situation and use it in this book. I haven't figured out how to use the two bat colonies in the walls, but it'll come to me.

Last but not least, thanks to all my wonderful readers who've bought my books and spread the word to their friends, and/or e-mailed me at haywood100@aol.com to let me know they like my work. We writers need encouragement, and my readers are so kind. God bless you all. For those who find fault with my books, I throw myself on your mercy and ask only that you keep it to yourselves. Health insurance ain't cheap when you're self-employed and decrepit.

For those of you who are Internet active, check out my Web site at haywoodsmith.net for upcoming appearances and book news.

Watch for my next novel in the fall of 2010, currently titled *Waking Up in Dixie*, a fun, uplifiting twist on the age-old midlife crisis.

Ladies of the Lake

· 1 ·

There's nothing wrong with this family that a funeral or two wouldn't fix.
—MY PATERNAL GRANNY MAMA LOU

....

*J*HAVE SOME family secrets to tell, but first, I need to make one
thing crystal clear: With two glaring exceptions, my mother is a
true Southern lady of infinite grace and discriminating taste.

The first exception—and by far the least—is the fact that as soon as the
four of us girls were safely on our own, Mama moved to a double-wide in
Clearwater, Florida, where in short order she married, then buried, two
"diamonds in the rough" who smoked cigars. Good men, but phew. Only
recently did she find the second great love of her life besides Daddy: retired rabbi David Rabinowitz, who loves her back just as much as our
sainted daddy did.

The second, and worst, exception is that Mama (who hated being
named Daisy) broke her own vow to give her daughters normal names
and succumbed to the centuries-old tradition of christening all female
descendants of our direct ancestor Lady Rose Hamilton with floral
names. Mama said she wasn't afraid of the ancient "unlucky in love"
curse that's supposed to fall on nonfloral daughters, but Daddy, romantic

that he was, loved the idea of siring his own little bouquet, so Mama finally gave in, sparing herself the infamy of breaking the chain of ages. Her only rebellion was naming me, the firstborn girl, Dahlia instead of Rose.

Frankly, I would have preferred Rose. Weird names like mine made me fair game for the Susans and Patricias and Nancys and Cathys of my era. Not to mention the fact that I still have to spell out Dahlia for everybody.

I was unlucky in love, too, so maybe there's something to that curse, after all.

Two years after I was born, feisty, colicky Iris arrived. After another two years, we were blessed with precious Violet, an angel-child from her first breath. I was eight before placid baby Rose was born and Mama made her nod to the woman who started the whole tradition back in England.

We've forgiven Mama for our names, but Mama hasn't been able to forgive our grandmother for her shortcomings, which were many, as you shall see.

My three sisters and I had the privilege of growing up in Atlanta during that golden illusion of domestic innocence between World War II and the sixties. For us, magic was real and had a name: Lake Clare. We didn't know and didn't care that the lake was Old Atlanta's premier summer watering hole, its rustic homes handed down from generation to generation, among them our great-grandparents' impressive three-story Hilltop Lodge and Mama's tiny Cardinal Cottage. We only knew we loved spending our summers in the little log cabin just down the hill from our beloved great-grandmother and our black-sheep grandmother Cissy (short for Narcissus), who was so vain she never let anybody—even Mama—call her anything but Cissy.

We never suspected how much Mama hated it at the lake, or why. All we knew was that there, in the cool beauty of the mountains, we could go barefoot, drink café au lait instead of milk with our eggs and bacon, and spend our days swimming and exploring and playing. And, in Iris's and my case, fighting. We were so busy, we never suspected the secrets that hid in the shadows of Hilltop.

. . . .

THE LAST TIME my sister Violet and I saw Cissy was two years ago, and she was trying to kill us—and enjoying herself immensely.

But that was Cissy for you. She never had been anybody's idea of a grandmother—or a mother, for that matter.

It was just before Christmas, and Violet and I were on our regular holiday run up to Lake Clare, bearing gifts and a perky little decorated tree along with the food we and my other two sisters took turns delivering every month. Normally, Violet and I really look forward to our December drive from her place in Clarkesville to the northeast corner of the state. We both love the bare-bones splendor of the mountains in winter, and the trip provided welcome escape from the pressures of the season and a chance to visit.

But this time, an unexpected Canadian Clipper had barreled down on us, sending the temperature plunging in the cold, hard drizzle. By the time I picked her up and got back onto Highway 441, the Bank of Habersham sign said 31 degrees, and the pine trees were already bowing slightly under a coating of freezing rain.

"I should have let you drive," I fretted, slowing down to fifty. There wasn't much tread left on my ten-year-old Mercury Sable's tires, but the home-building crisis had put a serious dent into my developer husband's income and his ego, so I'd used the car maintenance fund to buy him a new golf club for Christmas to cheer him up. "These tires are okay for regular driving, but not ice."

"Nothing's okay for ice," Violet said without alarm. "But we'll be fine. WSB said it wasn't going below freezing, even up here." As always, her blue eyes and soft expression radiated calm and reassurance.

It took a lot more than the prospect of running off the road to ruffle Violet. Of the four of us Barrett sisters, she was the most stable and well-rounded.

"Oh, gosh." Violet delved into her huge purse. "I almost forgot to call Cissy." We were nearing the fringes of the cellular network, and it wouldn't do to arrive unannounced in our grandmother's isolated mountain realm. Even when we called ahead, there was no guarantee what we'd find when we got there.

After dialing, Violet stuck her finger in her ear (we all have midrange nerve deafness) and waited, then hollered, "Cissy? Hello? Cissy!" She frowned at the phone and muttered, "Still plenty of signal. She just hung up."

Our grandmother Cissy was almost as hard of hearing as she was crazy, so even the special amplified phone we'd gotten her didn't make communicating much easier. You have to pay attention to the other person for it to help, something Cissy never had mastered.

Violet dialed again, waited, then hollered hello again. After a brief pause, she brightened. "Hi! It's Violet! We're on our way with your groceries!" Pause. "Violet! Your granddaughter!" Her soft alto voice wasn't made for yelling. "No, Daisy is my mother! I'm Violet!" She gave the thumbs-up (Cissy had remembered Mama, at least), but she crossed her eyes at me when she did it, which made me laugh. "Dahlia and I have your groceries!" Pause. "Dahlia! Your granddaughter Dahlia! We're coming with the groceries!" A sigh of resignation and renewed volume. "We're on our way with the groceries! Your groceries are coming today!" Her lips folded briefly. "No, we're bringing groceries to *you!*"

The routine was so familiar, I could hardly keep my tickle box from tumping over, which would only set Violet off, too.

Violet enunciated every word emphatically. "We . . . are . . . bringing . . . your . . . groceries . . . today!" She frowned, then gave up and flipped the phone shut. "Boy, that wears me out. I have no idea if she ever connected with what I was saying before she hung up on me."

Based on experience, things wouldn't be much easier when we got there, even though Cissy seemed to be having a fairly good day. I mean, she'd remembered Mama, which was something.

Beside the road, pine saplings were bent double now. I gripped the steering wheel. "Let's get her the food and get back home ASAP."

"Works for me," Violet said.

Thirty minutes later, I was relieved to turn off the slick pavement onto the rough tar and gravel road that led over the mountain to the family compound where we'd spent our summers as children. The way was steep, but offered a lot more traction than the highway's slick blacktop. It took us another twenty minutes to navigate the cutbacks up and down the other side, but at last we reached the single-lane dirt road at the edge of Cissy's fifty-three acres, and scraped our way through ice-laden rhododendrons and mountain laurels down to the turnaround at Hilltop Lodge.

"Let's take the stuff to the side door, so it won't get wet," Violet said as we broke out the umbrellas and hurried to unload.

Nobody ever used the side entrance on the verandah, but there was no protection from the elements at the kitchen door, so I agreed. I didn't hear Foxy (Cissy's mangy old red mongrel that she insisted was at least half fox), but the dog was as deaf and ancient as she was, so I didn't think anything of it.

Worried that a huge branch might break off and kill one of us any second, we skirted the thick laurel hedge that shielded the little vegetable garden and the kitchen door, then carefully picked our way up the mossy flight of native quartz stairs to the verandah.

Built in 1919 from virgin timber as a hunting lodge, the rambling old three-story place had sunk and sagged till it seemed to have grown up out of the sodden drifts of leaves like a giant mushroom fantasy, with thick moss on the log walls and curling shingles. Down the slope of the orchard beyond, Lake Clare lay shrouded in mist like a Turner painting.

I put down the gifts and groceries on the ancient wicker settee, then turned to gaze across the lake and breathe of the cold, clear air, mold be damned. No other place on earth had the power to calm me like this one.

Sending me half out of my skin, Violet shattered the quiet with an ear-piercing rendition of the distinctive five-note whistle that had been our family's summons for generations.

"Violet!" I scolded, heart pounding. "You scared me half to death."

She just smiled her graceful little smile, but I knew her calm façade hid a streak of mischief a mile wide.

We listened for some sign of life inside, but there was none.

Violet whistled again, but this time, I was prepared.

After the brief echo died, we heard nothing but the rain and the ominous creak of ice-coated branches from the surrounding forest.

I jumped at the crack of a breaking branch in the big hemlock by the kitchen, but when I whirled toward the sound, there was only the soft whuff, whuff, whuff, *whump* as it fell through the foliage to the ground.

"She's probably holed up under the electric blanket," Violet said. "I can't blame her." The screen door was hooked, so we picked up our umbrellas and headed back out into the rain toward the kitchen door.

When we got there, we found its screen hooked from the inside, too, so we circled around to the terrace. Violet and I both peered into the sliding glass doors that made up the corner of the master bedroom—a sixties renovation the Captain and Cissy had made that included a sunken tub (the only one in the whole house) overlooking the terrace, the verandah, and the path to Mama's now-derelict guest cottage. Amid the piles of old magazines, clothes, newspapers, and junk, Cissy's unmade bed was empty except for the black plastic mesh hair protector she wore to keep her French twist in place as she slept. She was a dead ringer for Queen Nefertiti with it on.

The sunken tub was full, a film across the cloudy, hard well water.

"Uh-oh," Violet said. "Her boots are gone." Summer, winter, rain or shine, Cissy wore those bright green rubber barn boots whenever she went out.

I checked the pegs by the hall door. The rest of her "uniform"—a tall-crowned, floppy denim hat stuffed with newspapers to keep it from coming down over her face and the Captain's WWII trench coat and wool army trousers—was missing, too. "Oh, lord. She's gone out in this weather." I scowled. "Perfect. We'll have to call Mountain Patrol to bring the search dogs." Again. So much for getting home before dark.

It never occurred to Violet or me that this time, something might have actually happened to Cissy. As our other grandmother was wont to say about people as difficult as Cissy, "The Good Lord wouldn't have her, and the devil's gettin' too much use out of her to kill her."

The Mountain Patrol had to be getting sick of finding Cissy when she got lost (which was often), but she was so fiercely determined to live out her last days in her own home that even the authorities didn't want to mess with her. They'd tried carting her off to a nursing home once, but she'd escaped three times in less than a week, leaving rampant destruction in her wake. So they, like us, left her pretty much alone, except for the visiting nurses, who—thanks solely to her—had the highest turnover rate in the state. Maybe even the whole Southeast.

"She might have just gone to get the mail," Violet suggested. "Let's check the boathouse." Which was where the postal boat delivered.

Wary of falling ice and debris, we headed down that way.

"Damn." I scowled when we found no sign of her there. God forbid, we should have to spend the night in Hilltop with the mildew and the fleas and who knew what else. And if we had an ice storm, there was no telling when we'd escape. I shuddered at the prospect, but at least we'd brought a HoneyBaked Ham we could eat without fear of ptomaine. "Crap, crap, crap. We'll have to call the patrol."

"At least we know she hasn't been gone long," Violet said. "She answered the phone when we called. Let's look awhile longer."

We were almost back to the house when the first shot went off.

At first, we both thought a tree had snapped, so we frantically scanned the oaks and white pines overhead to see which way to run.

Only when the second shot blew a huge hole in the furled rhododendrons not three feet from Violet's shoulder did I realize what was happening. But sound plays tricks on the steep slopes beside the lake, and I couldn't tell where it had come from.

"Run!" Violet shrieked, dropping her red umbrella in the path as she took off for the neglected orchard's open spaces.

Hearing the click of reloading nearby, I dropped my umbrella, too, and launched myself toward my sister, barely catching her raincoat in time to drag her down into the vinca minor beside me. "Stay down."

It never even occurred to me that it might be somebody besides Cissy shooting at us. A crack shot, she had hunted with Hemingway in Africa and taught us all how to use and clean a shotgun. Even with cataracts and arthritis, she posed a very real threat.

"Head for the basement," I whispered to Violet. It was hidden from the yard by an overgrown hedge that offered the closest cover, and the doors hadn't been lockable in decades.

When the third shot blew Violet's umbrella to bits, showering us with red nylon confetti, we screamed and flinched in unison, then made a break for the hedge.

"We got rid of all her guns," Violet panted out as we cowered behind the ancient tractor stashed behind the hedge. "We both went over every square inch of that house. Where did she get this one? Nobody in the county would be stupid enough to sell her one!"

"I don't know," I snapped, in mortal terror for my life. "Maybe Santa Claus gave it to her."

Another blast sent my umbrella soaring, sieved with holes. "Hah!" Cissy crowed from somewhere nearby. "Got the other one!"

Better my forty-five-dollar Brookstone umbrella than me. My son thought I was an old stick-in-the-mud, but he'd miss me if I was gone. And he'd be mortified to have to tell everybody his great-grandmother had killed me.

I peered gingerly over the tractor and was hugely relieved to see no sign of Cissy, so Violet and I picked our way over to the only pair of functional French doors that led into the basement, and tried to pull one open. When we did, ice cracked and fell from the wisteria and honeysuckle that covered it, so we retreated back to the tractor.

Then we heard a rustle from the woods, followed by heavy steps treading up the path toward the house.

"Vile rapists!" Cissy's voice rang out. "My womanhood is all I have left for them to take, but they shall not have it, my Captain." Our step-grandfather the Captain had been dead for fifteen years. "I know I sought the ideal lover many times before we met," she went on dramatically. (She did everything dramatically.) "We both dipped our oars into many a lake of passion, but all that's over now." I heard her start up the stone stairs, followed by the click of Foxy's labored pace behind. "It was war. But my chamber of treasures opens to no one but you now, my darling. No one but you." She started toward the side door.

Gripping each other's hands, Violet and I pressed ourselves hard against the stone foundation under the verandah so she couldn't see us.

Several steps onto the floorboards, Cissy halted, and I heard her open the breech, slide in two more shells, then snap it shut. "Filthy rapists. I'll kill every man-jack of them if I must, but I shall not be defiled."

Her steps came closer above us, then stopped directly overhead. "Here, now! What's this?"

Violet and I both winced and tightened our hold on each other, expecting the worst.

Cissy's strident tones abruptly became almost dainty. "Presents. How lovely. Look, Foxy. Santa Claus has been here." A rustle of wrapping paper. "From Violet. From Dahlia. Who the hell are they?" More rustling. "From Iris and Rose." Her voice sharpened. "What, they're too cheap to get me a gift apiece?" Another rustle. "Rose. Rose." There was recognition in the way she said it. "That child is the spitting image of my mother, Foxy, only she lacks backbone. Isn't she a nurse or something?"—no, a preschool director—"I do believe she is, a talent she undoubtedly got from me—all those years in the Red Cross, you know." Just as abruptly, she became suspicious again. "They weren't so picky about official training back then. The government's absolutely destroyed individual liberty in this country. It's those industrialist whores, the Republicans, who did it. Ike, indeed! Rapists, all of them."

After a hard thump, we heard cans rolling on the verandah and the sound of something being dragged. "Foxy, no," Cissy ordered. "Put that ham back!" So much for safe eating. "Obey me, cur!" She swatted at her pet, who sounded a feral growl that made me wonder if she really might be part fox after all.

After a brief scuffle, we heard tinfoil ripping, then the smack of meat on the boards. "There. That should tide you over till supper. Come." Cissy's boot steps schlepped toward the French doors to the two-story living room. "Let's bring these presents in, then clean our gun. Only the basest sort would put a gun away dirty."

The phrase took me straight back to pistol practice and skeet-shooting sessions in the orchard with Cissy that were our rite of passage from childhood to adolescence. "Every woman should know how to handle guns, dear," she had confided to each of us in turn. "Men find it incredibly sexy."

Mama had been horrified, but Daddy had said learning gun safety was a good thing. I'll bet he never dreamed we'd end up being her targets.

Cissy's voice grew fainter as she went inside. "Can you believe they just dropped these boxes at our doorstep like a bastard child in a wash-basket?" She clumped to open the side door. After a plink and skreek of rusty screen-door spring, she came back out. "They didn't even bother to ring the doorbell or let me know they were here," she fumed as she started moving things inside. "Not so much as a hello. Probably those sneaky Christians. I am nobody's charity case. Thank the Buddha and the Great Creator for Transcendental Meditation, that's all I can say. Without it, those sneaky Christians would drive me insane."

A pause.

"What do you mean, the grandchildren, Captain?" Pause. "Oh, they did, did they? The little ingrates. It's why I'm glad I never had any more children of my own. No respect for their elders. And I'll bet one of those presents is another cursed cotton nightgown. Same thing every year, underwear and coarse cotton nightgowns I wouldn't inflict on the maid. I've got a chest full of those wretched things upstairs, but they're not the ones I like. I've told them a hundred times, I like the nylon Madame Lillie peignoirs and the Madelaine silk-knit tap pants with six-inch legs, but do they ever listen? No."

Never mind that those hadn't been made for a generation.

"Should we make a run for it?" Violet whispered tightly as Cissy continued her delusional conversation in and out of the door with small loads from the boxes.

"Not yet," I breathed into her ear. Cissy was so deaf, we could have spoken normally without fear of being overheard, but both of us were too rattled from being hunted. "She still has the shotgun. Let's wait till she closes up and goes to her room. Then we can sneak across the path and cut through the woods to the car."

A bolt of adrenaline sent me groping for keys in the pocket of my coat, but they were there, thank God. "Whew!"

"Double whew," Violet said in a more conversational tone.

It seemed like hours, but was probably only about ten minutes before we heard Cissy retreat to her room.

With painstaking care, we crept back out into the freezing rain, made our way to the path, sprinted across its ten-foot span into the woods, then beat it for the car. I clicked open the doors, and we jumped in. Then I started the engine and threw the car into reverse, backing out with such force that I didn't realize I hadn't taken off the emergency brake till I whipped into the turnaround at the blackberry patch, and the smell of burning rubber caught up with us. With tingling fingers, I reached for the release and popped the hood instead. "Oh, damn!"

"Don't panic," Violet said. "Put your foot on the brakes and take a deep breath. I'll get out and close it. Deep breaths."

I did as ordered, managing to find the proper release and pull. Violet got back in and away we barreled, heedless of the branches lashing at my car as we bounced up the rutted road toward safety. Halfway up the hill, we both burst into a hysterical mix of laughter and tears.

"Can you believe that? Can you?" Violet asked. "She really tried to kill us!"

Jouncing and lurching, I pleaded, "Oh, please, don't make me laugh. I'll wet myself."

"Merry Christmas!" Violet said, hilarious.

"No, really, don't," I said, wracking my memory for the nearest restroom and remembering that the one at the River Road convenience store had holes in the floor and smelled of sewage.

"Under the circumstances, inappropriate laughter is perfectly understandable," Violet said. "It releases the tension." As dean of women's athletics in her little college, she counseled lots of her students, but I was in no mood to be counseled.

"Don't give me that psycho-pop lala. Cissy really, truly tried to kill us. We need to call somebody. Have something done. She's dangerous. Next time, she might kill one of the nurses. Really."

Violet sobered. "Who do we tell? Mountain Patrol? They don't have a SWAT team."

"Nobody said anything about a SWAT team." We reached the tar and gravel road, and I increased my speed to a reckless thirty. "But somebody has to do something."

"Maybe we should do what Rose suggested and have State Game and Fish dart her for real," Violet said. Our baby sister Rose was a certified angel, but she had a wicked sense of humor underneath.

"That would be perfect except for the fact that sedatives make Cissy psychotic," I reminded her. "Extremely intelligent and psychotic, or have you forgotten the Ativan incident at the nursing home? Or the time she climbed naked out on the ledge at the hospital after her breast cancer surgery?"

"This really isn't a police matter," Violet said. "It's mental health."

"Yeah, well, call it what you will, I don't want anybody to get killed dealing with it, not even Cissy. We'll phone the sheriff from the convenience store on River Road." Holes in the floor or not, I'd have to use the bathroom there.

A thought occurred to me. "Maybe Iris might have an idea what to do." Iris loved telling people what to do, under the guise of concern. "I mean, I certainly don't want to take responsibility for what might happen. The more, the merrier," I suggested.

Usually, that was Iris's corporate-minded modus operandi, not mine.

Normally, Violet backed me up a hundred percent, but this time, she shook her head. "Honey, this is a job for the sheriff. He gets paid to handle things like this, so let's let him."

I tried to convince her otherwise all the way to the convenience store, but even though she validated my point of view, she wasn't persuaded.

So we called the sheriff, who spoke with us personally and told us not to worry, he'd take care of it, then insisted we go back home before the roads iced up. I made him promise to call and tell us what happened, which he did.

Three hours later as I neared the Perimeter in Atlanta, my cell phone rang, displaying a Clayton exchange.

"Hello?"

"Mrs. Cooper?"

"Yes. Is this the sheriff?"

"One and the same. Everything's fine." He sounded almost offhand. "We contacted a friend of hers on the lake, and he went over and talked her out of the gun and ammunition, so everything's back to status quo."

I was horrified. "You sent a civilian into harm's way with an armed crazywoman?"

He just laughed. "Well, technically, he's a deputy, and your grandmother sets great stock in him. It was his gun; apparently, your grandmother snuck over to his place and took it. He's promised to keep his arms under lock and key from now on, and make sure she's unarmed before y'all come up for your regular visits."

"But—"

"I'm sorry, but I've got another urgent call coming in," he said. "Y'all have a merry Christmas, and don't hesitate to call if you need any more help with Miss Cissy. Bye, now."

I hung up, never dreaming it would be two years before I got back up to the lake, or that I'd be divorced and alone.

· 2 ·

Things ain't the way they used to be. Fact of business bein', they never was.
—HORACE HANSON, PROPRIETOR, HANSON'S BOATHOUSE

Cardinal Cottage, Lake Clare. June 1960

*N*APTIME WAS SACRED at Lake Clare on weekdays when all the daddies were back working in Atlanta. From one to three every afternoon, everybody took to their beds for two hours of peace and quiet, including the mamas.

When I was ten, there was nothing better in the world than swimming all morning, followed by sandwiches made from Great-grandmother's home-grown tomatoes and washed down with cold, creamy Nantahala milk at lunch, then peeling out of my clammy bathing suit to settle naked between warm, age-softened sheets in the top bunk for a good long read. July flies sang our lullabies in the towering poplar above the tin roof of Cardinal Cottage, but in the bottom bunk my six-year-old sister Violet never lasted long enough to hear them. Her straight, silky hair permanently askew with child sweat, she fell asleep like a stone the minute she hit the bed, worn out from playing with all her might. Bless her heart, little Vi did everything with all her might, including loving me, from the moment she was born.

My next-younger sister Iris was another matter altogether. She'd come into this world taking everything personally, including me. Don't ask me why. If anybody should have been upset, it should have been me. After all, I'd had Mama and Daddy to myself those first two years. But Iris had been a grumpy baby who'd grown into a grumpy second-grader who considered it her mission in life to get on my nerves and contradict me.

Some people, you just can't please.

That particular Tuesday afternoon late in June, I was asleep with my copy of *The Good Earth* on my chest, happily dreaming of O-Lan and Wang Lung's rise in fortune, when Iris's voice intruded with, "Wake up. Naptime was over half an hour ago. It's time to go swimming. I want to play battle."

She always wanted to play battle, which gave her the excuse to splash me. She liked any game that gave her a chance to do me bodily harm, like Swing the Statue or tag.

I glared at her through a slitted eye. "Leave me alone. Play with Vi." If I went right back to sleep, I could recapture my dream. I turned my back to her, poking myself in the chest with the corner of my book. "Ow. Go away."

"No. Mama said to get you up, or you'd never go to sleep tonight," Iris ordered, smug as ever at the chance to tell me what to do.

The journey from my dreams to reality had always been a long, hard one. I stretched, letting out a long moan of protest, then opened my eyes to stare at the rough pine beams and decking above me.

Iris poked me, hard. "Come on."

I swatted her hand. "Stop it."

"Mama," Iris called, her expression sly. "Dahlia hit me!"

Fortunately, Mama didn't respond.

Back home on our street in Collier Hills, Iris had plenty of friends to keep her occupied, but at Lake Clare, the four of us only had each other to play with, and Iris's idea of fun didn't exactly mesh with mine. I liked reading and playing prima ballerina and Barbie and Nancy Drew and chess, while Iris preferred house and store. Bor-ing.

"I'm just the middle child," she whined for the thousandth time since she'd overheard Mama talking to Daddy about an article on birth order in *The Saturday Evening Post*. "Nobody ever pays any attention to me. It's always Dahlia, the firstborn. Dahlia, the *star*. Dahlia, Miss Perfect and Brilliant. Everybody ignores me."

As always, she knew exactly how to push my buttons. "Like it's my fault?" I responded, compulsively driven to be justified. "Can I help it if I'm good at ballet? I worked very hard to get that way." I took the usual shot back at her. "Would you be happier if I was lazy and made Cs like you?"

"Mama," Iris tattled, "Dahlia said I was lazy!"

Lying there, I forced myself to count to ten to keep from smacking her again.

Then I heard the familiar thump, thump, thump of my grandmother's walking stick approach from the orchard, and I sat up with a happy, "Cissy!"

Cissy never came down from Hilltop without a reason, and the reason always had to do with me. Except for criticizing Iris's swaybacked posture, she rarely paid any attention to the others—a fact that I probably should have felt guilty about, but didn't.

It wasn't easy being a prodigy. I had almost nothing in common with any of the other kids I knew, especially Iris, who hated reading as much as I loved it, and resented my ballet lessons, but didn't want to dance, herself. The fact was, she didn't want to work at anything; she just wanted to complain about me.

I leapt out of bed and raced past Iris to meet my grandmother at the door.

I didn't run out to hug her. Unlike Great-grandmother, Cissy wasn't the kind of person you could hug. But I knew she loved me, anyway, because she took me seriously and paid attention to me, even if she was gruff about it.

Posture still erect from her long-ago career as a prima ballerina, Cissy glided in without bothering to knock, as usual, as if she were queen of the whole lake, including our house. "Good afternoon, Dahlia," she said, glancing past me to the living room. "Where's your mother?"

"*Je ne sais pas*," I said with the perfect Parisian accent she'd drilled into me since I was four. "*Je viens de me lever.*" (I don't know. I just got up.) I topped it off with a perfect pirouette, earning a glimmer of stern approval, which was the only kind of approval anybody ever got from Cissy, making it precious, indeed.

"Daisy?" she trilled dramatically. As I said, Cissy always did every-thing dramatically, which would have been enough to make me love her, even if I hadn't always been her pet.

Mama came in from the front porch, carrying two-year-old Rose on her hip. Violet followed close behind, wide-eyed, to cling to Mama's long, full cotton skirt as if Cissy were the big, bad wolf instead of our grand-mother. "Yes?" Mama said, her expression guarded.

"I'd like to have Dahlia spend the night," Cissy told her. "That sweet Lenny Bernstein sent me a rough cut of the movie they made from his Romeo and Juliet musical, and the Captain's oiling up the projector. I'll send her back home after her French and ballet lessons in the morning."

"*West Side Story?*" I gasped out. Cissy had always said she knew Leon-ard Bernstein, but I'd thought she was just exaggerating, as usual.

Everybody in my ballet classes back home had been talking about *West Side Story* since it had debuted on Broadway, dying for the movie to come out so we could see it. "You really know Leonard Bernstein?" I asked in awe.

"Of course," Cissy clipped out. "I've told you often enough. Didn't you believe me?"

Monumentally impressed, I stared at her with new respect. "Wow. Leonard Bernstein." All my friends would be green with envy.

"I helped him get his start," she went on. "Such a bright young man, even if he does like the boys a bit too much."

"Cissy!" Mama scolded, shooting a warning glance my way.

"Well, it's a fact of life in the arts," Cissy dismissed. "Do you mean for her to be ignorant about such things? She's going to be a prima ballerina one day. She might as well know the truth."

"Not now," Mama scolded. "And not from you."

Unrepentant, Cissy turned her attention back to me. "Get your things. We can do an art project while the Captain finishes setting up."

I looked to Mama, knowing better than to accept without permission. "*Pleeeze,*" I wheedled, worried by the grim set of her mouth.

Mama shifted Rose, who curled into her shoulder for protection from Cissy's disturbing presence. "Iris might like to see it, too," she said to Cissy. "Did it even occur to you to invite her?"

"Mama," I moaned, "Iris hates ballet. And she never can sit still. She'll ruin everything."

"Iris," Mama called across the cabin. "Would you like to spend the night with Cissy and watch *West Side Story* with Dahlia?"

Iris skulked into the doorway from the screened porch. "What's *West Side Story*?"

"It's a ballet movie," I told her, praying for the reaction I got.

Iris glowered. "I hate ballet."

"Well, it's really more of a musical," Mama coaxed.

Iris wasn't persuaded. "I hate musicals."

I couldn't conceal my relief. "See? I told you she wouldn't want to." I did two pirouettes.

Seeing my delight, Iris went sly. "You know," she said to Mama, her eyes locked on me with grim satisfaction. "Dahlia stole three cigarettes from your purse, Mama, and smoked them in the woods."

"Dahlia!" Mama gasped out. "Is this true?"

Damn! I'd be grounded for life!

Blindsided by such unprovoked—and accurate—treason, I launched at Iris in fury. "You little bitch! I can't believe you spied on me! And told Mama!" I grabbed a hank of her curly brown hair and gave it a ferocious yank. "I'll teach you to tattle-tale, dog dammit!"

"Maamaa!" she yelled, genuinely scared by my reckless reaction. "Help! She's gonna kill me!"

I could have sworn Cissy was trying not to laugh, but Mama was anything but amused. "Dahlia! Let go of your sister this instant!" She shoved Rose at Violet, then headed our way to break it up. But I was so furious at Iris for ruining my chance to see *West Side Story* that I started slapping at her and cussing with all my might, consequences be damned.

Ever allergic to conflict, little Rose started to wail, and Vi patted her in consolation even as she grimaced to witness my self-destruction.

But Iris, eyes alight to see me digging myself in so deep, dodged the blows and laughed at me. Laughed! Which made me so furious, my string of cusswords dissolved into gibberish, making me even madder.

"Dahlia! Stop it!" Mama grabbed my forearms from behind and pinned me hard against her, lifting me off my feet. Kicking at my sister as Mama dragged me out of range, I vowed revenge, but even that came out garbled.

Meanwhile, Cissy just took it all in with a mildly amused expression.

"Dahlia!" Mama's arms tightened around me. "Calm down, honey. Stop. Breathe."

Mortified, I went limp and started to cry.

Mama subsided into the wicker armchair, drawing me into her lap. "That's it. Just take deep breaths."

"Yeah," Iris goaded, "like the ones you took when you inhaled those cigarettes."

"That's enough from you, young lady," Mama scolded her. "Go to your room!"

"Me?" Iris protested. "She's the one who stole your cigarettes and smoked!"

"And she'll have consequences to deal with for that," Mama said. "Just like you will for spying and tattling on your sister." She pointed toward the bedroom Iris shared with Rose on the other side of the cabin. "Now go. And don't you stick that lip out at me."

Iris stomped away.

Drained, I closed my eyes and accepted the fact that I would probably be stuck in the house doing chores for the rest of the summer.

"And you," Mama said to me, "you could have set the whole woods on fire. Why did you take my cigarettes and smoke them?"

"I just wanted to know what they tasted like," I said dully, which was at least partially true. The fact was, I'd wanted to act grown, like Cyd Charisse, and I'd enjoyed every menthol-soaked molecule.

"One puff would have told you that," Mama responded. "Three whole cigarettes is a pattern, and a dangerous one. Not to mention the fact that you took them."

I'd figured I could get away with it, since Mama smoked at least a pack a day—all our parents did, back then—but I hadn't taken my spying, sneaky grease-spot of a sister into account. "I'm sorry," I said, genuinely regretful that I'd been caught. "I won't do it again."

Not till I was at least sixteen, anyway. Or maybe twelve.

Mama let out a short, hard sigh. "All right. Back to your room. And no swimming or trips to Hilltop for the next week. You can stay here and help me with the chores."

Only a week? My heart rallied. I'd expected at least a month.

"A week?" Cissy said, reminding us both of her presence. "Isn't that a bit severe? The child's inquisitive. Children experiment with such things. It's only natural."

Mama stiffened, her features congealed. "Not my children."

Uh-oh. I shot Cissy a pleading look, willing her not to make things worse by taking up for me. "It's okay, Cissy, really. I deserve it."

Mama patted me, then urged me to my feet. "Off you go, then. I'll call you when it's time for KP." She stood to face Cissy. "A week, Mother. I mean it."

It was the first and last time I ever heard her address Cissy that way, and my grandmother actually flinched when she did it.

"Very well."

That night when Mama came in to hear my prayers, she insisted I ask God to bless Iris, too.

"But Mama, it won't count," I argued. "God knows I don't mean it."

"The Bible says to pray for those who despitefully use you," she countered, "so you must always pray for Iris. It isn't easy for her, being your little sister, you know. You're a pretty hard act to follow. She feels like everybody's disappointed in her compared to you."

I sighed. "But all she has to do is tell people she's herself, not me."

Mama kissed my hand. "To whom much is given, much is expected. I'm counting on you to be kind to your little sister, even when she's not kind to you."

"Okay," I said. "But I won't like it."

"Just do it," Mama told me. "In time, your heart will follow your actions."

I tried, really I did. Forty years later, I was still trying, and Iris was still driving me nuts.

· 3 ·

There's nothing like a death and a dollar bill to tear up a family.
—MY WONDERFUL FRIEND ROSLYN CARLYLE

The present. The second Tuesday in April, 9:00 A.M. Habersham Road
. . . .

*A*NOTHER BIRTHDAY. I'D never paid much attention to the numbers, but this particular one seemed a whole lot older than the last. Felt that way, at least.

I was worn out from two years of trying to make ends meet since my husband Harrison had hocked our house for more than it was worth and embezzled millions, then fled with his Barbie-doll secretary to a tropical paradise with no extradition treaty. Worst of all, he'd bribed our eighteen-year-old son into dropping out and going with him—halfway around the globe, in another damned hemisphere.

Granted, things hadn't been great between us for a long time, but it had never occurred to me that Harrison would steal, much less steal our son. But two years with Divorce Anonymous had made me face the fact that my husband had been stealing Junior from me ever since the boy had realized he could go to Daddy for a *yes* whenever Mama said *no*.

Even so, I'd done my best to be the responsible parent, providing boundaries and consequences and decent values. Harrison, on the other hand, had been the fun one whose motto was "boys will be boys." Always overruling me, he'd spoiled Junior rotten, overlooked his failing grades, given him a fast car and let him drink beer at sixteen, paid all his speeding tickets, and hired a lawyer to get him off on two DUIs. But the cruelest cut had come after the alimony stopped and Junior wearied of living on a shoestring with strict, boring old Mom. So he'd informed me he was moving to Paridalla where his dad had gotten him a beachfront condo in the same building with him and *Brandi*, who treated him like an adult. Translate: didn't make him go to school or get a job, and let him do whatever he wanted, including smoke pot, which was legal there, along with God knows what else.

Who could compete with that?

Junior's defection had left a hole bigger than the Holland Tunnel in what was left of my heart, and even after more than a year of "detachment with love" and "letting go and letting God," the cold wind of that betrayal blew through me afresh as I faced turning a year older on this chill, gray morning.

My son, my son. That was what I wanted for my birthday. I wanted my son back.

Well . . . not exactly.

What I really wanted was the precious five-year-old who'd cupped my cheeks and gazed at me in adoration, telling me I was the best mama in the whole, wide world. Not the selfish college dropout who'd left me to face destitution alone because he was sick of pinching pennies and hearing people "bad-mouth" his Dad (never mind that Dad was a fleeing felon and everything they—never I—said was true) and Junior wanted to have *fun*.

I wanted my little boy. But life doesn't work that way. My little boy had become the prodigal, living with the pigs (my ex and his girlfriend).

I wanted some alimony, too, but had just about the same chance of getting it.

So for the second birthday since The Exodus, as I called it, I woke to an empty house and an empty heart.

As a present to myself, I decided to sleep for another half-hour, but before I dropped back off, the phone rang, jarring me awake.

My sister Violet's name appeared above her number on the caller ID. "Hullo," I mumbled out.

"Happy birthday, honey," she said with conviction. "I sure am glad you were born."

"Thanks. I'm glad you were born, too." I yawned hugely and stretched in my king-sized bed, which—like the house I loved—was way too big for just me.

"How are you planning to celebrate?" she asked.

"I wasn't. This one's depressing. Seriously depressing biggie." Sixty. This could not be.

Violet remained cheerful. "Malarky. Nobody would ever guess how old you really are. Thanks to Daddy's Viking genes, you look ten years younger."

Genes we shared, along with our sister Rose. "Only ten years younger?" My mind was barely thirty. We won't discuss my ballet-abused body.

"Be glad for that," she said, direct as always. "Did you get my card?"

"Not yet." She always found really funny ones, and since the divorce, included a modest check, which was all she could afford. Small colleges like hers didn't pay well, even to their deans of men's and women's athletics, positions she and her husband Taylor had held for the past five years.

Call waiting beeped on my end, showing "out of area." "Could you hang on a sec? I've got another call. Maybe it's Junior." I could always hope, even though he'd only called me four times in almost two years.

"Hello?"

A man's voice said, "This is Lieutenant Howard Poole of the Mountain Patrol. I'm trying to reach a Dahlia Cooper." His somber tone spoke volumes.

Mountain Patrol. Cissy?

"This is she."

"Mrs. Cooper, I regret to inform you that your grandmother, Mrs. Howell, has died. Please accept my condolences."

Cissy.

"Oh." When Great-grandmother had died, I'd felt as if the world had ended. It really had ended when I was fifteen and the aneurysm took Daddy. But oddly, I felt no sense of loss about Cissy, just guilt for not having gone to see her since the divorce. Fiercely independent despite her failing health and memory, she'd refused to leave Hilltop or let anyone stay with her there. And without any alimony, I'd been working so hard to pay the mortgage that I'd kept putting off going to see her.

I should have gone. Should have made time, no matter what it cost me. Now she was gone, but I couldn't believe it, not really. "What happened?" I heard myself asking, dazed.

There was a pregnant pause, then, "A neighbor out fishing found her floating in the lake. She had on an old trench coat"—the Captain's, from World War II—"that held enough air above the belt in back to keep her floating, but her feet were weighted down with rubber boots,"—the green ones she always wore with six pairs of socks—"and a denim stovepipe hat stuffed with newspapers kept her facedown." Thanks to the leather thong she tied it with.

"That's what she wears every day for her morning walk." Wore. "How could she drown? She hasn't been in the lake for years."

"Judging from the tracks, she walked around the cove to a point opposite her boathouse, then bent to look at something in the water and toppled in. The bottom drops off pretty steeply there," he said. "The man who found her tried to revive her, but she was already cold. We don't suspect foul play."

She must have looked like a sea turtle, drifting in the frigid water. Drama queen that she was, it seemed appropriate, somehow, that Cissy would end her solitary life in the lake she loved.

Even if she'd fallen in on purpose, a sharp inner whisper suggested.

If she couldn't live on her own terms, she might very well have decided not to live at all. But that, I kept to myself.

"There's one more thing," the officer said. "Her dog." Foxy. "It looked pretty bad, so one of the guys took it to the vet in town, who said it was so eaten up with cancer, he'd like to put it down."

Poor Foxy. Cissy hadn't been able to put her out of her misery. "It's for the best, I'm sure. I'll pay for it."

That took care of Foxy, but what about Cissy? There are things to be done when someone dies, and I was good at getting things done. "What about the arrangements for my grandmother?" I asked. "She was a member of the Georgia Cremation Society."

"I'm afraid that will have to wait," the officer said. "Under the circumstances, there'll have to be an autopsy. Just a formality."

"Of course." Cissy's high-handed manner with the locals had made her unpopular, but nobody had hated her enough to kill her. Frankly, they were too superstitious to do anything worse than cut her boat loose occasionally.

My phone beeped in again. Violet. I'd completely forgotten she was holding. "Officer, could you please hold a moment? I was talking to my sister when you—"

"I'll let you go," he said. "The coroner's office will contact you with the autopsy results. Feel free to call them if you have any questions. Good-bye."

"Thanks." I clicked over to Violet.

"Was it Junior?" she asked in a tone that told me she knew it wasn't.

"No," I said. "It was the Mountain Patrol. Cissy drowned." Even saying it, it still didn't seem real.

She reacted with the same sense of disbelief I had. "Drowned? How?"

"They think she bent over to look at something and just fell in. She had on the Captain's old trench coat and those big green boots. They must have weighed her down."

"Who found her?" Vi asked.

"Some fisherman. He tried CPR, but she was gone."

"Good."

I did a double take. "Did you just say, *good?*"

"That I did. Cissy was failing badly. She hardly made any sense when I talked to her last week, but when I told her I was coming up to check on her, she had a conniption and absolutely forbade it. For her sake, I'm glad she went quickly."

Maybe that was why I hadn't felt any grief. "You've got a point. But drowning?"

"The water can't be over forty degrees at this time of year," Vi said, flat-footed as ever. "Her heart probably stopped when she fell in."

"The autopsy will tell."

"Do you need me to go up there and take care of anything?" she asked. "I can." Clarkesville was fifty miles closer to Lake Clare than Atlanta, but Vi had classes.

"No. She'd already made arrangements to be cremated, but that will have to wait for the autopsy and the coroner's verdict."

"Did she have a will?"

"Yes. Her lawyer's Mr. Johnson in Clayton, but she made it perfectly clear that she's leaving everything to the Dalai Lama for a Buddhist retreat, so I don't see any reason for us to make a trip just to hear the bad news."

Vi didn't mince words. "She knew how hard up you were. She should have at least left you a little land to sell."

"It was hers to do with as she pleased, Vi," I reminded her. "Lord knows, she scrimped enough for all those years to keep that land intact while she was paying for my ballet training. That was a lot." Never mind that she treated the rest of my sisters like redheaded stepchildren.

After a pregnant pause, Vi begrudged, "Maybe so, but she should have helped you out now, at least a little." Knowing how uncomfortable such talk made me, she shifted the subject. "So what happens now?"

"I guess I'll call Mama." Not that Mama would be upset. She'd long since buried Cissy emotionally for making no secret of Mama's illegitimate birth and dumping her on Great-grandmother and Poppy Jack, then sending her to boarding school at five. When it came to love, Cissy had reserved hers for a succession of lovers and husbands.

"Why don't you let me call her?" Vi offered. "The birthday girl shouldn't have to tell anybody their mama died."

I let out a huge sigh of relief. "Thanks. I really appreciate that."

"This is your day," Vi consoled me. "Try not to think about Cissy. Use my birthday check to take a friend out to lunch someplace nice."

"In case you've forgotten, I don't have any friends anymore. Poverty isn't popular in Buckhead, it seems. I think they think it's contagious. Same with divorcées."

"Ask Rose to come, then. Her assistant can look after the preschool."

Our sweet baby sister would probably drop everything and do it, but . . . "Lord, then I'd never hear the end of it from Iris." Rose and Iris had been joined at the hip since Iris could pick her up, and I wasn't about to spend my birthday money getting indigestion from Iris.

"Take Rose anyway. Iris'll get over it." I heard her start the car. "I'll call and tell them about Cissy, too. Try to forget all this and take it easy."

As if I could. I had heaps of laundry to do, then ballet classes to teach from two till ten. "Thanks, sweetie. And thanks for calling the others."

"You're welcome."

After a rebelliously long bath and breakfast, I went to the mailbox and found cards from Mama, Rose, Iris, and Vi. And a letter from the mortgage company, to whom I owed four payments, thanks to a plumbing disaster that had used up the last of my credit and emptied my scant reserves.

I looked at the evil envelope. Might as well get the bad news over with first.

I opened it to read: "Dear Mrs. Cooper: We regret to inform you that we cannot issue any further grace periods and must institute foreclosure proceedings on your property. Though your ex-husband may indeed have forged your signature on the loan documents, our representative acted in good faith, and your legal recourse lies with your ex-husband, not our company. Again, it is with deep regret that we must take this action in the interest of our shareholders." Blah, blah, blah.

I looked up the gentle slope to the azaleas blooming in my perfect gardens surrounding my perfect Georgian house. Happy birthday, Dahlia. Your grandmother drowned, and you're going to lose your home, the last thing left of your marriage.

I opened Vi's card next, which would have been funny under other circumstances, and found a check for a hundred dollars with *Splurge* scrawled across the *For:* line. Mama sent a check, too, for fifty. So did Rose, God bless her. Iris just sent a card that reminded me I'd always be older than she was, to which she'd added *two years* with an exclamation point.

For a fleeting moment, I envied Cissy for being beyond the mortal cares of this world.

Then I went for a manicure and pedicure, followed by lunch at the Ritz Carlton in Buckhead, where I toasted Cissy with a glass of Evian and enjoyed myself immensely one last time before I got packed off to the homeless shelter.

So there.

. . . .

THE CORONER RULED Cissy's death accidental. The autopsy showed her heart stopped with her first gasp of frigid water, so she probably didn't even fight, just fell in and gave up the ghost.

I still had my suspicions, but it served no purpose to dwell on them. And I still didn't feel like she was really gone.

As for the will, my sister Iris had been adamant that we be there together to get the bad news, and when Iris insisted on something, you might as well give in, because she'd drive you nuts with endless phone calls and wheedling till you agreed. Despite all the super-sweet, touchy-feely noises she made, she sure was pushy.

It made no sense that she was always so obsessive about getting us together. Every time, she ended up with her nose out of joint—usually about something I did or said that she took personally, adding it to her lifelong list of grievances with my name on them. But some perverse compulsion kept her doing it. Maybe she hoped things would be different, but that would require some change on Iris's behalf, which wasn't likely after more than half a century.

She wasn't a bad person, really. Lots of people—especially Rose—loved her to pieces. But when it came to me, Iris was one big booby trap, loaded with sugar-coated resentment.

As crisis junkie of the family, Iris was going to love the reading of the will. Plenty of feelings to "share" when we got confirmation that our grandmother had donated her estate as a Buddhist retreat.

The members of the Lake Clare Association were going to *love* that.

My grandmother's land was worth a fortune, but I was going to lose the one thing I had left from my marriage: my beloved home. And I was having to use up a whole tank of gas to go hear it.

So a week after Cissy drowned, I headed for Clarkesville at the crack of early in Queenie (my trusty 1995 Mercury Sable, named Madam Queen—Queenie for short—after Sapphire's mother on *Amos and Andy*, a character I'd loved as a child) to pick up Violet on my way to the reading of the will in Clayton. Traffic was so light that, even though we took the old road for nostalgia's sake, we ended up approaching Clayton half an hour before our appointment with Cissy's lawyer.

When we got to the city limits, Violet pointed to a sign posted in the yard of a stone cottage on my side of the road. "Slow down. I want to see what that says." She started rummaging for her trifocals in the huge purse she carried.

I pulled over by the sign and read aloud, "RABIES NOTICE." I scanned the smaller type beneath. "Oh, for cryin' out loud. It says they've had twenty documented cases of rabies since the first of the year, and there's a ten-dollar vaccination clinic for pets this Saturday at City Hall."

Vi stopped rummaging and tucked her chin in alarm. "Great for the pets, but what about the *people*?"

I chuckled, speeding back up to the thirty-five mile an hour limit. "They don't give people rabies shots . . . unless you're a dogcatcher or a vet, or something bites you."

Vi shook her head. "Well, honey, if I was gonna spend any time up here, you can bet I'd want a rabies shot."

"Lucky for you, you won't have to."

Little did I know.

Three blocks farther on, the trees gave way to town—a decidedly upscale version of the sleepy mountain hamlet we'd visited as children.

Vi pointed to a worn sign that said HORATIO J. JOHNSON, ATTORNEY AT LAW in front of a little stone bungalow ahead. "There it is." She checked her watch and frowned. "We're half an hour early. If we go in now, he's liable to charge the estate for the extra time till the others get here, and you know they'll be late."

Rose's chronic tardiness with friends and family—often resulting from her inability to pass up a flea market or garage sale—was the sole manifestation of passive aggression in her sweet, enigmatic nature.

"I think the Dalai Lama can afford to pay for the time," I said, "but I know the lawyer won't start without the others, so why don't we do some window-shopping?" Never mind that I didn't have a cent of cash or credit to spare. My birthday money was long gone.

A spark of the old mischief flashed in Vi's blue eyes. "Let's shock the others and be even later than they are." She motioned to Clayton's renovated storefronts. "We can see the lawyer's from one end to the other, so we'll know when they get here. C'mon," she wheedled. "Let them wonder where the heck we are, for a change." With a flourish, she turned off her cell phone—a cardinal sin to Iris.

The prospect of giving my tardy sisters a taste of their own medicine overrode both my manners and my punctual nature. "Okay. Let's do it." I turned off my cell phone, too, then found a parking spot on the old main drag.

My "little" sister Violet unfolded from Queenie like a graceful white egret, stretching out her long, muscular legs that were still athletic as a thirty-something's, thanks to her years of coaching women's basketball before she got kicked upstairs as dean of women's athletics.

I got out and stretched, too, standing even with her five eleven, my dancer's body ropier than hers, but both our bustlines still high and proud, even though I had to bend almost upside down to coax mine into my supersupport bra. Not bad, for a couple of old broads. We happily browsed away more than an hour till we saw Iris's huge, gas-guzzling SUV pull into the lawyer's at the top of the hill.

"They're here," Vi said. She looked at her watch. "It's a new record. One full hour late for our appointment."

I got out my keys. "I'd say better late than never, but considering what we're about to hear, *never* sounds pretty good."

On our way to my car, it struck me afresh that I hadn't been to see Cissy in two whole years. I'd been so caught up in my own problems that I'd abandoned her, just as surely as Cissy had abandoned Mama at the lake with Great-grandmother and Poppy Jack so she could go right back to dancing and living the bohemian life in Paris.

Served me right, not to inherit anything but bills and funeral expenses.

As always, Vi read me like a book. "Ah-ah," she chided gently as we got in. "I know that faraway frown. None of that guilt. Lord knows, Cissy never felt guilty, even when she should have. She'd be the first one to tell you to get over it and move on."

Even as a little girl, I'd always been afraid that a just and wrathful God would punish me for accepting Cissy's blatant favoritism by letting me end up being just like her. "Please tell me I'm not like Cissy," I pleaded for the millionth time.

Vi gave my leg a reassuring pat. "Trust me, ballet and book-learning were the only things y'all had in common. Cissy was the most selfish person I ever met. You're wonderful, a fabulous wife and mother, just like Mama was to us."

"So fabulous that Harrison deserted me, then coerced Junior into doing the same thing."

She gave my arm a squeeze. "Honey, it's all gonna be okay. Teenagers are selfish. Junior hated school and having a curfew. Harrison played into that, the scumbag. It wasn't you Junior left, it was house rules and accountability and responsibility. But one day, he'll come to his senses. He'll grow up eventually."

"Not with Harrison as his only role model," I said. Boys will be boys, and so will men.

Deep down, I knew that God would take care of me. I still had a lot to be thankful for. I had my faith. And Mama and my sisters. And my health, such as it was. And my ballet school was doing as well as any ballet school in Atlanta could.

If I lost the house, I lost the house. It would hurt, but I'd survive. Nothing could hurt as bad as my son's defection, and I'd survived that.

I could always move in with Rose for a while, if I had to. Or Iris, perish the thought, who'd love to get her CPA fingers into the minute details of my existence, especially my finances.

By force of will, I silently thanked God for my life, just the way it was, then pulled into the lawyer's and parked. "Time to go get the bad news."

*W*E BREEZED INTO the lawyer's without a word of explanation. The gray-haired receptionist motioned toward the open door of his cramped office. "Mr. Johnson and the others are expecting you."

Rose and Iris twisted in their chairs. "Oh, thank God!" Iris said at the sight of us, leaping to all five feet one of her short, fluffy self.

The plump little old man behind the desk rose immediately with a smile, showing no hint of irritation as we entered. "Welcome, ladies." His classic three-piece suit was subtly expensive, his white hair and personal grooming immaculate.

Iris threw her arms around me, pinning mine. "When y'all didn't answer your cell phones," she said against my chest, "we were sure you'd been in a wreck or something." The bear hug lasted past concern and into control. "I told Mr. Johnson, y'all are *never* late."

"Mrs. Cooper," he acknowledged to me. "Mrs. Hansell," to Vi. Clearly, he knew who was who, but how? "Please make yourselves comfortable."

He motioned to the two empty chairs beside Rose and Iris, prompting my sister to let me go.

Mr. Johnson made sure we were settled before subsiding into his chair, where he put a pair of pince-nez onto the bridge of his nose, a charmingly archaic affectation.

He was so nice, I felt compelled to say, "So sorry we were all so late."

His deep green eyes went merry in contrast to his professional decorum. "Think nothing of it. In the fifty years I had the privilege of representing your grandmother, I grew quite accustomed to accommodating her unpredictable schedule. Especially near the end, may God rest her soul." He gestured to a heaped in-box. "I always have plenty of work to keep me busy while I wait."

He sobered in deference to our reason for meeting and shifted a thick folder to the center of the desk. "Is everyone comfortable?" When we nodded, he opened the file. "Then we'll proceed.

"First, I'd like to ask if any of you were aware that your grandmother's cancer had metastasized extensively in the past few months."

"No," I rasped out. She'd been clear for so long after her double mastectomy, I'd taken it for granted.

I should have gone to see her! *Made* the time.

"She came to terms with the fact that she was dying," he reassured us, "but she made me promise not to say anything till after she was gone. I thought knowing might make it a little easier to let her go. She softened in her last few weeks, even made her peace with God in Christ."

"Cissy?" we all said in shocked unison.

"But she was a die-hard Buddhist," I blurted out. "I tried to witness to her countless times, but Cissy just said she *had* been born again, to Transcendental Meditation."

"Which is valid, too," Iris snipped, her liberal universal-salvation Episcopal sensibilities ruffled.

Mr. Johnson turned to me, radiating affection for Cissy. "If Cissy was anything, she was unpredictable. And seriously spiritual, however misdirected that might have been over the years. But she came full circle in the end."

For the first time since hearing of her death, I had to choke back tears, but they were tears of relief to know her soul had come home at last. "Thank you. That means the world to me."

Mr. Johnson opened the file before him and took out what looked like a deed and dropped the first bombshell. "Before we get to your grandmother's estate, your mother has asked me to inform you that she has deeded Cardinal Cottage and her acre of lakefront property, fee simple, to all of you in equal measure."

We all did a double take. "What?"

Great-grandmother had given Mama the cottage as a wedding gift, but I thought Mama had sold it to Mrs. Pendergrass after Daddy died. We all did.

"Didn't Mrs. Pendergrass buy it?" Rose asked.

"Actually, no," he corrected. "In exchange for Cissy's maintaining and paying the taxes on the cottage, your mother allowed her to lease it out to Mrs. Pendergrass, who didn't want anyone to know she was just renting, so we all kept that under our hats."

I couldn't help wondering what else Cissy hadn't told us. And Mama.

"Why didn't Mama *tell* us she still owned it?" Iris demanded, indignant, as if Mr. Johnson were responsible.

Rose raised a finger. "The fact is, she chose not to. More importantly, she's just given it to us, which is very generous. I think we can all be happy about that."

"Speak for yourself," Iris grumbled, sulking about not being in the loop. "All those spiders." She shuddered, phobic—probably because I'd tortured her with daddy longlegs every summer. "And scorpions in our shoes. And *snakes* in all the wisteria. Yuk."

"Well, I loved it there," I said. "Still do." Despite the mold and mildew, to which I was violently allergic. But as the oldest (and Cissy's pet) I had the most happy memories of our summers at the cottage.

"Unfortunately," Mr. Johnson said, "during the last big storm a few weeks ago, a huge branch fell from that giant poplar over the cabin and pretty much destroyed the back two-thirds of the place. But the lot alone is worth about seven hundred thousand."

Cardinal Cottage, destroyed? My heart twisted even as the practical side of me was calculating. One-fourth of seven hundred thousand was a lot, but still not nearly enough to pay off the mortgage.

The others digressed into a hopeless din of second-guessing and crosstalk about the cottage and the land it sat on.

Mr. Johnson let us go on for a bit, then looked pointedly at the clock and asked loud enough to be heard over our voices, "Perhaps you ladies might like to discuss this after we dispense with the will. I'd hate for you to end up stuck in gridlock getting back to Atlanta this afternoon." A polite way of asking us to put a sock in it.

Mr. Johnson took two regular envelopes from the file and handed them to me. One had my name inscribed in Cissy's still-strong hand, the other, Mama's. "Your grandmother asked me to give these to you and your mother."

None for the others. One last display of favoritism. Cissy might have gotten saved, but she was still Cissy.

Embarrassed, I tucked the letters into my purse, then promptly forgot them when Mr. Johnson dropped another bombshell with, "Your mother has also asked me to inform you that she has legally given up any claim to your grandmother's estate. She's fully aware of the terms of the will, but made this decision of her own free will, for reasons that should become evident when the terms are made known."

"She what?" Snapping erect, Iris gripped the chair, every fine, dark hair on her forearms standing up as she confronted the lawyer. "I talk to Mama every day, and she never mentioned anything about that to me!"

I was surprised, but couldn't figure out why Mama would bother, since Cissy had made it clear none of us was included in her will.

"First, giving us the cottage," Iris fumed, "now this. I talked to her *on the way up here,* and she never said a word about any of this. Not one word."

Probably because Mama had no more patience than I did with Iris's third degrees and didn't want to have to explain herself endlessly, in minute detail.

Iris spun to Vi and me accusing, "Did she say anything to y'all?"

Both of us shook our heads in denial, so distracted by her reaction that we put our own on the back burner.

As usual, Rose tried to make peace. "You know Mama can't stand it up here," she told Iris. "I'd probably hate it, too, if my mother had dumped me in the backwoods with my grandparents as a baby."

"Anyway," I told her, "we all know Cissy left everything to the Dalai Lama, so it doesn't matter."

I swear, there was a glint of mischief in Mr. Johnson's eyes, but it passed as he pushed the legal document Mama had signed across the desk for Iris's perusal. "Your mother said you might need a little time to accept her decision, Mrs. Browne, but she knows exactly what she's giving up and made her decision without duress of any kind."

Recognizing Mama's signature and the letterhead of her Florida law firm, Iris went beet red and dropped her usual sugary façade. "Damn." Mama had committed the cardinal sin in Iris's book: She'd kept her out of the loop about something major. Worse still, she'd talked to Mr. Johnson about Iris's reaction—*behind her back.*

Mr. Johnson cocked his head in concern. "May I get you some water, Mrs. Browne? Or perhaps some sherry?"

"Bourbon would be more like it!" Iris snapped as she pored over the brief, lucid wording as if she'd find some sort of explanation between the lines.

"Sorry, but the strongest thing I have is port."

"Then it'll have to be port," she said harshly.

Mr. Johnson asked his receptionist to bring in the port, which the rest of us declined, but Iris took full advantage of. After chugging a hefty serving without so much as a shudder, she tossed the document onto the desk and flopped back into her seat, jabbing a finger at the lawyer. "I'm going to verify that document Mama's supposed to have signed, I hope you know."

Mr. Johnson remained unruffled. "Of course. It's only prudent."

"All right then." She sniffed in derision, but finally eased.

Boy, was Mama gonna get an earful on Iris's way back home.

Mr. Johnson resumed as if nothing had happened. "Now to the will." He handed out copies for each of us, a scant three pages of dense type. "Would you ladies prefer I read it aloud, or cut to the chase with a brief summary?"

Rose and Vi and I all said, "Cut to the chase," at the same moment Iris said, "Read it."

Mr. Johnson aimed a conciliatory smile toward Iris. "It seems the consensus is for a summary."

Rose patted Iris's thigh. "The two of us can go over it together later, word for word, if you want to."

Always impatient, I looked at my copy and was caught by the date— just a few weeks ago—and the words *of legally adequate mind and unsound body.*

Cissy's mental competence was debatable, but before I had time to consider the legal ramifications, Mr. Johnson captured my attention with a cheery, "First, your grandmother willed her banking stocks"—*what banking stocks?*—"to be equally divided between the Rabun County Council for the Arts and St. James Episcopal Church in Clayton. At today's values, those stocks exceed four hundred twenty-four thousand dollars, with annual dividends of roughly thirty-two thousand."

Not the Dalai Lama! Not *us*, but not the Dalai Lama! Hope flared inside me.

Heart thumping, I blurted out, "I didn't know she had any banking stocks left."

"Oh, yes," the lawyer said. "They've split and merged more times than I can remember. Fortunately, Sunbelt Credit Union is one of the most solvent in the country."

All this time, Cissy had let us think she barely had the money to pay her taxes!

Iris went livid. "I've been sending her a check every month," she said in indignation. "And she took it!" She glanced at me as if it were my fault. "I thought she was starving. I couldn't stand her, but I couldn't very well let her starve."

Before I could digest the fact that Cissy hadn't been as land-poor as we'd all thought, Mr. Johnson dropped another bombshell that made the previous ones look like firecrackers: "As for the remainder of her estate, she's left it all to your mother and the four of you, to be disposed of as you see fit. Since your mother has chosen not to participate, that leaves the four of you."

My sisters and I sat, drop jawed, in shock.

Questioning my own ears, I raised a staying finger. " 'Scuse me, but could you please repeat that last part?"

Eyes twinkling, Mr. Johnson obliged, confirming that I had, indeed, heard what I thought I'd heard.

This was the miracle I'd prayed for! Cissy's land was worth . . . *millions and millions*! I was saved! Maybe if I had money, Junior might come home. Or at least come to see me. Or I could go see him . . .

"There is, however, one condition." The lawyer paused dramatically.

Hope took a nosedive.

"In order to inherit," he said, "the four of you must spend ninety contiguous days and nights together, without friends or family, at Hilltop—excepting necessary day trips or medical emergencies; or service work, maintenance, or conditions that render the house unsafe or uninhabitable—respectfully going through your grandmother's belongings and reacquainting yourselves with each other."

Iris picked up reading aloud from the condition on the last page of the will. " 'An exercise that I hope will strengthen their love and understanding for each other, as well as their forgiveness for the many wrongs I have visited upon them, especially Daisy, Iris, and Rose.' "

Cissy, admitting she'd been wrong? That was even more improbable than her leaving us her land!

I was speechless, but Rose popped up with, "She didn't do anything bad to me."

Mr. Johnson reminded us, "If any of you fail to meet the condition, you'll forfeit your share of the estate. As I said, your mother has chosen not to participate."

Little wonder. Mama was financially secure, and when she'd married David, she'd told us she meant to spend every day the two of them had left together. Three months was a long time to be apart when you're in your eighties.

I looked at the last sections of the will while Iris read on. " 'It is my fervent prayer that my family will make better choices than I have in this life, and comply with my wishes. As for the dispensation of my home and property, my heirs may use or dispose of it as they see fit, provided they are of one accord, and the natural beauty of the land and lake are not destroyed, the determination of which I leave to my lawyer and beloved friend' "—Mr. Johnson's eyes welled—" 'Horatio Johnson, Esquire, or, in the event of his unwillingness or inability to execute that responsibility, my granddaughter Dahlia.' "

Me? But I was an heir—a clear conflict of interest.

Mr. Johnson pulled out a clean white handkerchief and wiped his lenses, then gave a brief swipe to his eyes with a leveling sniff before he said to us, "I assure you all that I will be responsive to any reasonable decision concerning the use or sale of the property." He sat back and waited for our response.

Lake Clare was *the* place to summer in Georgia. Buildable land there was scarcer—and more expensive—than oceanfront at Sea Island. The last time I'd visited, Cissy had told me the power company was selling ninety-nine-year leases with a thirty-day vacancy clause at half a million an acre for what few undeveloped lots they had left.

Cissy's fee-simple fifty acres and half-mile of virgin shoreland were worth a Middle East fortune.

As soon as we completed our ninety days there, we could sell.

For that much money, I'd drop everything and move into Hilltop the next day, mildew be damned. Surely the bank would grant me another extension when they saw the will!

My ears rang and I forgot to breathe. I'd be able to pay off the house in Buckhead and have a comfortable nest egg left over. Maybe I could even sell the school to my assistant and cut back to tutoring only my most promising students. I could try to get Junior to come home.

After the past two mentally and physically exhausting years, the prospect of rest and security rose like a bright, sturdy zinnia in the bleak landscape that had become my life. I bent double and sent a wordless hymn of gratitude to God and to Cissy.

I heard Mr. Johnson get up, but the sound seemed far away. "Mrs. Cooper, are you all right?" he asked from a great distance.

Iris's voice came from all too close. "Dahlia?" Somebody was shaking me, only I wasn't really there.

Iris forced me upright and got in my face. "She's white as a sheet."

Detached, I saw her grab a glass and the port as the others moved to see how I was. Iris splashed a liberal serving into a glass, then thrust it to my mouth. "Here, drink this."

The familiar aroma wafted, rich and strong, into my nostrils. Oh, port. I loved port.

"No!" Vi hollered, reaching over to stop me, but fool that I am, I drank anyway.

The liquor burned a golden path across my tongue and down my throat.

"Iris," Vi scolded, snatching the glass from my hand. "Are you trying to kill her? You know how allergic she is to anything fermented, *especially* wine!"

Abruptly, I came to my senses. There'd be hell to pay for that one, long sip. And my antifungal drugs were back at home.

"I'm sorry," Iris responded. "She looked like she was going to keel over. I was only trying to help. I swear, I completely forgot about the wine thing."

"Forgot?" Vi bowed up with indignation on my behalf. "We've all known this for twenty-three years! How in the hell could you possibly forget?"

"Well, she cheats all the time," Iris justified.

"With sugar," Vi said. "Or a hamburger, once in a blue moon. Never with wine or cheese! She'll be sick for a month from this!"

Mr. Johnson frowned in concern. "Should I call 911?"

"Oh, it's not an emergency," Iris dismissed. "Dahlia tends to exaggerate about her health. She's had this problem forever, but she always looks just fine to me."

That did it. Furious and humiliated that Iris had force-fed me something she knew I was allergic to, then broadcast my weird health problems only to dismiss them as if I were some kind of hypochondriac, I lost it and started swatting her about the head and shoulders with my copy of the will, which proved to be a most unsatisfactory weapon. "You sanctimonious little bitch! Pretending to be so solicitous, treating me like a child, then giving me something you knew I couldn't have. You probably *were* trying to kill me, but you'd never be honest enough with yourself to admit it!"

"I was only trying to help!" Iris fired back from behind her sheltering forearm. "I didn't think. You never made a mistake, Miss Perfect?"

"Not one that put somebody on liver-destructive antifungals for a month!" I got in an ineffectual swat from the side. "You never fix anything I can eat when it's your night at the beach," I vented, "or if you do have anything I can eat, you make such a huge production about it that it embarrasses me to death. And you never put away that damned cat when I have to come to your house, either! I have to take antihistamines for a week afterward."

"Nobody makes you pet it," she shot back.

"I wasn't petting it! I was trying to get it off me."

Iris's eyes narrowed, and the gloves came off. "Oh, give it a rest. My doctor said there's no such thing as chronic yeast. And as for that diet of yours, I know about all those midnight trips to Wendy's for chocolate

Frosties! *And* the raisin toast at Waffle House, so don't come down on me. Look in the mirror, missy! If you're sick, you only have yourself to blame!"

"That's irrelevant," I snapped. "Don't try to wiggle out of what you just did by putting the blame on my dietary shortcomings!"

"Well, you drank the stuff!" Iris accused. "Nobody put a gun to your head."

"She didn't do it on purpose, Dahlia," Rose intervened. "It's such a complicated, unconscious mechanism at work here. Iris loves you, really, but—"

"Unconscious mechanism?" Iris turned on our baby sister. "Who asked for your opinion? The last time I looked, you taught preschool, not psychology. And Dahlia's the one who's acting like an idiot, not me."

I pointed to Rose. "Oooo, hoo, hoo. How does it feel to be on the receiving end of that *unconscious mechanism,* Miss Rosie?"

Which prompted Iris to start whacking me with her copy of the will. "Leave Rose alone. She was only trying to help."

Vi let loose with the ear-piercing whistle she'd developed to get her lady basketball team's attention during games. "Stop this, both of you. You're both acting like idiots and embarrassing Mr. Johnson."

To the contrary, Mr. Johnson had sat back to enjoy the show and interlocked his fingers behind his head. "Oh, don't stop on my account," he said with a happy little smile. "These things are usually so boring, but this is better than cable. Which stands to reason, considering you're from Cissy's bloodline."

"Kindly do not compare me to that woman," Iris bit out.

Sobering, Mr. Johnson straightened in his chair to say quietly, "*That woman* was my friend."

"Who just left us millions," I pointed out.

Iris turned a canny glare on Mr. Johnson. "Did you sleep with my grandmother?"

"Iris!" all three of us cried in dismay.

Instead of being offended, Mr. Johnson waxed nostalgic and removed his glasses, his eyes losing focus above a soft smile of reminiscence. "Your grandmother was a true bohemian. At one time or another, every healthy, unattached male worth his salt in this county had the privilege of sleeping with her, and it was quite a privilege, I can tell you." He replaced the glasses and resumed his professional demeanor. "Only when she was single, of course."

Vi and Rose and I burst out laughing. It was all I could do to keep from kissing the guy. He'd one-upped Iris, in spades.

Mr. Johnson spoke into the intercom. "Judy, could you please bring in the obituary information and the ashes?" He turned back to us. "As I said over the phone when we spoke last week, your grandmother left her last wishes with me." He gave us each a copy in her own strong, unique handwriting.

Still glaring, Iris snatched hers, then recoiled into her chair.

"As an officer of the court," Mr. Johnson said, "I am compelled to inform you, as I did your grandmother, that it's illegal to dispose of human remains anywhere in this state but a cemetery, mausoleum, or columbarium. Especially not on a public body of water. But as your grandmother's agent in this matter, I am also bound to make you aware of her last wishes."

We all read in silence.

It is my desire that the County be invited to a memorial service some Saturday afternoon during the summer following my death, at Bishop Childers' convenience, who has agreed to preside because of my return to the fold, however tardy, and the testimony my decision might make for all the other stubborn, misguided reprobates who show up for the open bar and lavish food I've arranged for—and paid—Livy Waycaster to provide.

My orchard would be a good location, unless it rains, in which case the verandah will suffice. After the service, it is my desire that my family scatter my ashes near the place I was happiest in this world, the little beach beyond the Point, and know that I am at peace with God.

"It would be illegal to scatter her ashes near or on the lake," Mr. Johnson reminded us. "Not that anyone would notice, if such a thing were done discreetly and never discussed."

We got the message. "Thank you," I said. "We'll decide what to do later."

Speak of the devil, the secretary brought in two boxes: a large, flat one of polished wood and an eight-inch, closed cube of heavy corrugated cardboard with a small typed label on the top. She placed each carefully on the desk, then left.

I guessed the wooden box contained Cissy's ashes, but I was wrong.

Mr. Johnson opened it to reveal several densely typed pages atop a crush of yellowed news clippings, ballet programs, certificates, and documents. He handed me the typed pages. "Here's the obituary your grandmother wrote for herself. The local paper will print it without charge, no matter how long it is. But at the current rates for death notices in the Atlanta paper, something this detailed and extensive"—read *long-winded*—"could cost thousands. Not to mention the fact that your grandmother was pretty confused there at the last."

I scanned through Cissy's flowery, dramatic recitation of her birth, schooling, and ballet achievements, then came to the section about having Mama in Paris. "Ernest Hemingway?"

I reread it, just to make sure it really said what I thought it did. "I'll say she was confused. She claims Mama was Ernest Hemingway's 'love child'!"

"No way," Vi blustered as she and the others leaned in to see for themselves.

"Love child," I fumed. "Right there in the middle of the obituary. Mama would die. Bad enough, Cissy told everybody she wasn't married when she had her."

I replaced the pages, then closed the lid and took the case into my lap. "Thanks so much for letting us edit this," I told Mr. Johnson. "Mama would be humiliated. And clearly, Cissy was senile. Ernest Hemingway."

Mr. Johnson didn't share my skepticism. "You never know with Cissy. She was the hottest thing in toe shoes back then, and they did meet in Paris. I've seen some of the letters he sent her. Who could say?"

"Not us, that's for sure," Iris clipped out. "And certainly not the obituary. Are we finished?"

Mr. Johnson glanced at the smaller box. "Except for your grandmother's ashes. What would you like to do with them until the memorial service?"

The others drew back, suddenly silent.

"I'll take them," I volunteered.

"What we all need to focus on now," Violet said, "is meeting the condition of the will. Then we can sell and be set up for life."

Iris straightened. "We don't even know if all of us want to spend three months in that creepy old house, much less whether we should sell."

"Oh, give me a break," Vi told her. "Of course we all want in. And of course we'll sell. We'll still have Mama's land." She turned to Mr. Johnson. "And Cissy's property will automatically be reassessed at current fair market value for its highest and best use, won't it?"

He nodded. "That's correct. Fortunately, the tax-free inheritance caps have been rising, limiting your individual exposures with the IRS. But the county's another matter. If you choose not to sell, the property taxes will be substantial."

"See?" Vi told Iris. "For that alone, none of us can afford to keep it. We'll stay, and we'll sell."

"Speak for yourself," Iris countered. "That house has got to be full of spiders and who knows what other kinds of bugs." She pulled a face. "Not to mention mold. There's no way we can get rid of either without spending a fortune, and we're not millionaires yet." She shook her head. "How are Dahlia and I supposed to manage for three whole months in that place?"

"We've got millions of reasons to figure that out," Rose said, "but we don't have to decide anything right this minute. Why don't we let Mr. Johnson finish? Then we can come up with a plan over some food."

I shrugged. "So you'll bring the bug spray and a gallon of insect repellent," I told Iris, "and I'll bring the bleach and a ton of antifungals. We'll manage. We have to. If we don't," I let slip, "I'll lose my house to the bank."

Iris's antennae went up. "I thought the house was paid for."

"It was," I confessed. "Till Harrison forged my signature so he could siphon off more equity than it's worth." Iris had been fussing at me forever about my "head in the sand" approach to finances. I hadn't wanted to give her any more ammunition by telling her about the house. But now that deliverance was at hand, it didn't seem to matter anymore that I'd spilled the beans.

For once, Iris didn't scold me. She even had the good grace to be ashamed. "So that's why you kept refusing to sell. You couldn't." Her expression softened. "I thought you were just being stubborn and unrealistic."

"I doubt the bank really wants your house," Rose reassured. "It needs so many repairs, and the mansion market in Buckhead has been flat as a flounder for years. But with your inheritance coming, I know you can talk them into giving you an extension."

God willing. "Assuming I can meet the condition." Three months "camping in" with Iris, not to mention the mold . . .

Violet's mouth firmed with resolution. "You will. We all will."

Iris gave my hip a less-than-gentle bump. "Just as long as you understand that you're not the boss of me."

Three whole months of that. Ninety long days.

And mildew. And decaying papers and old clothes and scorpions and no air-conditioning and . . . I raised my eyes toward heaven.

"Are we finished, then?" Iris asked Mr. Johnson.

"Think so," he said, closing the file. "For your protection, I'll have the will and deed to Cardinal Cottage recorded today."

I shook Mr. Johnson's hand. "Thank you so much." The others added their thanks, too. "We'll fax you the obituary as soon as it's finished."

He nodded, then paused. "Oh, I almost forgot." He retrieved another, smaller corrugated cardboard box from his desk drawer, then placed it atop Cissy's ashes. "Foxy," he said with as much gravity as he could manage.

"Oh." The Mountain Patrol hadn't said a word about cremation. I looked to Rose. "You're the dog person in the family. How about taking custody of Foxy till the memorial service?"

"Okay." She gingerly lifted the box off Cissy's "cremains."

Iris grabbed the obituary box and started for the door with Rose in tow. "We can work on the obituary after lunch."

"Or not," Vi said as she followed them out, which left me alone in the office with Mr. Johnson and Cissy's ashes.

How does one carry one's grandmother in a cardboard box? Under the arm seemed a bit casual, but I found it surprisingly heavy, too heavy for one hand. "What if I accidentally drop it?" I asked Mr. Johnson, conjuring visions of Cissy-dust all over my feet and shoes. I couldn't very well just suck her up with my Oreck. "I'm so clumsy. How would I—"

"Don't worry." He smiled. "The remains are fairly granular, and they're in a resealable, flexible waterproof container inside the box." Translate: freezer bag. "You'll do fine."

"Okay, then." I slung my purse over my shoulder, then lifted Cissy with both hands.

After lunch at the Dillard House, we came up with a reasonably brief and factual obituary that left out the part about Ernest Hemingway and Mama's illegitimate birth, then we all headed back home in time to miss the traffic.

That night, I dreamed of secrets and surprises. And money. Lots and lots of money.

Followed by one of those endless ordeal nightmares, where nothing you try works, about being stuck in an elevator with Iris—for ninety days.

· 5 ·

The Scene of the Crime

Friday, June 1. Lake Clare, in the North Georgia mountains

THANKS TO THE strain of air-conditioning, overload, and sorry, newfangled gas, my trusty Queenie car only got thirteen miles to the gallon on the hundred-mile trek up to Cissy's, so I had to stop for an extra fill-up near Cornelia to keep from arriving on fumes.

When I finally got to Ridge Road's tar-and-gravel pavement just below the dam at Lake Clare, I noted that the ramshackle houses on either side of the old riverbed had been remodeled into quaint cottages with concrete driveways and posh landscaping. It was a good omen. If people had gone to that much expense for property off the lake, heaven only knew what we'd get for Cissy's.

That happy thought eased my annoyance at having to spend a chunk of my precious remaining cash for gas, an expense that proved to be a wise one when I shifted into low for the steep climb to the ridge overlooking Lake Clare. Even in low gear, Queenie strained so hard on the way up, I could almost see the fuel gauge falling.

Not that I could have packed lighter. When you go somewhere for three months, you might as well move, for all the stuff you need, especially when you're as allergic as I am. Hilltop Lodge was rife with dog hair, mold, mildew, dust, and piles of decomposing papers, so drastic measures were necessary. I sneezed merely thinking what we faced to make it habitable.

Just when Queenie's aged transmission threatened to bust a gut, I reached the straight, level stretch atop the ridge that allowed me to catch glimpses of the cool, misty march of mountains to my left, and far below to my right, the sparkling green waters of Lake Clare. As always, ornate fixed docks dotted the edges of its narrow basins, the houses hidden by old-growth hardwoods and evergreens.

Time always seemed to stand still at the lake. No matter how crazy my life—or Cissy—had become, the magic of that place comforted me like my mother's arms and took me back to those simple, peaceful summers when the worst thing I faced was chiggers and putting up with Iris.

A pang of loss hit me. Come September, I was going to sell away all those magic, childhood places to save my home. We'd still have Mama's lot, but our beloved cabin was beyond repair. Even the boatload of Lexapro, Wellbutrin, and trazodone I took couldn't erase the sting from that.

Determined not to let the blackbirds take roost in my mind, I focused on the last leg of the trip. After heading back down toward the lake at a gentler slope, I finally reached the little bridge over the spring-fed creek that marked the southern boundary of Cissy's land.

Despite years of drought, the cold, clear waters still tumbled, wild and clean, past sandy shoals where my sisters and I used to catch crawfish and shriek with proper horror when we discovered a leech on us. The stream then cascaded over moss-draped falls to the little rock house at the back of the cove, where we'd discovered the biggest, shiniest copper still I've ever seen in my life.

Halfway up the next hill, I turned onto Laurel Lane, the private dirt road that had once been a riverbed. Under towering oaks and poplars, overgrown rhododendron and mountain laurel obscured Hilltop Lodge and the lake below. To my surprise, the road was in even worse shape than it had been when regular afternoon thunderstorms sent torrents down its narrow banks.

"Looks like where you'd go to dump the body," Cathy, my assistant at the ballet school, had said when she'd kept me company on a visit to Cissy.

Amen to that. But whenever I'd suggested having it graded and grav-eled, Cissy had refused, saying it kept out curious strangers, which was probably true. In the two years since I'd been there, the undergrowth had tried to shake hands across the stone-littered ruts between the narrow banks. Easing through as gently as I could, I winced at every ominous screech of limb across Queenie's fragile, dark-green paint.

Finally, I emerged into the wide, level junction of Cissy's driveway and the point road. "Just a teeny bit farther," I promised Queenie, "and you can rest."

Iris doesn't talk to machines or understand people who do. She's far too literal for such nonsense.

I turned right, into the long shady allée of towering trees, and there it stood, just beyond the woods: Hilltop Lodge, bathed in morning sun. I deliberately didn't look past it down to the ruined cabin, where a glimpse of blue tarp served as a sad reminder. I focused instead on Hilltop.

At first glance, the old lodge still looked like something from an English fairy tale, the glossy gray floorboards of the verandah contrasting with the deep brown of the log walls and narrow, white French doors. Ram-pant wisteria bloomed up the side and along the porch roof and gutters, like a frothy lilac summer shawl draped across the bodice of a beautiful old woman who sat enthroned in the remnants of Great-grandmother's English gardens. The magic was still there, undiluted.

Until you got close enough to see the sags and buckled floorboards and crooked openings and peeling paint.

But for just that moment, it was still the meticulous kitchen where Great-grandmother had taught me how to make her dark, rich potato bread. And the dusky cellar woodshop filled with fascinating tools Poppy Jack had used to make the ornately carved rosewood settee and side table in the parlor. And the sleeping porch/studio where Cissy had taught me to read and draw and make clay statues, and schooled my palate to speak French like a native. And the dramatic two-story living room, where I'd fallen in love with classical music as Great-grandmother held me in her lap and told me the stories in the music from her crackling LPs of *Peer Gynt, Peter and the Wolf, The 1812 Overture,* and *Night on Bald Mountain.*

I slowed Queenie to a crawl, wanting to prolong the illusion. Then the biggest red-tailed hawk I'd ever seen glided down to perch on Hilltop's leaning river-rock chimney. The creature turned directly toward me, peering my way with huge, amber eyes.

And suddenly I was ten again, lying on the dock with my father after a swim. *Oh, look, Daddy! A hawk, your favorite. First one of the summer.* I flashed on the scent of his Coppertone and bleached cotton T-shirt, and suddenly he seemed so real, so present, that it took my breath away.

My fifteenth summer had been our last at the lake. After the aneurysm took him, Mama couldn't bear to go without Daddy, and now I finally understood why. The memories wakened grief as fresh as the day he'd died.

Rather than feel the loss anew, I directed my thoughts toward busyness.

I had a lot of work to do if I was going to get set up before Iris arrived to hassle me about all I'd had to bring.

But as fate would have it, I turned into the parking area beyond a bank of concealing laurels to find Iris's honkin' huge SUV already taking up two spaces. And already unloaded, from the looks of it.

What in blue blazes was *she* doing there? She was supposed to be late. I'd counted on it.

Criminy. I was so busted.

I parked as far away as possible to make room for the others, then leaned back against the headrest, bracing myself for my sister's inevitable second-guessing about every little thing I'd brought. *I am peaceful, I am calm. I am peaceful, I am calm.*

I was beginning to feel that way—till Iris snuck up on me and rapped on my window, blaring, "Good morning! Are you okay?"

Total jolt! I went bolt upright, heart pounding. "You shouldn't sneak up on people our age like that," I scolded as I got out. "You almost gave me a heart attack."

She pursed her lips. "Sorry. I just wanted to make sure you were okay," she said in that annoying baby-talk voice she used when she got oversolicitous, which was most of the time.

She meant well, I reminded myself. She always meant well.

"I'm so glad you got here. This place is too creepy by myself." Iris enfolded me in her usual bear hug, the top of her head not even reaching my shoulders. "I came up yesterday so I could bomb the house for bugs. I wanted all the fumes to die down before y'all got here."

"You stayed in the house all by yourself?" Spray or no spray, I was shocked that Urban Iris had spent the night alone at Spider Manor.

"Lord, no. I slept in the car," she said as she released me. "Which was scary enough, believe me." She aimed a wary glance at the tall canopy above us. "There's all kinds of loud bugs and critters out here. And in the lake. I swear I heard an alligator slither ashore at midnight." Which had actually happened nearby when we were kids, though we'd only heard about it.

"Every time I started to drift off," she told me, "something else cranked up or moved around in the bushes. And after I finally did fall asleep, some"—her petite features and hands twisted in revulsion—"*creature* dropped onto my moon roof from God knows where at three o'clock in the morning. Pure-D scared the life out of me." Palm to heart, she shook her head. "I heard it run away, but I didn't sleep a wink after that."

"You were really brave to stay up here alone at all," I told her. "I'd have been on my way to the nearest hotel."

At the mention of such an extravagance, tacit disapproval congealed her expression, speaking volumes about her scorn for my "spendthrift" philosophy.

I should never have mentioned the hotel. Drat. Why did I always have to personalize everything? One sentence too far, and I'd summoned her critical parent, who summoned my defensive child.

Chill out, I reminded myself. This was only Day One of ninety. "Did the bug bomb kill all the spiders and crawlies?"

She shook her head in consternation. "Couldn't find a one, which is pretty weird, come to think of it. But I did find a notice from a local pest control company that Cissy had paid to have the house treated for wood borers, and arrangements had been made for us to stay with a neighbor while they did it. Maybe she had a bug man."

Prophetic words, as it turned out.

Her eyes fell to the orderly crush of plastic-encased pillows, linens, yeast-free food, and clothes that filled every inch of Queenie's interior but the driver's seat. She looked to the tires. "Holy crow, Dahlia," she said. "What in heaven's name have you got in Queenie, anvils? The tires are half-flat from the load, and I don't see how you could drive safely with all that *stuff* blocking your windows. We only assigned you the cleaning things and bath soap."

And so it began.

Determined not to let her get to me, I flashed on cool breezes at St. Bart's and chanted silently, *It's only gnat bites. Detach.* When that didn't work, I thought about the huge outdoor hot tub at the grand hotel in Banff, surrounded by pristine snowdrifts. *I can do this. I am peaceful,* I willed, to no avail. *I am calm.*

Then on its own, my imagination formed a gleaming gas station with Iris's SUV at the pumps and $147.50 on the meter.

A warm glow permeated my chest, then spread into a genuine smile. "Unfortunately for Queenie," I said without a smidgen of rancor, "I need every bit of that *stuff* to make it for three months in this place, weird as I am."

After a minuscule flicker of skepticism (she'd never said it, but clearly thought I was a hypochondriac), Iris's features smoothed. "If you'll pop the trunk," she offered, "we can get started unloading all this."

Even though I knew it was fruitless to delay the inevitable, I still wanted to. Iris was going to have a field day with what was in that trunk. "I'd rather wait till later." When she was busy with something else.

"Oh, don't be silly," she dismissed. "You're always the one who has to do everything right this instant. Let me help you. I really don't mind. Really."

Translate: She was going to make a big thing out of it if I refused. My stomach tightened, but in the interest of tranquility, I gave in. "Okay. Thanks."

I popped the trunk with dread, but when she looked inside, I got praise instead of criticism. "Oh, I was hoping you'd bring this! I completely forgot to ask you." She pulled out my super-duper, deluxe hypoallergenic, light-weight upright vacuum cleaner, a remnant from better days. "And all the attachments, too. Great."

When she set it down beside her, some deeper level of my conscious-ness noted that the usual carpet of moldy leaves beneath our feet had been replaced by a clean cushion of long, white pine needles. No cones, though. Definitely unnatural. But I attributed the resulting pinprick of uneasiness to Iris's unexpected presence.

Iris cocked her head to the seats. "What about the stuff in the car? Do you want to bring it in now?"

"No." I picked up a box of nuclear-grade cleaning materials, hoping she wouldn't notice the hazmat supplies underneath. "I want to wait till everything's been treated with CitriSafe before I put anything absorbent in the house."

Iris scowled. "What's CitriSafe?"

"It's a nontoxic fungicide made from botanicals. I was going to use bleach, but Rose"—our family eco-Nazi—"found this stuff on the Internet and insisted I not 'poison our living environment,' so I gave in and got it." To the tune of a hundred twenty dollars a gallon, as opposed to a dollar-fifty for the bleach. But my allergist had said it was worth the money. "I brought a sprayer and two gallons of the concentrate for all of us to use. Bleach only treats the surface, but if you mix the concentrate with distilled water, you can soak things with this, even fabrics, and it won't hurt them."

She gave me one of those "here we go again" looks. "And how much did *this* stuff set you back?" she asked, as if I'd gotten it from a snake-oil salesman.

"None of your beeswax," I said in as pleasant a tone as I could manage.

Iris sniffed. "Well, for your sake, I hope it works."

Another subtle dig. For ninety days, she was going to pass judgment on every penny I spent or had spent, and every inconvenience imposed by my allergy to mold.

Oblivious to her own judgmentalness, she said, "Good thing you picked Mama's old room upstairs. The afternoon sunshine makes it less moldy than the others."

Precisely why I'd chosen it. That, and the fact that it shared a sleeping porch with the room beside it Vi had chosen.

Shifting aside my blow-up bed to get the case of vacuum attachments, Iris let out a dry chuckle. "We both had the same thought. I brought a blow-up mattress, too." Like everything at Hilltop, Cissy's mattresses were ancient and moldy. Iris cocked a thumb toward the house. "It looks like somebody made a stab at cleaning in there, but it's musty, musty, musty." For once, her tone was without subtext. "It's a miracle the mildew didn't spread all over Cissy and digest her while she slept."

An attempt at humor. In Iris, a very good sign.

"I think it did get her," I responded, "only by degrees."

" 'Watch out,' " she quoted Cissy, " 'or the microbes'll get you.' "

Miracle of miracles, Iris was actually trying to lighten up.

Buoyed by that, I fell into my best John Wayne imitation. "Wal, let's go make that filthy establishment safe for democracy."

Though Iris rarely watched movies, preferring golf and the Weather Channel (!) on TV, she actually recognized my impression. "John Wayne, right?"

"Give the little lady an A plus," I imitated with an arcing point of the finger worthy of the Duke.

Pleased, Iris smiled as she followed me toward the tunneled shortcut to the kitchen through Great-grandmother's huge azaleas.

Keeping a careful eye on my steps on the uneven ground, I navigated through the hedge, then emerged into the sun, expecting to find the abandoned kitchen garden beyond. But it wasn't abandoned. I was standing on a smooth stone walkway flanked by neatly mulched vegetables brightened by colorful beds of zinneas and geraniums, and all kinds of marigolds, including my favorite giant African variety.

My garden-loving heart did a jig. "Where did *this* come from?" Cissy couldn't have done it. She'd died way too early in the year to plant in this climate.

"Beats me," Iris said as she passed me to open the oddly sturdy screen door. "I knew you'd like it."

Looking closer, I saw that somebody had cleaned out Poppy Jack's narrow stone irrigation trenches and reconnected the waterfall to the cistern.

"Somebody who loves gardens even more than I do did this. But why?" I called after her. The only response from the kitchen was the sound of drawers opening and closing, and metal clinking.

The heavy box in my arms forgotten, I stepped to the edge of the walk and used the toe of my ballet flat to scrape aside the thick mulch. Then I tested the black earth with a downward push. My foot sank easily into loamy soil instead of sterile, sunbaked clay. Somebody must have excavated the whole plot and replaced the clay with rich, black earth—a massive undertaking.

The garden's intricate design was as beautiful as it was functional. I looked at the plantings more closely and counted a dozen tomato cages cleverly made to look like minigazebos and filled with neatly labeled varieties already setting fruit, with *organic* on every label. Perfect patches of lettuce and sweet peas were ready to pick. Six-inch Silver Queen corn sprouts sprigged a wide circle on one side, and a matching plot of Early Girl bicolor outpaced it on the other. And red and yellow bell peppers! Yum. Burpless cucumbers and straight-necked yellow squash bloomed profusely beneath their leaves in four latticed cages. And beyond it all, pole beans had already reached their tidy bamboo trellis. All my favorites were there, as if someone had planted it just for me.

And strawberries!

And asparagus, the thick, tender kind that took two years to yield. So this was nothing recent.

Clearly, I'd missed a lot in the past two years, yet Cissy hadn't said a thing.

Quite a mystery. "Who *did* this?" I hollered rhetorically.

"I told you, I have no idea," literal Iris hollered back from the kitchen.

"Cissy alienated all the locals," I reasoned aloud. "And the lakies thought she was crazy. Why would somebody do this for her?" I noted the size of the annuals. "Or us? This was planted after she died."

"You read too many mystery novels," Iris declared, emerging from the kitchen. "Look at you, still holding that heavy box," she scolded. "Here. Let me take that in."

When she pulled it from me, my arms rose spasmodically, but I barely noticed, my middle-aged brain spinning. *This garden. The pine straw in the parking lot. No bugs. A new screen door. The prepaid fumigation.*

Like a nearsighted person finally given glasses, I took in the telltale details all around me.

Hilltop's curling shingles now lay flat. All the windows had screens that actually fit, their frames neatly painted to match the fresh white of the trim. The slate terrace outside Cissy's room now lay flat, too. And all the weeds were gone from between the stones and beyond in the deep green vinca minor under the surrounding trees.

My eyes shot to Great-grandmother's restored rose beds that bordered the freshly mulched and leveled path that stepped down the hill to the boathouse.

"Iris," I croaked out. "Somebody has spent a huge amount of money repairing the house and grounds."

"Good," she said as she came back out. "Maybe it was Cissy. She paid for her memorial reception. God knows, she had the money to fix this place up," she said, still miffed to have been taken in by Cissy's illusion of poverty. She looked askance. "The rest of the place still looks pretty wild to me. I'd have hated to see it before." She turned her attention back to me. "So why do you look like somebody just canceled your pool service?"

"I don't like not knowing something important." That was an understatement. "Doesn't this seem . . . a bit too perfect?"

She shrugged. "Not to me. I don't like corn, and cucumbers give me terminal gas, and too many tomatoes make my tongue break out in sores. But you like them all. Why look a gift horse in the mouth? It's here. Enjoy it."

I shook my head in baffled denial. "Nobody does something this enormous without a reason. All these repairs and all this yard work took time. Cissy was senile and dying. I don't think she had the wherewithal to supervise all this. But why would somebody else do it?"

Iris sighed. "I swear, Dahlia, that mind of yours. Why do you always have to trouble trouble? You only make yourself miserable. And everybody else."

She had a point. Still . . . "What if it's somebody trying to butter us up for a cheaper sale?"

"So what if it is?" She pushed me back toward the car. "C'mon. Let's get your trunk cleared out so we can start on Mama's room. Maybe that miracle cleaner of yours will whiten up those dark suspicions. Then you can help sterilize Cissy's room for me."

"So you finally decided on Cissy's room. Good." Vi and I had picked our rooms right away, but Rose and Iris had done their usual "no, you take it" dance ad nauseum about Cissy's, since it was the nicest.

She pulled a heavy shopping bag from the trunk. "Rose kept telling me to take it, so I'm taking it. After what I went through last night, I earned that sunken bathtub."

The sunken tub Cissy had put in her bedroom was the only one in the house. Never mind that it sat at the intersection of two huge sliding glass doors that offered an unobstructed view of the front verandah and side terrace, and vice versa.

Iris always had liked to run around naked when she was a kid. For all

I knew, she still did, but Lord help us if our mystery gardener turned up to weed while any of us were soaking. Now, *that* would give the lakies something new to talk about at the gas docks.

On that cheery thought, I grabbed a box of meds and respirators and braved mildew mansion.

Once inside, I was shocked to see how clean the kitchen was. "*Some* cleaning?" I turned to Iris. "You have no idea how filthy this place was. I thought the cabinets were tan." They were actually butter yellow. Or had they been repainted? No. Vintage yellow.

While Iris rummaged around in the kitchen, I passed the supplies she'd piled on the Jacobean table Poppy Jack had carved for the tiny dining area, then I ventured across the floor furnace in the hall and entered the library. "This is great. Somebody's been sorting through the papers." Cissy's random heaps of typed memoirs and correspondence had been consolidated into neat piles atop the daybeds that served as seating and overflow bedding. The vintage forties fabric on the mattresses and drapes looked like it had been washed. "I can actually see the floor. And the inlays on Poppy Jack's desk."

Cissy had always said she was going to separate the trash from the treasure. Maybe she finally had, once she knew her time was running out.

All her local newspapers and *New Yorker* magazines were now neatly stacked beside the big inlaid Raj desk, and tidy piles of bills, tax info, correspondence, and checks had been given their own labeled plastic bins on top. There weren't even any "doodlebug" cones of ultrafine sawdust on the floor. "This is awesome."

I spotted my favorite piece in the whole house. "Oh, look, Mama's little slipper chair." Poppy Jack had carved it from one of the oak trees they'd felled for the house, decorating its flat legs and slender back with perfect bunches of wildflowers. "This is the only thing I want from this house."

"Fine by me," Iris said from the kitchen, "I don't want any of this old stuff. But you really ought to ask the others."

With Iris, everything had to be by committee. God forbid somebody would actually ask for what she wants.

Nose atingle, I let out a huge sneeze. Not a good sign. My lungs had already tightened just shy of a wheeze. I searched my purse for my antifungal inhaler, and wouldn't you know it, Iris walked in just as I was taking a deep hit.

"Oh, dear," she said with unconvincing concern. "Already?"

Involuntarily, my eyes narrowed and nostrils widened. "I'll manage."

Oozing cosmic superiority, she arched a skeptical brow without comment.

Day One. Shake it off.

I left her standing there. After passing the oak spiral staircase, I emerged into the two-story living room to find it as junk-free and clean as I'd ever seen it since Great-grandmother died. Even the smooth river rocks of the two-story fireplace had been dusted, and cobwebs no longer clung to the chinks or the ornate frames on our family portraits. Somebody had gone a long way to make our job easier. Looking up to the sparkling clerestory windows and log rafters high above me, I saw that even the family flags the Captain had made looked clean and pressed.

Still, the tickle in my lungs became a faint wheeze.

I heard Iris retreat into Cissy's room—sulking, probably. Iris considered it rude when anybody left her presence without permission, but I took advantage of the coast's being clear to head for some fresh air and another load from my car.

On the way through the kitchen, I sidled over to the vintage refrigerator and gingerly pulled it open. Gone was the cracked, blackened door seal, replaced by a fresh one. And the interior had been cleaned till it sparkled. No more moldy produce and leftovers, or neglected jars of apple juice going hard.

Instead, Iris had filled the whole interior with tofu, cheese, eggs, and other ovo-lacto vegetarian staples, plus fresh organic vegetables, leaving no room for the red meat and poultry I'd brought for my high-protein, low-glycemic, yeast-free medical diet.

"Remind me to take the casserole out of the freezer this afternoon," she said, aloof, as she came in. "I brought several."

"The ones with tofu and cheese and mushrooms," I shot back before I could catch myself. "With bread crumbs on the top?" All things I couldn't eat.

Instead of getting defensive, she said, "I brought homemade chicken pies for you. Just the crust with chicken and hardboiled eggs in plain gravy." My favorite recipe. "Twenty of them. They're in the hall freezer. Which, by the way, somebody cleaned out."

I was touched, and contrite. "That's really nice, Iris. Thanks. Thanks a lot."

I pulled the huge plastic bag of prescriptions and vitamins from the box I'd brought in, then took out the masks and hot-pink respirators underneath them. "Let's get started." I tossed a respirator to Iris, then took out one for me. "With luck, we'll be finished with both rooms in time for lunch."

Iris eyed the respirator, but didn't put it on. "Okay. Mildew, here we come."

After an unnecessarily long discussion of who would do what, we barely finished Mama's old room before our stomachs started growling. So I picked us a nice mess of asparagus, sweet peas, and lettuce from the garden, then came back into the kitchen to find Iris filling a pan with water to boil the veggies. "Oh, no," I cautioned. "Don't even try the water. It's got so much iron in it, it'll make you gag."

Iris frowned. "That yeast in your system must have done something to your taste buds. It seems fine to me."

The screen door opened behind us and Violet stepped in, weighted down with bulging shopping bags of food and paper products. "Hey, y'all." She set them down and opened her arms, clearly pleased about something.

I got to her first for a big hug. "We didn't hear you drive up."

She gave me a smug smile, then deflected, asking Iris, "What seems fine?"

"The water," Iris said, closing in for a hug.

Violet made a face. "That horrible well water? Makes me gag just to think about it."

"I swear," Iris told us, "it's better than what we get at home."

Skeptical, I pulled a plastic cup from the huge stack Iris had bought at Sam's. Noting the lack of rust stains in the kitchen sink, I drew a small sample from the spigot, then looked into the cup. Clear as a bell. "Okay, here goes." I took a sip. The cool, crisp nothingness on my tongue was almost sweet. I looked at the cup again. "This is great!"

"So why do you look like it's awful?" Vi asked.

"It's not supposed to be great. It's supposed to be awful." The spring had dried up twenty years before, necessitating a well with water so hard the wash came out brown and able to stand by itself. But this tasted great.

"Maybe Cissy had a new well dug," Vi conjectured.

"Or found a new spring," Iris added.

I shook my head no. "She was forgetful, but something like that, she would have told me." The last few years, the old house had been a real burden to her, especially as she became more senile and less able to deal with even simple things. "Somebody's been working on this place," I told Vi. "Inside and out. A fortune's worth, and Cissy never said a word about any of it. Something's rotten in Denmark."

"There she goes again," Iris told Vi. "Nancy Drew lives." She hijacked the conversation by turning her back to me and asking Vi, "How was your morning?"

"I thought I'd never get out of the house," Vi said. "Every time I started to leave, I remembered something else I'd forgotten. No way would all of it fit into my Mini Cooper. I had to bring Taylor's SUV."

An ancient Suburban. I got a headache just thinking how much it must cost to run the thing. "Whoa. Getting up here must have really set you back."

Vi flushed with embarrassment. "Well, actually, it's not the Suburban. When I told Taylor about the will, he insisted we go straight to the dealership and get a hybrid, so the mileage is great." She grinned. "Just so y'all know, if I screw this will thing up, we have no hope of paying for it."

"You're not gonna screw anything up," I assured her. She never did. "I might, but you won't." I stepped toward the screen door. "Let's go look at the new car. What kind is it?"

"Black, with a silver interior and tinted windows and power everything, including a GPS and a backup camera," she said proudly. "And it has that great new-car smell."

Iris didn't budge. "We're just fixing lunch," she said, getting a box of pasta out of the cabinet. "Can we please do it after?" She put another pot of water on the propane burner, and everybody knows you shouldn't go off and leave things on the stove with the burners going.

Control, control, control.

"We're having fresh peas and asparagus from the garden," she told Vi. "I plan to toss mine with some pasta and Parmesan. Dahlia's making salad."

"No, thanks," Vi responded with a wry wink for me. "I had a Whopper and fries on my way up." We both knew how it galled Iris that active Vi could eat junk food till the cows came home and still keep her slim figure. She opened the refrigerator. "Good grief, Iris, you took up all the space with your tofu and cheeses and mushrooms. What's Dahlia supposed to eat?"

"She made me chicken pies, just the way I like them," I defended. "I can freeze all the meat I brought."

Validated, Iris motioned Vi to the stool at the counter under the kitchen windows—the same counter beneath which I'd curled with a book while Great-grandmother's bread was baking. "Sit. First, we'll eat. Then we'll see your new car before we sterilize the rest of the rooms and unpack the cars."

Iris always had a plan, and we were always supposed to go along. But since it was only Day One, I went with the flow. "Any idea when Rose might show up?" I asked her.

Iris set the pot on the burner. "She said she was going to leave early and take the scenic route."

Vi shot me a wary look. "There have to be a hundred flea markets and garage sales between here and Roswell. We may not see her till midnight."

"I'll call her." Iris flipped open her cell phone and hit speed dial, then frowned and peered at the screen. "No signal? How can there be no signal?" A fate worse than death for Iris, who would be first in line when they finally came up with cell phone implants. "This is the twenty-first century!"

She'd been there twenty-four hours and was just finding out? "This is the mountains," I reminded her. Frankly, I'd always considered my cell phone a necessary evil, but Iris was a communications junkie.

"Remember those pale little blotches in the cell phone coverage maps?" Vi said. "We're in one of them."

"The regular phone's in Cissy's room," I told Iris. "You can use that."

"*The* phone?" she responded, appalled. "As in, only one, for the whole house?"

She really was jonesing. "You didn't notice when you were bombing the house?" I asked.

"I was busy bombing the house!" she snapped.

"Bombing?" Vi said in mild alarm, giving the whole exchange a Three Stooges feel.

"For bugs," Iris and I said in unison.

"The phone," Iris said to me.

I tried to keep a straight face. "The old-fashioned kind. With a cord."

Iris's eyes narrowed. "Please tell me there's cable here, at least."

Vi and I shook our heads in denial.

"Some people up here have satellite," I offered, "but Cissy never even owned a TV. She said they were mind-eaters."

Iris straightened, her lips pursed. "You might have told me when we were talking about coming up here." She headed for *the* phone, saying over her shoulder, "I'm calling the satellite company. I'll pay for it, but I have to have my e-mail. And I'm getting the premium channel package." Her voice got louder in the hallway. "And tomorrow I'm going to Wal-Mart in Clayton and buying a TV and some cordless phones." Thanks to her successful CPA business, she could afford it.

I turned to look out the kitchen windows, and Vi followed my line of sight to the huge trees on the mountain southeast of the house. Smack between Hilltop and the satellite that serviced our region.

"Will a dish even work here?" Vi asked.

I slowly shook my head. "Don't think so." I hadn't had time to watch TV for ages, so it wouldn't bother me. But I couldn't help feeling just a pinch of satisfaction that Iris was going to have to suffer a little this summer, too. She was always on that damned cell phone, as if the people who called her were more important than whoever she was actually with, or what she was really doing. She could stand to do without it for a while.

Reading my mind, Violet grinned and sat to keep me company while I made the salad.

Ten minutes later, Iris fumed back in with, "Three weeks! They can't come for three weeks! I never heard of such a thing. And I have to use *dial-up* for my e-mail, dog dammit." Her sole cussword, reserved for the most dire of circumstances.

Vi and I stood there like hear no evil, speak no evil.

Iris threw the asparagus and peas into the boiling water with a vengeance. "How are civilized people supposed to live in this backwoods place?" she fumed to nobody and anybody, "Are we *camping out*, here?"

"Camping *in*," I corrected.

Vi changed the subject. "Did you talk to Rose?"

Iris dumped the pasta into the boiling water. "Yes," she clipped out. "She hasn't even made it past Buford."

Buford? Not even forty miles. "Well, she'd better get here before midnight," I said, "or we'll have to start over tomorrow." I did *not* want this to end up being Day Zero.

As always, Iris defended her. "She'll be here. Buford's only seventy miles, and it's only noon."

If I had been the one to show up late when there was work to be done, I'd never have heard the end of it from Iris, but Rose hung the moon, as far as Iris was concerned. The fact was, Rose got away with a good bit, simply because she was so darned quiet and sweet.

Five "progress" calls from Iris later, Rose turned off her phone at three.

By eight o'clock, all four rooms had been sprayed and cleaned to within an inch of their lives, our three cars were unloaded, beds were made, and dinner was ready, but there was still no sign of Rose.

We were just about to sit down to supper accompanied by the sound of tree frogs and lapping waves when we heard her approaching from the shadowed driveway.

"Thank goodness." Channeling the Cable Guy, I stood and said to Vi, "Let's git out to Rose's car and git 'er done."

"I wish you wouldn't do that," Iris snipped out as she got up.

"Do what?" I asked, surprised.

"Talk movie or TV, the way you and Vi always do with each other, like it was some kind of foreign language. You know I don't get it, but you always do it anyway. It makes me feel left out and less than."

Oh, for cryin' out loud.

Vi looked at me askance. "We do, don't we?"

Iris nodded.

My compulsive need to be justified prompted, "It's just that Vi and I love all the same movies, and we've seen so many of them that it just sort of . . . evolved."

"Well, I'd appreciate it if you didn't do it," Iris said.

Please. "Well, I'd appreciate it if you wouldn't act like I'm a hypochondriac," I countered.

Vi spread her hands like a referee. "Foul. Time out. It's way too early in the game for you two to start squabbling." She eyed me with her best stern-professor look. "Cut it out. Don't make me separate you." Mama's severest threat when we fought as kids.

I let out a bark of laughter just as Rose breezed in with her hands laden with bulging reusable grocery bags. "Hey, y'all," she bubbled. "Boy, did I have fun on the way up here! You won't believe what I found at the flea markets."

Iris brightened up at the sight of her. "I'm so glad. I was beginning to worry about you."

Rose was our peacemaker. With her there to buffer Iris, maybe I could make it through Day Ninety without committing murder—or suicide. Maybe.

· 6 ·

See me. Feel me. Touch me. Heal me.
—THE WHO

. . . .

*W*E LEFT THE table to help her. I took a completely disorganized bag of clothing and wigs, and Vi did the same.

Iris gave Rose a big hug. "What treasures did you find today?"

Rose beamed. "A great sledgehammer for only fifty cents, and a pickax for a dollar." As if she'd ever touched a tool. "And a shop vac for only ten dollars, good as new. And a mason's trowel for a dollar. But the pièce de résistance is a fabulous cast-iron cauldron on legs. It's a bit rusty, but for three dollars, I couldn't pass it up. I'm thinking Halloween."

I shook my head, constantly amazed by her thrifty impracticality. The shop vac, we could use, assuming it didn't spew dust out the exhaust. But a sledgehammer, a mason's trowel, a pickax, and a cast-iron *cauldron*? Give me a break.

Even Iris couldn't think of anything positive to say about Rose's latest haul, so she just hugged her again. "Ooh, I'm so glad you're finally here," she said with an affection she'd never spent on me or Violet. "Come eat. Your room's all ready. We can help you unload after supper."

Rose sneezed, then fished out one of the wretched tissues that she left like a trail of bread crumbs wherever she went.

"Aaagghh!" Vi and I made the sign of the cross with our fingers to ward off the evil tissues. "Nasties!" Our nickname for them.

"Away, away," Vi pleaded.

"Totally gross," from me.

Rose just laughed and dangled one at us. Despite her quiet demeanor, our baby sister was so green it was mean. She reused, repurposed, and recycled with a vengeance. Only toilet paper was exempt from an eco-logical afterlife. (Thank the Good Lord.)

Vi and I had given her countless pretty white handkerchiefs for her hay fever, but she always lost them. Always. Can we say, passive-aggressive?

"You two," Rose said with a doting smile for Vi and me. "I swear." She sat on the bench and slid over to make room for Iris, then blew loudly into the nasty once more, just for good measure.

Besides those nasties—and her tardiness; and her need for innumer-able transitional activities going from point A to point B; and her turtle pace in stores—the woman was close to perfect, with one of the tender-est hearts I'd ever known.

Not that I felt I really knew her. She'd never shared anything intimate or dangerous with me or Vi, only with Iris, who never leaked a word. But our pairings were just a normal function of temperament and personal-ity, something we'd all accepted from childhood. Neither Vi nor I resented the touchy-feely, shades-of-gray sensibilities that bound Rose and Iris, and I hoped they accepted the practical, black-and-white dispositions that held me and Violet close.

Two and two, we took our places across the circle of yellow light cast on the table, then joined hands, heads bowed, and waited for the Spirit to move somebody to say grace. The silence resonated with sunset song from the deep woods and the lake, a blessed sound that brought back other, happier times.

Just as I was about to launch into an off-the-cuff prayer of thanks, Rose's thready soprano piped up with the blessing she used with her preschool students, to the tune of "Frère Jacques." "Lord, we thank you, Lord, we thank you. For this food, for this food. And our many bless-ings, and our many blessings. Ah-amen, ah-amen." She lifted her head. "How was that?"

" 'That'll do, pig,' " I quoted from *Babe*.

Iris scowled.

Shoot. Movie talk. "Sorry. That was a quote from *Babe*. I promised Iris I'd stop doing that."

"Good." Rose sat poised with a bite on her fork. "I do not like being called a pig."

"It's not calling you a pig," I explained, compelled, as always, to be justified. "It's what the farmer said to Babe whenever he did something wonderful."

"I've seen *Babe*," Rose said mildly. "But I still don't like being called a pig." Rose rarely spoke up about anything that bothered her, so for her sake, I stiffened my resolve to quit.

If only my brain would get the message. I'd been living on autopilot since Harrison had left, so it wouldn't be easy. I'd have to second-guess my every word for three whole months. Talk about self-conscious.

"I don't like it when you do that, either," Iris had to put in.

I looked to Vi. "You'll have to help me. I don't even know when I'm doing it."

Before she could reply, Iris usurped that responsibility with, "Don't worry. I'll call you on it."

Oh, joy.

Rose changed the subject, pointing her empty fork toward the single bulb and paper shade that hung over the table. "I brought compact fluorescents for the fixtures."

Vi and I exchanged pained expressions. Even Iris let out a sigh.

Rose straightened. "Well, don't everybody thank me at once."

Vi spoke for both of us. "That was really nice of you. It's just . . . we tried those at home, but they're so dim, I could hardly see to read."

"They ought to be called darks, instead of lights," I seconded.

Rose refused to take offense. "The old ones were that way, but not these. I got the bright kind." The smile never left her voice when she added, "But if you still think you need to use one of those heat-producing, power-hungry incandescents, so be it. At least give these a try, first. We can save a lot on the power bill."

Never mind the sky-high cost of the bulbs. Or the fact that they had toxic mercury in them, a problem to dispose of. Or that somebody else would end up getting the use from them after we sold. But tree huggers like Rose never wanted to hear the real bottom line.

I broke the crust on my steaming chicken pie, releasing its divine scent into the humid air, and shifted the topic. "We have an extra full-sized blow-up mattress, if you'd like to use it."

Rose's blond eyebrows lifted. "Thanks, but I brought one, too. It's a queen, only ten dollars at a garage sale, complete with frame. Repurpose, reuse, recycle."

"How in blue blazes did you get all that stuff you bought and all your food and clothes and bedding into that little Honda you drive?" I couldn't help but ask.

Rose's cheek dimpled for the first time in a long time. "I didn't. Martin got me a hybrid SUV."

"A new one?" Vi asked in a subtle bit of one-upmanship, knowing perfectly well that Rose would never buy new.

"Gracious no. That would be hideously wasteful." Riding her own little cloud as usual, Rose obviously hadn't noticed Vi's new SUV, but Vi didn't take the comment personally. "A distant cousin of Martin's bought it for his teenaged daughter, but she flunked her first quarter as a senior, so he decided to sell it. We drove all the way down to Waycross day before yesterday to get it. The mechanic we took it to said it was fine. And we only had to pay thirteen thousand for it."

New, they were going for almost thirty. "How much mileage?" I asked.

"Only eight thousand," Rose boasted.

"Only you," I said with admiration.

"That's great," Vi said. "What color is it?"

"Silver fox," Rose answered with pride, "and a black and gray interior. And stowaway seats. Big enough for a dresser, even."

"Good," I said. "We can take it to the store for supplies. The kitty will pay for the gas."

"Speaking of the kitty." Iris got up and pulled some papers from her briefcase, then handed one to each of us.

MEAL UNITS was centered in bold type above an impressive grid with teeny captions. While the others did the same, I groped through my pockets for my readers, then put them on and tried to decipher the thing.

"As you can see, I've done a chart for each month," Iris said in her CPA voice, "with four columns, one for each of us, and three lines for each day's breakfast, lunch, and dinner. Below that, there's room to put in what you spent on food before you got here, and another line for how much we each put into the kitty." She'd already warned us to bring at least a hundred dollars cash for the kitty. I'd had to borrow mine from my assistant Cathy.

"At the end of each month," she went on, "we'll add up the total meal units for all of us, then divide what we've spent by that number, to figure out our actual cost for each meal unit."

"I hope by *we*, you mean *you*," I qualified. I got a headache just thinking about all those numbers.

Iris nodded in affirmation, then resumed. "Then we'll multiply the actual meal-unit cost by the total meal units for each of us to fairly determine our shares. Subtract that from the total money we each put in, and we come up with exactly how much we each owe the kitty, or the kitty owes us."

Way too complicated for me and Vi. We were split-the-check-down-the-middle, round-it-off overtippers, but Iris hadn't gotten as rich as she was by doing that. A real penny-pincher, she always wanted her share to be computed exactly, so that's the way she'd set up the meal-unit plan.

" 'I bow before your superior intellect,' " I quoted from *Star Trek* before my brain went into gear.

Shoot! I'd done it again. Trying not to was only making me worse. Which stood to reason, since I've always been my own worst enemy.

Thank goodness Rose and Iris were too literal for *Star Trek,* so my lapse went unnoticed.

Iris beamed, even as Vi pinched my leg under the table.

Just to be safe, I clammed up. Maybe I could find somebody to anesthetize my vocal cords for the first few weeks till I got the hang of it.

After supper, we helped Rose bring in her bare necessities. Passing my room after we had finished, I remembered the letter from Cissy and excused myself to read it.

I was expecting something flowery and typically overwritten, but Cissy surprised me once again. The note was short and sweet:

My dear Dahlia:
I told you once that for dancers of our abilities, our art means far
more than happiness. I see now that I was wrong. I know you've been
hurt, but keep your heart open to whatever happiness you might find.
It's not too late.

Cissy

A bit cryptic. Sitting there, I couldn't help wondering if she'd ever really been happy, even with the Captain. The words *obsessed* and *driven* seemed more appropriate.

I thought of the letter to Mama in my purse and wondered why Cissy had asked Mr. Johnson to give it to me instead of mailing it to Mama. It wasn't sealed, just tucked closed, which, to my way of thinking, amounted to tacit permission to see what was inside. Cissy knew how curious I was, and Mama would never have to know. Compelled to see what her last words to Mama were, I got it out and carefully opened the envelope to read:

Precious Daisy,
I have marveled daily that you turned out to be such a wonderful
mother after having such a selfish one as I. I have wronged you and
your children in so many ways that mere apology seems an insult, but
I shall ask this of you when I am gone: forgive me, daughter, and bury
your disappointments with me. Not because I deserve it, but for the
sake of your own gentle soul. Though you may not believe it, I have
loved you.

Mother

Sadness and anger rose inside me. Why hadn't Cissy picked up the phone and called Mama, told her in her own voice, while there was still time? Surely she wasn't afraid. Cissy hadn't been afraid of anything, even God, except maybe at the last when she knew she was dying.

Sealing the envelope, I wondered if Mama would ever tell me about Cissy's message. And if she could forgive Cissy. I hoped she would.

"Dahlia!" Iris called up the stairs.

Propelled by guilt, I almost jumped out of my skin.

"Come down," she told me. "We're going to sit out on the porch."

Ah. The "schooling" had begun, as Harrison called it, referring to fish, not education, and Iris's insistence that all of us be there for whatever group activities she had planned.

"I'm coming." I put the letter back and resolved to mail it the next time we went out.

Downstairs, Iris sprayed me and the others down with Deep Forest Deet, then we all took our decaf coffee out onto the verandah. Gingerly, we sat in the vintage wicker rockers whose rusty springs and ancient upholstery felt none too sturdy.

Across the lake, the last glow of dusk on the mountaintops gave way to darkness, revealing the wide swath of the Milky Way across the sky.

A companionable silence settled between us. Till Iris piped up with, "Isn't this great? No streetlights. No traffic sounds. No sirens. Just quiet." Except for Iris's compulsive narration. "No husband to take care of. No kids wanting me to babysit. No problems at the office."

"No cable," Vi added in the same dreamy tone Iris had been using. "No cell phones. No air-conditioning. No dishwasher."

"Talking like that isn't going to make this any easier," Iris chided.

As always, Rose tried to deflect even the possibility of confrontation. "What's your favorite memory of being here?" she asked me.

"Oh, so many." I reached back to those long-ago summers. "The taste of sugar bread, fresh out of the oven." Great-grandmother had carefully packed the moist surface of each narrow slice with table sugar for me, then shaken off the excess. "Swimming with Daddy at the point. I could almost beat him before . . ." I couldn't bring myself to say it. "And playing slapjack, and sardines." I cocked my head at Rose. "You were so funny. You wanted everybody to win." Remembering brought on a flood of emotion that threatened to spill over, so I passed the baton to Iris. "What about you? What do you remember?"

She exhaled briskly, peering into the darkness. "You, throwing daddy longlegs on me when I made you mad. Playing high-heeled dolls with Vi and Rosie while you were up at Great-grandmother's." Her mouth flattened. "Cissy, always picking on my posture. Oh, God, and the slop jars."

How could I have forgotten the slop jars? Or more properly, the chamber pots.

"Aaagh," Violet chimed in. "Do I remember those. Gross."

What with scorpions and black widows and the six stairs up to the "new" forties-era second bathroom Poppy Jack had added on our side of the cabin, Mama hadn't wanted us risking a trip to the potty alone in the night. "I had to empty them every morning and scrub them out with Babo," I said.

"We took turns," Iris corrected.

"Babo," Vi mused. "I remember that. It had a blue label with bubbles."

I nodded. "So it did."

"What about you, Vi?" Iris asked. "What do you remember?"

Vi leaned back against her chair and rocked, considering. "Daddy. And Saturday nights over at the boathouse, dancing to the jukebox." She looked across the water to where the old Clare's Boathouse had once been. Only Hanson's, next door, remained. "I wonder if they still do that at Hanson's?"

"They do," Iris said. "Every Saturday till Labor Day. I looked it up on the Lake Clare Association Web site."

"Oh," Vi said with enthusiasm, "let's go tomorrow night."

"We have a lot of work to do," Iris reminded her.

"And a whole summer to get it done," I said. "You don't have to go if you don't want to, Iris, but Vi and I will. How about you, Rose?"

Rose loved to rock and roll. "Sounds like fun."

"Well, I certainly don't want to stay here by myself," Iris grumbled. "So I guess I'll go, too."

Vi looked to Rose. "What do you remember best about our summers up here?"

Smiling, Rose focused in the middle distance and rocked. "Square dancing at Mountain City. I loved that. And going to Clayton to spend our allowances while Mama got groceries."

My nose remembered the comforting scent of the five-and-dime. "I got cloth to make tutus for my ballerina dolls." I smiled in Iris's direction. "And you always picked out something right away, then spent the next half hour swapping out every other twenty-five-cent toy in the store. But you always ended up getting Cracker Jacks." Pieces of the past managed to surface from behind the chaos of the past two years. "And Vi loved balls and bats and jump ropes."

I looked to Rose, remembering her little white pinafore tops and the musky summer-child smell of her, and her wistful little face as I'd held her in my lap. "You always wanted books."

Iris nodded. "I had to read them at least six times before you'd finally go to bed, even when you were so sleepy you could barely keep your head up." She yawned hugely, then got up. "On that note, I've got to hit the hay. I hardly had any sleep last night, and I'm beat from all that cleaning."

The rest of us got up, too. After hugs and good-nights, we locked up (an exercise in futility) and went to our newly sterile rooms.

By the time I finished my nighttime rituals and climbed into bed, I was insensible with fatigue, too tired even to pray.

My last thought before I fell into a dreamless sleep was that our remaining eighty-nine days might not be so bad, after all—if only I could remember to lighten up.

And quit speaking movie.

7

*[Dreams are] that which permits each and every one of us to be quietly
and safely insane every night of our lives.*
—WILLIAM DEMENT

. . . .

$\mathcal{I}$N MY SLEEP, I was five again, and vivid colors brought the summer
of 1955 to life.

Great-grandmother was still alive and sturdy, emanating the subtle
scents of lilac and talcum powder from her old-fashioned voile dress.
She never stirred from her room unless she was dressed up, which made
everything she did seem special, and me when I was with her.

"Dahlia, where's your snake-stick?" Her aristocratic face was stern,
but her tone far nicer than when she corrected Cissy, which was a lot.

I halted, trained from the cradle to be still and face my elders when
they addressed me. "I lost it." A lie, but, having been born with a hyperac-
tive imagination and a seriously elastic conscience, I knew better than to
trouble trouble with the truth. And my fantasy world was still far more
vivid than mere reality.

The truth was, I'd started out pretending to be the Great Wallenda
crossing Tallulah Gorge with the snake-stick as my balancing pole. But
the next thing I knew, I was a Georgia Tech cheerleader, and it was a

flaming baton. I'd tossed it so high that it had stuck in the branches of a white pine.

"We're not really in the woods, anyway," I rationalized to my great-grandmother. "Just the creek bed. So I'm okay."

I could con most anybody, but not Great-grandmother. She ignored what I'd said, closing the distance between us. "It hasn't rained in a month." Her capable hands snapped off a yard of skinny poplar sapling. Any other eighty-five-year-old might have struggled to do it, but even that tree knew better than to argue with my great-grandmother. She handed it to me, then waved her walking stick toward the lake. "Dry as it is, every snake for miles will be heading for water. We'd best keep alert. There might be a little rattler or a copperhead hiding under those stones you're hopping on, and I wouldn't want either of you to hurt each other." She said it without scolding or complaint, simply stating a reasonable concern.

Great-grandmother didn't hate the snakes, so I didn't, either. She'd explained to all four of us from the beginning that these woods belonged to all the forest creatures first, so we had to respect them and learn to live together safely and in peace.

I believed her. Everything Great-grandmother said was absolutely, perfectly true. You could ask anybody.

Steadying herself with the polished walking stick Poppy Jack had made her, she dabbed a hankie at the deep vee of her lace collar, shaded by her wide-brimmed straw hat.

At five, I had little control when it came to my antsy body, but I tried my best to stay close to her. "Why do you always wear that black dress, Great-grandmother?" I did an arabesque in the dry riverbed, grateful for my brief outfit of shorts and an eyelet midriff top with pinafore sleeves. (And cotton underpants with an eyelet ruffle at the legs, of course. Everybody in the world had to wear underpants; it was a law.) "You could wear shorts, like Cissy. Isn't it hot, always wearing a dress?"

Great-grandmother kept her steady uphill progress toward the hillbilly's cabin, our source of fresh eggs. "Dear child, I have never worn shorts, nor shall I ever. Unlike your grandmother"—her head shuddered briefly, the way it always did when she mentioned Cissy to me—"I have a sense of decorum and modesty. Even with good cotton stockings, I feel salacious showing my ankles."

"What's *salacious*?" Arms outflung, I turned almost all the way around on one toe.

Great-grandmother cocked her head. "Oh, dear. Well, in this instance, let's just say it means embarrassed."

"Mama wears shorts," I worried aloud, then defended, "but I don't think she's salacious about it. She wears them all the time, except when we go to town."

"Your mother is nothing like your grandmother," Great-grandmother ruled. "She's young and fit, and modest. She never shows bad skin."

I stopped. "What's bad skin?"

"Skin that should only be seen in private, or by a doctor," she answered without the slightest hint of irritation.

That was one of the things I loved most about Great-grandmother. No matter how many questions I asked her, she never got that weird look and told me to go do something else the way everybody else did.

A brief reflection caught my eye, so I bent to inspect it. At that time of day, a narrow, wending strip of sun lit the center of the old creek bed, igniting the mica in the sandy soil so it sparkled like Tinkerbell's fairy dust. Great-grandmother had showed me how to find many treasures there—arrowheads, rocks with real garnets in them, layered slabs of mica big as my five-year-old palm, and nuggets or crystals of beautiful rose quartz for my collection. But this time, the sparkle turned out to be just a little piece of mica, small as the scales on a brim.

Great-grandmother waited till I was ready to move on before she resumed speaking. "As for why I wear black," she said, "I do so in memory of your sainted great-grandfather, may God rest his soul."

"Oh." I'd never met Poppy Jack, who'd died before I was born, but I'd seen the pictures of him on the walls of the round staircase at Hilltop. He looked really nice (except for his bushy ole mustache), with a true smile and thick, wavy hair, and round little glasses just like Great-grandmother's. "Did you ever kiss Poppy Jack?"

Great-grandmother tucked her chin at my impertinence, then smiled. "Every chance I got."

I circled her, leaping from rut to rut on the washed-out riverbed. "Wasn't it icky, with that big ole mustache?"

Her gray eyes narrowed. "And whose big old mustache made you think that was icky?"

"Mama's godfather." Pirouetting, I scowled, remembering the stink of cigarettes and the prickly hairs on my cheek. "You know, Mr. . . . Davies. He came to our house from Paris and brought us some wine that he snuck out of France, just for Mama and Cissy. He even let me have a sip."

Great-grandmother arched her left brow in disapproval. "Oh, he did, did he? And what did you think of this illicit wine?"

I assumed *illicit* meant wonderful, because that was what it was. "I think it tasted like sweet sunshine."

Great-grandmother let out a sigh, her sturdy lace-up heels halting. "Come here, child." Shifting her egg basket to the crook of her elbow, she took my hands in hers, and I gazed up into the shaded face I loved. "The water's so foul in France," she explained, "that they sterilize it with a little wine for the children, so I don't suppose it was too terrible that Cissy's friend, Mr. Davies, gave you a taste. But in this country, we have excellent water, and wine is for adults only. It's against the law for children to drink it." The threat of arrest would have sent Iris running for Mama's skirts, but for some reason, I wasn't impressed in the least. "I disapprove strongly of cultivating a desire for spirits in the innocent," Great-grandmother went on, "so please reserve such things for when you are grown and married."

"But that's forever," I argued, my busy feet shifting automatically through the basic ballet positions Cissy had taught me. "And wine is so good. Especially with Circus grape drink."

Great-grandmother's eyes widened behind her spectacles. "And when, pray tell, have you tasted *that*?"

I smiled, remembering the sweet, pungent flavor of Mama's red jug wine mixed with the sugary drink. "I make it after kindergarten." Seeing her dismay, I added, "But not every day. Just sometimes."

Her expression grave, Great-grandmother sat on a boulder at the edge of the path. "And does your mother know about this?"

I smiled, swinging from a sturdy branch that hung from the old riverbank. "Of course not. She wouldn't let me." At that point in my life, getting away with things posed a far more appealing challenge than my underdeveloped conscience did.

"May God preserve you," she sighed out, "from my daughter's wayward blood."

"Don't worry, Great-grandmother," I comforted. "Cissy's never bled on me. We're always very careful when we do our art projects."

"Bless your poor mother's heart. She's got her work cut out for her." Great-grandmother stood, her posture as erect as my ballet teacher's. "After we get our eggs and finish making bread, I need to have a little chat with Daisy." (Mama's real name.)

Convinced that Great-grandmother had hung the moon, it never even occurred to me that she was going to tattle.

"Come along then." She resumed plodding up the ever-steeper path.

Twenty minutes and a hundred pliés, arabesques, pirouettes, and tour jettés later, Mr. Slocum's blue-spotted coonhounds scattered the chickens and raced to meet us when we emerged from the last curve at the head of the trail. Breathless from the climb, Great-grandmother waved her hankie in greeting to Mr. Slocum, who sat on the porch at the end of the lane, smoking his stinky pipe and rocking, as always. Overalls were his favorite clothes, because he was always wearing them, without a shirt.

When he saw it was only us, he shouted a harsh command for the dogs to come back, which they did, tails wagging.

"Does Mr. Slocum ever get out of his chair?" I asked Great-grandmother from behind my hand.

"He must," she answered, "he has eight children."

I didn't get the connection, but all eight of the Slocum kids materialized like shy forest creatures, peering through the open windows and from the edges of the house.

I thought they were the luckiest children in the world. They never wore shoes and didn't have to bathe but once a week. And their back-yard was filled with great toys: a tire swing and a real-live rusty tractor, and three old iceboxes, and two wringer-washers on their sides, even an old wood-burning stove that really worked, out under a huge oak. Better still, their daddy was always home; how I wished mine didn't have to go to work all the time. But my deepest envy was for the fact that they'd never had any shots. At least the older girls who'd spoken to me hadn't. The boys never came close enough to say anything; they just spied on us from the trees and bushes.

"Does Mr. Slocum have a job?" I whispered to Great-grandmother. He was always talking about his old war wound.

"It is perfectly legal for the head of a household in this state to manufacture several hundred gallons of spirits for his household," she said quietly, another answer I didn't understand. "The mountain people have their ways. We must respect them. Though how the man feeds his family is beyond me. As long as he keeps smoking that wild mountain flower, he'll never make anything of himself."

Daddy smoked a pipe sometimes, but he liked cherry pipe tobacco, which smelled wonderful. I'd never heard of wild mountain flower, but Mr. Slocum's didn't live up to its name. It stank like burning hemp twine.

"That's enough, now," Great-grandmother cautioned as we reached the hard-packed yard in front of the porch. "Good morning, Mr. Slocum," she called in a respectful tone. We mounted the porch. "How is Mrs. Slocum's cold? I hope the chicken stock I brought was helpful."

"Waal," he replied in a harsh mountain accent, "it didn't kill 'er."

That wasn't very nice, considering Great-grandmother had gone to all that trouble, but when I started to say so, her hand tightened on my shoulder, so I didn't point it out.

Mr. Slocum cocked his thumb back toward the house. "Cold's gone, but she's abed. A branch broke and spooked th' mule when she wuz plowin' fer mah second crop, and she pulled her shoulder."

Oh, the mule! "Can I pet the mule?" I asked Great-grandmother. "Pleeeeeze."

"Ortn'ta do that, missy," Mr. Slocum decreed. "It ain't settled down good yet." He rocked, inhaling slowly. "I'll shore be glad when them wild young'uns is strong enough to plow, and so will Mertice."

"Should I send the doctor?" Great-grandmother offered.

Mr. Slocum's eyes went narrow. "Naw." He kept on rocking. "The girls bound her up good with rags'n turpentine. She'll be okay."

That was the way mountain people treated hurt dogs, not humans.

The wrinkles in Great-grandmother's upper lip deepened and set, letting me know what she thought about Mr. Slocum's "sorry" treatment of his wife, but when she spoke, her tone was mild. "Perhaps I should look in on her."

Mr. Slocum's eyes went sly. "Better not. Might be sleepin', ya know."

Great-grandmother's posture got even straighter, if that was possible.

"We've come for eggs," she said briskly, pulling three dollars from her pocket—a lot of money for eggs back then. "Can you spare four dozen? I'd be obliged."

"Kids!" he yelled from the corner of his mouth, pipe still tight in his teeth. "Git me four dozen, and make it snappy. Don't wanta keep Miz Stuart, hyere, waitin'."

Kids scrambled from everywhere, happily searching out the chickens' nesting spots as if it were an Easter egg hunt. Just a few minutes later, they arrived, panting, with precious eggs caught up in their skirts or shirts.

"Thank you so much, children," Great-grandmother said as she carefully transferred them to her basket. When she finished with each child, she winked and pressed a quarter into his or her hand, out of their father's view.

No wonder they'd been so fast. Back then, a quarter bought an order of homemade fries and a Coca-Cola at the café by Hanson's Boathouse.

I waited till we were on our way home to ask, "Can I have a quarter, too?"

Great-grandmother shook her head. "Precious one, you have your allowance. Those children have nothing but cares. It might be the prosperous fifties for us, but for them and many others like them in these mountains, it might as well be the Great Depression."

I'd heard a lot about the Great Depression from Cissy. Her husband had been a banker when the Great Crash happened, and he'd lost all their money, then gone crazy, so she'd had to divorce him—the very first divorce in all the history of our family, Mama had told me when I asked about it.

"That's nice of you, then," I told Great-grandmother, "giving the Slocum kids those quarters."

"The children," she corrected. "Goats have kids. Human beings have children."

I glanced at the brown eggs in her basket. "Better take care of those eggs. They cost five whole dollars."

Great-grandmother laughed. "That's correct, but let's just keep that our little secret, shall we? Just between you and me." She cocked her head.

"That was very good, totaling the quarters and the dollars. You're doing quite well."

"Oh, I know all about money," I boasted, bigheaded from her praise. "Cissy said it's the most important thing."

"Ah, child," Great-grandmother said, her expression intense when she looked at me. "Cissy is misguided. Faith and family are the most important things, and neither costs a cent. Don't ever let anyone tell you otherwise."

We'd been studying about Moses and the Hebrew slaves in St. Luke's Episcopal Sunday school back home, and the idea of having Iris for my slave had sounded pretty good to me, if only she wasn't such a pest. Maybe Great-grandmother could take her off our hands. "I'd sell you Iris for only a nickel," I offered, completely sincere.

"One cannot sell another person in this country," she chided. "Especially one's sister. Slavery is evil and illegal."

"But she's always ruining my things and getting in my way," I complained. "And she can't wait to tell on me."

"Then don't give her anything to tell," she counseled.

If only it were that simple. I leapt from stone to stone, imagining I could fly. "I try to be good. It's just . . . well, it seems like a good idea at the time, then the next thing you know, I'm in trouble."

Great-grandmother shook her head again, eyes on the ground. "Poor, poor Daisy." She straightened. "Come along. I want to get the bread into the oven before lunchtime."

So did I. I closed my eyes and savored the thought of fresh, moist slices packed with table sugar.

Then someone shook me. A distant, grown-up voice seemed urgent. "Dahlia, wake up."

I shot one last look at Great-grandmother, whose sad smile told me she was dead even as the dream faded into darkness.

A half sob, half groan escaped me. "What? Leave me alone! I need to go back . . ."

The shaking didn't stop. "Dahlia, honey, wake up."

Iris.

I might have known. Irritation eased my grief, and I burrowed deeper in my synthetic down pillows. "Go away." It was still dark!

The smell of coffee wafted into my nostrils. I peered through one slitted eye to see a dim hand holding a steaming mug beside me. "Two Sweet'n Lows," she murmured, "just the way you like it."

It would take caffeine by IV to get me up at such an ungodly hour.

"Come on, honey," she coaxed. "We're all going down to watch the clouds rise off the lake. You can go back to bed later, if you want to."

My other eye pulled open, and the shadowy room came into focus. "Good Lord, Iris," I rasped out. "It's still dark." I turned my back on her and her coffee, whereupon every muscle in my body complained. "Ow."

She had the nerve to pull down the covers, exposing my skin to the cool, clammy air. "Come on. You can wear your robe. Everybody else is already up."

Murder and mayhem bloomed in my brain, but I banished them, sitting up abruptly. "Nobody said anything about getting up before dawn!"

Across the room in Mama's old mirror, I saw that my hair was slabbed up and tangled on one side, and I looked as featureless as an alien, the only color in my Scandinavian pallor provided by red crease marks from the sheets. *Eerie* was the only word for it. "Aaagh!"

I turned to Iris, whose dark features didn't disappear without makeup the way the rest of ours did. "Clearly, you are deranged," was the most charitable response I could muster up. "Y'all go without me, and that's an order. And don't ever come into my room without permission again. I mean it." I rolled back onto my side, my back to her as I pulled up the sheet and thin cotton blanket. "Ow."

Blast. All that moving and cleaning had insulted muscles I didn't even know I had.

"Well," she said, "excuuuuse me."

I heard the door squeak open, then shut. A few seconds later, Vi's muffled voice rose from the room below. "I told you she wouldn't want to," she said. "Give it a rest."

God bless her.

I started to drift away, but more voices rumbled downstairs, then somebody clanked across the floor furnace in the downstairs hall, followed by footsteps up the spiral stair.

Flipping my pillow to the cool side, I groaned and pulled the covers higher.

A gentle tap at my door. "Dahlia?"

Violet. *Et tu, Brute?*

I stayed where I was. "Oh, hell. Come in."

I heard her scuffies swish across the floorboards, then felt her sit on the side of the bed. She stroked my arm through the covers. "Iris couldn't sleep," she said gently. "She waited hours and hours to wake us up." Vi was far more compassionate than I ever thought about being. "This is really hard for her, staying here with all the bugs and critters. Especially without Wilson. You know she doesn't do well alone."

"Then why doesn't she room in with Rose?" There was plenty of space for another bed in the long room above Cissy's.

"She needs to be downstairs. She won't say so, but her knee has really been bothering her. Rose said the orthopedist told Iris it was time for a replacement, but you know how that went down."

Not well, with Iris's mind-over-matter philosophy about ailments she'd never had to endure. "God forbid, she might actually have to admit something's wrong with her." Still, I wasn't moved to stir. "So Rose can room with her downstairs."

Let the early risers have the main floor to themselves. Vi understood how dancing and teaching till almost midnight for all those years had rendered me *non compos mentis* before nine.

"I know it's not your time of day," she soothed, "but it's such a simple way to make Iris happy." She stroked back my hair and played her ace in the hole. "Could you do it for me, sweetie?" she asked gently. "Pretty please?"

Oh, rats, but okay.

One molecule at a time, I dragged my soul and body into the world of the living.

I rolled onto my back, then stretched and yawned a blast of dragon-mouth into the room. "Eeyew." Cupping my hand for a test blow-back, I winced at the result, one eye closing spasmodically. Yuk. "You know it's bad when you offend yourself."

I launched to a sitting position and hugged Violet's dark silhouette, expecting to encounter the ragged terry cloth of her ratty old robe, but feeling smooth cotton knit instead. I peered into the dimness to see she had on the expensive pink knit kimono wrap I'd given her two Christmases before. "You're finally wearing my Christmas present," I complimented, my eyes closing as I laid my head to her shoulder.

"I've been saving it for my funeral." Vi rubbed my back, which felt so good that I realized how long it had been since anyone had, and how much I'd missed it. "My old one was so ratty that Aster"—her older daughter—"and Lily ganged up on me and talked Taylor into burning it in the fire pit so I couldn't bring it."

Pink robes and scuffies were a family tradition the four of us had pinkie-sworn to be buried in, a vow that thoroughly embarrassed all of our children, who'd threatened closed coffins if we insisted on going through with it.

"What time is it, anyway?" I mumbled.

A deep chuckle rode Vi's bones to my ear. "You don't want to know."

Her answer triggered, "That's the same thing Great-grandmother said whenever I asked what was behind the walled-up doorway to the old root cellar."

"Thank you so much for bringing that up." Vi's shiver ended my backrub. "Now I've got snakes and spiders on the brain."

"Mmm." I nodded, drifting.

After a moment of transitional silence, she brought the conversation back to the matter at hand. "Iris is dead set on all of us going down to the cottage to watch the clouds rise the way we used to with Daddy."

Daddy and the clouds. Boy, did Vi know how to work me.

The mere mention was all it took to resurrect the long-ago drama of Daddy's scooping me out of bed, covers and all, then carrying me in silence to curl in his arms at the edge of the dock and watch the "clouds" slowly rise from the lake while the rest of the world, even the birds, still slept.

He'd done it with each of us, saying we'd miss God's miracles all around us unless we learned to be quiet and still so we could see and hear Him. Something I'd forgotten as I struggled through the last two years on fast-forward.

Propping my chin on Vi's shoulder, I looked beyond the screens of my open windows toward the heavy mist now faintly brightened from the east. "Why do y'all always give in to Iris?" I grumbled.

Vi pulled free to smile at me. "For the same reason you do sometimes: We love her."

Not at that moment, I didn't.

"Will you join us?" she prodded gently.

The truth was, if I could recover even a shred of that long-lost peace and security, I'd be there with bells on.

"You can talk me into anything, and you know it," I told her. "Scoot." She stood, and I forced myself to follow. "Ow. You'd think, as much as I stretch and dance, that I'd be able to clean and unpack without every muscle in my body screaming, but no." I stepped to the foot of the bed and launched into my morning stretch routine without even thinking about it. "I'll be down as soon as I work out the kinks, but no gloating." I pointed a warning finger at her as she opened the door. "If there's any gloating, I'm coming back to bed."

"I'll make that clear." Beaming with affection, she handed me my toothbrush. "See you in a minute. There's plenty of coffee." All too aware how rotten my low-carb, yeast-free diet made my breath, I took the hint and flossed, brushed, *and* gargled before going down in my mandarin-style pink jacquard robe and scuffies.

Two cups of coffee and a pit stop later, the four of us lit our way with flashlights through the misty orchard, cold-natured Rose in pink chenille and Iris in a zip-up seersucker housecoat that was probably supposed to be mid-calf, but hit her at the ankles. At least she still had features. Sans makeup, the rest of us looked colorless, lipless, browless, and lashless, our blond hair lank while Iris's brown curls bloomed into a giant frizz.

Illuminated by our flashlights, beaded moisture weighted down the grass and low-growing weeds in the orchard, and our slippered feet picked up damp bits of mulch from the path. With every step, the mist grew just an atom brighter. When we reached the huge poplar at the bottom of the hill, Cardinal Cottage loomed silent and ghostly through the clouds still hovering low to the water.

The blue tarp over the collapsed roof sent a shiver of loss through me. Though the surrounding periwinkles and tiny front lawn looked well tended, sheets of plywood on the side windows glared in harsh contrast to the hundred-year-old log walls. I turned my eyes toward the low wisteria that cushioned the lakefront retaining wall. That, at least, looked the same.

Iris's flashlight brightened a shaft of fog toward the front porch. "This doesn't look so bad. The front wall and windows seem sound." She climbed the three shallow stone steps, then moved toward the front door with confidence.

"I wouldn't—" The sharp crack of collapsing porch boards cut off my warning as Iris dropped knee-deep into the crawl space filled with old wisteria vines, dried leaves, and who knows what else.

"Aaaagh!" She levitated, I swear. Two feet straight up, faster than I can say "charge it."

I turned to rescue her, but Rose held me back. "Wait. The whole thing might fall in."

The words weren't even out of her mouth before Iris stood beside us, wriggling in disgust, her housecoat hiked above her knees. "Snakes. Spiders. Rats. Ticks."

"Hold still." I inspected her calves and feet carefully by flashlight for telltale double punctures or spider bites. Black widows and brown recluses loved dark, relatively dry places. "I don't see anything. I think you're clear."

Her body shuddered. "Eeyew. I feel all crawly." She turned her beam toward the fog-shrouded dock. "Do you think it's safe to go out there?"

"*Now* you're asking if it's safe out there?" I grumped.

The dock, its ramp, and its low-floating platform looked sturdy enough for me—decking, cleats, and clad Styrofoam intact, white bumper strip still in place.

Vi looked at me askance. "Well, is it?"

"Yes," I told her. "Cissy and Mrs. Pendergrass had it replaced with pressure-treated wood not long ago." Well, maybe ten years ago, I computed. Fifteen, at the earliest.

Still, we were all cautious on the slickened surface, especially going down the gentle slope of the ramp. By the time we made it to the floating platform, the shroud of mist had gone silver and lifted to just above the weathered planks, exposing the glassy green surface of the lake. I kicked off my damp, mulch-peppered slippers, then sat beside the cleat on the left-front corner, promptly soaking the back of my robe to the skin. "Whoa. Wet here. Very wet."

The lake felt just cool enough to be refreshing on my bare feet, though.

Vi eased down past the cleat on my right, leaving both of us plenty of elbow room. "It's okay. We won't melt."

Rose left a polite interval as she sat down beyond Vi, but Iris braced her hands on their adjacent shoulders and asked, "Would y'all mind if I scoot in between you?" Without waiting for an answer, she lowered herself between them, which left the rest of us to butt-wriggle over in compensation.

"Okay. Quiet game," I invoked, something Mama had often used when we were little to buy some peace. "First one to say anything or make a sound—except sneezing, farting, or coughing, which don't count—owes the kitty five dollars. Starting now."

The only thing Iris hated worse than being cut out of the loop was having to pay more for anything than everybody else did. If she argued with me over the rules, she'd end up losing the game, and she'd be five bucks deeper into the kitty than the rest of us. So we settled to a forced, but gradually easing, silence.

I looked down at our feet lined up in the water and suddenly saw them with fresh eyes: my nine-narrows gnarly, callused, and distorted from all my years on point; Vi's long, slender, and unblemished, the way mine would have been if I hadn't abused them; Iris's tanned, short, and as pudgy as the rest of her; and Rose's a bit more delicate than Vi's and mine, immaculately manicured with toenails polished to match her nails.

The only thing our feet had in common was a second toe longer than the rest, which was supposed to mean we were the bosses in our marriages, which—in my case—couldn't have been further from the truth.

Looking deeper into the clear water, I could see every detail of the golden algae beds on the bottom ten feet down.

I remembered another time, at dusk instead of dawn, when I'd seen the bottom so clearly. Iris was sitting on it, her footed blue pajamas sending off little puffs of mud from where she'd landed. Her short, dark hair spreading like a halo, she held her breath with brown eyes wide in fascination as friendly brim swam over to check her out.

It had all happened so quickly and so quietly. Clean and in our pajamas, we'd been lying on our stomachs to look at the fish in the shadow of the platform, while behind us in their folding chairs, Mama held newborn Vi and Daddy talked to some friends. Iris got uncomfortable lying on the snaps at the waist of her footed pajamas, so she sat up, Indian-style, and leaned over to look.

I was busy watching the fish when I heard a gentle plop, then looked over to see Iris completing a tidy somersault underwater, apparently unconcerned, her hands to her knees and her legs still crossed as a trail of tiny bubbles traced her progress.

I remembered the panicked thought that I was supposed to be watching her. If she drowned, I was *really* gonna be in trouble!

Daddy! Iris fell in! my childhood soprano shrilled across the memory.

Mama shrieked and jerked me to her just as a huge, drenching splash hit us both, then Daddy came up with a furious, red-faced Iris who wailed between choking coughs, "Daddy scared me!"

I couldn't help smiling, remembering how grateful I'd been that she was okay, and how mad she'd been at Daddy for saving her. I looked over to see Iris looking back at me with the same nostalgic smile.

Five dollars was the only thing that kept me from telling her I was glad she hadn't drowned.

For all we'd gotten under each other's skin over the years, whatever would the world have been like without Iris? I didn't want to know.

A flash of sound drew our attention from each other to a big bass that leapt for its dragonfly breakfast, then disappeared into a spreading circle of tiny waves. My soul and body easing, I lay back onto the dock, propping my head on my right hand, and one by one, the others did the same.

So quiet, there. So peaceful.

I gazed left beneath the rising clouds to the red banks snaking toward the point beyond our boathouse cove. Cissy and I had dug pure, clean clay from those banks for our art projects. By the time I was twelve, she had taught me every bone and muscle in the body, and how to shape statues of fairies and goddesses and Shakespearean characters.

Wondering what had happened to those figures, I closed my eyes to wakening birdsong and another plop from the falls cove. The world was getting up.

I let out a sigh and pretended that Daddy was next to me instead of Vi.

Warmth spread through me, taking me to a deep and comforting place, the same place from which I'd ordered my dreams as a child till reality became more vivid than my imagination. I could feel Daddy's presence there with us, hear his relaxed breathing in my own.

There was a gentle whirr, then lapping at the shore that lulled me even deeper.

Just as I was about to achieve the bliss of oblivion, Daddy said, "Good morning, ladies. Is everything all right?" Only it wasn't Daddy.

Iris let out a cry of dismay, and the four of us shot erect as one, caught at our very worst.

Rod and reel in hand, a tall, ruggedly good-looking outdoorsman of indeterminate middle age glided closer to the dock in an expensive fishing boat, his electric trolling motor all but silent. His weathered face communicated relief, then amusement. Looking straight at me, he tipped the brim of his fishing hat.

Men are so visual, my dear, Cissy had always told me. *Never let one see you at your worst. That's how he'll remember you forever.*

"Good morning," Iris said stiffly, pulling Rose to her feet as she got up. "Please excuse us, but we haven't had our coffee." They turned and headed for Hilltop.

The stranger nodded, granting them only brief attention, then reverted to looking at me in expectation.

Mortified, I bit out, "Good morning." I was ready to escape after my sisters, but when I saw the soggy backs of their robes, I realized that my thin robe and gown were probably transparent with dew, so I stayed put, devoutly wishing I'd thought to put on a little makeup, at least.

Only Vi seemed unruffled. "Hey," she said to the stranger. "Who are you?"

He cocked his head back toward the falls cove. "A neighbor."

No name, but frankly, I didn't want to know the identity of the only man in the world who had seen me without a shred of makeup—and I do mean only. Even when I was married, I'd worn a little bronzer and some lip stain to bed, right up to the divorce.

Again, the good-looking fisherman eyed me with bald assessment.

The one cute man who'd noticed me since the divorce, and I looked as featureless as a sugar cookie. It's vain, I know, but I couldn't have felt more exposed if I were naked, so I decided to escape, even if I had to back all the way up to the house.

"I'll just leave you two to talk," I said, rising, then backing over to my slippers and fumbling my feet into them.

The fisherman watched in obvious amusement as I haltingly backed toward the ramp, my progress punctuated by numerous sidelong glances to make sure I didn't make an even bigger fool of myself by falling in.

Fortunately, the fog bank hadn't yet lifted in the orchard, so once I got that far, I could turn around and flee.

Vi didn't help. She just watched me, smiling, the same way he did.

We'd have words about that, later.

Before I finally subsided into the fog, I heard him tell Vi in a nice baritone, "I didn't mean to scare y'all off. I fish here every day."

Vi said something back, but I didn't hang around to listen. I turned and sprinted for the shelter of Hilltop. At last, I reached the kitchen, where the clock said five-fifteen. Panting, I collapsed beside Iris at the breakfast table and stuck out my palm. "You spoke first," I gasped out. "That'll be five bucks."

8

RIS SHOVED MY hand aside. "Don't be ridiculous. That doesn't count. Even though he scared the life out of me, the man greeted us. Somebody had to respond."

Rose pressed her fist into a stitch in her side. "What kind of person would sneak up on us like that?"

"A gentleman would have turned around and given us our privacy," Iris accused.

"I don't know if he's a gentleman," I weighed in as I got up to rinse out my special lab-glass coffee mug, then helped myself to my third cup of the morning. "But he's rich; that fishing rig and equipment cost a mint. I've seen them at the boat show with . . ." I stopped short of saying Harrison's name. "And his clothes. Those shoes, alone, cost three hundred dollars." I should know. Harrison had bought an identical pair right before he left, leaving me to pay the Visa bill.

"His *shoes*?" Iris tucked her chin at me when I sat back down with my coffee. "You sure noticed a lot, considering the circumstances."

"I always notice a lot," I said, then took a welcome slug of coffee. Perfect. Way sweet and not too hot.

"So he's a *rich* jerk," she retorted. "So what? He snuck up on us."

Violet strolled in, hiding something behind her, and joined the conversation as if she'd been there all along. "He's not a jerk," she said. "He was very nice. Apologized and explained that he was casting toward the back of his boat and accidentally bumped his electric motor and ended up too close to the dock. He didn't even see us till he turned around to correct his course."

"He should have turned his *boat* around the minute he saw us," Iris complained.

"Iris," Vi said. "Think about it. The guy fishes the same route every morning. Only one morning, he turns around and sees four women, three of them white as paste, all showing no visible signs of life, stretched out side by side in pink bathrobes on the dock of an abandoned house. If you saw that, would *you* turn around and leave them?"

Excellent point.

Rose chuckled. "I'd think it was some kind of bizarre suicide pact."

"See?" Vi asked. "He offered genuine condolences about Cissy. Said they were friends for a long time." Only then did she pull out two impressive bass and a big rainbow trout, already cleaned, on a string. "Then he gave us his whole catch to make up for scaring us."

Rose made a face. She'd spit out her first bite of fish stick at six months and hated seafood ever since.

"Friends with Cissy?" Iris repeated, skeptical. "Cissy didn't have any friends. Who is this person, anyway?" she demanded of Vi. "Where does he live?"

Vi shrugged and headed for the kitchen. "We didn't get around to names. I figured y'all would worry if I didn't come on back." While we waited for any further revelations, I heard her flop the fish into the kitchen sink, followed by the squeak of a bottom cabinet, then the clank of the cast-iron skillet on the propane range top. "Who wants bass fillets for breakfast? I'm gonna sauté them in butter with lemon and almonds."

Fish, even fresh bass, before noon didn't sound so hot to me, but Lake Clare was the one place I'd never be afraid to eat a catch. Strict regulations kept its waters and the river upstream clean to the source.

"None for me," I told her as Iris opted out, too. "I brought breakfast chops."

"I'll cook a whole one, anyway," Vi said. "Just in case."

The rest of us followed her into the little kitchen to start our breakfasts, constantly bumping into each other.

"Aaagggh!" I cried when I discovered one of Rose's "nasties" in the pocket of the apron I put on. "Get it," I ordered.

She smiled sweetly and retrieved it. "It's not used, you know."

I wasn't convinced. "So you say."

Undaunted, she announced in her capacity as eco gestapo for the family, "I've brought cloth napkins and distinctive silver rings for us to use. They're right over here." She pointed out a wire holder full of them atop the breadbox on the narrow strip of counter below the windows. "Get a fresh one whenever you really need it, but Martin and I find that one a day works well." Whenever Rose made a personal reference of that nature, it amounted to instructions. "And I've put a compost bucket beside the garbage under the sink. Please remember to put in vegetable matter only. And I brought lots of paper bags."

"Paper? What are we supposed to do with those?" I asked.

"Use them for the garbage, then take them to the Dumpster when we go for supplies once a week," she said cheerfully.

"In what?" Vi asked.

Rose smiled. "In the garbage can," she said in her slow, preschool-teacher voice.

Sounded pretty stinky to me.

I personally generated more garbage than a caravan of Gypsies, and there were four of us. A week's worth would reek for three counties.

I broke out my preschool-*parent* voice. "Rose, honey, I'm all for being green. But wild as it is on this side of the lake, there are hungry bears who've been known to eat screens and flatten the doors behind them when they smell garbage inside. Not to mention the raccoons and foxes that Cissy's been feeding for years. Garbage isn't their natural food, but if they can smell it, they'll try to get it. Plus, we'll draw bugs, especially those big old—"

Iris stopped me from finishing with, "I move we use plastic."

Rose glared at her in consternation. "I thought you were as committed as I was to living green."

"Your way," I told Rose, "we'd have to take everything to the Dumpster every night, which doesn't make sense, either. Ten miles is a lot of gas. That's why I brought plenty of three-mil contractor-grade trash bags: So the critters won't be able to smell our garbage."

"I second Iris's plastic motion," Vi said, putting the smaller bass and the trout into freezer bags, then adding water to keep them from getting freezer burn.

"I third," I said, knowing it wasn't unanimous.

"Yaaalll," Rose implored.

"You're welcome to compost," I offered in consolation, "I'll be happy to contribute. But be sure to do it away from the house. And don't be surprised if most of it's gone when you bring more."

"I'll manage," Rose snipped out, pushing past me to get her whole-wheat bagels. "I may be outvoted, but I, personally, will dump the paper bags into the Dumpster and rinse out those plastic bags for reuse."

"Whatever floats your boat, honey," Vi said, "but if they stink, we're gonna have to go back to plan A. Agreed?"

Rose went haughty, jerking open the drawer for a knife. "They won't, but okay." She moved to the far side of the kitchen and started slicing her bagel.

"This time," Iris murmured to me under her breath, "you were right on the money."

I smiled, buoyed by her rare praise.

Then I turned to Vi and went back to what I'd been wondering before the whole green thing interrupted. "What kind of friends do you think that guy at the dock meant," I asked her, "when he said he and Cissy were friends? He can't be much older than we are."

"Who knows?" Vi sharpened one of the fancy knives she'd brought from home. "It would hardly have been polite for me to give him the third degree." She cleaned the blade, then laid the biggest bass on the now-sterile dish drainer and started removing the skin with a deft touch. "Surely Cissy had *some* friends."

"She didn't mention any to me." I got out silverware and napkins for all of us. "She alienated everybody, even Great-grandmother." A long-ago summer afternoon came to mind as I laid four places at the table. "I remember sitting between Mama Lou"—Daddy's mama—"and Great-grandmother late one afternoon on the terrace. I couldn't have been much older than four.

"Mama Lou was smoking her daily cigarette." Her personal limit. "And she and Great-grandmother had their bourbon and branches." One a day, as well. "I remember them talking and laughing. They really liked each other. Then I heard the screen door open onto the verandah, and we all looked over and saw it was Cissy, coming out to join us. But Great-grandmother shot her such a hateful look that she stopped dead in her tracks and backed up into the house and left." I returned to the kitchen for the punch line. "Then Great-grandmother turned to Mama Lou and said, cool as you please, 'Why couldn't *you* have been my child?'"

Retrieving cream cheese from the fridge, Rose let out an empathetic, "Ouch."

I'd felt the same way then. "I remember thinking it wasn't fair, Great-grandmother wishing she had another daughter instead of Cissy. It shook me. Made me wonder if Mama really loved all of us, or was only pretending, the way Great-grandmother had been with Cissy." I swapped places with Rose to get the eggs. "I felt sorry for Cissy from then on. It made it easier to overlook things and love her."

"It didn't hurt that she spent all her time and attention—and *money*—on you instead of any of the rest of us, including Mama," Iris commented as she pulled a bowl from the open shelves above the sink.

"Cissy wanted to be loved," I said. "She wanted to show love, too. She just didn't know how to do it right."

"She should have learned, already," Iris said, unimpressed. "The one I'm sorry for is Mama."

"Mama learned how to love somehow," Violet added, laying the thick, gorgeous fillets with a sizzle into the hot butter, followed by a generous sprinkle of sliced almonds around the edges. "God knows, she didn't get it from Cissy."

The aroma from the pan, not the slightest bit fishy, made my mouth water. "Maybe I will take you up on that fish."

Rose picked up one of the organic tomatoes she'd bought on the way up and started slicing it. "Thank goodness for Great-grandmother and Poppy Jack. But it had to be hard for Mama. She must have wished Cissy would come back and be a real mother to her."

"I asked Mama about that," Iris said, opening her box of bran, twigs, and dried fruit. "She said she got these icky-poo, lovey-dovey letters from Cissy all the time, postmarked from all over Europe, but Mama couldn't write her back, because by then, Cissy'd gone somewhere else." She retrieved her soy milk from the refrigerator. "Then when Cissy did come back, she was penniless with a suicidal banker in tow. Can you imagine what that was like? Mama said she was afraid to make a sound, because Cissy told her he might kill himself if anybody upset him."

"That's horrible," I said, appalled. Mama had never said a word to me about that.

But then again, my conversations with her had always focused on life in the present, never the past. Beyond the bare facts of Mama's history and a few happy anecdotes she'd shared about Great-grandmother and Poppy Jack, what little else I knew of her childhood had come from Great-grandmother—who never broached the embarrassing or traumatic—or from Cissy, whose dramatic reminiscences always starred herself as heroine and conveniently skipped all the awkward parts.

Iris poured her cereal. "And no sooner was Cissy shed of the crazy banker, than she left again to teach ballet to rich people's children in Paris, sending Mama to boarding school at five. Mama said she cried herself to sleep every night till she was in third grade."

Mama had never shared any of that with me. From Vi's reaction, this was the first she'd heard of it, too, but tenderhearted Rose's silence meant Iris must have told her already. Otherwise, she'd be reacting with much more empathy for Mama.

"The reason Mama graduated so early was she didn't have anything else to do but study," Iris revealed. "Cissy wouldn't even allow her to go to school dances." Iris's features tightened with disapproval. "Then after Pearl Harbor, Cissy joins the Red Cross and takes up with a married man in California, and writes Mama all about it—how they were true soul mates, and nothing else mattered. Mama was mortified. No wonder she married Daddy so young." She poured soy milk over her nuts and twigs. "Considering what Cissy did, I think it was only fitting that she died alone and friendless."

"She wasn't friendless," Vi reminded her. "She had that fisherman from this morning."

"Fisherman, schmisherman," Iris dismissed. "The guy probably just knew her and said that to be polite."

"Cissy had *me*," I said. Even though I'd been woefully absent for the past two years. "*I* loved her."

"That you did, and she was lucky to have you." Vi flipped the fillets, which added the heavenly scent of butter-browned almonds to the kitchen. She turned to Iris. "When did you and Mama talk about all this, anyway?"

"After the reading of the will," Iris said as she squeezed past me to put away the soy milk. "I went down for Mother's Day weekend to try to convince Mama to come with us so she'd get her share, but she wouldn't budge, and David completely refused to cooperate."

The trip was news to me, but I wasn't surprised by David's reaction. After all his years as a rabbi, he was far too wise and far too sure-footed to let Iris coerce him into anything.

"You never said anything about that to me," Vi told her.

"Me, either," I chimed in. If any of us had done that to Iris, she'd be incensed to find out after the fact.

Iris shrugged. "I knew y'all would try to talk me out of it," she said. "Didn't work, anyway, so why mention it?"

"You mention *everything,*" I reminded her.

With a haughty look, Iris closed the refrigerator door just a little harder than necessary. "That's what *you* think." She and Rose exchanged pregnant glances, then headed for the breakfast-room table.

Vi cut a lemon and used a fork to ream fresh juice over the fillets. Whoa, did it smell good. Then she served our plates, adding sliced tomatoes beside the almond-covered fillets, plus a few captain's crackers on the side for me. "Breakfast is served. Here you go, sweetie."

"What other Dickensian horrors did you coax out of Mama?" I asked Iris on my way to the table with Vi behind me.

Iris's mouth pursed into two quick pouts of irritation. She'd always been sensitive about the disparity between our vocabularies, accusing me of using ten-dollar words when ten-cent words would do, just to make myself look smarter than everybody else. "What the hell is *Dickensian?*" she demanded.

"Sorry," I offered. At least I hadn't quoted any movies so far. "It means twisted and awful, like the situations Dickens put his characters in."

Iris let out a long breath, then lightened up. "We can talk about Mama later. I'm starving." She ended the conversation before I could argue by bowing her head and offering her hands. "Who wants to say grace?"

"I will," Vi volunteered as we closed the circle. "I'm starving, too."

After a brief, meditative silence, Vi chirped, "Grace." Then she pulled her hands free and rubbed her palms over the fish. "Boy, does this fish look good, even if I do say so myself."

I laughed, enjoying Iris's consternation, while a smiling Rose bit into her bagel.

Iris lifted a brimming spoonful of her cereal and retaliated with, "I brought a spreadsheet that breaks down the cooking responsibilities for the summer. I was thinking we could draw numbers to see who gets to sign up in what order. We could always swap with each other, if we needed to. What are y'all's thoughts on the subject?"

Spreadsheet? Was she kidding? " 'Scuse me, sweetie," I said as she crunched so loudly it sounded as if she were eating whole paper-shell pecans, "but I'm busy introducing myself to this god-awful hour of the morning for the first time since I was breast-feeding Junior." Despite our encounter with the fisherman, my brain wasn't really awake yet. "I'm not exactly ready to hammer out any major decisions." Much less let Iris lock us into some cast-iron boardinghouse KP routine.

Iris sniffed and kept on chewing.

I took a bite of fish and was transported. "Mmmmm," I said behind my napkin to Vi. "This is fabulous." But even the delectable fish wasn't enough to keep me from obsessing about Iris's scheduling the whole summer for all of us.

I'd always loved my alone time at home, even after my son deserted.

Suddenly, the next three months loomed before me as an apocalypse of forced togetherness. Breakfast at seven, together. Chores by the chart in allotted time. Work on the house till lunch, together. Eat at one, together. Work on the house again, together. Dinner at eight, together.

Shopping trips en masse to save gas. All recreation, group only, by vote. Every fart tallied by Iris. Everything we did or didn't do evaluated and recorded in her mental dossiers. Every decision subject to discussion. And God forbid anybody leave a dirty dish in the sink for her to find.

Lab rats went crazy and started eating each other under conditions like that.

I must have looked like a deer in the headlights, because Iris waved her hand in front of my glazed stare. "Dahlia, are you okay?"

"Fine," I lied, snatched back from the brink of madness.

Iris's dark brows knit as she peered at me. "You're always wandering away in the middle of conversations, which is very rude. Where do you *go* when you do that?"

I quoted Great-grandmother and Vi. "You don't want to know."

Iris's features hardened. "You mean, *you* don't want to *tell* me."

"No, I meant what I said," I said calmly. "You really don't want to know."

Radiating conflict alerts, Rose glanced from me to Iris.

Vi gave me a sidelong hug and a wink. "Easy does it, sweetie. One day at a time." She rose from the end of the bench. "I'll be right back. Forgot the extra lemons. Can I bring anybody anything?"

"My diet cranberry juice from the fridge," I remembered aloud.

Rose gave Iris a consoling sidelong hug of her own. "That was sweet of you, going to all that trouble for us, and I'm looking forward to the four of us finding a system that works for everybody. Why don't we have breakfast and decide what we want to do today, first? Then we can pick a good time to talk about the meals and things."

God bless Rose. "I vote we all go back to bed and wait till Monday to start anything," I said. "I'm too pooped to peep."

For once, Iris didn't wait for a consensus. "I hear what you're saying. We're all tired. But I think we should go ahead and at least make a beginning in the basement. You can stop, if you need to, to rest."

Now there was a booby trap if ever there was one. If I did quit early, I'd never hear the end of it.

"Until we get downstairs cleaned out," Iris went on, "all that dirt and mold is seeping up into the house. You can smell the mustiness rising from the floor furnace. Plus, that's the only dry place we have for storing the stuff we're not keeping."

More damp than dry, but she had a point. Air circulated through the furnace whether it was on or not. And the rusty barn roof was about as watertight as a pair of panty hose, so we couldn't put anything out there.

Vi returned with my juice and a bowl of lemon wedges.

A generous squeeze of citrus made the fish even yummier, shifting my focus from Iris to my gourmet breakfast.

But Iris wasn't finished with me. "You're always telling me not to procrastinate," she said, "to do the hardest job in the beginning so I can get it out of the way."

Normally, I was the first to dive right into a challenge, but in addition to being sore, I was exhausted from making arrangements to be away from the house and my school for three months. For that matter, Iris had to be worn out, herself. She'd done the same for her CPA practice. "We have ninety days," I reminded her.

"Eighty-nine," she corrected.

Vi frowned. "Did yesterday count?"

"Mr. Johnson said it did," Iris answered. "I called last month and asked."

Heaven only knew how many times she'd called him. "You know he's on the clock every time we call," my voice said even as my brain hollered an internal, *Don't!* Lord, now I was sounding like her.

Iris glared at me. "Of course. I kept it brief."

Even Rose had her limit, and she got our attention with, "Just listening to you two is wearing me out. Could we please drop this till after breakfast? This is our first morning here. Can't we just relax and enjoy it?"

"Brava!" Vi clapped the tips of her first two fingers on each hand together the way her baby daughter Aster used to.

Chastened, Iris and I both backed off.

Somehow, the two of us had to figure out a way to coexist for three months under the same roof without rubbing each other raw—for Vi's and Rose's sake, if not our own.

Like every morning of my life, I picked up my A.M. pill-minder and dumped my morning allotment of thyroid, antidepressants, supplements, time-released potassium, and antifungals into my left palm. Then I got my juice and sat up straight in preparation. After a brief swallow of juice, I threw back the whole handful of pills and washed them down with a generous swig.

Rose shuddered. "How do you *do* that?"

I grinned. "It's like the song about the old lady who swallowed the fly. I just open my throat and swallow the goat." I chased off the lingering bitterness from my antifungal with a couple of captain's crackers, savoring the crispy texture with each minibite.

"Why are you eating your crackers that way?" Iris asked, critical.

I answered with the truth. "To make it last longer."

"Oh," she said, exchanging her criticism for sympathy.

Awkward with her pity, I rattled on, "I don't get to eat many crispy things. You gotta get your kicks where you can when you're a host organism."

The rest of breakfast, we both behaved ourselves. Once we'd finished, I felt a lot better and realized that the sooner we got the mold out of the basement—or the Underworld, as I called it—the better.

Good thing I'd come prepared. "Okay," I conceded to Iris. "I'm game to start today."

Iris looked to the others. "What about y'all?"

"As long as you give us time to rest for a while after we get the kitchen done," Vi qualified.

"You cooked," I told Vi, "I'll clean." We'd always worked it that way.

"A rest before we start sounds like a good idea," Rose said. "What time were y'all thinking to start?"

Iris looked at her watch. "It's twenty to seven. What about nine?"

"Okay with me," I said. "But for future reference, I don't want to do anything before nine again. And I'd rather not talk till I've had my coffee and looked at the paper."

"Can we even get a paper up here?" Iris asked.

"Hanson's gets the *AJC*," I said, as all natives call the *Atlanta Journal Constitution*. "I guess I could get one for tomorrow morning today."

"Count me in," Vi said.

"Me, too," said Rose.

Papers! Of course. We all did the crossword and the jumble. That was enough to get us through breakfast in peace.

"Do they have *USA Today*?" Iris asked.

If it kept her quiet through breakfast, I'd make sure they did. "I'll find out."

"Thanks," she said. "If not, the *AJC*'s fine."

Things were definitely looking up.

Iris stopped me on my way upstairs after we'd cleaned up. "I'm glad you brought the respirators. You'll need them down there."

She sounded sincere, so I took it as an olive branch.

Encouraged, I volunteered, "I brought enough for everybody, and a few extras."

Vi came up and curled her fingers into claws, quoting Cissy in a witchy voice, "Watch out, or the microbes'll get you!" She finished with a witchy cackle. "Aaaaah-hah-hah-hah-ha!"

"No microbes for me," I said with a smug look. "Just you wait and see." My white Tyvek hazmat suit had double-sealed Velcro closures and covered everything from top to toe but my latex-gloved hands and my face, which would be sealed up by the full-visored industrial respirator that filtered the air I breathed down to a single micron.

By nine, the others had been down in the basement for ten minutes before I got to the main floor, already perspiring despite the cool morning, but that was to be expected. My hazmat suit didn't breathe. Before I put my respirator on, I opened the deep freeze by the basement door and sucked in a few long, cooling breaths, focusing on the sensation so I could invoke it later in the basement.

Then I finished suiting up, pulling the rubber straps of the visor tight to my head. I couldn't resist a few Darth Vader breaths before I crossed the floor furnace and opened the door to the Underworld. Bending almost double so I could see my Tyvek booties, I carefully descended the open stairway into the crammed basement below.

No sooner did the others see me descending into the dim light of the only two working ceiling bulbs, than they turned my way and started laughing. Even Violet.

The farther down I came, the harder they laughed. Vi's and Rose's hilarity was muffled by the hot-pink plastic painter's respirators they'd put on, but Iris's derision rang loud, her respirator unused on the bottom step.

I *knew* they were going to make fun of me. The heat of embarrassment rose to my face, but I managed a smile anyway.

"For cryin' out loud, Dahlia," Vi hooted, "you look like *Andromeda Strain*. Where in the world did you get hold of that getup?"

"I thought you were broke," Iris criticized. "How much does a suit like that set you back?"

Considering the fact that it was critical to my health, and the suits were mass-made for white rooms and hazardous-waste removal, it hadn't cost all that much. "My pal Jenny who does research for the CDC got it for me wholesale, so it wasn't that much." A hundred fifty dollars, including a box of heavy-duty vinyl gloves and a full-face visored respirator with each. So I'd bought an extra, just in case, with the last of my credit. But I wasn't about to tell Iris any of that.

I smoothed the Tyvek over my chest and said, "Laugh all you want, but my allergist wrote me a prescription for this, and he told me not to set foot in the basement or the barn without it. And even with it, he said I could never go to New Orleans. Ever." I looked down the narrow swath of dirt floor that led to one of four sets of French doors on the west wall, all so overgrown with wisteria that no extra light made it in from outside. Then I scanned the damp, rusty junk and mildewed footlockers and boxes piled at least four feet high everywhere else. Mold, mold, mold. "This suit is not overreacting," I told Iris, knowing what she was thinking.

Iris's mouth flattened. "I never said it was. And I already apologized ten times for what I said at the reading of the will." She had. But she'd also remained subtly critical of all my precautions. "Do I have to keep apologizing for the rest of my life?"

"Only when you laugh at my efforts to keep from croaking while we're here," I told her frankly. "It's embarrassing, being such a weirdo. May you never know what it's like."

"Oh, sweetie," Rose said with her arms spread wide, heading my way. "We didn't mean to hurt your feelings." She hugged me with a crinkle of Tyvek.

Vi wasn't the touchy-feely type. "Face it, Dahlia," she said. "You look like the marshmallow man in *Ghost Busters*, and I mean that with all respect."

Translate: Lighten up, sis.

Setting aside my injured sensibilities, I struck a pinup pose. "Pep Boys, eat your hearts out."

"Okay," Rose said to all of us. "I think this basement needs a plan."

"I vote for piles," I responded. "Like on those cleanup shows. Keep, sell, donate, and toss." The local volunteer fire department had agreed to pick up anything decent we didn't want for their annual sale, barbecue, and Chris-Craft parade on the Fourth.

"Don't forget recycle," Rose added, then rattled off, "Newsprint, books and magazines, PETE plastic, natural plastic, colored plastic, clear glass, colored glass, cans, and scrap metal."

"I hereby nominate Rose as a committee of one in charge of recycling," Vi declared.

"I second," I added.

"I third, which makes it unanimous," Iris said with a smile. She picked up an old broom handle and dubbed our sister's shoulder. "Rose, you are hereby delegated to set up the recycle piles and rule on what goes where."

Something clicked in my memory. "Wait a minute," I said. "Are we even sure they can handle that kind of a breakdown here? Do they even *have* recycling? Need I remind y'all about that time at Fripp? My minivan never smelled the same again."

Clearly unrepentant, Iris and Rose exchanged amused looks.

In a disastrous experiment never to be repeated, Mama had rented a beach house on Fripp Island that wasn't quite big enough for us and all our toddlers and kids. After a rainy week of who-hit-who and "She was playing with that. Give it back," I was way past ready to make a surgical exit and head for home and sanity. But Rose, a recent convert to the eco gestapo, decided my new minivan was the only vehicle with room enough to haul out our final load of garbage—which included eight stinky bags of recyclables she'd carefully sorted out all week, lecturing the bearer of every can, bottle, newspaper, and scrap of plastic about the environmental impact of using, much less discarding, such substances. After endless delays and rechecks by the you-know-who duo, the kids and I were finally given permission to reek our way over to the island's Dumpsters, where we watched the others zoom by with waves and smiles as an island resident informed me they didn't recycle, period. Suffice it to say, I didn't take any of it home.

"You gotta admit," Vi told me through her respirator, "that was choice."

"Looking back, yes," I acknowledged. "But it was hugely frustrating at the time, so I don't want us to end up in the same situation."

"I can call," Iris offered with an eagerness generated by almost two days without her cell phone, "and find out what they recycle here and what they don't."

"Great," Rose said.

"And I second the piles," Iris added.

"I third," Vi voted.

"Then it's unanimous." Rose moved on. "Now. Who wants to do what?"

As the book lover among us, I spoke first. "I want to go through all the old books and papers. You never know what we might find." Even better, it was a job I could do alone, the way I worked best.

"Great," Rose agreed. "I'd like to go through all the old furniture." She glanced past the furnace to the hillside section of foundation where all the damaged and discarded pieces had been shunted against the walled-up door to the old root cellar. "We might find some treasures, too." Lord knows, if there were any, she could find them, after thirty years of auctions, flea markets, garage sales, and *Antiques Road Show*.

"I'm strongest," Vi said. "I can haul out whatever's not too heavy, but I'd really like to work with Rose so I can learn more about antiques and collectibles."

Which left Iris the odd man out.

Uh-oh. I prayed she wouldn't try to team up with me.

"Iris, what would you like to do?" Rose asked her. "You're welcome to work with us."

"Okay," she conceded, warily peering at the heap Rose and Vi were about to tackle. "That looks pretty spidery to me."

"Didn't you bomb down here?" Vi asked.

"Yep," Iris said, still on the lookout anyway.

Rose's brows converged in disapproval. "I really wish you hadn't done that. Boric acid powder works just as well."

"Speak for yourself, Rosie." Iris only used that nickname when Rose had stepped on her toes. And *only* Iris was allowed to use it.

Another thing occurred to me. "Has anybody thought about how we're supposed to get all this junk and trash off the property? Cissy always told me the garbage people around here were thieves."

"Cissy said all the local people were thieves," Iris reminded me.

We decided to see if we could get a Dumpster delivered, then Iris cheerfully went upstairs to check on that and the county's recycling capacities.

I rustled up a hammer and a rusty screwdriver, then picked my way through to a haphazardly piled stack of footlockers on the one small area with a concrete floor.

Man, but it was "close" down there. Out of habit, I tossed my hair to cool it, but my tidy bun was cocooned in Tyvek strapped down firmly by my respirator.

Trying to focus without my reading glasses (should have thought of that), I had to use several strategic whacks and wheedles to get the top trunk's rusty lock open.

Inside, atop a hodgepodge of the Captain's war memorabilia, a folded piece of letter-sized paper with a floral border caught my eye. I unfolded it and found Cissy's strong handwriting from top to bottom, with numerous cross-outs, corrections, and rearranging arrows.

Thanks to the boldness of her writing, I was able to read it at arm's length without my glasses. *Paris, 6 October 1922. Dear Sergei* . . . Aha. A man.

With all the scribbled corrections and oblique language, it wasn't easy on first reading to figure out exactly what she was trying to say. The only thing that came through loud and clear was cold fury. So I read it again. And again. It wasn't till the third time, when I was able to piece it together the way she'd indicated, that I finally got the message between the lines.

"Hah!" I cackled. Cissy was chewing this guy out for leaving before breakfast after they'd spent the night together!

Sergei . . . Wasn't that the name of the White Russian prince Cissy claimed to have had a "romantic interlude" with?

"Y'all," I hollered, waving the rough draft. "There really was a White Russian prince!"

Rose and Vi straightened as one, then said, respectively, at the same time, "Great. We'll look at it later!" and "We'll never get anywhere if you start reading things at this point."

"Remember what we said," Vi reminded. "Only four piles: recycle, keep, donate, and toss. We'll go back through the keep piles once we've cleared some space."

"But there's no room for piles yet," I argued logically.

Vi raised a pointer finger in her work glove. "Wait a sec." She rooted through an open box beside where she'd been working, then came up with a set of Cissy's pastels. "Here," she said, handing the flat metal box to me. "Mark the trunks, so we'll know where to put them."

After placing Cissy's letter on the bottom step, I took a coral pastel and marked *keep* on the footlocker. Maybe the Captain's grandchildren would want his things.

It took a lot of effort and levering and tossing, but I managed to clear a space beside the haphazard pile of trunks, then shoved the footlocker onto the concrete. "I hereby christen thee the keep pile," I announced through my respirator.

Rose struggled past Vi, lugging a long bent piece of rusty metal. "Could you please open the door for me?"

When Vi obliged, a blessed breeze blew cool, fresh air inside, and sunshine from beyond the shadow of the house brought light to supplement the two bare bulbs.

Vi helped Rose heave the metal into a patch of weeds outside. After a swipe of her gloved palms, Rose announced, "I hereby christen thee the scrap metal recycle pile."

The first step in a journey of a thousand miles.

When they came back in, I could see from their eyes that both of them were smiling behind their masks.

Then I heard a slow-mo avalanche behind me and turned around to find I was completely boxed in. I summoned the others with, "Heeeeeelp," and was rescued, but that meant we had to restack everything, so without planning it, we ended up working companionably to deal with everything that had toppled loose. Iris returned from upstairs with news that we could get a Dumpster delivered, and the county did, indeed, recycle all of Rose's categories.

Halfway through the tumbled boxes, I came upon one full of letters bound in ribbon, all of them from me. I poked around to see if there were any underneath from anybody else, and found the bottom loaded with letters to Mama, some at the lake, but most of them postmarked in the thirties, addressed to Mama at boarding school, and marked *return to sender.*

Ignoring Vi's instructions, I opened one up and read in Cissy's handwriting:

> *My precious child,*
> *In the interest of preserving your privacy, I've waited to respond to your earlier letter so you would be home for the summer, and Mother could read this to you.*
> *Dear one, Mummy loves you so much. I would love nothing better than to bring you here to live with me, but circumstances do not permit it. Europe is becoming a very dangerous place, and I fear the French did not learn the lesson of history from our Great War to End All Wars. But Paris is where I must be in order to ply a living.*

*As I have explained so often, America does not cherish the Dance
as Paris does.*

*With every day my heart breaks to be apart from you just as much
as yours does to be parted from me, but Mother and Poppy are there
to be my arms and my lap, always open to you. Do not despair,
little one. You have warm clothes and shelter, plenty to eat, and the
freedom to come and go as you wish, which is more than I can say
for the poor, downtrodden Jews here, who have been forced to live in
ghettos and endure unspeakable abuse, especially from the Poles and
Austrians.*

Cissy went on about the political situation there. Mama had written
that her heart was breaking to be separated from Cissy, and this was
Cissy's response? A lecture about anti-Semitism and European politics?
And "Buck up. It could be worse"? I looked at the date and saw that Mama
had been only nine. Then I read on.

*You mustn't let the other children upset you with their jibes about
your parentage. You are descended from the only royalty that truly
matters in America: strong people of exceptional talent and artistic
accomplishment. Mummy will be so proud if you could muster the
courage to live up to such a standard.*

*How are your piano and dance lessons going, by the way? I wrote
your instructors, who wrote back that you were trying valiantly, and
it pleased me to hear it. Remember, practice makes perfect.*

*Mummy thinks of you every single minute. Please remember me in
your prayers, as another attempt to find a man worthy of my high
standards has gone awry, but for your sake, precious one, I shall
continue trying to find you a father worthy of your heritage. But as I
have said so many times before, a bad father is far worse than no
father at all. Whatever I have done or shall do in future is for your
best interests, alone.*

Your ever devoted,
Mummy

Poor Mama. I'd never read such a load of hogwash in my life. The burden she must have borne at such a tender age was no longer a detached

concept, but a tragedy to me. My heart literally ached for the little girl she had been.

"What's got you so quiet?" Vi asked from over my shoulder.

I handed her the letter. "See for yourself. It's awful." I glanced through more of the letters, finding them about the same—florid declarations of love, excuses for Cissy's abandonment, and no emotional comfort for Mama, just ridiculously adult objectives from which to fall short. I'd have stopped accepting them, too.

"No wonder Great-grandmother said what she did to Mama Lou," I told Vi as she read, her brows peaked in sympathy. "If a daughter of mine treated a precious granddaughter of mine like Cissy treated Mama, I'd probably feel the same way."

I still loved my son deeply, even though he'd left me for the luxuries his father offered, but since he'd become a teenager, I honestly couldn't say I liked him very much. I'd tried all his life to give him sound values and a sense of responsibility, but his father's obsession with luxury and appearances bore bitter fruit in my son as he'd entered adolescence, that most selfish of phases. Focused solely on popularity and *things,* Junior had quit trying in school and acted as if the world existed to satisfy his whims. So I couldn't help empathizing with the way Great-grandmother must have felt about Cissy.

Rose and Iris came over and read some of Cissy's letters for themselves. When they were done, Iris poked through the box again. "Not a single letter from Mama or any of us. Just yours and her own." She peered at me in indictment. "Typical. And you loved her."

"The woman who wrote those letters wasn't the Cissy I knew," I told her. "True, she was self-absorbed and gruff, but she was a much better grandmother than she was a mother, very generous with her time and concerned about my life."

"Well, she wasn't with any of us," Iris stated for the jillionth time since we were kids.

Rose and Vi didn't say anything, but I knew they agreed and had to resent it at least a little. "And I'm at fault for that?" I countered, more weary than defensive. "Have you ever considered it from my perspective?"

"Of course we did," Rose said, "and we don't hold you responsible. You were just a child, craving attention, and she delivered. No one can blame you for accepting what she offered." Iris did. "And you had dancing in common. Maybe that was the only emotional bridge Cissy could cross."

It suddenly occurred to me with chilling clarity that my choice of what Cissy had offered, over my loyalty to my sisters, hadn't been that different from my son's choice of what Harrison offered, over loyalty to me, and the parallel struck me like a javelin to the heart.

Vi pulled the letters from the others and shoved them back in the box, closing it. "Okay. That was then. This is now. In spite of all of this, Mama's happy." She shot a pointed look at Iris. "You're happy. The past is past."

Would that it could be between me and Iris. But I'd picked Cissy . . .

As if she'd read my thoughts, Rose said, "Cissy's dead and can't hurt us or Mama anymore. Except through letters like these. I think we should have a cleansing ceremony and burn them, releasing all those old resentments once and for all." Normally, Vi and I pooh-poohed such New Age rituals, but in the case of Cissy's letters to Mama, I agreed with Rose.

Iris looked skeptical, too comfortable with her grudges to want to let any of them go, but there was always hope.

"I'd like to keep my letters to Cissy, though," I said. "I've almost forgotten what my life was like before I married. It might be nice to remember."

The others glanced to each other, then settled on me in agreement, nodding. "Okay."

Vi placed the box of letters on the stairs. "We can sort through them later."

We went back to work in silence, but pretty soon, we were hollering to each other through our respirators and sharing ridiculous finds.

Vi opened one of the footlockers. "Oh, y'all." She carefully lifted a tiny, disintegrating empire gown of pale green silk organza over a column of deeper green satin. Hand-painted florals peaked just below the tiny, high waist on the right side, then trailed in an elegant arc down to the hem in front and back, leaving the opposite side clear. "Cissy's wedding gown from the war." We'd all seen her formal black-and-white photo in the dress and the portrait the Captain had commissioned from it, but the real thing looked like a miniature, and the colors were still surprisingly fresh.

Iris fished out an open-toed pump with a really high stacked heel, its footprint so small, it wouldn't have reached from my heel to the base of my toe pad. "Look how tiny she was," Iris exclaimed.

"I sure don't remember her feet being that tiny." But by the time I came around, age had taken its toll, the way it was doing with me, now. Cissy's abused feet had been gnarled and swollen by arthritis ever since I could remember, and mine were well on their way to being just as bad.

"It's the shoes," Vi pointed out. "They're made to minimize the foot size. See how far toward the toes the base of the heel hits? Look." She measured the length of the shoe compartment between her thumb and middle finger, then turned the span level horizontally, revealing a much more normal foot size.

I nodded. "That's more what I remember."

Holding the dress open by the bodice, Iris peered down inside. "That waist is smaller than my thigh."

The gown was hand-stitched in perfect rows, beautifully put together. No label.

I tried to button the puff sleeves over my wrist, but the narrow hem lacked almost an inch, conjuring visions of the teensy Mrs. Simpson, who'd made her diminutive royal lover look tall. Cissy and the Captain had seemed normal in my memories, but Daddy must have towered over them. "All those pictures hanging in the stairway," I commented. "I knew they weren't tall, but . . ."

Vi pulled Cissy's Red Cross uniform from the trunk. "How about this?" Moth holes riddled the wool fabric of the salt-and-pepper gray peplum jacket, but it still looked natty with its badges and button-up pockets. "Dang. This waist would make Scarlett O'Hara look like a cow. It's almost unnatural. Did Cissy wear corselettes?"

"No. Great-grandmother wouldn't let her," I said, "because she knew they were unhealthy."

Iris whistled low. "We are talking seriously teeny."

"She must not have eaten anything," Rose commented, "or drunk anything but water."

Iris lifted a finger. "Speaking of water . . ." She headed upstairs, leaving the rest of us to marvel over the other clothes we found, including a genuine Mainbacher suit.

Then Vi rolled up a pair of tap pants and shot them at me using one of Cissy's old torpedo-front bras that still had a surprising amount of snap to it as a slingshot.

Rose and I grabbed two more bras and started a lingerie blitz.

"Ooo," Vi said when we heard Iris cross the floor furnace on her way back down. "Let's all get Iris."

Rose hesitated. "I don't know. I don't think she—"

Too late. Iris's legs appeared on the stairs, and Vi and I let fly with balled-up underwear. "Aha! Take that, you varlet!"

Iris didn't laugh. She just bent over and peered our way, a tray in her hands bearing a pitcher of ice water and four glasses. "Not one more shot, or no water for you two."

No water for me, anyway, in my full-face respirator—as if she didn't know.

Vi brightened. "Cease-fire." She pulled off her respirator, then rubbed the red marks it left behind. "Thanks." She poured a glassful and started chugging.

Just watching her, I immediately went parched, but there was no way I could have any without taking off my gear, which I knew better than to do in that miasma of mold. Seeing the condensation run down the sides of the pitcher had another adverse effect: Four cups of coffee and twelve ounces of diet cranberry juice picked just that moment to ask for the exit, stat.

Flashing on how long it would take me to get out of my hazmat suit, I suddenly felt trapped.

The others and the box of letters blocked the stairs, so I raced outside, pulling away my respirator to take in deep gasps of unpolluted air as I shouted back, "Don't worry. I'm okay."

Now there's a whopper for you. I was about to pop, but I did make it to Cissy's bathroom in time.

If I'd known how the day was going to end, I might have been more cheerful when I had to suit back up, but I didn't.

9

Nothing sets off fireworks like a long, slow dance on a hot summer night.
—CISSY STUART GARDNER ETHERINGTON

. . . .

*A*FTER TAKING CARE of business, I stripped to my underwear, drank tons of iced water in front of a fan, then got calm and cooled off enough to go back to chain-gang duty in the Underworld. Regular breaks for the same routine helped me get through the rest of the day without ending up in the booby hatch.

It's true that many hands make short work, even if four of them function only by committee. We accomplished a surprising amount for our first effort, clearing wide paths to the major piles, the largest of which, of course, was the one we needed to go through again. (Three guesses who put the most on that one.) When we finally uncovered Poppy Jack's heavy antique woodworking machines, we found them hopelessly rusted up, good only for scrap—assuming we could get them to the dealer in Clayton.

We also uncovered a refrigerator-sized Wells Fargo safe that was in the same sad condition, its door rusted open, the inside stuffed with rough drafts of Cissy and the Captain's Great American Novel they'd tried to write after World War II, about what would have happened if the South had won the war. As an avid reader all my life, I'd managed to get through everything from *The Canterbury Tales* in Middle English, to bound physics treatises, to Gibbon, but it took only one of Cissy and the Captain's endless, rambling, flowery paragraphs to leave me cross-eyed, with thoughts of burning the thing lest it be inflicted on any other unsuspecting reader.

I could only hope the Captain, not Cissy, was responsible for what I'd read. They must have showed it to Great-grandmother. Surely, she would have offered constructive critique.

Not that Cissy accepted critique, even when it cost her thousands. Just a year ago, *Women's Forum,* a major magazine, had accepted an article she'd written about being an emancipated woman among the Lost Generation writers when she was dancing in Paris, but when the magazine had refused to let Cissy have the final word about their edit, she'd torn up the check and sent the pieces back with a scathing indictment about exploiting women writers.

We designated a footlocker to all of Cissy's writing efforts, then forged ahead.

By the time we quit at five, the pile of scrap metal had grown to substantial size, and we'd filled thirty—count 'em, thirty—construction-grade plastic bags with moldy old books, magazines, cushions, sickroom supplies, and household castoffs.

Worn out, we took turns showering or bathing away the dirt and microbes, then had our happy hour with wet hair out on the verandah in our pink robes and scuffies. I savored the fizz in my cut-rate Splenda-sweetened decaf cola. Iris had her usual weird martini-of-the-month. Rose sipped a totally organic gin and tonic, but Vi opted for plain old white wine.

We were all peacefully rocking in the late-afternoon sun when a huge red-tailed hawk swooped down to glide above us in the verandah, then came to light on the far railing, in the shade.

We all froze, transfixed—Vi and Iris and I in awe, and Rose in fear, because her 1961 Easter duck had sat on mine, smothering it, a trauma that lingered in her aversion to anything feathered. For that matter, feathers in general.

"It's okay, Rose," I reassured her, my voice low. "He won't get close."

I touched Iris's arm. "That's the same hawk I saw when I got here. Cissy must have fed it, trained it to roost with her out here."

"Just as long as it doesn't head this way," Rose said loudly enough to scare him off, but he didn't budge.

"That is the biggest hawk I've ever seen," Vi murmured. "He's gorgeous."

"Makes me think of Daddy," Iris said with nostalgia.

As if that were what he'd waited to hear, the hawk swooped away into the orchard, then flapped into the sky, disappearing toward the cove around the bend.

We watched in silence, then all started talking at once.

Vi wanted to feed it. Rose wanted us to hang aluminum pie pans from the rafters, keeping it away. And Iris and I swapped memories of sitting in Daddy's lap and watching hawks fish when the lake was still, or capture voles in the orchard.

Her memories were so different from mine. She'd been afraid, comforted by Daddy's protective presence. I'd thought Daddy had the power to conjure the regal birds, and I'd wished I could touch one, stroke his brown feathers and see what lay in the depths of those enormous eyes.

Our discussions bled over into our supper of lasagna (chicken pie for me) and fresh salad from the garden. After Iris sprayed us all down with insect repellent, we took our decaf coffees back out onto the verandah by the bright light still glowing from the west. I was happily contemplating a bit of reading before an early bedtime when the sound of Beach music wafted across the lake from the Boat Church pavilion next to Hanson's Boathouse.

Every Saturday night since Clare's Boathouse had been condemned and demolished in the seventies, the nondenominational Boat Church had hosted the traditional summer jukefest for all the lakies, plus a few brave locals.

Iris leaned forward. "Oh, y'all, listen. The Four Tops." She stood and tugged at Rose's hand. "Let's go, pleeeease. Wilson hasn't taken me dancing in a million years."

If you could call Iris's awkward efforts dancing.

Rose stayed in her rocker. "And who, pray tell, do you plan to dance with? No way am I gettin' up in front of a lot of strangers and dancing with a woman, even if you are my sister. People might get the wrong idea."

"God forbid anyone might mistake y'all for lesbians," Vi teased good-naturedly. "Usually it's me that gets hit on." More than a few students and waitresses had mistaken Vi's lack of frills, androgynous sporty attire, and athletic build to mean she had an alternative lifestyle, but she always put them straight with a laugh.

Tired though I was, I stood and offered, "I'll dance with you. Who cares what people think? Lord knows, Cissy wouldn't."

Iris took my hand and formally led me to the clear space beside the rockers, where we started the stroll. (Even Iris could do the stroll.) The others couldn't resist and joined us. Laughing when the music stopped, we agreed to slap on clothes and faces and meet back in fifteen minutes to take the boat across the lake. (A five-minute trip, versus thirty in the car.)

After eye makeup, lipstick, and some bronzer to keep me from looking like Casper the friendly ghost, I threw on a red tank top and black capris that showed off my still-fit dancer's body, then I twisted my hair into a tight chignon at the nape of my neck. I hid my gnarly feet in a cute pair of Kate Spade rubber flats and grabbed a lightweight white overblouse in case the ride back was as cool as I remembered it.

When we met on the verandah, I saw that the others had brought their wraps, too.

Poor Iris. Hot weather left her with only two wardrobe options: let it all hang out to keep from melting, or roast in something flattering and concealing.

She'd opted for the former, her "muffin top" and fluffy arms on display above her black jeans. No way would I say a word. What she ate was her business, not mine, a concept she had trouble reciprocating as an ovo-lacto vegetarian.

Flashlights in hand, we went down to Cissy's boathouse, accompanied by a travelogue of possible complications from Iris. "Did everybody freshen their Deet?" We had. "If you didn't, I've got the bottle in my purse. The mosquitoes are awful this time of day." After a two-second intermission, she resumed with, "I can't drive a boat. Can any of y'all?"

"I'll drive the boat," I volunteered, though it had been several years since I'd piloted Harrison's Sea Ray or taken Cissy across the lake in her little aluminum fishing boat.

Iris shot me a worried look. Since I was prone to fender benders, she was probably wondering if I'd run aground, or worse.

"I'll be very, very careful," I assured her. I hadn't ever driven a boat at night before, but how hard could it be? The Boat Church was in plain sight across the narrow basin, a straight shot of less than half a mile from our cove, and there was still plenty of twilight. Dark fell fast once the sun set on the flatlands, but we'd be there before then, with time to spare.

"There better be life jackets," Iris went on. "If there aren't, we'll have to go back and drive over. No way am I gettin' in that old boat without a coast-guard-approved life jacket." Et cetera, et cetera.

The faded orange Mae Wests we found hanging above the slip had cotton covers, which tells you how old they must have been, but they were coast guard approved.

Vi took one down and whacked at the dust on it, raising a cloud that sent us all sneezing. She stepped into clean air to give it a wary sniff. "Phew! Sour. Maybe we should test one to make sure they still float." She grabbed the long waist strap from a ratty one and threw the vest into the water. It floated fine. "Okay. They're stinky, but serviceable." After pulling it back to the narrow gangway, she picked the best of the lot. "Here, Dahlia. This one looks the least moldy."

"Thanks." I dared not think of the mildew and who-knows-what-else fungal poison that was probably growing in all of them, so I resolved to sit on mine.

Vi handed two to Rose and Iris, then picked one for herself and got into the boat. While the Dithering Duo stayed on the dock to inspect theirs for bugs—or, God forbid, spiders—Vi helped me aboard, then I carefully made my way to the ancient fifteen-horsepower outboard in back.

Locating the rubber hose from the gas tank under my seat, I remembered Cissy's instructions the last time I'd taken her to Hanson's Boathouse for a fill-up. *Firmly squeeze the bulb on the gas line twice, and only twice. Make sure the engine is in neutral, then pull the cord till it starts. But don't choke it again, no matter what happens, or you'll flood it.* It had taken me fifteen pulls to get the motor going that day, but by golly, I hadn't squeezed the bulb again. No, ma'am.

To my surprise, this time took only four pulls, but the motor smoked and sputtered till I gunned it a few times, then tapered back down to a steady idle, something Daddy had taught me way back when. It was all coming back.

"Okay," I called to Rose and Iris, still on the dock and clearly confounded as they helped each other with their life jackets. "You don't have to use the straps that go between your legs," I told them. "Just make sure the waist strap is snug and the chest ties are secure." I made a mental note to have the kitty buy new ski vests with Velcro closures. They looked like the lifeboat drill on a cruise ship.

Poor Cissy, all those years of holding on to every square foot of this place, too miserly to buy decent life jackets. She was hardly cold in her plastic bag and cardboard box, and there I was, desperate to sell it all away so I could keep *my* place back in Buckhead. I knew her will said it was okay, but it sure didn't feel okay now that we were seeing hard evidence of what she'd sacrificed.

Guilt, guilt, guilt.

"All aboard!" Vi hollered to Rose and Iris. "This means you."

Our combined weights strained the twelve-foot fishing boat to its limit, so we had to shift our positions to balance the load. When we finally reached an equilibrium, Vi sat in the prow, Rose and Iris in the middle, and me at the stern. Even so, the gunnels were disturbingly low to the waterline.

"Okay," I announced. "Everybody sit tight. No sudden movements, and I'm not kidding. Got it?"

Iris bristled. "You don't have to give orders. Who made you captain?"

"Whoever drives the boat is captain," I told her. "If you'd rather do it, I'll be happy to hand over the helm."

She refolded her sweater. "You know I can't drive a boat." No. She'd rather ride and criticize. "But that doesn't give you permission to start barking orders. Have you completely forgotten your please and thank-yous?"

I hated it when she patronized me that way. Especially when she was right. I *had* forgotten my please and thank-yous, maybe because of my decades of ballet training—first as a dancer and then as a teacher—where time could not be taken up by such amenities. "Before this summer is over," I said to Iris by way of amends, "I promise to teach you how to drive this boat. Now, would you ladies please help me cast off? Thank you."

Iris granted me a smug smile. "Of course. You're welcome."

I backed out into the cove very carefully, letting the boat stabilize before I shifted to forward and accelerated to a comfortable speed for the motor, which was so slow that every mosquito in the neighborhood caught up with us. They whined around us but didn't bite, thanks to Iris's heavy-duty insect repellent, which she brought out of her purse as her lips shaped *West Nile* in disgust. After a fresh application, she spritzed each of us without bothering to ask if we wanted any.

We made it safely two-thirds of the way across the lake before it got really dark. We could hear the echoing words to the golden oldies and see the people in the Boat Church pavilion laughing and talking along the railings.

Something seemed . . . different, out of parameter, but before I could put my finger on it, Iris ducked abruptly and groped the top of her head, glaring skyward. "What was that?" she hollered over the motor. She flicked on her flashlight and shined it haphazardly toward the stars.

"What was *what*?" I asked.

Rose ducked next, but this time, I saw a flicker of darkness streak away. I remembered the same thing happening when we were little. Daddy even tossed them huckleberries. "It's only a bat," I reassured the others, but Iris and Rose went stiff with alarm. "It's normal for them to feed on bugs at nightfall. Don't worry. They don't bite humans."

"Unless they're rabid!" Iris shouted back, covering her head with her sweater like the Virgin Mary in a Christmas pageant.

Rose followed suit with her windbreaker.

"Relax, y'all," Vi told them, "Dahlia's right. They're just going after the bugs."

Not a good choice of words around Iris. If there was anything she hated more than bats, it was bugs. She hunkered down and scanned the skies for invaders.

I throttled up to outrun the mosquitoes so the bats wouldn't have reason to dive-bomb us, but that put the back of the boat in serious peril of taking on water. Before I could ask Iris to move forward, she screamed and jumped to her feet, frantically scrubbing away at the back of her neck and hair. "Aaaaaggghh! Get it off me! Get it off me!"

It was all I could do to keep us from capsizing.

Dear Lord, had she really been attacked by a rabid bat? "What? What?"

"Spider!" she shouted back.

Rose quailed. "Where? Where?"

Suddenly we looked like the bad guys trying to find E.T. in the midnight forest, our flashlight beams crossing haphazardly inside the boat, which started rocking dangerously as we moved along.

I slowed, but Iris did a panicked little circle dance that rocked the boat even more. "Freeze!" I roared, shifting to neutral, then throwing it into reverse just long enough to bring us to a stop. "Or we're all gonna end up in the lake!"

Rose and Vi tried to get her to sit down, but only made things worse.

In the heat of the moment, I completely forgot that, while we had to shout to hear each other over the motor, our voices carried across the placid water to anybody within a quarter mile. Quite a few people at the pavilion railing turned our way and pointed, only to turn right back.

Meanwhile, Iris went right on having a hissy fit.

"Do not move," I bellowed, finally getting through to her over the noise of the sputtering motor. She froze, and the boat started to settle.

I used to hate spiders, too, but daddy longlegs never really qualified because of their tidy little orange bodies and clean, abstract legs. As the engine sputtered to a stop, I shined my flashlight into the center of the boat and spotted a fairly large specimen halfway between me and where Iris had been sitting. "Okay. Everybody stay calm. Please." I kept my voice cool and deliberate, like somebody defusing a bomb. "I have found the spider." I captured it by one of its legs, high enough not to break it, but low enough that it couldn't climb onto my hand.

Rose whimpered, leaning as far away from it as she could without upsetting our fragile balance.

Poor daddy longlegs. He was fish food, for sure. "I am throwing it into the lake."

Iris cracked an eye to see for herself.

I whisked it behind me. "No, don't look," I scolded. "You'll have nightmares."

She dutifully closed her eyes again.

I flung it as far as I could, then rubbed away the feel of it on my clothes. "Okay. It's gone." I scanned the boat again with my flashlight while Vi and Rose did the same. We found no spiders, but apparently, I was the only one who noticed that we had started taking on water in the back, because none of them mentioned it.

Perfect. But first things first. "There are no more spiders," I told Iris. "It's okay to sit back down."

"We all made sure," Rose added.

Only then did Iris relax her arms and open her eyes, but her feet remained firmly planted.

"You're safe." Rose took her hand. "Crisis over, sweetie. You can sit down again, but be very careful. We seem to be taking on a little water. Nothing to get upset about," she hastened to add.

Iris nodded like a sleepwalker and descended to her seat.

"Don't worry about the water," I said. "There are some cups in here to bail with, but we'll be there before we need them. I'm just gonna start the motor and get us to the dance, and we can all forget this upset." I squeezed the bulb twice, made sure the outboard was in neutral, then pulled.

Nothing. Not even a hiccup.

I throttled up a little, then tried again.

Still nothing. Even though the starter wheel turned freely, I checked the gearshift and reset it on neutral, just to be sure.

Nope.

Above us, the sky went deep indigo, the western ridges in stark silhouette against a band of tangerine. I looked to the east and saw Venus gleaming brightly.

It would be dark soon. I needed to get us going.

Several more efforts yielded the same lack of results. When I'd been with Cissy, the motor had at least put out a smoky little cough with every pull. "Okay. It must have gotten a little mad at me for putting it into reverse while it was still going forward. We'll just keep trying." Was it me, or was the water under the gas tank getting deeper?

I pulled again. And again. And again. And lots more agains.

Zip.

Flushed, I sat down in frustration, shallow water under my feet. Meanwhile, night fell like a ton of bricks.

Iris turned and asked me, "Did you check the gas?" She wasn't catty about it, but the question alone was enough to make me feel the fool.

Judas, Jonah, and Jezebel! I hadn't even thought about looking at the gas. How stupid could a person be! I let out a doom-struck sigh. "No."

The others exchanged pregnant looks.

I bent over and turned the beam of my flashlight onto the tank beneath my seat, trying to lift the bottom corner. It didn't budge. Way too heavy to be empty. Or . . . I pivoted into a squat for a better look and saw the bailing cups and the two aluminum brackets that secured the gas can. Rats.

Praying I would find gas, I unscrewed the cap on the tank and shined inside. "At least half full," I reported with relief, "and the tank's clean. No rust or debris to clog the fuel line."

I made an executive decision. After replacing the cap, I ignored Cissy's warning and squeezed the bulb twice more, have mercy on my soul. Then I pulled again.

Still no sign of life.

I throttled up a little more. After several tries, I hadn't smelled excess gas, but I checked the water by the prop with my flashlight, just to be sure. No rainbow slick coated the surface, so I hadn't flooded the motor. Still, I gave it several more tries before announcing, "This is futile. It's dead as a carp." Though why a carp, of all things, deserved to be held up as the gold standard of being dead was beyond me.

The water was inching forward with increasing speed. "I do believe it's time to start paddling. And bailing." I said a brief arrow-prayer that somebody would come along to help us, but it appeared that everyone who was going to the dance had already arrived, except us. The rest of the lake was deserted. "Iris and Rose, would you mind getting out the paddles, please?"

"Okay," Iris said with trepidation, "but not till we've made sure there aren't any spiders in there."

"Of course." There were bound to be, but I hoped otherwise, and was delighted to hear there weren't. Which was the good news.

The bad news was, one of the paddle blades had split lengthwise, which left us with only half.

Uh-oh.

The water was now halfway up my shoes and rising ever faster. "Okay," I said, "we can do this." I kicked into solution mode, handing out cups. "We need to start bailing back here *now*." I put my shoes on the seat. No way would I ever find my size in Kate Spades at the thrift shop again.

Iris looked at her heavy plastic cup as if it were full of spider eggs.

I spoke past her to Vi. "We'll just have to find a balance when we paddle. Probably best to do it from the center seat. We'll figure out how to balance our strokes. Would you please swap places with Rose? And Iris, you can come back here and bail while we paddle." I remembered to tack on, "Please."

Rose was only too happy to oblige, but Iris balked.

Scowling, she crossed her arms tight over her chest, refusing to bail. "Why don't *you* bail?" she asked me. "And let *me* paddle? You're already back there."

"In case you hadn't noticed," Vi told her, "there's water in the middle, now, too."

"You've got a cup," she retorted. "So bail, already. I want to paddle."

I pressed a fist to my lips to keep from getting into it with her. She was just coming down off a hissy fit and clearly wasn't thinking logically. Nobody in her right mind would pull this passive-aggressive ca-ca in our kind of fix.

With typical selflessness, Rose plucked Iris's cup from her and quietly started to bail with both hands, scooping and emptying over the side in steady, graceful arcs.

When I trusted myself to speak calmly, I told Iris, "Honey, you haven't picked up a paddle since you were ten. Vi and I kayaked through the rapids in Colorado."

"Oh, please," she snipped out. "This is hardly the rapids. You're just rationalizing because you want me on poop detail, bailing out dirty water. In the dark."

Lord, give me patience.

Vi bristled. "Iris, that is absurd. It's gonna be hard enough for me and Dahlia to keep this thing straight." I winced. When was Vi going to realize that taking my side only made Iris worse? "If we wait for you to get the hang of it," Vi argued, "we'll be waist-deep in water. Swamped."

"Sunk," I corrected compulsively. "This thing doesn't have positive flotation." And the wind had shifted, wafting us downshore from the Boat Church. "Please, Iris," I begged, feeling the water rise. "Please, please, please don't make this the hill you pick to die on."

The set of her mouth told me I was wasting my breath.

There was always behavior modification. Knowing better than to try logic, I decided to let her find out firsthand why it wouldn't work. I forced a smile and a cheery tone. "Okay. You can paddle." I carefully avoided any more "orders" or absolutes. Instead, I put her in the driver's seat. "Which side would you like to sit on?"

There was a fifty-fifty chance she'd pick the left, the one I wanted her to, so her strokes with the whole paddle wouldn't be as strong against mine with the skinny one.

For once, she made up her mind in a blink, with an unerring instinct for the perverse. "The right. I'm right-handed."

Perfect.

Watching from the bow, Vi turned her face skyward, lips folded inward, knowing exactly what had just happened.

Iris and I traded sides, scooting close to the gunnels.

"Great." I handed her the whole paddle. "You can have the good one. Just set your own pace, nice and easy, and I'll try to balance my strokes to yours with the skinny one. We'll be fine, as long as you find a steady, comfortable pace and stick to it. Try not to pay attention to how I'm paddling. Just find your rhythm and keep it up." I knew she couldn't. "It helps to keep the paddle perpendicular to the boat," I couldn't resist adding.

To my amazement, she quickly adjusted her pace and grip to a long, powerful stroke that made it impossible for me to keep up.

"We're going the wrong way," she warned as we veered toward my side.

"Who knew you would be so good?" I admitted. "I can't keep up."

Fueled by that small praise, she suggested, "Maybe we should switch sides."

Thank you! "Good idea."

Vi turned her flashlight toward Rose in the back. "Rose," she said, "let me spell you with the bailing. You're lookin' a little peaked, there."

"Thanks," Rose panted out. "I'm starting to see stars, but when I slow down, the water starts gaining again."

Vi nodded. "Once Dahlia and Iris are settled, we can slide past each other in the middle."

"Why don't you try paddling with Iris?" I suggested to Vi. "I don't mind bailing."

"Fine," Vi said with a hint of annoyance, "but we'd better do it quick, before Rose faints."

Talk about too many cooks. But this time, we'd end up *in* the soup instead of serving it.

We changed out in slow motion, then I started to bail with a vengeance.

It soon became evident that Vi couldn't keep us straight, either, despite Iris's efforts to lighten her stroke.

From the bow, Rose leaned toward Iris with a consoling hand on her knee. "Sugar, this isn't working. Maybe we ought to give Vi and Dahlia a chance."

Thank you!

Easy as you please, Iris nodded and shipped her paddle. "Sure."

She and I swapped places.

The kicker was, Vi and I couldn't work it out, either. We had to keep swapping paddles to correct our heading, which took us only a few yards closer to shore, but back on course, at least. Then a strong gust of wind rustled through the trees, sending us back where we'd started.

Totally frustrated, Vi smacked the water again and again with her paddle, letting loose a string of cusswords that would have made an NFL coach proud.

After a pulse of shocked silence, we all burst out laughing, which was quite cathartic despite the fact that we were in a sinking boat with a broken motor in the middle of the lake, with only one and a half paddles.

"There's one more thing I can try," Vi offered, pointing to the prow. "I'm the strongest. I can paddle in the front by myself. Maybe that'll work. Y'all shift back a little so we'll balance."

We did, but the plan didn't work. The boat was so overweighted, she barely made any progress. By then, all three of the rest of us were bailing away with all our might. A rivet must have come loose in the hull.

I realized we might actually have to swim for it.

Talk about embarrassing. We'd managed to get a little closer to the pavilion, but the dark banks near it were way too steep and rocky to get out there. The only place we could was right at the dock. No way would we escape detection. The only other spot we could safely get ashore was at the gas docks three hundred feet farther, in the boathouse cove.

Just damn.

As we bailed away in silence, my sisters' faces reflected the same thought.

Then I heard something behind us and turned around. "Shhh!" I said, and the others stopped bailing. "Listen."

My sisters pivoted to follow my line of sight to the cove left of Cissy's land.

The undeniable sound of an old Chris-Craft roared in the cove, then settled to a guttural hum. A white light emerged from the boathouse across from Mama's deserted cottage, then swung slowly around till we saw a red and green one slightly lower, moving our way.

Oh, please, let them rescue us.

Be careful what you wish for.

"Iris, give me your sweater. Please."

The boat picked up speed, heading right for us, its bow high into the wind.

I waved Iris's white sweater, and the others started yelling, "Help."

Yep. They were coming. We cheered.

But as it neared, still barreling along at full speed with its prow riding high, we stopped cheering. It wasn't slowing down.

Then I realized what was wrong. "Lights!" I shrieked. "We don't have any lights! They're riding so high, they can't see us!"

We scrambled for the flashlights and stood, aiming them toward the boat, but saw only the front of the keel. A very large keel, as in "smash us to smithereens."

"Get ready to jump!" I told my precious sisters. "Wait till you're sure it's not going to stop, then get as far from the boat as possible!"

FOUR ATLANTA SISTERS DIE IN FREAK BOAT COLLISION. The caption flashed behind the news anchor who not-so-subtly wondered why we had crossed the lake at night without any lights in such a small boat.

One foot braced on the gunnel so we could abandon ship, as our flashlights waved frantically toward the looming boat, I turned my face heavenward and shouted a petition to God from the bottom of my soul. *God, this is all my fault. I should have realized we didn't have any lights. Please don't punish my sisters for my stupidity.*

At that very moment, the Chris-Craft jerked sharply toward the pavilion, sending up a huge wake that sloshed another forty gallons or so into our boat. It circled safely away from us, then cut its engine. A tall man stood, silhouetted against the lights of the pavilion. "God! I didn't even see you till the last second! I almost ran over you." His exclamation sounded shaken, not accusing. "What happened? Did you lose your lights?"

"We'll talk about it after you pick us up," Vi called back. "We're taking on water, here."

He sat immediately and turned his spotlight our way, which blinded us. Wincing and shielding our eyes, we heard him restart the engine, then throttle down and head our way at a cautious, wakeless putter. "I am *so* sorry." The voice was deep and masculine, with just a hint of mountain twang.

Weak with relief, we watched him draw expertly alongside. Only then did he cut the light, leaving us all seeing spots.

"Is everybody okay?" he asked with what seemed like genuine concern.

"We are now. Heads up." Vi tossed a rope toward his voice.

He caught it and drew us close against his shiny Chris-Craft. I grabbed the side of his boat near the inboard housing and pulled us snugly alongside, stabilizing our escape.

One by one, he helped us into the interior of his beautifully restored boat, then secured ours to a ski ring at the back of his. Without us in it, Cissy's boat rode high enough to waggle along behind us without a huge strain on the Chris-Craft.

Still seeing spots, I took the seat beside the rescuer who'd almost killed us. "This was all my fault," I confessed when he returned and started the motor, my voice unexpectedly sultry from shouting.

Lit from behind by the stern light, he kept our speed slow and steady.

"There was plenty of daylight when we headed for the dance," I went on, "but the motor quit on us, and we started taking on water. It's my grandmother's boat, and I've never been out with it after dark. Then the bats came, and then a spider got on my sister, who's textbook-phobic about them. I was so busy trying to calm her down so she wouldn't capsize us that I never even realized we didn't have any lights till you kept on coming. By then it was almost too late." The enormity of what had almost happened finally sank in, and I went queasy, closing my eyes. "I sure am glad you saw us. I was getting ready to meet Jesus." My voice cracked with emotion on the last.

My lids brightened as we came into the pavilion's security lights.

"You're not half as glad as I am," he said with candor, not resentment. "I'm not sure I could live with something so terrible on my conscience."

A man with a conscience. Rare, indeed. And forthcoming about his feelings. I found myself warming to our rescuer. I opened my eyes for a better look at him.

"You!" The dad-gummed gorgeous fisherman! In *very* expensive classic casual.

A slow smile lifted one side of his mouth. "I might say the same thing, myself."

He glided alongside the end of the pier to a seamless stop, then cut the engine and leapt out to tie us up. Vi tossed him the rear rope with a wicked little grin.

He helped the others out first, then pulled me easily up onto the dock. After a brief nod to the others, who were taking this all in, he made the suggestion of a bow to me. "Allow me to say that you all certainly clean up nicely."

"You may not," I bit out, covering my embarrassment with haughtiness. "And if I hear one word about this morning from another living soul, I'll . . ." What? "Tell everybody you deliberately splashed us with your wake when we were already sinking."

His smile spread. "Be my guest. They won't believe you. I'm beloved in these parts."

"Humble, too, I see."

"Nope. Just honest." He cocked a thumb toward Hanson's. "If you lovely ladies will excuse me, I'm going to tow your boat over to the repair shop before it sinks. They know every screw and bolt in that motor."

"And how would you know?" I challenged.

He sobered, his eyes darkening. "Your grandmother was a very close friend."

A likely story. "Funny. She never said a word about you, Mr. . . . ."

Unfazed, he responded smoothly with, "Considering the fact that I've seen you and your sisters in your matching pink bathrobes and slippers, then almost killed you, I think first names are in order. I'm Clete."

Vi swooped in to pull me toward the stairs that led up to the pavilion. "Thank you for rescuing us, Clete. She's Dahlia."

Before I could recover my dignity, he hopped back into his boat, then started it with a throaty roar. With a brief salute, he headed slowly toward Hanson's with ours in tow.

Rose and Iris repeated their thanks and waved.

"Have you lost your *mind*?" Vi whispered at me as we headed up to the dance. "He's gorgeous, just the right age, and he's not wearing a wedding ring. And no mention of a wife."

"Have you lost yours?" I countered. "My life is unmanageable enough. The last thing I need is a man."

Rose and Iris caught up with us, their lack of conversation betraying the fact that they were listening to our every word.

"I'm telling you," Vi said, "this one's a keeper. And he's very interested in you."

"And how would you know? You only met him this morning."

She looked ahead, smiling. "True, but I talked to him, and you didn't. And I watched him watch you run for the house in your bathrobe. His body language is very wholesome. Good men are rare as hen's teeth, but I only need a few minutes to spot one, and he's a good guy."

"You and your instant truth." I shook my head. "Like I said, the last thing I need is a man. Even a good one."

We reached the crowded landing, and Iris pointed across the dance floor. "Oh, look, y'all. A real jukebox. Come on, Rose." She pulled Rose past us. "Let's check it out."

Suddenly I felt hugely self-conscious. I hadn't been to anything like this without Harrison for decades. Hadn't been to anything like this *with* him for the last few years of our marriage, except charity events and League socials, where he'd circulated like a hungry politician, leaving me to my women friends, most of whom had disappeared almost as suddenly as Harrison had after the divorce.

When had he and I stopped going on dates? Having fun?

When had our marriage become a cage instead of a sanctuary for him? Could I have done anything to change that?

Stuffing away my self-indictments, I focused on the chatter among the well-heeled lakies around me. They were far too sophisticated to be obvious about it, but I picked up immediately on their subtle awareness of our presence.

It wasn't attention like the admiring or jealous kind we used to generate. I couldn't remember exactly how long it had been since men noticed me as a woman. I hadn't consciously sought that kind of recognition, but I sure did miss it now that it was gone. Call me shallow, if you want, but it gave me confidence.

"I think they know who we are," I whispered to Vi.

She read my expression, then took my arm and drew me close to her side. "Who cares? Come on. Let's go see what Iris and Rose find so fascinating on that jukebox."

Thank God for Vi, even if she did keep trying to set me up with total strangers. Bolstered by her presence, I was able to recover my composure.

When we reached Rose and Iris, they were reading each other the CD selections and laughing.

"What's so funny?" Vi asked with a grin.

Rose pointed to the titles. "See for yourself."

We did and started laughing, too. The selections were a wild mix of old-fashioned, foot-stomping bluegrass, golden oldies, classic country western, a little salsa spiced by a tango or two, and rock-of-Gibraltar classic shape-note hymns that made me think of the tiny little church by the creek near Clayton where Daddy had loved to sing along in his strong, sure baritone. Thinking back, I realized the little congregation hadn't even had an organ or piano, just a pitch pipe to start them off.

I spotted a title I remembered from the real jukebox at Clare's. "Oooo, they've got Hank Williams Senior's greatest hits." I reached into my pocket for the stash of quarters I'd brought, but Iris punched the numbers into the keyboard.

"Put your money away," she said. "It's free."

We listened as "Lonesome Whippoorwill" drew slow-dancing couples onto the dance floor.

I closed my eyes and savored the undiluted purity of the music and Hank Williams's narrow, mournful voice. "I just love that song." Then I watched the dancers who looked into each other's eyes with affection, some old, some young, and some in between.

Iris listened with a worried expression for a while longer before saying, "You're kidding, right?"

I turned to find her sincere. "No. I'm not."

Her jaw dropped behind pursed lips as she shot Rose a sidelong, wide-eyed glance.

I couldn't help smiling. "You made that exact same expression when Mama made you eat a bite of tomato aspic." Affection welled inside me.

She grinned. "Aaaggh. Don't remind me." She shook a finger my way. "You told me gelatin was made out of cows' hooves, and I barfed."

"Well, it is," I said innocently.

"I remember that day," Vi contributed. "I never touched Jell-O again till Taylor's mama served it at the preengagement his-parents-ask-our-parents dinner. Taylor made a big deal about how it had been his favorite as a kid, so I had no choice but to eat it. There wasn't even anything in it to cut the texture." She shivered. "Every bite just got bigger and bigger. Yuk."

I couldn't resist invoking the one food we all detested. "It could have been worse," I told her. "It could have had *cottage cheese* in it."

"Eeeyew!" the others said in unison.

Rose beamed. "I've always liked Jell-O just fine. Even Mama's aspic."

"Suck-up," I said cheerfully.

Iris pointed to the jukebox. "I've enjoyed about as much of this guy as I can stand. Do you mind if I switch to something peppier when this song is over? I'm ready to boogie, baby."

Judging from the decreasing number of dancers, I realized her opinion was shared by a lot of the people present. "Go right ahead."

After Hank was done, "Give Me Just a Little More Time" cranked up, and Iris pulled me toward the dance floor, joined by most of the other couples. "C'mone, baby," she said in a decent imitation of Jerry Lee Lewis. "Let's dance." She started doing the mashed potato. Badly, but with abandon. Never mind that it was completely wrong for the song. Despite my embarrassment, I joined her.

We hadn't been going at it for more than a few minutes when two lake ladies forced their husbands to cut in and introduce themselves, providing each of us with a proper partner, which hit me sideways, I must say. Those women thought their husbands were *safe* with us. Talk about a blow to the ego. Never mind that we were all monogamous to the bone. No woman worth her salt wants to be considered sexless.

Apparently, everybody there knew exactly who we were, because one by one, the inner circle offered all four of us their husbands, who dutifully pointed out their wives and told us their history on the lake, most of it relatively recent.

"Our family built up near the dike back in the seventies," bragged one nouveau riche guy with way too big a Rolex and *way* too much chest hair showing. "When did yours come?"

I batted my eyelashes at him. "Nineteen nineteen. Our great-grandparents built the first house up here, before the dams were finished. Everything but the timbers came by wagon from Savannah, then a barge took the goods across the river, and mules finished the trip to the site. My great-grandfather talked the power company into running a direct line from the generators on the other side of the mountain to our house."

"Oh." He managed a pained smile till a vaguely familiar guy cut in and took me off his hands.

The heavyset newcomer peered at me through his reading glasses. "Dahlia?"

"Yes?" I gave him my stage-door-Johnnie smile. "You look familiar. Have we met?"

And there it was, that fuzzy hubba-hubba look I'd been missing, but he maintained a respectful distance as we danced. "I'll say we've met. On a Saturday night just like this one, over at Clare's. You were the very first girl I ever kissed." A deep dimple in his right cheek triggered something of note, but I couldn't come up with a context. "In the shadow of the concession stand. I was eleven, and you were nine and the most gorgeous thing I'd ever seen. Still are."

God bless him.

He caught the attention of a rotund woman who stood frowning at the edge of the floor, then pointed to me and mimed, "It's her." Then he turned back with a jolly, "That's Patsy, the love of my life."

It was clear Patsy didn't like his dancing with the first girl he'd ever kissed.

He chuckled. "You wore my ID bracelet for exactly three days, till I burped in your presence and you sent me packing."

"Joey Finnerman?" the depths of my memory spat out. "You were the cutest, skinniest, boldest redheaded boy I'd ever met." I saw him still in those bright blue eyes. "That was the first time I ever kissed a boy. You did a good job of it, as I recall. I haven't stopped—" I left off the word *since* because it wasn't true. Harrison had quit giving me anything but an absentminded peck years before I wised up. I recovered with a brittle, "What the heck have you been up to all this time?"

He grinned. "Not skinny anymore, as you can see, but I sure had fun getting this way. Patsy's a fabulous cook." He waved to her again, but she peered back like a schoolteacher who'd just heard a firecracker go off in her desk drawer. "That's my Patsy. We've been married two years."

I'd expected him to say forty.

"I love being married," he confided, "I'm just not very good at it. But I have high hopes this time." He waggled his eyebrows at me. "Unless you're available."

I could tell he was only kidding. "What did you grow up to be?" I deflected.

"An internist. Best one in Greenville, South Carolina. But things with the insurance companies got so bad that I converted my practice to custom care with an annual fee. Fewer patients, cash or check only. My retainer's a couple of thou a year, but I make house calls and everything. Just have a small office with an answering service. Patsy does the books and keeps up the records. That's how we met. My patients come to see me, they see *me*, not some Rottweiler receptionist. On time, unless I have an emergency, in which case I'll call right away and work them in before the end of the day."

"Sounds great. I wish I could afford something like that."

"You? Our prima ballerina?" he scoffed. "You're a legend in your own time."

"That was then. This is now, after getting fleeced by the husband of my youth." Why was I telling *him*? I certainly didn't want that on the local grapevine, a tidbit Patsy looked like she'd just love to share. "Could we consider that last remark doctor-patient privilege?"

"Absolutely. I hereby waive my fees and accept you as a patient. Gratis."

"For that, I might invest in the trip to Greenville and back." Not that I could ever get naked in front of the first boy I'd ever kissed, but I appreciated the offer.

I couldn't help wincing when he stepped on my toe for the third time. "It's been so good to see you. I'm sure we'll cross paths before the summer's over. I'd love to meet Patsy. But right now, I think she's ready to drag you out by your ear." I lowered my voice. "I think we're having too much fun. Better go reassure her. Good cooks are hard to come by, these days, especially at our age."

He laughed. "You've still got it, kid."

A deep, familiar voice said from behind me, "May I cut in?"

"Thanks for the dance," I told Joey, then turned to Clete. Feeling sassy, I curtsied. "But of course. Did Patsy send you?"

"No, but it was good of you to be so nice to Joe. Even when a man's happily married, he appreciates being flirted with by a beautiful woman." A seductive undercurrent resonated in the last, but it didn't come across as glib.

Hallelujah. Twice, in one night, even if this time it was from the nosy fisherman! I was full of myself, indeed.

The jukebox struck up "Seems Like a Mighty Long Time" and Clete effortlessly led me into a leisurely collection of ballroom moves.

For a man his size, he moved with surprising elegance.

"Wait till the next song comes on," he said as if he'd read my thoughts.

Disconcerting. So was the realization that the husbands had shifted their attention to my sisters, who were happily chatting away and meeting wives as if I'd been taken off the dance card.

If there's one thing I can't stand, it's being the last one to know something, especially since that something had been a secretary in a condo in Paridalla. But I definitely got that feeling.

Then the song came to a close, and Clete spun me to a graceful conclusion. A smattering of the spectators applauded.

He cocked that half-smile. "Get ready."

"For what?"

The music answered for him. It was a tango. God, I loved to tango, but Harrison had never bothered to learn.

Clete lifted a hand my way like a pro, and I took it, grateful that I looked up to his face instead of down on his hair plugs the way I'd had to with Harrison.

I will not make a spectacle of myself, I vowed. Just keep it simple.

But Clete's tango was anything but simple. He guided me into the steps with coiled grace, leading me into more and more complex moves until I let go all the stops, and there was only the music, the man, and the movement.

Something woke up low inside me.

Eyes locked, we functioned as one, cheered on by our audience, who had given us the floor. I hadn't felt such a rush in decades.

All too soon, the last few passages brought us toward the conclusion, where Clete leaned me backward, supported by his strong hand, and angled over me at the final dramatic clash, close, but not touching.

Cheers and applause broke out.

"Dang, Clete," a local buck perched on the railing shouted through his cupped hands. "Git a room."

Clete pulled me to my feet, then lapsed into his unassuming smile and let go of my hand for a bow to his friends.

"Encore," the lakies called, clapping louder.

He lifted his hands to calm the applause. "Please, enough. I'm old," he called back, "and it's getting late." They laughed, then went back to their cold drinks and coolers.

He turned to me in the hum of conversation that followed. "Thanks. That was fun."

I was panting, heated from the exertion, but he wasn't even breathing hard. "Where in this good green earth did you learn to dance like that?"

"Rio," he stated simply. "And São Paulo." He pronounced the latter like a native. "But mostly from your grandmother."

"Cissy?" I couldn't hide my skepticism.

His expression went aloof. "Yes, Cissy. She was a very good friend for many, many years."

Then why hadn't I heard about it? "What kind of friend, specifically? Please tell me you weren't one of her boy toys." Oh, Lord, I hadn't just said that, had I?

He clearly didn't like that one bit. "I knew your grandmother for a long time, and I never saw a single boy toy, as you call it."

Ouch. "Sorry. I stand corrected."

"Then I'll overlook it," he told me, still aloof.

I took that foot out of my mouth, then promptly inserted the other one. "You said you learned to tango in Rio. I thought you were local."

His eyes narrowed. "And what made you think that?"

"Just a feeling. It wasn't a put-down."

He eased, but only a little. "I am local."

I waited for what he wasn't saying, and he finally spoke. "I met someone when I was seventeen who made me realize there was more to life than repairing boats, so I joined the navy and ended up repairing carriers, instead."

A mechanic? He sure didn't look like any mechanic I'd ever met.

"Do you know any other dances besides the tango?" I asked, hoping my eagerness for a skilled partner didn't show.

"All of them," he said, dead serious.

I love a challenge. "Prove it."

He warmed immediately, his smile spreading. "You're on."

Before I knew it, we were the main attraction. I hadn't had that much fun since . . . I would have said since Harrison left, but the truth was, I hadn't had that much fun since I'd hung up my toe shoes.

We went through almost every dance I could think of, then finally sat one out. "Were you always a dancer?" I asked between sips of the cold bottled water he'd brought me.

He swiped his bottle flat across his forehead. "It didn't come easy," he said, "but I had my pay on shore leaves, but nothing to do. Nothing constructive, anyway. Never did drink. So I started taking dance lessons at every port of call. All night, if they'd let me. It was good exercise." There was that half-smile again. "I let the guys on the ship think I was out whoring. But your grandmother was the one who helped me the most. I never told anybody but her, and when I did, she started teaching me herself. That's when it went from work to fun."

Cissy, fun? Especially when she taught . . . She was good, but I'd never describe my sessions with her at the barre as fun. Yet Clete's expression remained candid. *Wholesome body language,* as Vi would say. So he was either telling the truth, or he was a sociopath. With my luck, he'd be the latter.

"A lot of my friends from around here think any man who dances well is gay," Clete went on. "They're good people, just uninformed." He cocked his head at me. "Now, thanks to you, I'm outed."

My heart tightened. "As in gay?" I had no reason to care whether he was or not, but I did.

He laughed, and it was magical—warm and infectious. "No, as in dancer."

Relief left me grinning like an idiot. Then I noticed that people were starting to leave the pavilion. Curfew was at ten, in fifteen minutes. "Well, thanks for dancing with me."

Clete nodded. "My pleasure. Let's do it again sometime. Now that everybody has seen me dance, we may as well. Good night." He crossed to the other side and started talking with a couple he seemed to know, clearly at ease in their presence.

My sisters closed in on me from three sides.

"Holy crow," Iris said, "but that man can dance."

Rose nodded in agreement. "Amen. It was worth almost getting run over to see it."

"I told ya he was a good one," Vi singsonged, giving my ribs a nudge.

"And I told you a dozen times, quit playing matchmaker. The guy could be a cocaine dealer, for all we know."

"I never heard of a cocaine dealer who got up before dawn to fish," she said sagely.

"You never heard anything about a cocaine dealer's habits, period," I told her. "The smart ones don't deal in it themselves. They just get people hooked, then keep the whole thing going like a giant Ponzi scheme."

"As if you would know," Iris challenged.

"I read," I defended. "All the time."

She snorted. "Fiction."

"Anything and everything," I clarified, "including nonfiction about drug trafficking."

"And what's a Ponzi scheme, anyway?" Rose asked.

"Like multilevel marketing, but without any product," I explained. "Just the fees. It's illegal."

"But there *would* be a product," she insisted. "The cocaine."

On the stroke of nine-fifty, her last two words came out in one of those supernatural lulls in conversation that are supposed to happen at ten till or ten after.

I felt myself color as all eyes turned our way in surprise, including Clete's.

"Great," I seethed through a forced smile. "Now everybody thinks we're cokeheads." I glanced to the jukebox. "Punch the button. Pick something and punch it."

Flustered, she stabbed away without even looking.

"When the Roll Is Called Up Yonder" boomed in twangy bluegrass perfection across the pavilion, spawning laughter and a blessed return of conversation.

Oh, for a trapdoor to drop through.

I couldn't even leave. We didn't have a boat. Turning, I leaned against the railing to look across Lake Clare to the yellow lights of Hilltop Lodge and the feeble bulb marking the boathouse. From here, the family compound looked absolutely regal, the golden glow of wood and stone shining through the clerestory lights of the living room. I breathed deeply of the cool mountain air. How were we going to get home? The last thing I wanted to do was ask Clete. Maybe one of the couples we'd met.

Speak of the devil, Clete came up behind me. "I brought you some more water." He handed me the bottle, then a set of keys. "The Kellys are dropping me off on their way home. Take my boat. It's yours for the duration. I've got two more."

"That's incredibly generous," I told him. "But I can't accept this. I hardly know you, and I hardly know how to drive a boat." He didn't budge. "I'm the one who forgot about the lights, remember? What if I wreck your Chris-Craft? I couldn't begin to replace it." I extended the keys toward him. "Thank you, really, but we'll get Patsy and Joey to take us home."

"Patsy and Joey have already left. And the boat's insured."

I spotted several of the couples I'd met through their husbands, but couldn't remember any of their names to save my life.

Clete stayed calm and silent beside me, waiting for me to give in, while I tried to think up some other way for us to get home without embarrassing anybody.

Rose came up beside me. "Honey, we're all about to fall out," she said in her sweet, soft voice. "Please say thank you and take the blasted keys."

Vi swooped in and relieved me of them. "Clete, you're a brave man to let my sister drive your boat, but we sure do appreciate it." She and Iris gave me the bum's rush toward the stairs. "Come along, Captain Cooper. Your yacht awaits."

"Thanks, Clete," Iris called to him, "for everything."

He looked to me. "We'll see each other again. Soon."

I bristled. "The nerve."

"Oh, give it a rest," Vi scolded as we headed down the stairs.

"What if his boat won't fit into the slip?" I realized aloud.

"Then we'll dock it at Mama's and walk up," Iris said.

One of the loaned-out husbands greeted us at the end of the dock. "Clete told me he was going to lend you girls his boat. Here, allow me to help you in." He got in without waiting, offering his hand. Once we were all seated and life-jacketed in Clete's state-of-the-art ski vests, the husband offered to get the boat started, and I was more than happy to let him. He hopped out to untie us, then I carefully pulled away.

We made it across the lake at a judicious pace, and by the time we reached the boathouse, I'd figured out the controls and gotten the feel of them. It was close—very close—but the boat fit inside.

I wasn't aware how tense I'd been till I turned off the key and suddenly felt all the juice run out of me. I looked to Vi and whined, "I cannot move."

Vi pulled me up by my hands. "You've had quite a night. Just a little farther."

Walking up the hill, she lagged behind me with one finger to my back, a trick that helped, though why it did was beyond me.

By the time I finally got to bed and took all my medications and put in my bite guard, I was so beyond beyond that I burst into tears, and I *never* cry. I tried to stop when I heard Vi get up on the other side of our shared wall, but I couldn't.

She crept in through the sleeping porch, then sat beside me, pulling me into a hug. "I know, sweetie. It's so hard, isn't it? But you're not married anymore, and that wasn't your fault. Harrison broke the covenant. It's okay to feel attracted to somebody else."

How could she know what I hadn't even known myself till I heard her say it?

I just cried harder, but she understood that, too.

"Don't you worry, honey," she soothed. "Just cry. You can sleep as late as you want tomorrow. I'll make sure."

What would I do without her? "I wish you were a man and not related," I told her between involuntary shudders as my tears subsided.

"Oh, sweetie. God's in His heaven, and He's watching over you. If He wants you to have a man, He'll send one."

It was my turn to read her mind and counter with, "Thank goodness He hasn't yet."

She gave me a final squeeze, then laid me back onto my pillows. "Just go to sleep, now." She rose and left, but I heard her soft murmur as she went. "And dream of tangos."

Instead, I dreamed of Daddy, seeing him as a young father at the lake as if I were a hovering observer, not his child. I could smell the sharp tang of his clean sweat mixed with Coppertone and bleached T-shirt and lake water. My grown-up self watched the way he flirted with Mama, and how she fussed, but ended up laughing when he pulled her away from the stove and started to waltz. They were so young. So much younger than my present self.

And then it was me dancing instead of Mama, and my partner was Clete, whose brown eyes looked at me the same soft way Daddy's blue ones had looked at Mama.

And then I was flying, scared at first that I would fall, because nobody can really fly. But with a paradox of effort and letting go, I began to rise, and then I was just above the ridges, flying through the night with the hawk, who soared just out of reach, looking back with huge, dark eyes to be sure I followed.

Then I was falling, falling, falling, and I woke up having my first orgasm in years. And my second. And my third. And, thinking of Clete, one more for the road.

· 10 ·

The truth is beautiful, without a doubt, but so are lies.
—RALPH WALDO EMERSON

THE NEXT MORNING, I woke up mad as blue blazes—not at the Boat Church pontoon for waking me with "forty minutes to Boat Church" from a megaphone as it cruised the shore, but at Clete, for rousing my mothballed libido.

Irrational, I know, but since when had anything to do with hormones been rational?

Grumpy as a she-bear in spring, I got up and did my best to wash away my senseless resentment in a long, hot shower. I peeked in on Vi, who could sleep through a tornado, and found her bundled in the covers, breathing deep. Then I went downstairs to find Rose and Iris sharing the Sunday paper they'd bought the night before during the dance.

Iris looked up from the Living section. "I thought you were going to sleep late."

With anything but Sabbath peace in my heart, I said, "I'd planned to, but that didn't take Boat Church into account."

"When did they start doing that?" she asked, catching my bad mood. "It's mighty nervy of them. Very bad karma."

"Cissy thought it was bad karma, too." I poured myself a cup of coffee and sweetened it. "It hardly puts me in a Christian frame of mind."

Iris tucked her chin. "You could go back to bed."

"I'm up," I snapped.

Rose glanced over her paper, eyebrows lifted, but remained blessedly silent.

"You don't have to take my head off," Iris said, rattling the newsprint in her hands. "I didn't do it."

"I don't want to talk about it."

I noted another pointed glance from Rose, who at least had the courtesy not to make things worse by saying anything before I'd had my first cup of coffee.

Grateful for the morning coolness, I sat and helped myself to the magazine section.

Rose waited till I was on my second cup to ask me gently, "Dahlia, would you mind taking me over to church in the boat? If I take the car, I'll be late. And there's hardly any parking over there."

I narrowed my eyes, irked that she'd waited to ask me till it was too late for her to drive over. But she so rarely asked anything of me that I could hardly say no. "Okay. When?"

We both looked at the vintage clock that sat on the plate rail above the outlet. It was only nine-thirty.

"Quarter till?" she suggested.

I sighed, wondering if I could get my face and my clothes on in time. "I'll do my best."

She turned to Iris. "Will you be coming with us?"

Iris shook her head. "No, ma'am. I'm not the one who thinks you're hell-bound if you miss a Sunday."

Translate: I was.

I went into the kitchen for a handful of shaved ham, then headed upstairs to get ready, wishing I were as sound a sleeper as Vi. My one consolation was that we'd all decided not to work on Sundays.

The sermon, broadcast on a PA system to the boats drifting near the pavilion, was on Jonah 4, about how God can use even grumpy, resentful people to do a mighty work. I took it to heart and repented of my ill mood. Then went home for a quick lunch and a three-hour nap.

The next day, we all slept till nine, had a brief, blessedly quiet break- fast, then headed back down into the Underworld for another session. As our reward, we got to go to Clayton for a status meeting with Mr. John- son. Vi decided to stay home (probably for some alone time, bless her heart), but Iris dawdled and dithered for so long that I made an executive decision and invited Rose to drive us there on time in her hybrid.

To my surprise, she accepted without challenge.

"I can't remember when just the two of us have been together," she said after the bone-jarring trip up our little road.

"Me, either." On further recollection, I realized aloud, "Rose, I'm not at all sure we ever have."

"We haven't," she said simply. "I thought about that a lot when I was planning the summer. One of my main goals for our time together is to get to know you better." She shot me a sympathetic look. "You've been in crisis for so long."

I nodded. "And before that, I was always bitching about the meaning- less little problems in my life instead of appreciating what I had. It's like Iris always said, I need to lighten up." Somehow, saying it made me real- ize how tough it must have been for my family to endure the standard of perfection I'd held for myself, and them. "How could you stand me? How could anybody stand me?"

"Don't be so hard on yourself," she scolded, thoughtfully keeping to a slow, controlled speed as we navigated the cutbacks toward the bottom of the ridge. "You're one of the most generous, creative, engaging people I've ever met. You're our go-to girl. If I ever need a job done, and done well, I know who to call." Not that she ever had. "It's your nature to get on task and block everything else out."

Translate: And ignore everybody else's feelings. But Rose's accepting nature took the sting out of that particular bit of insight.

She had that effect on everybody. Total strangers confided their deep- est fears and disappointments, and Rose kept them safely bundled in a warm blanket of reassurance and encouragement. But there was a catch. She guarded her own just as carefully.

"I'd like to get to know you better, too," I told her. "I mean, I know you're one of the kindest, sweetest people I've ever known, but you always play it so close to the vest. I don't have the slightest idea what makes you tick."

Rose laughed. "Maybe that's how I like it."

Frank. "But it keeps you at a distance," I told her. "Makes me think that you think I'm dangerous."

Rose chuckled, affection in her expression. "Dahlia, darlin', all of us aren't the stars of our own lives. Some of us are in the chorus, and it suits us just fine." She shot me a warm smile. "I'm just private. And you're not. That doesn't mean either of us is wrong. We're just different."

"But you share everything with Iris," I said, realizing it sounded petty the second the words came out.

"Aha," she said with a twinkle of mischief. "Maybe Iris isn't the only one who's jealous."

"I'm not jealous," I blustered, realizing for the first time that I might have been. "I mean, I don't resent your closeness. I just wish we could be closer, that's all."

Rose turned onto the old road to Clayton. "We can be. But I don't think it requires picking my brain. Iris does enough of that for all the rest of you."

"Do you mind it?" I dared to ask her.

"Nah." Rose kept her sunny expression. "It's always been that way between us, so I don't mind. Not that there's much to tell. My life is pretty boring, and it suits me and Martin fine. As far as I can tell, it suits Christian, too." Her oldest, a math whiz at Georgia Tech. "Cam's another matter." Free-spirited Cam (short for Camellia) had always marched to her own drummer, a lot more like me than her mother.

"How do you and I get closer, then?" I asked her.

"Just like this," Rose said evenly. "Go places occasionally. Chat, when Iris isn't there to get on your nerves."

Guilty. "I'm gonna do better about Iris," I vowed. "Really."

Rose just grinned and kept on listing ways we could bond. "Survive almost sinking in the middle of the lake, then nearly getting run over by another boat. That'll be a fine war story we can reminisce about."

I remembered Iris's having a hissy fit in the boat and couldn't help laughing. "That was pretty rich, in retrospect."

Rose waggled her blond brows my way. "Or we could talk about the good-looking fisherman who saw you without any makeup, then almost killed us, but still wanted to dance you out of your shoes."

I felt myself flush with a mixture of embarrassment and remembered heat. "Or not talk about him." I lightly tossed her own words back at her. "I don't think it requires picking my brain about him."

"Touché!"

I shifted the subject. "How's Martin these days?"

"Overworked and underpaid, as usual," she said with a quiet smile of empathy, referring to his job as a child psychologist for the Atlanta schools. "With these recent cuts, it's only getting worse for all of us."

"You, too?" She had taught Head Start special needs children for years.

"Not my salary," she answered, "just what I have to do to get it. Administration is drowning everybody who has anything to do with Title Nine in paperwork and procedures. Even in the classroom, every little thing we do has to be documented, in case we're sued. Every little bump and bruise the kids get has to be recorded and reported. Which only steals time away from helping them, which is the reason we're in it, in the first place. I swear, I'd gladly take a thirty percent cut in pay if I could just kiss the skinned knees and teach and do my lesson plans."

"Don't you ever get discouraged?"

She exhaled heavily, but didn't lose her gentle, secretive smile. "Every day, but whenever I do, one of my kids comes over and gives me a big hug. I swear, they can sense it."

Little wonder. It must be nice having a saint like Rose as a teacher, always patient, always kind, even when she was reinforcing boundaries. Not that it had been easy being the sister of such a saint. I hadn't seen her cry or get mad since she was a little girl, in glaring contrast to my own fits of temper and very human failings. "So," I asked, shifting to a brighter topic: her children. "How are Cam and Christian these days?"

"Great." She warmed. "Cam is so excited about being with the medical mission in Africa this summer."

"That's our Cam." It had always been easy for me to love my brilliant, hardheaded niece, but that was because I wasn't her mother. Her adolescence had just about done in Rose and Martin.

"You know, if there was any justice," Rose said, "she'd be yours." For Rose, that was quite a declaration.

I laughed. "I paid for my raising, and then some, with Junior." But I didn't want to talk about my son; it made me too sad. I looked to the blooming rhododendron flanking the road. "If Cam had been mine, neither of us would have survived it. We're too much alike."

"She's a pistol." Rose's personal substitute for *pain in the ass.*

I watched the scenery for a few minutes, then Rose piped up with, "Would it be okay with you if I take Poppy Jack's settee? I asked Iris and Vi, and neither of them wanted it."

No surprise, since the heavy, ornate piece hardly fit with Iris's country cottage or Vi's well-worn traditional décor. Or, for that matter, my comfy contemporary spiced with a few really good antiques. "You're welcome to it. It's amazing, but not my cup of tea." As far as I was concerned, good Edwardian was an oxymoron.

"I sure wish the matching armchairs were still around," Rose mused. "They look so beautiful in that photograph of Poppy Jack and Great-grandmother over the piano." She slowed to thirty-five when we got to Tiger. "Did Great-grandmother or Cissy ever tell you what happened to those?"

"I asked Great-grandmother one time," I said, "but she just told me I didn't really want to know, which was her stock answer for anything she didn't want to discuss." That included anything the slightest bit troubling or embarrassing. "Maybe somebody broke them, or they got stolen."

"Makes sense." Rose focused on the road ahead, dropping her speed to the posted twenty-five at an intersection, then maintaining it for blocks and blocks.

"I think we can speed up now," I said.

"I'm waiting till the sign," she answered.

"What sign?"

"The one that raises the speed limit." That was Rose. She always played it by the book, no matter what.

We rounded a bend, and there were no signs for at least half a mile. "In Georgia," I prodded, "it's fifty, unless posted otherwise."

Rose's nostrils flared. "It was posted otherwise, back at the intersection."

I looked at her intently. "Rose, don't you ever break the rules, even a little?"

"I try not to."

"But there are so many stupid rules out there."

"Rules are rules," she said firmly. "They're supposed to be for every-body."

Not in my book. I remembered what she always did when she came to a notice that her lane was ending. "What about when the lane ends? There isn't any rule that says you have to switch lanes right away, but you always do."

"Some of us learned to take turns when we were little." She shot me a mildly scolding glance. "Some of us obviously didn't."

"Please tell me you're not one of those people who block both lanes," I said.

"No." We finally came to a sign raising the limit to fifty-five, so she slowly began to accelerate. "If other people want to cheat and endanger the safety of others, it's not up to me to stop them. I just do my best to stay out of their way"

"Waiting till the lane actually ends helps keep the traffic moving," I rationalized. "And it's not cheating. Cops do it all the time. It isn't endan-gering anybody, either."

"Cops are some of the biggest cheaters ever," Rose observed. "They speed all the time without their hazard lights or sirens, which is illegal."

If speeding was cheating, ninety-nine percent of Atlanta drivers were cheaters, including me.

I'd always known Rose disapproved of my pragmatic approach to life, but it stung to know she thought of me as a cheater. "Let's just say we agree to differ, then."

"Fine."

We passed the rest of the trip in silence at only forty-five, and arrived at Mr. Johnson's office right on time. As we approached the door, who should we run into coming out but Clete, rolling up a thick set of plats?

After a brief glance of shocked recognition, we both looked away—me, because of the dream I'd had, and Clete, as if he'd seen it.

He tucked the roll of drawings behind him. "Hi. How's the boat work-ing out?"

This time, his body language was anything but forthcoming. Even a child could have realized he was hiding something besides those plans.

"Fine," Rose answered. "We both got to go to Boat Church and enjoyed it very much."

"The mechanic called and said we need a new outboard," I told him stiffly.

"Sorry to hear that." He started edging toward a hybrid SUV. "Well, my offer stands. The boat's yours for the summer. Consider it a fee for all those dancing lessons." He got into the car and drove away.

Why had he been so shocked to see us, and what was he hiding?

"What dancing lessons?" Rose asked me.

"From Cissy," I answered absently, staring at his car as it disappeared behind the building supply. "She taught him to dance."

"Cissy?" Clearly, Rose was as skeptical as I had been.

I turned back to her, the wheels in my mind spinning up all kinds of dire motivations for Clete's behavior. "I wonder why he seemed so upset to see us."

Rose smiled broadly. "Looked like chemistry, to me."

"Not chemistry. Suspicion," I said.

"Well, whatever it was," she told me, "it sure flustered you both."

I decided that maybe, if I confided in Rose, she might feel more comfortable confiding in me. "I had this dream about him Saturday night." I couldn't think how to articulate the shifting imagery, but my embarrassment must have showed.

"Oh," Rose said with dawning comprehension. "One of *those* dreams."

"Ummm-hmmm." Suddenly I felt as awkward as I had after kissing Joey that first time. I looked at my watch. "We'd better get inside. The last time Vi and I were deliberately late to teach you and Iris a lesson, but I can't stand to keep people waiting. It's rude."

"As rude as breaking in line or interrupting all the time?" Rose shot back.

"Ha!" I grinned, opening the door and motioning her through first. "Touché."

Smug, Rose glided past me. "Glad to see you can take it as well as you dish it out."

Inside Mr. Johnson's office, he reviewed how he'd advertised our sale on the Web, multilist services, and in selected publications like *Town & Country* and *Southern Living* and the *AJC*.

"We've had a slew of offers, many of them above the four million reserve," he told us, "but all of them are contingent on financing, which makes them speculative, at best, in the current market. We got a lot of joint-venture proposals, too, but I rejected them, as y'all instructed."

I flashed on a foreclosure sign in front of my house, and my heart sank. "You mean, we might not be able to sell it?" Disaster!

"No, not at all," he hastened to tell me. "I mean yes, it will sell. It's just a question of when and for how much. I've countered the offers, asking them to remove the finance contingencies, but so far, none of them has. I know several buyers are working really hard on that, but only time will tell."

Clete? I wondered, remembering the way he'd acted. Did he have an ax to grind? Was that why he'd been so nice to us? To *me*?

Was that why he claimed to be Cissy's old friend?

The idea left me feeling betrayed. "Is Clete one of those buyers?" I asked point-blank.

Rose looked to me in surprise.

Mr. Johnson's features went bland. "I really couldn't say at this time."

"And why not?" I challenged. "I thought your fiduciary responsibility is to us, not the buyers."

Comprehension dawned in Rose's expression, and she turned to stare at him in question.

Mr. Johnson didn't rattle. "It is. Your best interests are my primary concern. But the legalities of something like this can get very complicated," he said calmly. "As an officer of the court, I have a responsibility to the community, as well."

Whatever that meant. "Please clarify," I insisted.

He relaxed. "As in, all terms of the offers being equal, I'd rather see low-density development win over something that will strain the county's resources and destroy the natural setting of the lake."

"Oh." That made sense, but which category did Clete fall into? Judging from his reaction to seeing us there, I guessed the latter. "That, I understand."

"Excellent," Rose said. "All of us are very concerned about the environment, too." She nodded firmly. "The greener, the better."

At that point, I was a lot more concerned with the kind of green that would pay off my mortgage—on time.

Mr. Johnson rose, signaling an end to the meeting. "Let's just hope we get a noncontingent offer that's environmentally compatible."

He shook our hands, then we left.

"I'm so pleased to hear that Mr. Johnson is looking out for the environment, too," Rose said as we got into her car. I did my best to keep my worried mood from bleeding over onto her good one. "Why don't we stop and see if there are any blueberries ripe at that organic pick-your-own stand at the Lake Burton cutoff?"

Still obsessing over dire suspicions about our sale, I could use a diversion. "Great."

An hour later, we'd picked two gallons of organic blueberries, and I'd conjured up a fresh bushel of worries about Clete, the fisherman, and what he was really up to.

And wouldn't you know it, but who should be sitting out on the verandah drinking iced tea with Vi and Iris when we got back, but Mr. Enigma himself.

· 11 ·

Oh, what a tangled web we weave when first we practice to deceive.
—WILLIAM SHAKESPEARE

....

WELL, SPEAK OF the devil," Vi said with a bit too much anima-
tion. "Here they come."

Clete stood and turned an assessing look my way. "Hello, again."

Iris frowned at Rose and me as if we'd gone to the ball without her,
instead of Mr. Johnson's. "Any news from the lawyer?" she asked, aloof.

"Not yet," I told her. "Everything that's come in is contingent on financing, which makes them all long shots."

After a brief, awkward pause, the phone rang in Cissy's room, and
both Rose and Iris leapt up to answer it, leaving me and Vi with Clete.

Clete waited to sit till I did.

"Guess what?" Vi said. "We're all going to stay at Clete's for a week."

I practically dropped my teeth. "Do what?"

Seeing my dismay, Clete hastened to clarify, "Right before she died,
your grandmother contracted and paid my pest control company to fumigate the house for wood borers this month. I'd have done it sooner, but
it's more effective in warm weather."

Pest control? "You're a *bug* man?"

I was having erotic dreams about the *exterminator*?

I know it might seem shallow to react that way, but when I was little, Cissy and my great-grandmother had always made it clear that they didn't consider *service* people our social equals.

Not that I was above anybody who was willing to do honest work, mind you. It occurred to me that I was being as shallow as Harrison, but maybe it was just an excuse to keep my distance. Still, Clete was a *bug man*?

"Yep," he said without apology. "I used to spray your grandmother's house."

"And get this," Vi said. "He lives in that gorgeous house on the ridge, across the side cove. The whole place is mold-free, and totally green. The air-conditioning comes from a system of ducts fifty feet down, where it's always fifty-five degrees, then it passes through two microbiological scrubbers with UV and filters to take out all the mold and germs. And he's got solar power, as well, his own Australian water treatment facility, sunken tubs, and a gray-water system for his organic gardens, and a windmill. And a *cook*. I can hardly wait."

"All that, from being a bug man?" I rudely blurted out. Maybe he grew wild mountain flower on the side.

Despite my bluntness, Clete remained calm. "In a way. When your grandmother found out how I liked to experiment with organic gardening, she suggested I come up with some environmentally responsible substances for pest control, particularly for living spaces and consumables. I did, and she loaned me the money to test them and get them into production. I hold the patents on quite a few that are in wide distribution. Tested a lot of them right here at Hilltop."

"So that was why Iris didn't find any spiders."

His quiet smile broadened. "Good. I just finished that particular product and tried it here the week before you came. It's a repellent, not a poison. Cissy told me how Iris felt about spiders."

He was there the week before we came, spraying for spiders because he knew Iris hated them?

That seemed creepy to me. And I didn't like the familiar way he kept referring to Cissy by her first name.

Vi alternated between frowning at me and smiling at Clete.

I thought of all the repairs and improvements. "Were you the one who had all the work done on the house and grounds?"

"Yes."

What possible motive could he have for that? Was he trying to talk Cissy into letting him inherit? "When?"

"A year ago," he answered. "After Cissy told me why you stopped coming."

Half the world knew of my humiliation, but I felt violated that Cissy had told a complete stranger. "Why?" I whispered, wondering what had possessed her.

Thinking I was referring to all he'd done, Clete responded, "Because I loved her, and she couldn't handle things here by herself." Only the subtlest shift in stature and expression betrayed the fact that he didn't appreciate being grilled.

"Nobody loved my grandmother but me," I countered.

He peered at me in assessment. "I did. Are you jealous, or just suspicious?"

The nerve. "That's absurd. Why would I be jealous? I never even heard of you till we got here." I straightened to a rigid posture in my rocker. "How do I even know you're telling the truth?"

"Dahlia!" Vi gasped out. "Why would you say such a thing? Clete has been nothing but kind and generous to us."

His eyes darkened as he said with deadly quiet, "I don't lie. And I did love Cissy."

And now he wanted us to stay at his house. But we had no way of knowing whether or not Cissy had really made those arrangements.

Shades of *Psycho.*

I eyed him sharply. "Cissy never said a word about any of that."

"I'd probably be skeptical if I were in your shoes, too," he offered affably, "but it's all true. Ask Mr. Johnson. Ask her banker. Ask anybody."

"What reason would she have for not telling me?" I challenged.

"Good ones. Maybe I'll tell you after we get to know each other better." His expression was earnest. "I'm just lucky she befriended a raw mountain boy like me and taught me to—" He stopped short, editing what he was about to say. "Dance."

Rose would have an orgasm when she found out how he'd made his money—assuming he'd been telling the truth—but I was still getting over the fact that he was a bug man, and not telling all he knew.

"I can see you're not convinced," he said.

"I can see you're hiding something," I countered. "Something big."

He studied me, his half-smile returning. "Cissy always said you were quite astute."

"And that's another thing," I told him. "I don't appreciate the fact that she talked about me to somebody I'd never even met."

Before I could question him further about what he wasn't telling us, Rose and Iris came back outside with a diet cola for me and iced tea for themselves, plus a pitcher for refills.

"That was Martin," Rose said, then added for Clete's benefit, "my husband. He and the kids send their love." She smiled at Clete, topping up his tea. "And he said to tell you he's glad you didn't run over us."

Clete relaxed. "I'm glad I didn't, too."

Rose handed me my drink. "Here you go, honey."

The phone rang again, and this time, I took advantage of the chance to escape. "I'll get it."

When I picked up the receiver, my assistant Cathy asked to speak to me. "It's me."

"Thank goodness." She sounded upset.

"What's up?"

"The condensation backed up from the air conditioners on the roof, and we've got water damage all over the office and the side walls."

Perfect. I let out a moan.

Harrison had gotten the two-story building off Buckhead Avenue as part of a property swap and given it to me for my birthday so I could start the school. But without his support, I'd barely been able to pay the taxes and utility bills, much less maintain it adequately. Still, I loved its gently shabby New York studio look and feel.

"One of the girls' fathers is a plumber," Cathy said, "and he's offered to fix it in exchange for tuition, if that's okay. And his brother-in-law is a commercial roofer who'll cut us the family rate to fix the leaks."

"That's more than okay," I told her. "It's brilliant. Do we have enough to pay him?"

"Just."

"You're the best," I said with gratitude and relief. "Do what you have to do."

"I'd love to. And don't worry. Bill and I can clean up the mess and do whatever we need to inside."

Besides being a wonderful instructor, Cathy was nothing if not efficient. "Thank you so much for taking care of this," I said.

"Consider it done."

I hung up and went back to the verandah to find my sisters waiting with expectant expressions.

"That was Cathy," I explained. "We had a leak at the studio, but she has everything under control."

"Oh. Good," Vi said, then turned to Rose. "Did Iris tell you about us going to Clete's while they fumigate the house?"

Rose nodded. "That is so kind of you, Clete, but I'm afraid I'll have to decline." A subtle spark of wit lit her eyes.

Vi and Iris both bowed up, ready to argue, but Rose finished smoothly with, "I couldn't possibly impose on someone whose last name I don't even know."

He eyed her with respect. "It's Slocum," he said as if he was expecting some kind of negative response.

The name jingled something distant in my memory, but I felt no sense of warning.

"In that case," Rose said, "we shall consider your kind invitation."

At least she hadn't accepted outright.

An awkward silence fell over us.

"How long will this fumigation take?" I asked him.

"Five days at the least," he said. "Ten, max. It depends how extensive the infestation is. And the product we use in the fogger sometimes takes longer to be effective. It's the trade-off for the fact that it doesn't have any residual toxicity."

Vi brightened. "He said they could start tomorrow, if we wanted." Clearly, she was ready for some of those creature comforts he'd bragged about.

The idea of air-conditioning appealed to me, too, but I wanted to know a lot more about Clete Slocum before we agreed to accept his offer. "We'll talk it over and let you know," I told him.

He stood. "Just call me when you decide. My number's in Cissy's address book in the bedside table drawer."

"Uh-oh," Iris said. She looked to me. "Did we throw that away? It was filthy."

For some reason, I flushed with embarrassment. "No. I put it in a plastic bag and stuck it back into the drawer, just in case we needed it."

Iris beamed at Clete. "We'll call. And we're coming. It's three to one." She shot me a look of triumph. "You lose."

Iris! I glared at her, but she completely ignored me.

Rose piped up with, "Dahlia, why don't you walk Clete back to his boat? You'd like that, wouldn't you, Clete?"

It was his turn to color up. What choice did she leave him, but to say yes? "Sure."

Iris grabbed the insect repellent from the windowsill and sprayed up a cloud on me. "Off you go, then." Then she sprayed him, marking him as part of our herd.

More amused than embarrassed, Clete waved at the fog. "Come on, nature girl."

We passed the walk through the orchard in strained silence, both of us conscious of my sisters' attention from the verandah. It wasn't till we got to Mama's dock that we both spoke at once.

My "Listen, I really am sorry I was so suspicious, but—" collided with his "Look, if it's all the same to you, I'd really like to—"

His "start over from scratch" finished last, unopposed.

"Only if you'll swear to tell the truth, the whole truth, and nothing but the truth," I qualified.

He didn't swear, but he did offer his hand to shake mine. "Hi, I'm Clete Slocum. Your grandmother and I were close friends for many years. She was so proud of you, she told me all about you. And your sisters."

So that was why he knew so much. It wasn't sinister. I shook his hand, finding it firm, dry, and very masculine. "Ah. I'm Dahlia Cooper. Cissy never mentioned you. How did you two meet?"

He eyed me with arresting intensity. "A long time ago, when I was just a raw mountain boy."

"I appreciate the information, but I asked how you met, not when."

He smiled. "You did, didn't you?"

"You must be a politician."

"No, I'm not. But I think my method of responding to prying questions is much more courteous than saying I choose not to answer that at this time."

That much, at least, was candid. And intriguing. I couldn't help smiling. "So please explain to me why I should trust a man who refuses to answer my questions. At this time. A man I've never met before."

"Oh, we've met. Many times."

When he didn't elaborate, I stepped closer to peer without recognition at his face in the dim light from the boathouse and pavilion. Then something he'd said popped up in my brain. *A raw mountain boy* . . .

Suddenly I saw a dirty, skinny, freckle-faced lank of a kid in too-short overalls, his expression glowing as Great-grandmother secretly handed him a quarter. "Slocum!"

Pain and pride mingled in his reaction. "Yes, Slocum."

I flashed on a taller, cleaner version of that same boy in tight jeans and a frayed Izod. He'd looked at me with such amazing intensity that night at the jukefest. "You asked me to dance at Clare's. I was only fourteen, and my sisters were all jealous. That was our last summer before Daddy . . ."

He nodded.

I'd never put two and two together till that moment. All he'd been saying suddenly fell into place. "So you weren't a stranger, after all."

"No. Cissy and your great-grandmother gave me far more than I could ever repay. They cared about me, something nobody else did after my mother died and I had to look after my brothers and sisters."

"I'm sorry I was so suspicious," I told him. "It just seemed so weird. She never said a word . . ."

"She had her reasons," he said without offense.

I could feel the heat from his body and knew I should step back, but I didn't want to. There was still something he wasn't telling—something big—but I didn't have to be a mind reader to know what he was thinking at that moment. Ears aflame, I was thinking the same thing, and it scared me to smithereens.

I stepped back to safer ground. "I'll call," I told him. "About the house."

He nodded, lingering for just a few seconds longer than courtesy demanded. Then he leapt into the boat. "G'night."

The word was hoarse.

"G'night." Mine was, too.

I felt like we were living a scene from a Merchant/Ivory production, all suppressed desire under a cast-iron shell of manners.

The engine of his bass boat roared to life, then settled as he pulled away toward the ridge house just across the cove, the one that almost blended into the mountain.

My newly resurrected libido keen as a paper cut, I watched him dock there, then ride the lift up to the house. Silhouetted against the warm house lights at the top, he paused before going in, then looked back my way.

Once again, I wished I had a trapdoor to fall through.

Then I came to my senses and reminded myself I was a . . . mature woman who knew better than to play such silly games with a man I barely knew. I wasn't some teenager at the mercy of her hormones. I knew who I was and what I wanted: my family and my home back in Buckhead, and the life Harrison had stolen from me. Resolute, I went back to the verandah, only to find my sisters all looking like they'd found Mama's diary.

"Did he kiss you?" Vi asked me.

I exhaled. "Don't be ridiculous. Of course he didn't. I hardly know the man."

"So what?" Iris said. "He's clearly got a serious case on you. If I were in your shoes, I'd have a fling. A good lay would work wonders. You're way too tense and crabby." Talk about the pot calling the kettle black! "What harm could a little safe sex do, anyway? You're going back to Atlanta in September."

"Iris," Rose chided as keeper of traditional values. "I can't believe you'd suggest such a thing. For one thing, there's no such thing as safe sex outside of marriage. And for another, Dahlia's not a fling kind of person and never has been."

"You never know till you try," Vi countered. "I'm with Iris. I think you should go for it. At least one of us should be getting some this summer."

I couldn't believe what I was hearing. "Vi? Since when did you consider affairs to be okay behavior?"

She looked at me with empathy. "Since right this minute." She lapsed into yenta mode. "He's got such a case on you, I'm telling you."

Iris chuckled. "You don't think I married Wilson without finding out how we did in that department first, do you?"

Arms extending, I spread my hands. "My sex life, or lack of it, is not open for conversation, by y'all or anybody else. Period. The end. And good night, ladies."

I let the screen door slam behind me as I fled to my room.

Vi and Iris had lost their minds.

And anyway, Clete was a *bug* man, for crying out loud. One of the Slocum kids!

Our worlds were galaxies apart.

Not that I'd sleep with him, regardless.

But my body didn't listen. It voted with Iris and Vi, so every time Clete intruded into my thoughts, which was often, I got a stab of O action, despite the fact that I knew he was keeping things from me.

Definitely not a good sign.

When I said my prayers, I ended with, "And Lord, could you please work things out between Clete and me the way *You* want them. I know You never tempt us, so I'm not blaming You, but I sure could use some help here."

That was one prayer, at least, that I knew He'd answer.

· 12 ·

It's an honor to be trusted with a desperate secret, but a curse to keep it.
—ANONYMOUS

....

FTER THAT, I stuck close to Hilltop, grateful for the distraction of
work, even if it was in the dreaded Underworld. Despite the res-
ervations I shared with the others about Clete, my sisters outvoted me
and scheduled the fumigation for the next Tuesday.

In the tradition of Scarlett O'Hara, I donned my hazmat suit on the
day before the bug men came and headed to the basement for the final
cleanup. By eleven, we had only a little work left before lunch break.
Outside, the Dumpster (a tasteful green at Rose's request) was half full,
and the recycling piles were neatly stowed in their contractor's disposal
bags. Inside, the basement was two-thirds empty, with only three remaining footlockers to be gone through, and a giant snarl of cast-iron bedsteads and springs to be liberated before we moved on to the upstairs, at
last.

"Dahlia, would you please come help us try to get these untangled?"
Iris called across the now-tidy space.

"Okay." I shut the footlocker full of Great-grandmother's old bills and bank statements, then headed over toward the corner by the walled-up root cellar, where we'd left the ironwork till last. It took all four of us, untangling what we could, then tugging in opposite directions with all our might, but at last, the heap gave, and three of us fell back with our newly liberated bedsteads.

Except Rose, who went airborne with the headboard she was gripping, straight for the walled-up door.

"Aaaagggh!" She and the headboard crunched into the stone base with a sickening thud and the sound of grinding stone, combined into one terrifying noise.

Oh, God! Rose!

The three of us leapt as one to rescue her.

"Don't move," Iris ordered. "You might have a broken neck!"

Her respirator knocked awry, Rose was coughing from the cloud of dust she'd raised on the dirt floor, but at least she was alive and appeared unscathed.

Vi grabbed the iron headboard lying atop her and pulled, but one of the bedposts had knocked a hole in the base of the wall, and it didn't give until she heaved it with superhuman strength, prying loose the quartz rock next to the hole.

We circled Rose. "What hurts?" "How are you?" "Don't move."

Iris gently probed the back of Rose's neck as if she knew what she was doing, which she didn't. "Vi, please go call the Mountain Patrol and get an ambulance," she instructed.

"Stay where you are," Rose told her, swatting away Iris's hands. "Quit that. I'm fine. The bedpost took the hit, not me. Landing just knocked the wind out of me, that's all." She started to get up, but Iris was having none of that.

"You might have hit your head and not know it," she said. "Just lie still. We'll let the paramedics decide whether you're hurt or not."

"Iris, that is absurd. I refuse to use up their valuable time. I am *not* hurt."

I grabbed a flashlight from atop a nearby carton. "I can tell if she's got a concussion," I said as if I knew what I was doing, which I didn't. Well, maybe I did. It was what the pediatrician always told me to do whenever Harrison junior had hit his head, which was often. "Rosie, I'm gonna shine the flashlight into each of your eyes. Just relax and look straight ahead."

"I know what you're doing," she muttered as she complied. "Christian and Harrison junior had the same pediatrician, remember?"

I checked her pupils and said what they always say on the emergency room reality shows. "Her pupils are equal and reactive." Of course, on TV they always ordered a CAT scan right after that, but Harrison's pediatrician had just told me to watch for irregular behavior or stupor. Illuminating Rose's face, I nodded to her. "Just let us know if you feel unnaturally sleepy or nauseated or get a really bad headache. Otherwise, you should be fine."

Blinking from the glare, Rose snatched the flashlight and shined it into my face in retaliation. "I told y'all, I know when I've hit my head, and I did not." She laid the flashlight across her stomach. "Just give me a minute to catch my breath. And please stop crowding around and staring at me. I feel enough like a fool without that, too."

Iris shot me a raised-brow look that said, *Testy! Not like her*, but I pulled her away with, "Rose knows whether she's okay or not. She asked for some space, so let's give it to her."

Iris balked, but I was strong enough to keep her moving. She scowled at me. "Who put you in charge of Rose?"

"I'm not in charge of anybody but me," I said, keeping my cool. "*Rose* is in charge of Rose, so we're leaving her to her own good company for a bit while she collects herself. Let's get some fresh air."

Vi joined us on our way outside, but we'd barely crossed the threshold when Rose's shout brought us back at the speed of light.

"Oh, my God!" she hollered. "I can't believe it! Y'all, come here!"

We found her still on her back, her head turned toward the flashlight beam that shined into the hole the bedpost had made.

"It's Poppy Jack's chair. It's in the root cellar!"

Rolling up into a sitting position, she handed Iris the flashlight. "You have to lie down to see it. I can just make out the corner of the chair leg by the wall, almost to the back."

We each took a turn looking. Sure enough, we could see one corner of the leg near the back of the concreted enclosure, the rest obscured by some rags and a rusty curve of metal. But the wood looked sound.

"It's definitely one of the chairs from the picture," Rose said with alacrity.

I nodded. "I wonder if the rest of the chair is as well preserved as the part we can see."

Little did I know how ironic my choice of words would turn out to be.

Rose positively glowed. "Let's find out. Boy, am I glad I knocked out that rock." She turned to us, as excited as I had ever seen her, tapping the tips of her first two fingers together in a baby clap. "Where did I put that sledgehammer and pickax I bought on the way up?"

"They're over by the footlockers," I told her, mildly creeped out that we needed exactly what she'd bought.

Iris scowled. "Please tell me you don't mean to tear that wall open."

Rose laughed like a little girl. "That's exactly what I plan to do. But don't worry. You don't have to participate. I want those chairs, even if I have to make like a gold miner to get them."

Vi grinned. "You'd better let me try first, Rosebud," she said, resurrecting Rose's childhood nickname. "I'm still the strongest."

I had an idea. "Maybe you won't have to dig," I said. "We could knock a small hole in the center of the doorway, then thread in some of that metal and tie it to the trailer hitch on Vi's car with that heavy nylon rope we found. Then we could just pull the wall down with the car."

"And the house with it," Iris protested.

"Nah." I scanned the piles for the rope. "The doorway's intact. It won't come down." Probably.

"Brilliant!" Rose said. "Did I ever tell you how nice it is to have somebody mechanical in the family?"

"Just to be safe, I could still whack around just inside of the doorjamb to loosen the mortar with the pickax," Vi volunteered.

I grinned at her. "Show-off."

"I can't believe y'all are planning to do this," Iris grumbled on general principle, though we all knew she would never come between her precious Rose and something she really wanted. "It'll just be more mess to deal with."

Boy, did that turn out to be a mouthful.

The old masonry was so stout, Vi could barely make a dent in it with the pickax, but eventually, she managed a hole big enough to accomplish our purpose. Something that looked like a rusty tank made it hard to get the crosspiece in, but Rose and I managed while Vi backed the car into place. Then we tied the rope to the trailer hitch while Vi whacked at the edges, which loosened a lot easier than the middle had.

Meanwhile, Iris continued to project gloom and disaster, not helping one bit. When the final pull came, she and Rose hid just outside the open French doors as I faced the SUV and directed Vi to tighten the rope, then pull.

It took several tries, but at last we heard a grinding groan, then watched a huge slab of the wall leap toward the orchard in an explosion of dust and mortar with such force that Rose had to slam on the brakes to keep from flying into an apple tree. As the slab started to break up, chunks hurtling dangerously close to the furnace and the stairs, the rest of us dove for cover. When all was silent, Rose popped up and started cheering her way toward Vi while we waited for the dust to settle. "It worked! It worked!" she sang as she jumped and hopped toward Vi like Cindy Lauper, then segued into Helen Reddy. "We are women, hear us roar!"

Her excitement was contagious, drawing our attention from the root cellar as she hugged and thanked us. Then she bounced inside, only to stop short as she stared at the opening we'd made. "Well, would you look at that!" she declared. "It's a Slim-Jim of a moonshine still!"

We turned to the hole in the wall to see a ramshackle still at least thirty inches in diameter. I was surprised (and relieved) to see that the first eight feet of the arched tunnel to the root cellar had been sealed off from the deeper reaches, blocking off whatever creepy crawlies lived beyond.

"Vi, help me move the still," I said. It wasn't easy for us to get a grip on it because of the irregular opening. Rose stood by, fingers tapping in excitement, as we tackled the last obstacle to the chair. After considerable effort, Vi and I managed to pull the still through the opening, but it was such a tight fit, it ended up on top of us when it popped clear.

Iris rushed to our aid. "Just sit tight. I'll get it off you." She shoved as we heaved, and it rolled clear. When we sat up, we found Rose staring into the cellar with a worried expression.

Iris followed her line of sight and let loose a horror-movie scream that bounced off the stone foundation and out the doors to echo from the far shore of the lake.

Rose spun around and clamped her hand over Iris's mouth. "Don't look, honey!" She turned Iris, who tried to keep looking, away from the cellar. "You've already had a hissy fit this week, so please stop screaming. You're only upsetting yourself more. Let me take you outside." She shoved Iris past us, clearing the way for us to see what had caused the meltdown.

"Aaaaagh!" Vi and I reacted in unison, grabbing each other close.

Poppy Jack's chairs were there, all right. Both of them. The only trouble was, they were occupied!

We stood transfixed in disbelief.

Two desiccated bodies gaped at us, their arms bent to rest on sheets of oilskin that draped the chairs beneath them. The mummified remains looked so bizarre, their muscles reduced to sinews, that they didn't seem real. Seated in the chairs, they seemed like a freakish parody of royal Egyptian effigies in an ancient tomb.

As Rose hustled Iris outside, Iris's screams subsided into a blubbering description of the mummies. "Honey, it's okay," Rose soothed. "They can't hurt you. Try to breathe. Don't think about anything but breathing." We heard the French doors scrape shut behind them.

The mummy on the right was much darker than the other, dressed in patched denim pants and a checkered shirt and a frayed, peaked hat that covered all but a tuft of kinky gray hair below the front of the brim. His short boots were past worn out, the laces spliced.

The other mummy was dressed in a World War I doughboy's uniform, the wrappings from his shins puddled around his cracked but tidy army boots, and his medals neatly pinned to the moth-eaten wool of his jacket. The flat-brimmed hat in his lap looked almost new.

I spied a suitcase behind the doughboy's chair and a burlap bag behind the other one's.

Vi moved closer to study them with a scientist's eye. "I think the one on the right was black, and the other one was white."

"Judas, Jonah, and Jezebel!" I said, unable to take my eyes off them. "Great-grandmother said I didn't want to know, and she was right."

Outside, Iris wound down to whimpers.

"Iris needs sedatives," I heard my voice say calmly, as if it were someone else's. "Did you bring any?"

"Never need 'em," Vi said, "but we've got plenty of vodka. That should do." She got almost nose to nose with the doughboy.

Thank God, I didn't detect any odor through my respirator.

"These are so cool," she mused. "Who do you think they are? Some of Cissy's old lovers?"

"Bite your tongue." I crooked my neck, trying to make out the print on the yellowed papers the mummies were sitting on. "There are newspapers underneath them, on top of the oilcloth. Maybe those can give us an idea of how long they've been here." I couldn't make anything out without my readers.

"Good thing you've got on gloves," Vi said. "We probably shouldn't touch anything, anyway. It could be a crime scene."

I stilled in alarm. "A crime scene, as in police, and yellow tape, and everybody in the county literally talking about, God help us, the skeletons in our closet?" Panic took hold and escalated with every dire possibility galloping through my mind. "Crime scene, as in, nobody will want to buy the place? Or nobody *can* till the police finish with their endless examinations? How long would that take? Months? I don't have months. This deal has to close on September first, or I lose my home. It's all I have left—"

"Dahlia!" Vi grabbed my arms and got in my face. "Calm down. Keep that up, and we'll have to commit both you *and* Iris to the psych ward."

I exhaled deeply, but my heart kept on racing. "Okay. It's gonna be okay." I licked my lips, suddenly parched. "Just let me think."

The door at the top of the stairs opened, and Rose leaned in to say, "Could y'all please come up here?" She must have gone around to the back door. "Iris is calmed down, but I barely got her back into the house. We need to talk." Then, of all things, she turned out the basement lights, leaving us with just the weak illumination that spilled down the stairs.

"Perfect," Vi said to me as she headed up. "We find two mummified bodies in the root cellar, and Rose calls a family council instead of 911."

We both pulled off our respirators at the top of the stairs.

"She can't call 911," I insisted as I followed her into the hallway. "We have to think of something else."

"There you go again," Vi chided gently, "hurtling to the direst of extremes. We don't have to jump to conclusions. There's plenty of time to think this over before we do anything. Those bodies have clearly been there for a long time. They can wait a little longer while we figure out what to do."

Appeased, I trailed her into the living room, the first time we'd used it since we'd arrived.

Still taking in an occasional shuddering breath from her waning hysteria, Iris glared at me as if I were responsible for everything.

"Why is she looking at me like that?" I asked Rose, indignant.

Vi answered before Iris could. "Probably because you figured out how to get the chairs."

"Vi," Rose chided, "she asked me, not you. I can speak for myself." She turned to me with a brisk, "So can Iris. She's right here. If you want to know why she's looking at you like that, ask her."

Before I could, my body responded to the crisis with an ever more powerful thirst and an even stronger pressure on my bladder. "Hold that thought. I'll be right back." After relieving myself, I filled a quart glass with ice, poured it full with cold decaf diet cola, then returned to the living room to find my sisters staring vacantly into the middle distance, Rose rubbing Iris's back.

"Okay," I said. "The way I see this—"

Rose laid a staying hand on my arm, providing a link between me and Iris. "Dahlia, honey, you're always so dynamic in expressing your ideas that it's sometimes overwhelming. Would you mind if the rest of us spoke first? You'll get the closing argument," she promised, "just like in court."

I went aloof, rebuffed, even though I knew I did have a tendency to monopolize the conversation, especially when a decision needed to be made. "Be my guest."

"Thanks so much for understanding." Rose gave Iris a sidelong hug, then released her. "Iris, honey, do you have anything you want to say?"

Iris came out of her trance loaded for bear. "Yes. I want to pack my bags and never set foot in this house again, even after . . . they're gone."

"But that will cost you your share," I argued. "Surely you—"

"Dahlia, please," Rose intercepted. "You'll have your turn. Iris has a right to express her feelings without being attacked."

Attacked? Since when was common sense an attack? Smoldering, I locked my lips.

"Go ahead, honey," Rose urged her.

Iris glared at me. "I don't care if this place sells by September or not. Unlike Dahlia, I have been responsible financially, so I don't need bailing out." She straightened, turning her torso to a narrower profile, a subconscious defensive gesture. "And unlike Dahlia, I think rules are made to be followed, not broken. The law is the law, and we need to call the police."

Rose frowned. "Let's try to stick to expressing your feelings," she suggested. "I know you're upset. We all are. But saying unkind things to each other doesn't solve anything, it's—"

Iris turned on Rose. "Oh, put a sock in it, Rose! I may not be married to a psychologist, but I know all that psychobabble as well as you do." She teared up again. "I've been violated, and I'm angry, and I don't want to be calm. Vi and Dahlia are calm enough for all of us. They act like they just found a load of cord wood instead of two dead human beings." Her eyes narrowed at poor Rose. "And you're not much better. I saw you looking at those chairs. All you care about is how to get those bodies out of them. So spare me the lecture and get out of my face. I've been traumatized, even if y'all haven't!"

"Iris," Rose warned, "that is no excuse to lash out against us because we responded differently. We have a right to our own reactions, too. And none of us had the slightest idea what we'd find in there!"

Iris struck some serious street attitude. "Who cares! I won't be able to sleep for months, and I'll never be able to erase what I saw!"

I couldn't help it, but seeing the touchy-feelys turn on each other left me with a completely inappropriate urge to laugh. It didn't help when I looked over to find Vi in the same condition. I managed to restrict my reaction to rolled-in lips and flared nostrils till Vi crossed her eyes at me, then both of us lost it.

Iris shot to her feet, livid. "Is this a joke to you?" she yelled. "Well, it's no joke to me. Those people are dead, and they were real people! Somebody in this family knew about it, but nobody bothered to warn us!" The veins swelled in her face and neck. "Just because the two of you never let yourselves feel anything doesn't give you the right to ridicule me. At least I care about things beyond the end of my own nose! You and Vi are both so self-absorbed, you never bother to think how other people might feel!"

Afraid she was about to stroke out, I considered slapping her to bring her to her senses, but decided to hug her instead. "Iris! We feel things, too. We just don't let it hang out for everybody to see."

"And I *do*?" She jerked free of me. "Well, that's really helpful. Any more criticisms?"

I lifted my hands, fingers splayed, between us. "I want you to think back," I said calmly. "I was in the eleventh grade, and you were a sophomore. Mama was out playing bridge, and we were in the downstairs hall, and I was freaked because you told Danny Carter I already had a date to the dance with gross-out George McKinsie. I was so mad, but you just laughed at me. Do you remember that?"

A twitch of Iris's lips said she did.

"You just laughed in my face," I went on, "and kept laughing. The madder I got, the harder you laughed.

"Fannie"—our maid and second mother—"heard me cussing and tried to break it up. 'Here, now!'" I imitated Fannie's nasal tone. "'Here, now!' And you just kept on laughing, so I finally got so mad that I couldn't even cuss. I started spouting gibberish at the top of my lungs."

Iris's lips flattened as she struggled to keep from gloating at the memory of how bad she'd gotten me. She lifted a brow. "So?"

"So," I said emphatically, bowing the way I used to after a performance, face lifted, arms spread. "We're even!" Then I looked down and waited. I was either forgiven, or royally screwed.

God must have promptly zapped Iris with a bolt of Holy Ghost happy, because she pointed to me and said, "That was good, wasn't it, that thing with Danny? I got you *so* good." She grabbed me for a reciprocal dominance hug.

Vi and Rose resumed breathing.

Once we all settled back down, it was my turn to play moderator. "Do you think Cissy knew about those bodies?" I asked Iris.

She shivered, but didn't climb her martyr's cross. "How could she? She lived here all those years, not six feet from that grave. I don't see how she could do that if she knew."

I did. Cissy only cared about things that directly affected her, but I kept that to myself.

"I think Great-grandmother knew," I said. "When I asked her what was back there, she said I didn't want to know."

"She always said that," Iris reminded me.

"Yeah, but that time, she shivered twice as hard as you just did and hustled me back upstairs." I searched my memory. "I don't recall her ever taking me back down into the basement after that. Cissy did, when we were looking for art supplies or nails and wire to make our sculptures, but not Great-grandmother." I braced myself and asked her, "Iris, why do you think we should call the police?"

For once, she didn't get defensive. "Those . . . men, they had to have relatives who must wonder what happened to them."

I turned to Vi. "What about you? What do you think we should do?"

"I think we should collect ourselves and consider our options," she said, "and what each option could cost us, individually and collectively." Bless her reasonable self.

I turned to our baby sister. "How about you, Rose? Is there anything you want to say?"

"Yes," she said, dead serious. Then an impish smile curved her mouth. "Dibs on the chairs."

That tore it. All of us collapsed in cleansing hilarity till we were chuffing and wiping our eyes.

"Oh, hell," Iris said good-naturedly. "I laughed so hard I wet my pants."

"Me, too," Vi seconded, her voice still thick with laughter.

Iris looked at her watch. "Ooo. It's past lunchtime. I vote we all go out. My treat. After I change, of course."

Rose raised her pointer finger, her eyes narrowed. "There's something we need to do. It's right on the tip of my tongue . . ." She shook her head. "Something really important. *Why* can't I think of it?"

"Quit trying," Vi advised her. "You'll think of it."

The phone rang, and I was closest to Cissy's room. "I'll get it." I exited to cut across the side verandah to the sliding door in front of the sunken tub, and made it to the phone by the third ring. "Hello?"

"Hi. Dahlia?"

Clete.

Oh, shit! I did a galactic inhale. "Clete!" I yelped.

They were coming tomorrow to fumigate. *He* was coming tomorrow! The bodies . . .

"Are you okay?" he asked as the others clambered in to see what was going on.

I looked to my sisters with a grimace. "It's Clete," I said a bit too brightly. "He's probably calling about tomorrow."

"*That* was what I was trying to think of!" Rose blurted out. "The fumigators are coming tomorrow!"

They couldn't come, not before we got rid of the bodies. I had to think of something, and there wasn't time to make it a committee decision.

Vi pulled a major uh-oh face, but Iris just looked from one of us to the other.

"Well, that is why I called, actually," Clete said. "What time do you want us to be there?"

The others started whispering dire instructions at me, but I just plugged my open ear and covered the mouthpiece of the receiver till I said, "Nine is fine, but not tomorrow. Next Monday."

Whispers of alarm went off behind me.

"Sorry. I must have gotten my wires crossed," Clete said, clearly perplexed. "I thought it was tomorrow. But next Monday is fine." After a pregnant pause, during which I covered the mouthpiece again so he wouldn't hear all of us whispering at once, he asked, "Is everything okay there?"

I motioned for the others to hush up. "Yep," I said through my fingers into the mouthpiece. "Peachy keen. We just hit a snag with the cleanup, so we'll need some more time. Nothing to worry about. Just need more time. Thanks so much for calling. See you then." I started to hang up, then tacked on, "Not before, please. We're very busy. Bye."

"Why did you do that?" Iris demanded.

I looked at them and burst into *I Love Lucy* tears. "Because he can't find those bodies here. Nobody can. If they do, there's no telling how long it will be before the police finish their investigation, and it'll be all over the known world via Internet before sunset." I slopped in Iris's direction. "And if you go home, everybody will want to know why. Please, y'all, I'm begging you. We can turn the bodies over to the police, just not here. Please. We have to close on time. If I lose that house, I'll . . ." My expression pinched in desperation, my voice going baritone. "I'll drink a whole bottle of white zinfandel. Two! With real cranberry juice! Then I'll lie down in the basement without any protection and die of anaphylactic shock, and I won't have to worry about money or my house or my wretched child or *anything* anymore. And I won't leave a note! Let y'all explain *that* to the cops!"

"You don't mean that, sweetie," a worried Vi told me. She turned to the others. "But she has a point about the bodies. Who knows what prospective buyers would think? And an investigation really could tie up the place for months. This isn't Atlanta. Murder is a big deal up here, but the county doesn't have the resources to deal with it quickly. The sheriff's office would have to take all kinds of samples, then wait for the state to process them. And a stale case about a couple of old mummies is hardly top priority. It really could be months before we could clear the basement." Her face softened in sympathy. "Please, y'all. At least consider an alternative. What if we wrapped the bodies in new plastic and put them somewhere safe, then called the sheriff anonymously. That way, they can find out how they died, and who they are."

I was beyond begging. This was the straw that broke my back. I turned my head toward the ceiling and closed my eyes, wondering what would happen if I simply never spoke again, just sat there, and let somebody else take care of me instead of the other way around.

I'd always thought that mental illness came from something in your genes or as a result of major trauma, but I could have detached from reality so easily at that moment. Just left the others behind and crawled inside myself and pulled up the ladder behind me.

The trouble was, I was a survivor, whether I wanted to be or not, just like so many of the women in my bloodline had been before me. So I let out a long sigh and sat up to find my sisters peering at me.

"Dahlia?" Vi asked. "Did you hear what I said?"

"No. I was trying to go catatonic, but it didn't work."

Relief brightened Vi's smile. "We decided to wrap the bodies in plastic and take them to county property, somewhere off the beaten path, then call in the location to the sheriff's office from a pay phone. Thanks to those hazmat suits of yours, we don't have to worry about leaving behind any evidence that could link us to the bodies. How does that sound to you?"

The weight of the world lifted off my shoulders. Happy tears streamed down my cheeks as I fell into Vi's arms. "Thank you. Thank you, Iris. Thank you, Rose." My voice fell to a confiding whisper. "Thank you, Vi."

"You're welcome," Iris said, then her tone went brisk. "Okay. If we're gonna do this, we need to get some plastic."

I wiped my cheeks, happy to shift to work mode. "We can't buy it locally. Everybody in town knows who buys what at the building supply, down to the last nail."

"Where's the nearest MegaBuild?" Vi asked.

I sniffed, wiping my nose with the back of my hand. "Dawsonville." It was at least fifty miles southwest of us.

"Then I guess we'd better get going," Iris said in a total role reversal with me. "I'll stay up here for my share, but only if those bodies are gone before bedtime." She shuddered again. "First, though, y'all need to cover over that opening. It wouldn't do for somebody to wander in and find the bodies before we get back. And I ain't going back to that basement, so hustle it up, ladies."

I saluted her. "Aye-aye, captain."

It took a lot of pushing and pulling, during which I might have lost my bladder tack, but Rose and Vi and I thumb-tacked a couple of Rose's dollar store plastic tablecloths over the opening, then shoved and stacked the "keep" footlockers in front of it.

That done, we securely blocked the French doors, then I went upstairs for a fast shower and change while the others moderately partook of some organic spirits and cashews.

By the time we got to the little town of Helen along the way, we were starving, and stopped for lunch at one of the ersatz Bavarian restaurants there. The others had big salads or sandwiches, but I ordered a large strip steak, medium rare, which turned out to be thin, barely pink, and tough, but at least it was protein. Fortified by lots of iced tea, we hit the road again.

Back in the privacy of the SUV, Iris frowned in concentration, then asked, "What about the cellar door? The bodies are sure to make the news, and everybody will be wondering where they came from. What if the bug people see the opening and put two and two together?"

"Iris, you would make a fabulous criminal," I complimented. "You're right. Maybe we should close the opening back up. The chunk we pulled out broke into manageable pieces when it hit the ground. It probably wouldn't be too hard to put things back the way they were."

"We could rub dirt on the mortar to make it look old," Rose said.

Vi chimed in with, "We can get the mortar at the MegaBuild when we get the plastic."

We all agreed that restoring the wall to its former condition would be prudent, but Iris still refused to go back down into the basement, which was just fine with me, as long as she stayed at the house. I sincerely appreciated her making that sacrifice, and said so.

Content with our plan, we made it to Dawsonville without once going over the speed limit, a definite concession to Rose and Iris on Vi's part.

As we approached the MegaBuild, Rose spotted a dollar store in the strip mall beside it. Inside the store's windows, a huge banner blazoned, CHRISTMAS IN JULY, 50% OFF ALL CHRISTMAS MERCHANDISE. "Pull over. Let's look in that dollar store first. Maybe we'll find a bargain."

Vi obliged, even as Iris argued, "Rosie, this is no time for cheap plastic. We need the heavy kind, at least three mils thick, so the bears and critters can't smell what's inside." She shivered, but carried on like a trouper. "It'll defeat the purpose if the police find the bodies half-eaten."

"Humor me," Rose said. Even when it was a matter of life or death, she couldn't resist a bargain. "Just drop me off, then y'all can go on over to the MegaBuild for the mortar. But don't buy any plastic till you talk to me. I've got really good vibes about this place." She got out. "Y'all go on. I'll meet you over there."

Vi drove us toward the building supply.

"Please drop us off at the contractor's entrance," Iris told her. "There are plenty of parking spaces there. We'll come get you when it's time to load everything. Unless you want to come in with us."

"I'll just wait out here," Vi said. "Unless I have to go to the bathroom." Always an issue with middle-aged women. "But you don't need to get a mason's trowel," she reminded us. "Rose got one at that flea market on her way up last week."

Eerie.

Iris and I looked at each other. "Do you think Rose is psychic?" I asked.

Iris waved her hand in dismissal. "I thought you were the one who believed God is in every little detail of your life."

"I do. He is."

"Well, there you are, then."

I narrowed my eyes. "I wonder what the cauldron is for?"

"I shudder to think," Iris said.

It occurred to me that we could put the rest of her finds to use, though.

"Those dress-up wigs will be perfect for tonight when we go to . . . you know. As disguises."

Iris balked. "I am *not* putting some garage sale wig on my head. Haven't you ever heard of lice, not to mention whatever cooties might be on there? Ugh."

"Yes," I said, "but you can kill them by microwaving the wig for a few minutes on high. Works for hats, too."

"This conversation is over," Iris announced, getting out.

"Dibs on the red wig," Vi told me.

"We'll flip for it." I got out and headed after Iris.

She stopped short of the entrance by several yards, making sure nobody else was around, then murmured, "Let me do all the talking in here. This is one time we don't want to draw attention to ourselves, and you always say too much."

I was so grateful she was cooperating that I gladly acknowledged her orders with another snappy salute. "Aye, aye."

Some customers getting out of a nearby truck looked my way, curious.

"See," Iris whispered. "That's what I'm talking about. I know it will take a miracle, but please keep your mouth shut, and don't do anything . . . odd."

Locking my lips, I nodded, then followed her inside to the masonry aisle.

Iris examined every word on every variety of masonry, but I just stood behind her, lips clamped, minding my own business. Silently.

I was innocently inspecting the inventory on the upper shelves of the deserted aisle when she turned in annoyance. "What are you doing?" she challenged in a whisper.

"Nothing," I said.

"I heard you back there, scraping on the concrete."

Oh.

"Sorry," I whispered back, even though there was nobody within a mile of us. "My feet go through ballet positions without even thinking when I'm bored." Could have done without the bored, I scolded myself.

"Well, think about it, and don't," Iris snapped. "Ordinary people don't go through ballet positions in the building supply."

I'd never been ordinary in my life and had no idea how to do it, but I tried to keep my feet under control.

A salesman in a red carpenter's apron—the image of a thirty-something quintessential redneck, complete with beer gut—rounded the end of the aisle and headed our way. "Good morning, ladies," he said, "or should I say afternoon? How can I help you today?"

"We're thinking about building a natural stone wall in our garden," Iris said. "Mostly quartz. What mortar would you recommend?"

He scanned the selection. "The Red Devil works really well, and it has a mildew retardant built in. But in this heat, I'd mix it a little wet, then keep it covered with damp newspapers or towels under plastic for a few days, so it can cure properly. How big is the wall?"

Iris had absolutely no spatial accuracy. "About four by seven," I said, overestimating for safety's sake. Better too much mortar than too little. "And it's shaded. Deep shade. No sun."

Iris put the toe of her shoe over mine and started pressing. "How much would we need, then?" she asked the salesman.

"That depends," he said. "How big are the rocks?"

While Iris hesitated, at a loss, I mimed the size of a large eggplant, then retreated behind her.

"I think six bags should do it," he said, going for a nearby empty skid.

Six bags? I looked at the price under the pallet of Red Devil. This wasn't going to be cheap! "Do you have enough cash to pay for all this?" I murmured to Iris.

"Yes," she whispered back, "but I expect the kitty to pay me back."

"Sure."

After positioning the skid, the salesman put on leather gloves, then gripped the corners of a bag. "Let me just get those for you." He transferred the sixty-pound load without a sign of exertion. "Could I interest you ladies in a mixer? Got a real sweet little electric number, just the thing for small projects like these. Half off. Only ninety-nine, including the rolling stand."

"Sounds like a great deal," Iris said, "but the mortar will be fine."

He heaved the last bags onto the skid. "You're gonna need some really good gloves to work with this stuff. It's pretty caustic. It'll ruin your hands."

Iris looked to me, and I nodded. My vinyl hazmat gloves weren't heavy enough.

"Okay," she said as if she made snap decisions every day. "Pick us out two pairs of the best ones for the money."

I smiled at her in approval. This was real progress. Normally, Iris had to call at least five friends for advice, then do three hours of online research and another three leafing through back issues of *Consumer Report* before she made a decision about anything for the house.

The salesman took down two pairs of heavily dipped black gloves with a fabric base and cuff. "These work just fine."

"The plastic," I reminded Iris.

"Oh, yes," she said. "Where could we find the heavy plastic? You know, the thick kind?"

"Ten-by-fifty, rolled," I clarified, knowing the heavy mil didn't come any smaller.

"A plastic drop cloth would keep the moisture in for a lot less," he advised, rolling the skid toward checkout.

"My . . . friend," Iris said, correcting herself before she called me her sister, "is right. We need the ten-by-fifty."

The salesman nodded sagely. "How long have you two been together?" he asked, clearly thinking we were a couple.

My eyes widened, but my lips stayed zipped.

Iris just sort of congealed.

Making sure nobody was around, he leaned in to confide, "Me and Rusty didn't come out till *Brokeback Mountain*. I thought our drinkin' buddies were gonna lynch us when we told 'em, but Rusty talked sense into most 'em. Explained how we're still the same people we always were, and we weren't ever gonna hit on *them*. God, no." He straightened in pride, grinning. "A few got nasty, so I beat 'em up good, and that was that. We're all back bowlin' and playin' pool, just like always."

I was dying to ask what Rusty did for a living, but my promise to Iris kept me quiet. If he was a mechanic, it would be perfect.

Iris glared at me as if it were my fault the conversation had taken a sharp left.

"You can leave the mortar up here till you're ready to check out," he told us as we neared contractor's checkout. He proffered a regular cart to Iris. "I'd go with you, but we're shorthanded. Cutbacks. Housing recession, you know." He nodded toward the far side of the store. "They can show you out in the garden center."

My mouth was cramping from keeping it closed and expressionless, so I had to let out a sigh.

"I swear," Iris grumbled as she pushed the cart. "It's uncanny. If there's a weirdo within a mile, they find you."

"How do you know it wasn't *you*?" I couldn't resist asking. "You were the one doing all the talking."

"Not all of it," she said. Then she actually smiled. "It was calling you 'my . . . friend,'" she said, "wasn't it?"

"Look at it this way," I told her. "He might remember us, but if it he does, we'll be that nice lesbian couple. Great cover."

She bumped my hip with hers. "Let's get the plastic and get out of here," she said.

I stopped. "Rose told us not to buy any till we talked to her."

Normally, this would have stopped Iris in her tracks, but now that she was on board with the plan, she waved her hand and said, "She won't find anything. Let's just get it and get out of here."

"I like you when you're being me," I told her. "A lot."

Flat-mouthed, she arched a brow. "That figures." Then her features brightened the way they used to when she was still a kid full of mischief. "To tell the truth, I like me when I'm being you, too."

"Want me to be you for a while?" I offered.

"Lord, no." She looked up her pert little Doris Day nose at me. "You'd irritate me being you to smithereens."

Humor! Yea!

When we arrived back at the car, we found Rose showing off her finds. "Look, y'all!" She pulled out a heavy plastic bag adorned with dancing Santas. "They're Christmas-tree bags. Three mils thick, ten feet long, and four feet wide. A perfect body bag for those seated mummies." She lifted a ten-inch-wide strip of red plastic "ribbon" from the package. "It even has ties. Double up the bags and wire them closed, and a drug dog couldn't smell marijuana inside." She was so proud of herself. "It took a lot of rooting around in the Christmas bin, but I finally found four. Only fifty cents apiece."

Talk about divine irony.

"They are beyond perfect," I admired, savoring the image of the "presents" perched on a park bench somewhere. And the police's reaction when they unwrapped the dancing Santa bags to find the bizarre mummies inside. Maybe their photographer would get a shot. *Too rich!*

Iris clearly didn't agree. "Well, could you *be* any more conspicuous?"

But there weren't any shoppers within earshot, or even eyeshot, for that matter, as Rose was inside the SUV.

"That's the thing," Rose said, thinking Iris disapproved of the bags themselves. "This way, nobody will mistake them for garbage. They'll look like presents!"

Iris put her hands to her head and called to the cosmos, "Is this my life? The last time I looked, I was a decent, responsible citizen, with a decent, responsible husband, and a well-respected business. My life was orderly. Predictable. Just the way I like it. Now there are dead bodies in the basement, and I'm probably abetting a major crime. And the only gay redneck in the world besides *Rusty* thinks my sister and I are a lesbian couple. What world did I just wake up in?"

"Actually," I said, "I think moving a dead body is a misdemeanor. It's only a felony if you disturb a crime scene, and frankly, there was absolutely no evidence of foul play visible. I don't know who those mummies are or what happened to them, but the house wasn't built till 1919, and Poppy Jack and Great-grandmother were not murderers."

"I wish I could be so sure," Iris replied. "Maybe Cissy did it, and they covered it up."

A more likely hypothesis, but one I didn't care to explore.

"We'll find out the truth soon enough," Vi said. "Or we won't. Either way, they can't trace the bodies back to us."

"That's what they all say," Iris retorted. "Tell it to the judge."

"You need a drink," Vi advised. "Or three."

Iris dropped her face into her hands. "I need a *steak.*"

Whoa. This was serious.

"Hang on, honey," I told her. "This will all be behind us before you know it, and we never have to talk about it again. Unless you've changed your mind about the bodies."

"No," she groaned out. "I haven't changed my mind. I've *lost* it. Completely."

The guys at MegaBuild loaded up the mortar, and we hit the road, stopping at a steak house on the way home, where Iris ate half the protein on the buffet. "I'm gonna have to get a high colonic, pronto, to make up for this," she said through a mouthful of medium-rare strip.

"This is too rich." Vi powered up her cell phone and started to snap a photo of Iris with steak when she wasn't looking, but I was able to stop her. "No phones," I whispered, pressing the off button. "They can be traced. I turned mine off and stole Iris's battery before we left. Rose didn't even bring hers. As far as anybody knows, we were just running routine errands this afternoon."

"What about tonight?"

I knew she was asking about more than the phone. "We'll do fine, just the two of us. Unless you want me to do it alone. I could, if the 'packages' aren't too heavy."

"Don't be ridiculous," Vi scolded. "I wouldn't miss it for the world."

"I don't know what I did right in this world to end up with you for a sister, but I sure am glad to have you."

"Ditto, honey. It's never boring when you're around."

"After tonight," I said, "let's hope it is. I could really use some boredom. And some rest."

"It's time things went your way for a change," she reassured. "We'll do fine, and some buyer will come up with a fabulous, environmentally friendly cash offer, and we'll sell the place right on schedule. Then you'll get your house, and I'll get to go back to coaching and teaching instead of adminstruating"—her term for her constant trials as dean of women's athletics—"and Rose will get to retire and travel with Martin the way they've always wanted to, and Iris will be even richer, and we'll all live happily ever after."

"Your mouth to God's ear," I said, though I couldn't believe God had anything to do with our moving those bodies.

The way things had been going for me, this was probably some trap of the devil that would snap shut right when I thought I was free.

I looked over to see Iris had cleaned her third plate. "Come on, sweetie. Let's get you out of here before you pop."

Vi and I had dark doings to accomplish, the sooner, the better.

· 13 ·

....

*B*ACK AT THE house, Rose and Vi and I moved the footlockers back
to the concrete, leaving the plastic tablecloths over the doorway to
cover the bodies. Then we unloaded the mortar, two to a sack. Even with
only thirty pounds apiece to carry, there was much groaning and complaint.

In the last of the twilight, we waited till no boats were around to
move the wheelbarrow from the barn to the basement. Once that was
accomplished, we transferred the tools and buckets we'd need to mix
the mortar, then carefully opened and doubled up the dancing Santa
bags out of sight in the woods, just to be sure the air inside them wasn't
from the basement. By the time we finished with all that, it was getting
dark.

We put Rose on babysitting duty with Iris in Cissy's room, and Vi
changed into the spare hazmat suit.

"Just give me a minute," she asked when I came at her with the respirator.

"It helps to stick your head into the chest freezer for a few minutes before you put it on," I told her. "That's what I do."

She perked up. "Why not put the mask in the freezer, too?"

I shook my head no. "Tried that. It fogs up. The mask won't bother you as much if you think about what we have to do instead of what you're wearing. With luck, we'll be home in our beds before midnight."

We'd decided to leave the bodies at a little picnic area by a stream between us and Clayton, down one of the few paved cove roads that wasn't a dead end.

The bulbs hanging in the basement were so dim, I didn't worry about anyone's seeing us through the hedge. Vi's SUV blocked the opening in the bushes, its interior lights covered with electrician's tape and the hatch open for our cargo of corpses. We lined the cargo space with heavy black plastic, with plenty of extra to cover the dancing Santa bags en route to their destination.

My biggest fear about bagging the bodies was that the mummies would start to come apart when we tried to move them. If that happened, I might well have a hissy fit myself. But that fear proved unfounded. The mummies proved far less brittle than I expected.

With infinite care, our vinyl-gloved hands slid the first set of doubled bags over the feet and lower legs of the raggedy man.

This time, I'd remembered to wear my granny glasses inside the respirator, so I could easily make out the date on the Franklin newspapers: 1922, the year before Mama was born. Cissy was still in Europe then, which meant she couldn't have done it. Assuming she really was in Europe. "We probably ought to leave the newspapers under their fannies," I said, "for the police."

"Good idea," Vi confirmed. "But let's do it after we get the bags above the arms. It's gonna take all the width we have to keep from knocking anything off."

Like a pinkie? Yuk. I shuddered.

I should have been horrified by the entire scenario. Normal people would be. But this seemed just one more onerous chore I had to do. I couldn't relate to the bodies as people, even when I tried. Was that sick? Were divorce and penury turning me into a criminal? "Vi, do you think I'm turning into a sociopath?"

Vi halted. "I'm bagging a mummy here, and you want psychoanalysis?

No, I do not think you are a sociopath. I think you're doing what you have to to survive." She resumed bagging, then stopped again. "Do you think I'm turning into a sociopath?"

"No." I grinned through my full-face visor. "Just a criminal, like me."

"Birds of a feather," she quoted Mama quoting Daddy, then focused on the job at hand. "I'm gonna need some help with the hands and arms."

"Okay." I got as close to the wall as I could and leaned over the torso, leaving Vi room to work. "I'll lift, and you shinny the bags under the thighs." I held my breath, then grasped the torso under the arms and lifted. The mummy was a lot lighter than I'd expected, but upon further consideration, that made sense, because water makes up most of a human body.

My brain told me what we were doing was foolhardy and bizarre, but my emotions didn't pay any attention. They were too focused on getting those bodies out and safely away from the house without leaving behind any telltale traces.

"How do you think they were mummified?" I asked Vi.

Vi eased the bag as far open as she could, slowly pulling it toward the hands. "Nothing like the Egyptian methods," she said, "which were basically like tanning leather. They weren't embalmed, either. The tissues wouldn't be dried out this way. The only thing I can think of that might do this is salt."

I eyed the bodies. "It sure would take a lot of it."

"People had plenty back before refrigeration, to preserve meat. If somebody salted down these bodies and let them cure for a long time, changing out the salt, they'd probably end up looking the way they do."

"But there's not any salt on their clothes."

"That one beats me," Vi said. "Unless whoever did this rinsed off the clothes last. Once the bodies were cured, the muscles were set, so you couldn't dress them afterward. They fit so well in the chairs, somebody must have put them there till rigor mortis set in, then salted them down."

"What would make somebody do something like that? There had to be a reason."

"Rose is the psychic in the family, not me," Vi said. "But her premonitions may only apply to secondhand merchandise."

It took some delicate manipulations to get the bags past the extended hands, but once they were safely cleared, we put the stack of newspapers back under raggedy man's heinie, carefully folded the oilcloth that had protected the chair, then tucked it behind him. I completed his travel preparations by putting his tall hat in his lap so it wouldn't get smushed. Not ten minutes after we'd started, the raggedy mummy was success- fully bagged, the pert plastic ruffle above his head secured tightly with a broken piece of scrap wire, then tied with a big red plastic bow. I added another bow just below his knees to keep the newspapers from shifting. The total effect was quite festive.

Very carefully, we carried the precious package to the car and laid it in the cargo area. "Put the feet in first," Vi advised. "They won't both fit unless we nest them on their sides, head to foot. We can cushion them with extra plastic before we cover them."

Bagging the doughboy was even easier. His newspapers were dated a week before the raggedy man's.

But when I picked up his hat, I found a name inked inside the crown in tidy letters above the band. "Augustus P. Hancock," I read aloud to Vi. "Hancock. Why does that name ring a bell?"

Vi frowned. "You've been going through all those old papers. Maybe you saw it there."

"Hang on." I fetched a pen and one of the old invoices destined for the burn pile, then wrote down the name on the back so I wouldn't forget.

Vi pointed to the paper. "Better not leave that lying around," she cau- tioned.

"I won't." I folded it neatly, then stuffed it into the cuff of my glove.

Once the second mummy was safely in the SUV, we put the suitcase and burlap bag—both filled with neatly folded clothing—into a contrac- tor's trash bag, then used that to keep the bodies from sliding, covering everything with the heavy black plastic, just in case anybody looked in a window.

Vi slammed the hatch. "So far, so good."

"Why don't you go upstairs and change?" I offered. "I'll handle the cleanup."

"Okay. I'll microwave the wigs and try them on, but if the other ones don't suit, I want the red one."

"We'll flip," I repeated. If I was going to participate in disposing of bodies, I wanted to do it as a redhead. Dressed in black, even if it was under my hazmat suit. "I'll wear the hazmat suit to the park. The bodies are light enough for me to put them on the benches. You don't even have to get out of the car."

"Oh, no," she said. "When I tell this story to my great-grandchildren, I want to get just as much of the glory as you, so I'll wear mine, too. We can change in the car afterward."

"Okay." How do I love thee? Let me count the ways . . .

Back in the basement with my HEPA vacuum, I carefully sucked every square inch of the still, the chairs (in pristine but dry condition), and the concrete enclosure, removing every molecule of dust and hair and cobwebs I could find.

Then I liberated the chairs and returned the still to its tomb, tacking the picnic cloths over the opening to keep anything else from wafting in.

Outside, I removed the bag from the vacuum and transferred it into a contractor's refuse bag, to be joined later by the plastic now enfolding the rest of the evidence. Those, we'd put in a Dumpster in another county, and nobody would be the wiser.

When I headed back upstairs for a pit stop and some ice water, Rose was waiting at the door. "Done?"

I pulled off my mask. "Phase one, anyway."

After a quick cold shower and a change into lightweight knit black capris and a black Polo T-shirt, I climbed back into my hazmat suit, then carried my respirator down to find Vi drinking diet cola while Iris was having yet another martini.

When she saw me looking at it, she leered my way with, "Iss called a mar-tweenie. Half vodka, half moonshine, with juss a splash of pink lemonade."

"Moonshine?" I didn't believe her. "Where did you get that?"

"Brought it with me," she said. "Made from one hunnerd percent organic corn, sweet as sunshine."

I looked to Rose. "Is she telling the truth?"

Brows raised, Rose smiled noncommittally. "It was in an unmarked flask in the freezer. I tasted it. Helluva kick, but she's right. It's corn sweet."

"Made right, in copper, like that still we found in the cove house."

I had forgotten all about that. "Well, this has been fun, but it's time for Vi and me to finish what we started. And we're not taking our cell phones. As far as anybody's concerned, we're back here with y'all."

"I'm going with you," Rose said.

"You need to stay here with Iris," I reminded her.

She shot me an odd look. "Nope. I need to go with y'all. Really. I have my reasons."

What was she up to?

"Wait a minnit," Iris said. "I am *not* staying by myself in this house, even without the you-know-whos. Or the you-*don't*-know-whos, as the case may be."

"You, madam," Rose said, "need to go to bed and sleep it off. I'm going to help the others. We don't need you there in this condition."

"I don't need me there in *any* condition," she argued. "Not with those not-know-you-whos. I wouldn' get within a mile of that SUV."

"Good." Rose was definitely up to something. "Because we wouldn't let you. You'd be nothing but a liability."

Iris's lower lip bulged, her expression wounded. "Rosie, why're you bein' so mean? You're never mean, 'specially to me."

"Iris, leaving you in this perfectly exorcised house is not being mean. I want to help the others, and you're in no condition to come with me."

"Yes I am." Iris stood up and had to grab the edge of the Victrola to regain her balance. "See?"

"But you know what's in that car," Rose said more softly. "We can't have you getting hysterical. We need to be able to count on you."

"You can." Iris saluted. "As long as I have a trash can with me, just in case I feel ill."

Perfect. The thought of Iris tossing her cookies into the trash can made me queasy. What in God's good green earth was Rose trying to accomplish?

"Rose, honey," Vi said, "I really think you should stay here with Iris. We'll be fine. Really."

"Oh, no you don't," Iris said. "We are goin', and that is that. Jus' let me git changed." She disappeared into Cissy's room.

"What are you thinking?" I whispered to Rose. "Have you lost your mind?"

"Listen, y'all," she whispered back. "Unless she sees us put those bodies on the benches and drive away, she's never gonna believe they're really gone, especially after we wall the door back up. She's gotta see it. She's always been that way." She looked to me. "You know what I'm talking about. You've tried to describe things to her."

"She never gets it," I confirmed. "I have to draw her a picture."

"That's why she's always taking pictures on trips," Rose explained. "She can only retain the memories if she sees the images."

Vi conceded. "I guess she needs to come, then."

"Don't give in too easily," Rose cautioned. "She needs to think she's getting the best of you."

I wasn't convinced, but I was outvoted. "Well, I think we should bring a pillow and some more of that mar-tweenie, in case we have to sedate her. And a *big* barf bag."

"Consider it done," Rose said.

Iris emerged in black from head to toe: huge black Jackie O sunglasses, black jeans, black sandals, black shirt over a black camisole, and a black china-doll pageboy wig from Rose's flea-market finds.

"Iris, that's perfect," Rose said. "If you cover your face, nobody can see you in the dark."

"Thenk yew." She sashayed toward the kitchen, picking up the empty plastic trash can from the breakfast room. "Last one to the hearse is a rotten egg." But she waited for Rose, who went for a pillow and the mar-tweenies.

Vi grabbed the long brown shag wig and her respirator, motioning with her eyes for me to follow. "I'll get the car unlocked."

I grabbed the red curly wig and my respirator, and we were off.

It was five minutes before the others joined us, making me wonder if Iris had gotten cold feet, but Rose had used up the time changing into black, herself, getting us all flashlights, then turning off lights.

Smashed, Iris had barely enough control of herself to make it into the front seat of the SUV. "Man, it's dark in here." I reached over and pulled off her sunglasses. "Oh. Thanks, Dal." Buckling her seat belt kept her so busy, she seemed to have forgotten that the bodies were underneath the plastic in the back.

Once we were on our way, I breathed a little easier. As luck would have it, we didn't pass a single car all the way to the old highway into Clayton. Vi kept her speed safely under the limit, so I was able to spot the remains of a wreck on the shoulder ahead.

A flash of reflective paint caught my eye. "Vi, pull over!"

She did, even as she said, "I thought we weren't going to stop for anything."

"Do you keep a screwdriver in the car?" I asked her as we drew to a stop, the shards of wreckage just ahead.

The green glow from her dashboard illuminated her frown. "Yes. In the glove compartment. Why?"

"Get it out." I jumped from the door and went straight to the reflective corner I'd spotted peeking from the weeds. "Aha!" Just as I thought. A license plate.

"Turn everything off," I instructed as I got the screwdriver, then retrieved my flashlight.

It was pitch-dark at first, but my eyes soon became accustomed to the gloom. Using my flashlight only to locate the tag screws, I switched the tags, then took Vi's back inside with me. "Lock your real one in the glove compartment. Without cause, the cops need a warrant to open it."

Never mind that two dead bodies in the backety-back definitely constituted cause.

Vi shook her head with a mixture of admiration and worry. "Have you been living a double life of crime that you haven't told me about? Because you sure seem good at this."

"I just project the worst that could happen, then try to prepare for it. Right now, the worst thing that could happen would be getting pulled over by the police."

"Bite your tongue," Rose protested, then said to Vi, "Let's get going, please. Somebody might see us here and think we need help."

Speak of the devil, two headlights rounded the corner behind us, and a pickup slowed to a stop alongside.

I slunk down in my seat so they couldn't see my hazmat suit, but Vi didn't seem concerned at all.

"Hey!" a guy who looked straight out of *Deliverance* called through his open passenger window. "Y'all okay?"

Vi rolled the window down just enough to answer, "We're fine, thanks. But it's so kind of you to check on us."

"Well, I'm a deputy, and I wouldn't want you gettin' out anywhere near here. We had a woman killed right where you're sittin', just last night. Some guy she picked up over at Cody's roadhouse cut her throat while she was drivin'. Totaled the car, but by the time we got there, he was long gone."

Perfect! I had been out there in a white hazmat suit with nothing to defend myself but a screwdriver.

"This is not my life," Iris roused to mutter. "Murderers in the woods. Bodies in the basement."

"Thanks." Vi spoke loudly enough to cover what she was saying. "We'll lock up tight!" She closed the window with one hand while pressing the other over Iris's mouth. We didn't get going till the pickup truck was well on his way.

Iris flung Vi's hand away. "I cannot believe this," she said, apparently shocked lucid by what we'd just heard. "This whole place is crazy. Are we in a Stephen King movie?"

The pickup turned left onto a farm road.

"Where is this park?" she went on. " 'Cause if it's anywhere near here, we need to pick someplace else for the you-know-whos."

"Don't get your knickers in a knot," Vi said. "It's miles away."

"You sure seem calm," I said, "considering what that guy just told us."

"I'm not convinced he was telling the truth," Vi said. "He didn't look like any deputy I've ever seen, and I could smell the booze on his breath through the window. Plus, he had this weasely little smile on his face, like he was in on some childish joke. I think he was lying. We'd have heard about something like that."

"How?" Iris challenged. "We don't have TV, we're a day behind on our papers, and the only radio station we can get is local fire-and-brimstone Bible-banging snake handlers who only tell you the weather, the crop reports, and what's on special at Winn Dixie at the top of the hour. And we haven't talked to anybody today but a couple of waitresses and a gay building supply clerk."

"And Clete," Rose added.

Ah, yes. There was always Clete.

Rose cocked her head at Iris. "Feel better now?"

"Much." Iris straightened in her seat.

We finally reached the highway that connected Clayton and Blairesville, then fell into a tense silence, watching the speed markers alternate between fifty, thirty-five, twenty-five, *fifteen,* and forty-five miles per hour.

Just as the trek began to feel endless, Iris pointed in the direction of a small green reflective sign ahead. "That's it," she blasted with moonshine-breath. "Bold Creek Road. Left. Left."

Vi turned onto the narrow tar and gravel road.

"How far down is this place?" Iris demanded, getting testy.

"About four more miles," I said. "There'll be signs for the picnic area."
The speed limit dropped back to fifteen, but we made it eventually.

To my relief, the park looked derelict, the same ancient green metal
shade still protecting the low-watt bulb that lit the front concrete picnic
table and benches.

Vi parked with the bench right in our headlights, then cut to the parking lights. At least we didn't have to worry about anybody taking down
our tag number.

I put my respirator on over my wig, then handed Vi her gloves. Once
we were both fully suited up, it hardly took any time for us to put the
bodies on the benches. We faced them toward the road, leaning close to
each other, their belongings beside them in the wan circle of light thrown
out by the bulb overhead.

Rose made sure Iris watched us do it. Then Vi and I went back to the
car. "Take off the booties and turn them inside out before we get in,"
I told Vi, "so there won't be any evidence in the car that we were here."

"Public enemy number one," she quipped as she did what I'd asked.

Still wearing my gloves, I accepted her booties, then put them into the
trash bag with the plastic and the vacuum cleaner bag, tying the top
tight.

"Okay," I said. "Let's get outta here."

"We might just get away with this," Vi said as we pulled onto the cove
road.

Iris cocked her head. "*Now* she says she thinks this will work? This
was your brainchild, sweetie."

"All we have to do is find a pay phone and make the call," I said, shuck-
ing down to my regular clothes beneath my hazmat suit. "Then a Dumpster for the last of the evidence, and the deed is done."

The Dumpster was easy. The pay phone wasn't.

We hadn't taken cell phones into consideration, because service was
spotty at best in the mountains, but even so, pay phones seemed to have
gone the way of the dinosaur. The first two closed gas stations we came
to had them, but neither worked. One lacked a receiver, and the other
had been smashed for the cash.

"No need to panic," Vi said. "Green Rock's not far, and it's nothing *but* gas stations and convenience stores. I'm sure we'll find one that works there."

Would that we had. After shooting four more blanks, we found one that worked at the local mechanic's, but it only took credit cards. Not what you need when you're phoning in an anonymous dead-body tip.

By then, all of us were getting really nervous.

"Okay," I said as we worked our way back toward Clayton. "There has to be a pay phone somewhere in Clayton that works. Nobody will recognize us in these wigs."

A light bulb went on over Iris's head. "Trailer parks," she declared. "Campgrounds."

"Why didn't I think of that?" Vi asked rhetorically.

"There's that trailer park in Dillard, off the beaten path," Rose said. "I check out the flea market just past it every now and then. I'll bet we can find one there."

Sure enough, after we very carefully crept through Dillard, Vi turned left at a sign for the flea market. A couple of miles down the road, we passed the ramshackle trailer park and our headlights came to a lighted pay phone beside the flea market.

Appropriating Iris's sunglasses, I said, "Y'all drop me off, then pull around so we can make a quick getaway. By the time the police find the you-know-whos, we'll be safely back in bed."

Replacing my glove, I dug a handful of quarters out of my pocket along with the dispatcher's number on a scrap of paper. My heart pounding, I paid, then dialed.

"Please deposit an additional fifty cents," a mechanical voice informed me.

Shoot a monkey! What a rip-off. I put the quarters in, then heard two rings and a click.

"Rabun County Shurruf's dispatch," a hard female voice announced, sending every hair on my body erect.

"There's a body at Bold Creek Park," I said as low and raspy as I could.

"I'm sorry, sir, I didn't get that. Could you please repeat it?"

"There's a body at Bold Creek Park," I rasped out again, then hung up without waiting for her to respond.

I'd planned to walk naturally back to the car, but being a potential criminal can make you do things you never intended to do, such as running like your fanny was on fire, then beating on the door because your sister forgot to unlock it after she turned around.

"Go, go, go," I gasped out once I was inside. "But don't speed. Mountain City's the worst speed trap in the state."

My fear was contagious. You could cut the tension with a knife.

"What did they say?" Rose asked.

"She asked me to repeat myself, so I did—not in my own voice, of course—then I hung up. I didn't want her to trace the call."

"Can't they do that anyway, these days?" Iris asked.

"Sure, but not on the spot. They'll find out where the call came from, but by then, we'll be home in bed."

I looked at the clock, surprised to see that it was well past midnight. Time flies when you're having crime.

It was one-fifteen when we reached Laurel Lane, and Rose got out to lead us back to the house by flashlight, so nobody could see us driving in.

Once we were back inside the house, we all collapsed around the breakfast table.

"I need chocolate," I announced.

"I need another drink," Iris said, smacking the flask of moonshine to the table.

"Do you always drink this much?" I blurted out before my brain went into gear.

She glared at me. "Only when I'm forced to leave my husband and live in a place that makes the Addams mansion look good, completely cut off from the modern world. With dead bodies in the basement."

"No bodies now," Vi corrected.

Safely home, I felt a huge letdown. "I wonder what that moonshine would do to my yeasty beasties," I mused aloud.

"At that proof, it would probably kill 'em," Rose said. "Kill anything."

"Could we please not talk about killing?" Iris asked. "I'm gonna have enough trouble getting to sleep, even with a sleeping pill."

I picked up the flask, but Vi took it from me. "We need to go to bed."

"Wait," Rose said. "I think a day like this one merits a ceremony. Y'all sit tight for just a sec." She grabbed the butane match and lit a candle, then put it at the center of the table. Next came mismatched little juice glasses with bloodred contents. Then she turned out the lights, leaving only the faint glow from the bathrooms, and sat, hands extended for ours. "It's pomegranate juice, but we can pretend it's . . . whatever."

We all joined in a circle without a word, even Iris.

"I hereby call to order the sacred Barrett sisterhood," Rose intoned, "to swear a solemn, binding oath of silence and of loyalty." She pulled her hand free and crooked her pinky safely above the candle flame. "Pinky swear."

The rest of us couldn't help smiling. We'd practiced this ritual many times at the cottage, usually after one of us had done something and didn't want the others to rat her out.

We crooked our pinkies together, fists touching.

"Repeat after me," Rose said. "I solemnly swear—"

"I solemnly swear," we chorused.

"Never to reveal—"

"Never to reveal."

"What happened today."

We repeated the phrase.

"Not even to husbands or best friends—"

Neither of which I had anymore, outside that circle. "Not even husbands or best friends."

"Or lawyers or investigators of any kind—"

"Or lawyers or investigators of any kind." Misgiving was evident in our tone.

"Which is why we have the Fifth Amendment, hallelujah—"

We all relaxed. "Which is why we have the Fifth Amendment, hallelujah."

"Amen and amen."

"Amen and amen."

We broke the pinkie circle as we always had, with a high arc and laughter.

"Now can we go to bed?" Vi pleaded.

"Now we can go to bed," Rose ruled.

"Can I bring my blow-up mattress to your room?" Iris asked her.

Rose hugged her, rubbing her back. "Of course you can, sweetie. For the whole summer, if you want to."

Iris pulled free, her touching gratitude channeling the sweet little girl she'd been before jealousy had built a wall between us. "Thanks. I might just take you up on that."

Vi and Rose headed upstairs, but I touched Iris's arm to keep her from following.

"I'm really proud of you, Iris," I told her, meaning it for the first time in a long time. "I can only guess how hard today must have been for you, but you waded right in, anyway. And you did it for me. Thank you."

She remained open, trusting me with, "To tell the truth, I'm proud of me, too. All these years, I've let my phobias own me, but today, I didn't let them win. I couldn't have done that without y'all. Without you. I just pretended I was you, and it worked."

The unguarded moment was fragile, yet profound. I prayed it would be a new beginning for us, sealed by a solemn oath.

Tears welled in my eyes, surprising me, but I didn't try to hide them. "I love you so much. Even when we're fighting. But I don't want to fight anymore. I want to be your friend, not your enemy. That can only happen if you let it."

"We're never going to think alike, you know," she said with a hint of regret.

I nodded. "We don't have to. We just need to accept each other as we are, and forgive."

"I haven't been very good at that, have I?" she confessed.

"Better than I have, I think."

Forgive us our sins as we forgive those who have sinned against us. It was a powerful contingency for our own relationships with God, one we shared with our fellow human beings—especially sisters.

Peace washed over the fatigue on her face. "You're on. Let's get to bed."

I nodded, suddenly exhausted, and hugged her gently. Then we both went up and crashed.

I didn't dream of bodies that night.

Neither did Iris. She told me at breakfast the next morning that she dreamed of me and Clete—in a ballroom-dancing porno flick.

· 14 ·

I changed my mind. I want to get Cracker Jacks.
—IRIS, AGES 5–7

July 26, 1957, Clayton, Georgia

....

*A*s SHE DID on most summer Saturdays, Mama dropped Daddy and Vi off at the hardware store on her way to get groceries in Clayton, because something always needed fixing at the cottage. By the time Mama headed for the checkout line at the superette, Iris and I had thoroughly inspected anything and everything that could be had for a quarter in the store.

Bored, I swung on the cart while we waited for the plump cashier to check out the scraggy-looking pregnant lady ahead of us in line. As usual, Iris—clutching a toy boat in her hand after endless rejections and substitutions—announced, "I changed my mind. I'm gonna go get some Cracker Jacks," and took off.

She always ended up with Cracker Jacks, just like I always ended up spending my allowance on fries and a Coke, or maybe a chocolate shake, back at the Rock House Café by Clare's Boathouse.

I looked at what the lady ahead of us was unloading from her cart and saw that she sure was buying a lot of dried beans. And lard. And cornmeal. And powdered milk—yuk! And a cheap brand of detergent I'd never seen before.

We used Tide, I was proud to know, just like the ladies in Mama's *Ladies' Home Journal*, and Mama used Breck shampoo on all of us, too, because she always said some things are worth the money.

My gaze fell to the worn-out loafers the lady was wearing, then rose to note how thin and shabby her dress was, and I realized she was poor. Next to Mama in her bright, full summer skirt, sandals, and white señorita top, the lady looked old. Even at only seven, though, I knew old ladies didn't have babies. Except Sarah in the Bible.

I studied the lady's face. If she wasn't so skinny and sad, with a little makeup and a nice hairdo and some nice clothes, she might have looked almost pretty. Being poor must have made her look so old, I decided, and felt a strong twist of sympathy.

The lady put a pack of Camel cigarettes atop the last of her order.

Just as the cashier was finishing ringing her up, Mama stuck a finger in the air. "Uh-oh. Forgot the cake mix. Dahlia, honey, watch the cart for me while I get it, please."

"Yes, Mama."

Back then, it was perfectly safe to leave a seven-year-old unattended in a small supermarket. Or even loose in a small town like Clayton, for that matter.

The cashier looked at the lady's big belly with disapproval. "Another baby?" she asked in a snotty tone. "How many does this one make? Four?"

Clearly embarrassed, the poor lady said quietly, "Five."

The clerk shook her head as if the lady had just cussed or something. "That'll be twenty-three dollars and fifty cents."

The lady opened her wallet and pulled out some kind of money I'd never seen. Instantly, my interest piqued. Then she unzipped the coin purse and reacted with alarm. Clearly, she'd expected to find some coins inside, but her searching fingers came up empty.

Having liberated a coin or two from my own mother's purse when I'd already spent my allowance and the Good Humor man came down our street, I wondered if that was what had happened, and felt a pang of guilt.

"I know I had some change." The lady groped all over the bottom of her purse, but still came up empty.

The cashier acted all stuck-up and said, "You'll have to put the cigarettes back. You know we can't accept food stamps for cigarettes."

Food stamps? What were those? The stuff she'd paid with looked more like coupons than stamps.

The lady acted like the cashier was going to arrest her. Desperate, she pleaded softly, "Couldn't you just make an exception, just this once. They're for my husband. He'll be real upset if I don't get them. I mean, *real* upset. I cain't go home without those cigarettes. It's only a quarter." Her big knuckles went white as she gripped the handles of her pocketbook. "Maybe you could put it on account. I'll sell some eggs to the lake people this week. I can pay it back on Monday."

The cashier didn't seem to care one bit. "Sorry, Mrs. Slocum, but we've already told you, the manager said no more credit."

I thought the lady was going to cry. Why a pack of cigarettes was such a big deal, I couldn't imagine, but it hurt my soul to watch that lady beg.

I weighed the prospect of fries and a Coke against the scared, beaten look in that lady's expression, and I offered up my quarter. " 'Scuse, me, ma'am, but here's a quarter for you." I placed it on the counter. "You can have it."

The lady looked at me with a mixture of shame and relief. "Thank you, little girl. You are used of God in this. Thank you." Grim-faced, she handed the quarter to the cashier. "It's nice to see they's some folks left with a little Christian charity."

She didn't look back as she started pushing her cart toward the door, but that was okay. I knew it must not have been easy to take money from a child, even when she needed it so bad.

The cashier leaned across the counter and frowned down at me. "That was throwin' good money after bad, little girl, but it's your money," she said as Mama returned with the cake mix and Iris gripping her box of Cracker Jacks.

Mama didn't take kindly to strangers scolding us. She straightened to all five feet of her with a frosty, "I beg your pardon, miss," to the cashier. "What seems to be the problem?"

Still acting all stuck-up, the clerk started ringing and bagging our order. "Your little girl just paid for a pack of cigarettes for the laziest, meanest piece of white trash in this county, that's what."

I didn't know much, but I knew better. "You're the one who was mean," I shot back at the cashier, indignant. I pointed out the window to the poor lady, who was unloading her groceries into a beat-up old truck that looked like it had been pieced together from a dozen others. "She wasn't mean. She was sad, and she needed the money."

For once, Mama didn't correct me for sassing off at an elder, which put the cashier in her place, at least a little.

Still ringing up our purchases, the clerk cocked her head toward parking lot. "I wasn't talkin' about her. I was talkin' about that sorry-assed moonshiner of a husband of hers." My eyes widened to hear such coarse talk from a grown-up. "Whole family on the dole. Houseful of starvin' kids with a daddy who won't turn a hand at honest work. Nobody in the county would touch that poison he brews, but he sells it down to Atlanta, then drinks up all he makes."

"Mama, can I open my Cracker Jacks?" Iris intruded, oblivious to what was going on, as ever.

"Not now, sweetie." Mama absently added them to our order instead of having Iris use her allowance. Iris's eyes widened, but for once, she had the good sense to keep quiet. Mama patted her. "You can open them after they're paid for."

Meanwhile, the cashier went right on gossiping. " 'Course, you cain't help some people. Everybody from the preacher to the sheriff to the social worker done told that woman to leave him, but she don't listen. Just keeps havin' more babies for the taxpayers to feed.

"I grant you," she went on as if she and Mama were best friends instead of total strangers, "he probably would have beat the snot out of her if she didn't bring home them cigarettes, but rules are rules. You cain't pay for alcohol or tobacco with food stamps, period." She waggled a can of Spam Mama's way for emphasis. "If my man ever hit me, it'd be the last time he saw this face, I can tell you. And he'd be lookin' through bars, so fast your head'd swim." She hit the total button with a flourish. "That'll be thirty-six dollars and forty-five cents."

Mama paid with a frosty look and a stern, "Situations like that are often far more complicated than they seem."

Then she drew me close for a fierce hug. "Dahlia, I'm very proud of you for helping that lady." She took a quarter from her wallet. "This isn't a reward," she said as she gave it to me, "because our good deeds are reward enough, all by themselves. I'm repaying you because I would have given the lady the money, myself, if I'd been here."

Feeling virtuous for keeping that poor lady from getting the snot beat out of her, I happily accepted the quarter. And as the cashier loaded the last of our groceries into the cart, I vowed, then and there, never to take another coin from Mama's change purse, no matter how hot it was and no matter how much I wanted a Popsicle.

The clerk rolled her eyes, but Mama ignored her, focused on me and Iris. "I want you two to remember how much a quarter can matter to some people. And I don't ever want you to gossip about another person's misfortune. It isn't Christian."

With that, she pushed the cart toward the door and our waiting Plymouth station wagon. "Let's go get Daddy." I could tell from the look on her face and way she said his name that she was proud Daddy was sweet and hardworking, just like *Father Knows Best,* and not a sorry-assed moonshiner like that poor lady's husband.

· 15 ·

No matter how old you are, skinny-dipping is really fun . . .
until you have to get out.
—MAMA LOU

Lake Clare, the morning after the Dancing Santa Caper

O I AND I slept late, along with the others, then the two of us rose and took the boat over to the boathouse to see if there was anything about the bodies in the newspapers. To our vast relief, there wasn't. Nothing on the grapevine, either.

Yet.

Which made sense, considering the fact that we'd called in the tip too late to make the papers.

Unless somebody had absconded with the bodies before the police got there, which worried the others, but sounded great to me.

As for our subsequent efforts to close the doorway to the cellar back up, I have only one thing to say: just because I was good with modeling clay and caulk didn't mean I could build a wall, much less rebuild one that was scattered halfway across the basement. It took the four of us the rest of the day just to lay out the remains on the floor so we'd know exactly where to put what, which was like doing a jigsaw puzzle—in Jupiter's gravity. By the time we got everything in place, all four of us were so sore and tired that we moved like we were a hundred as we moaned and groaned our way upstairs for supper, hands bracing our backs.

Advil and hot baths occupied us for the rest of the evening.

The next morning, Vi and I met early at the coffeepot and decided to go get our daily papers before breakfast. While the others were still sleeping, we took Clete's boat over to Hanson's to see if the police report on the last page of the local paper mentioned anything about the mummies.

If it wasn't for that wretched Sammy Tate, that's probably where we would have found it.

As it was, we weren't prepared for what was waiting. Half a dozen lakies and the checkout clerk in the boathouse store stood reading their *AJCs*, the A section spread wide as they finished the rest of the front-page article whose headline shouted 'DANCING SANTA' MUMMIES FOUND NEAR CLAYTON above two huge full-color renditions of the gift-wrapped bodies—frontal, and in profile—stark against the bench and picnic table in the flash photo.

Shit!

A small gasp escaped Vi. I froze with a fake smile on my face as the universe went into triple-slow, excruciating disaster time frame.

No, no, no, no, no! This couldn't be happening.

Survival mode kicked in. Get the papers and get out. Run!

No, don't run. Try to act casual. Breathe. Can't breathe.

There were only four *AJCs* left in the rack, and none of the local weekly. Usually, they didn't run out till afternoon.

I took all four copies. "What's happened?" I asked inanely through my fixed-grin smile when I set them on the counter. As if I couldn't see for myself.

The clerk (one of the boat mechanics' wives) lowered her paper, clearly thrilled to be able to fill me in. "The shurruf is fit to be tied. That Sammy Tate who lives out Bold Creek Road was listenin' to the police scanner the other night when he heard a deputy tellin' the dispatcher there was two giant body-shaped Christmas presents sittin' on a picnic bench at Bold Creek. So Sammy gits in his pickup and goes over there 'fore the shurruf comes, and takes all these pichers with his digital camera." She leaned in close to murmur, "I wouldn't be surprised if he promised that deputy a little green, if you know what I mean." Then her tone returned to normal. "So then Sammy goes home and sells them pichers over the Internet to some big news agency for tons o' money, and here we are. They's reporters all over the county interviewin' anybody who'll talk to 'em. It was even on *Good Mornin' America*."

Damn, and double-dog damn!

I tried to lower my eyebrows, but they wouldn't cooperate. Fortunately, the clerk was too caught up in what happened to study me. She returned my fixed grin with a genuine one. "Musta been a slow news day."

Hell, hell, hell!

I began to see stars, then reflex took over and I remembered to breathe.

One of the lakies folded his paper, then tossed three quarters on the counter. "I don't think it was a slow news day. I think people are so sick of bad news and devil-or-the-deep-blue-sea politics, the papers picked up the story to boost sales."

"Well, it sure worked here," the clerk said. "When we called the paper to order some more, the folks in Atlanta said there'd been a run on this edition, so they was gonna repeat the story tomorra on the front of the Metro section."

I could hear God laughing, and I didn't appreciate it one bit.

Vi and I deliberately didn't look at each other. She just slipped Iris's copy of *USA Today* into the stack under my arm. "It's on the front of *USA Today*, too," she said in a cheery little voice. "Only smaller."

"Wow," I said, sounding phony even to myself. "We can't wait to read it."

The clerk rang us up. "Well, don't feel guilty 'bout takin' the last ones of these. The early bird gits the worm, I always say."

"Thanks."

Vi waited till we'd putted halfway across the lake to lean close to me and read: " 'AP, Reuters: Clayton, Georgia. Rabun County Sheriff's Deputy Luther Gaddis responded to an anonymous midnight tip and found two seated, mummified bodies, wrapped in large dancing Santa plastic bags tied with giant red bows, sitting on a public picnic bench at Bold Creek Park.' " She went on to read that initial inspection of the mummies revealed no sign of foul play—thank God—" 'but at the urging of the governor, whose aunt lives in Clayton' "—"dammit," Vi interjected—" 'the state has assigned high priority to the autopsies, and the GBI and FBI were clarifying jurisdictions. Great care had apparently been taken to preserve the mummies, intact, when they were moved.' "

In an interview, the sheriff said the bodies appeared to have been dead for quite a long time, possibly more than eighty years, but were remarkably well preserved.

"If that was well preserved," Vi commented, "I'd hate to see badly preserved."

I shook my head. "After eighty years, anything in one piece qualifies as well preserved."

Then the story quoted several locals who lived in the area near where the bodies had been found, none of whom had seen or heard anything unusual recently. But all of them, when asked by the reporter, had theories as to where the bodies had come from. A local mechanic said aliens. The minister of the Lord Almighty Church of the Redemption said they might have been stolen, then returned because of a guilty conscience. A professor at the technical school said the whole thing was probably a practical joke, and the mummies fake. And a retired county clerk blamed "some evil outside developer" for digging them up at a new development, then not wanting to dispose of them properly.

"Whoa," I said. That was too close for comfort.

And the last one interviewed—a local granny—said they might have been hoboes who died during the Depression and were found by some well-intentioned soul too poor to give them a proper funeral, so they'd been preserved, then disposed of when their presence became inconvenient.

Way too close for comfort. "Between the last two, I'd say they've got us nailed," I told Vi.

She shook her head, unfazed. "It's all conjecture. We don't even know how they got into the you-know-where. And the article doesn't mention any evidence."

"This is a nightmare," I told her as she helped me pull Clete's boat into the slip. "A freaking nightmare. And I got y'all into it."

"You didn't put a gun to our heads," Vi retorted. "We're in it because we chose to be in it. End of discussion. Recriminations aren't gonna make this any easier, so no guilt trips, okay? What is, is."

Back up at the house, the others hadn't even stirred. I laid the papers on

the table, then poured an illegal bowl of raisin bran and doused it with va-
nilla Rice Dream and lots of Splenda before reading the story for myself.

Vi and I ate in silence. When we'd finished our cereal and second cups
of coffee, I leaned close to her and said softly, "I vote we go downstairs
and get started building the wall. Iris and Rose can read the story for
themselves."

She nodded. "Brilliant."

After tiptoeing to get ready, we came down and slipped out the side
door, then went around to the basement from outside to avoid the floor
furnace and squeaky door in the hall. Clad in my usual hazmat getup,
except for fresh gloves and booties, I'd just finished hooking up the hose
outside and bringing it in to mix some mortar when we heard footsteps
overhead, then the clank of the floor furnace, followed by muffled voices
in the hallway.

Both of us stilled for what was probably only a few seconds, but felt
like long minutes.

Then there was a loud yelp in Iris's voice.

Boom, boom, footsteps, then *bam*, the door at the top of the stairs flew
open. "Ohmygod! Did y'all see these papers?" Iris hollered down.

I winced, and Vi raised her respirator to her forehead. "I'm assuming
that question was rhetorical," she called in Iris's direction. "But you might
want to consider lowering your voice. Sound carries near water, remember?"

"Ohmygod! Shit! Shit, shit, shit, shit, shit!!" Iris spat out. She'd lowered
her decibel level, but not her consternation. "Shit, shit, shit!"

"My sentiments, exactly," I called toward the stairs.

Rose interrupted Iris's cuss fest with, "Would y'all like to come upstairs and discuss this?"

Vi and I looked at each other, both of us pulling faces. "No, thank
you," we said at the same time, then couldn't help laughing at the perfect
unity of our responses.

"This isn't funny," Iris scolded. "And yes, ma'am, you *are* coming up
here."

Rose overruled her. "Y'all just keep on working. We'll be down to help
after a while." She closed the door, muffling Iris's protests.

Vi and I waited, poised, till we heard them settle at the breakfast table, Iris still having a hissy fit.

"Whew," Vi said. "That was a close one."

"I never thought I'd be grateful to be down here in this getup, but I am."

"Iris will be fine," Vi told me. "She just needs to vent, and aren't we lucky that Rose doesn't mind being the ventee?"

"Amen to that, sister." I didn't want to think about it. I just wanted to get that wall back the way it had been before I'd had the bright idea of how to tear it down. After that, I planned to act innocent for the rest of the summer, no matter what happened. I just prayed the others could do the same.

The phone rang in Cissy's room, and Iris's familiar steps hurried to get it. After a brief silence, she called to Rose, "It's Wilson. He saw the paper."

Uh-oh.

I looked to Vi. "Should we go upstairs and make sure she doesn't tell him?"

As always, Vi remained calm. "Nah. Rose'll keep her straight."

For the rest of the morning, the phone practically rang off the hook. After Wilson, Mama called next. Iris summoned us upstairs to talk to her, then overheard me tell what the clerk had said.

She was waiting to pounce when I hung up. "You might have told us about the clerk."

"We were busy working downstairs," I defended. "But now you know, so feel free to spread it around."

Which was a good thing, because everybody in Atlanta who knew Cissy's phone number called to see if we'd heard any of the skinny on the story. We voted that whoever took the call would field it, so every time the phone rang while we were all working in the basement, Rose and Vi and I just ignored it, evoking Iris's compulsion to respond. So she spent most of the morning repeating what the clerk had said instead of working. Frankly, that suited me fine. I hoped that passing on the clerk's story would satisfy her need to talk about what happened, for good and all.

The calls stopped by one, and fortunately, we didn't hear from the press or the police, and no squad cars pulled into the driveway.

Iris finally rejoined the chain gang.

"Glad you're here," I greeted her. "The sooner we get this closed back up, the sooner we can close the book on this whole thing and rest easy."

She aimed a scolding finger at Rose. "You and your bargain Christmas tree bags. Now look what's happened." She turned on me. "I knew I shouldn't have let you talk us into this."

I cocked my head. "Do I hear blaming? I thought we were going to start over and be nice to each other. Allies."

She pointed the extra mason's trowel we'd resurrected from Poppy Jack's shop. "I changed my mind. When I picked up the paper."

Over the next three days, the furor about the bodies died a natural death without providing any leads, beyond the fact that the men had been mummified in salt after dying from lead poisoning.

Meanwhile, the four of us worked like Hebrew slaves in Pharaoh's brick pit to reconstruct the wall. In the process, despite our gloves, we all sacrificed every one of our fingernails to the Goddess of Masonry, but she rewarded us well. It was slow going, first getting the mortar mix right, then positioning the stones and making sure the mortar between them wasn't too wide or too narrow. But after we finished early Thursday afternoon and blended everything into the background by scrubbing mud into the fresh-dried mortar, then rinsing, the result was close to perfect.

With the end in sight, we swept the dirt floor clear of masonry fragments and mortar stains, sterilized the soil and foundation walls with a strong bleach solution, then dried out the whole basement with fans, so I could wear a regular respirator down there instead of the heavy-duty one. As a final chore, we freed all the French doors of vines and polished every pane.

Nobody would ever be able to tell what had happened.

To celebrate the end of our personal purgatory, we all slept till ten on Friday, then, after a quick breakfast, congregated in the basement one more time with coffee, still in our pink robes and scuffies, for a final inspection.

The odor of bleach lingered strong, but morning sun streamed through the sparkling panes of the eastern window in Poppy Jack's old shop, giving a warm glow to the native quartz in the foundation. And the open French doors let in a cool breeze that scoured away the dank. Our sorted piles had been reduced to mere fragments of the original mess, making the whole basement look bigger.

I started to say, "That'll do, pig," but managed to stop myself in time.

Looking at our handiwork, Rose nodded in satisfaction. "It's perfect. The rest will be easy, compared to this."

I nodded. "I vote we cut way back on our hours. I'm whipped."

Iris bumped my hip, careful not to spill either of our coffees. "Honey, starting Monday, we're all taking a vacation . . . for at least a week, and I can't wait."

Clete's.

Now, why hadn't I thought it was a good idea to stay there? For the life of me, I couldn't remember.

Nothing like a couple of mummies in the root cellar to put things in perspective.

I still didn't trust him, but I surely did lust him—for his creature comforts, if nothing else. "Air-conditioning," I rhapsodized, eyes closed.

"Soaking tubs," Vi seconded.

Iris let out a contented sigh. "A real bathroom."

"A cook," from Rose.

"Assuming he was telling the truth about his house," I felt compelled to add. "He is a bachelor, you know."

Iris smiled. "Brenda, the little college student who works at the gas dock at Hanson's, said a bunch of magazines had featured the house. Her brother works for Clete's factory in Dillard, so every year, she and her family get to go to a huge Christmas party at Clete's for everybody in the company. She said the place is amazing." She certainly had the lowdown. "Brenda's going for a degree in chemistry with a minor in ecology, so she can develop biofriendly pest controls for ornamental and agricultural applications, too. Her favorite color is red, and her favorite song is 'Rhiannon.' "

Vi and I turned to her in amazement.

"And when, pray tell," I asked, "did you find all that out?"

"At the dance," Iris said, then took another sip of her coffee.

"Anything about anybody else?" Vi questioned. "Or did you spend the whole night grilling Brenda?

Iris went smug. "I didn't grill anybody. People like to talk about their lives, and I like to listen." She shot me a mischievous look. "As for Brenda, she provided the narrative while we watched you do that tango with Clete. People around here love that guy. You might be missing something really special if you don't encourage him."

Warmth bloomed in my neck and cheeks. "We have nothing in common. He probably hasn't ever seen a ballet."

"Ballet, schmallet," Iris dismissed. "He's the only man I ever saw who could dance your shoes off, and that's saying something. Sexy, sexy, sexy."

I still didn't trust the guy, but now that we had our own giant secret to keep, I was a little less vehement about it. "Image is one thing," I said, a lesson I'd learned all too well from Harrison. "We have no idea what he's like behind closed doors."

"Next week will be your opportunity to find out," Iris said with a sly smile.

Shoot! That hadn't come out the way I'd wanted it to.

The others started laughing salaciously.

"Forget sex," I said. "All I want is his air-conditioning." I turned toward the stairs. "I'm going back to bed," I told them. "Don't wake me till supper."

Iris frowned. "Oh. I was hoping we could play some bridge this afternoon." She shot me a pointed glance. "To get my mind off things."

Ah. I'd gotten her into the mess with the bodies, so now I needed to provide a distraction.

I told myself not to get defensive, but felt it, anyway. The truth was, though, I could use a distraction myself, and bridge required just enough of my concentration to take my mind off whatever I might be worrying about—like Dancing Santa headlines and fit-to-be-tied sheriffs.

I loved bridge, but hadn't had a chance to play since the divorce. So I relented. "Okay. I'm in. But not till later, after I've had a long nap followed by some bacon and tomato wraps." Unlike Iris, I played for fun, not blood, so I looked at her and added, "As long as we remember it's just a game, not a contest."

She did that compulsive little lip-pursing thing, but said, "Of course."

Vi wasn't convinced. "Y'all, I'm awful. The last time I played was probably that horrendous week at Fripp when the girls were just toddlers."

Rose put a consoling arm around her shoulders. "Don't worry, sweetie. It'll all come back to you after a few hands. And if you don't like it, we can quit."

Vi looked askance at me, but gave in. "Okay. I'll try it, but only because you need a fourth."

So we all napped, then ate, then played hand after hand on the shady verandah, soothing away our unspoken fears about the Dancing Santa Caper by sharing the mundane gossip of the ordinary lives we'd left behind in Atlanta. The few times Iris tried to critique our games, I put her firmly in her place, so even Vi eventually relaxed and enjoyed herself.

Two gallons of artificially sweetened iced tea and a raft of baked tortilla chips and salsa later, twilight mosquitoes were whining past our Deet-soaked selves as Vi and I won the last hand of our fifth rubber (a bridge term that has no sexual connotation whatsoever, even though it still embarrasses me to use it). When Iris tallied the scores, she won by a large margin—no surprise there—but the rest of us had racked up decent scores of our own.

After a light supper, we watched the light die, then Rose stood. "I'm hot. Let's all go swimming."

"Great idea." Iris whipped out the Deet again and started spraying. "But y'all have to promise to do spider patrol, okay?"

"Okay," I promised.

Friday nights were quiet on the lake. Even a decade into this new century, daddies still arrived for late suppers after working in town for the week.

Twenty minutes later, clad in assorted modest one-pieces, we carried our towels and dollar store inflated rafts down to the little beach by Mama's dock. Graceful and precise as ever, Rose put her raft in, straddled it, then lay forward and started paddling with her hands toward deeper water. Iris tried to do the same, but ran aground, so she waded in deeper with hers, squealing about the cool water and the gooshy bottom.

No death by degrees for me. I went to the platform, tossed in my raft, then dived toward it. To my dismay, a week at hard labor had left my muscles uncooperative, so I barely made it up to grab the middle of the float and heave my chest across it, sending the ends into the air. "Damn. I seem to have forgotten how to swim. Y'all be careful. If you get into trouble, I'd probably drown us both trying to help."

"I'm glad you admitted that," Iris confessed, "I can't swim the way I used to, either."

I tried to remember the last time I'd gone swimming in a lake instead of a pool, and couldn't. "This is pitiful. I was a Red Cross certified lifeguard for fifteen years, and now I couldn't even save myself, much less anybody else. Total bummer."

Vi sighed. "Every time I have a birthday, I tell myself it's just a vicious lie, but my body keeps reminding me it isn't."

Rose paddled over, her perfectly manicured feet safely up on her raft. "There are plenty of women's ski vests in Clete's boat. Nice ones."

A totally unexpected flash of territoriality made me wonder what women he had them for, but I didn't let on. "Sounds like a plan to me," I said, squelching the image of Clete with a boat full of beauties.

While the others put theirs on, I snapped mine closed, grumbling, "Can't even swim anymore." Then I slipped below the surface to wet back my long hair, savoring the tug as I resurfaced with it smooth against my skull. "These beat the heck out of those sour old Mae Wests."

Confident in our vests, we paddled around, splashed each other, did somersaults underwater, then stretched out on our backs to study the star-swath of the Milky Way above us as the air cooled, leaving the water warmer than the atmosphere.

It was so quiet and peaceful there, serenaded by frogs and sounds of the night.

I had a brilliant idea and sat up to unhook the halter of my bathing suit.

Iris sat up next to me. "What are you doing?"

"Goin' skinny-dipping. The water's perfect." Shielded by my float, I loosened the plastic clasps on my ski vest, then pulled my suit down. After buckling the ski vest back up, I swam bare-assed to the platform and heaved my suit onto the dock.

"How's it feel?" Iris asked.

I swam back out to my float. "Fabulous."

Vi grinned and took hers off, too.

To my surprise, even self-conscious Iris shucked down to the skin, her extra pounds hidden by the float. Rose had to consider for a while, then made it unanimous.

Despite the ski vest, feeling the water against my bare skin made me remember when we'd all been little enough to wade naked whenever we wanted, while Mama or our maid watched us. "How old were we when Mama made us start wearing clothes all the time?"

"Young," Iris said. "I was probably only three. And I didn't appreciate it."

Lying back in the water with the stars overhead, I thought about us as children, and the women we'd become. And it struck me that, aside from her relationship with me, Iris was a far kinder person than I was. So was Rose. Iris knew every personal detail about everybody who worked with her, right down to the dog-sitter and the housekeeper, and she cared about their lives and needs—often to the point of excess, but she always meant well. Rose was more diplomatic about it, but she, too, made herself aware of the emotional needs of those around her. Even Vi was able to relate to people better than I could.

I'd always been so caught up in trying to reach a goal or make my own world perfect that I hadn't had time or emotional space for other perspectives.

Vi floated closer. "Don't fall asleep," she said softly.

I took in a long breath, then eased it out. "You caught me self-obsessing."

"Well, honey," she said, her tone warm, "you just go right back to it, then."

I did, till I heard a high whine in the water, getting louder with every second.

"Boat," I said, sitting up and scanning the lake.

The others popped upright, too. "Uh-oh," Vi said, turning toward the point. "I see lights."

"Shoot!" Abandoning her float, Iris swam for her suit. Rose followed.

"What do you think?" Vi said, not going anywhere.

I watched the boat—a pontoon—slowly clear the point, then take up a leisurely course toward us, close to shore, the lights inside its cover illuminating at least ten partygoers. Several of them were singing "Sloop John B" in excellent close harmony. Facing the stern, one man leaned against a roof support in back, his tall body as tense as it was familiar.

"Clete." The water next to my bare shin all but boiled from the heat of my embarrassment. Never had I been so aware of my nakedness.

Vi peered his way. "Uh-oh. C'mon." She grabbed her float and mine, heading for the dock. "Shoot!" she said when we got there. "The towels are all on the chair by the beach, and I can't reach my suit. Or Rose's. We threw them too far up onto the platform."

"I can get mine," Iris said, but when she pulled up to grab it, she let out a shriek. "Dahlia! There's a huge spider on my suit. Get it, get it!"

All spiders were huge to Iris, but I swam over as fast as I could, my bare behind beaming like two full moons behind me. "Don't worry, I'll—" I took one look at that spider and thought twice. "Whoa."

This was no daddy longlegs or narrow dock spider. It was huge and hairy, and there was no way I was flipping him into the water with us. He might try to climb up on us. On *me*. Suddenly my scalp felt alive and spidery. "Iris, that's no spider. It's a mutant arachnoid from outer space."

"*Get it, get it, get it,*" she repeated in panic.

When Vi and Rose swam over to see it, they drew back, too, as scared as I was.

Meanwhile, the pontoon was bearing down on us, their spotlight close enough to make out the fact that we were butt-naked below our ski vests if we tried to go for our towels.

"Forget the spider," I said, pulling Iris toward the space between the clad Styrofoam floats under the platform. "We can hide under here, where they won't see us." The cracks between the boards weren't big enough to see through.

Iris started back-paddling with a vengeance. "Are you nuts? That place is full of spiders. No way am I going under there in the dark."

"Here they come," Vi said tersely.

I saw Clete bend to speak to the overweight, florid man in a captain's hat, with a drink in one hand, who was driving the pontoon. Clete's voice carried across the water over the sound of the small motor. "Come on, Commissioner. It's rude to drop in on people. I've already embarrassed them once, doing that. Let's just go back to the party, okay? I'm askin' it as a favor."

"Please tell me they're not planning on dropping in on *us*," Vi whispered.

"We're not gonna embarrass 'em," the commissioner boomed as if he were addressing a crowd at a rally instead of one person. "We're just gonna welcome the little ladies to the neighborhood and invite 'em to the party."

"Shoot!" Vi said. "They're coming here."

The pontoon veered even closer, heading straight for us.

"Quick," I told the others, "under the dock, before they see us. Bring the floats, for extra cover." It didn't occur to us till later that we could have deflated the floats and wrapped them around us. I pulled mine into the dark passage between the Styrofoam, making for the back of the platform with Vi close behind me.

Rose reached for Iris. "Come on, honey. I'll make sure no spiders get you."

"No way in hell am I goin' under that dock with those spiders," Iris repeated. Shoving her float after us, she struck out at an amazingly fast crawl for the boathouse, taking the deep way for speed. We watched her just long enough to erase any chance of making the boathouse ourselves, then we scrambled under the platform in time to see the pontoon's spotlight stab through the slits between the decking. Slowly, it pulled alongside to an uproar of laughter.

"Oh-ho-ho." The commissioner leered. "Looks like our little ladies forgot something."

Ears aflame, I felt like I was caught naked in the middle of the aisle on Easter Sunday.

"Ernest!" Clete reprimanded. "I like a good time as much as any man, but if you don't move on immediately, I'm afraid I'm suddenly going to remember that little thing I forgot three years—"

The motor gunned, stirring a cloud of bubbles and wake as the pontoon abruptly took off. "No harm intended," Ernest the commissioner blustered as they pulled away.

Talk about close calls.

"Let's go for the towels," Violet said when they were a decent distance away.

"They could still see us," Rose protested. "And they're probably coming right back on their way home."

"What's that?" Vi asked, pointing to a dark object the size of a small plum that traced an erratic passage toward us from the direction of the pontoon.

"What?" Rose asked, squinting in the dark.

"That!" Vi said as it got closer.

"Turtle?" I hoped aloud. But it was moving too fast. Not turtle.

"Snake!" Rose screamed, all but levitating.

Adrenaline sent me toward the boathouse at Olympic speed with my sisters close beside, pontoon be damned.

There is nothing, and I mean *nothing*, creepier than being in the water with a snake, regardless of what kind it is. Halfway to the boathouse, I paused to make sure it wasn't coming after us—it wasn't—and discovered Iris's life jacket floating in the middle of the cove.

Meanwhile, the pontoon left Clete's in the direction of the Little Basin, moving away from us.

Rose and Vi swam up beside me. "It's okay," Vi panted out. "I think we scared off the snake, and the pontoon's not coming back."

Rose grabbed the ski vest. "Surely she wouldn't have taken off her life jacket in the water," she worried.

"She probably left it on the dock and it fell off," Vi surmised.

"Iris?" I called. Her name echoed slightly from the boathouse.

We paused, listening to the uninterrupted night sounds broken only by the faint whine of the retreating pontoon boat.

"Iris?" Rose called a little louder.

No answer.

"She's just messing with you because you wouldn't take on that humongous spider," Vi wished aloud. "Come on. Let's head for the ladder at the boathouse. I'm sure she's there."

"Iris!" This time, there was a definite note of fear in Rose's summons, but still there was no answer.

I got to the ladder first, but found no wet footprints there. A stab of fear hit low in my gut and resonated in my summons. "Iris!" My voice echoed loudly from the other side of the cove, followed by silence. Even the bugs and frogs went mute.

Mindless of my nakedness and bare feet, I climbed the ladder and raced through the darkness toward Mama's dock, calling along the shore all the way, "Okay, Iris. You've made your point. Please let us know you're okay. We're getting worried here."

I grabbed the towels, wrapped mine around myself, then doubled back to the dock and sped down to the platform, where I kicked the giant spider into the lake with my bare foot, then snatched up our suits, calling louder and louder. "Iris! Where are you? Answer! Iris!" My calls echoed from all the way across the lake, but there was no answer. She'd have heard me in the house, too.

With rising panic, I sprinted back to the boathouse and handed out the suits. I flung off my vest and scrambled into mine without any thought of modesty.

"I'll check the house," Vi said. "Maybe she went up without us."

"How?" I challenged, breathless. "No way would she have climbed out into that spidery wisteria on the wall, and there's no sign that she got out anywhere else."

Vi ran for Hilltop. "I'll let you know."

"She's all right," Rose said as if she was trying to convince herself as well as me. "I'd know it if anything had happened to her. I'd know it."

Driven by fear, I hooked the ski vest over my arm. "I'm going back out to where we found the vest and start diving."

"No, Dahlia!" Rose grabbed my arm. "You're not a strong enough swimmer. We'll get help."

"Who? The Mountain Patrol takes at least thirty minutes. By then, she could . . ." I faltered, my mouth dry and my words rapid. "I should have killed the damned spider with my bare hands. I know how terrified she is. Hell, I should have gone back up on the dock myself and handed y'all your suits. I don't care if the whole town saw me naked."

"Dahlia," Vi's voice called from the verandah. "She's up heeeere!"

Thank God! Thank God! Thank God!

I braced my hands on my knees and let out my breath in short, open-mouthed blasts.

"See? She's okay," Rose consoled me. "Okay."

There was no way she hadn't heard us calling. Anger followed close on the heels of my relief. "Good, 'cause I'm gonna kill her."

· 16 ·

A truth that's told with bad intent
Beats all the lies you can invent.
—WILLIAM BLAKE

....

I WAS SO mad, I don't even remember getting from the boathouse to
Hilltop. I have a vague impression of Rose's flitting around me like
a hummingbird, pleading for reason, but there is no reason after someone's deliberately let you think she'd drowned and it was your fault.

"That tears it," I yelled when I came through the kitchen door and
found Vi.

She stepped back, making a major uh-oh face, and pointed toward
Cissy's room as I blew past.

"Come out and take your medicine, you passive-aggressive little snot!"
I roared down the hall. "I am gonna kick your can from here to Atlanta
and back!"

I tried the bedroom door and found it locked, all the proof I needed.
"Don't even think about pretending this wasn't deliberate! You threw that
life jacket into the lake and deliberately didn't answer when we called
for you, all because I wouldn't kill that spider. Admit it! And don't you

dare try to hide!" Getting no response, I slammed against the door as hard as I could, and bounced.

Wouldn't you know, the only solid thing in that whole house stood between me and retribution.

"Iris. Let me in! You are not getting away with this one." Rubbing my bruised shoulder, I pressed my ear against the wood panel and heard the sliding glass door that led to the verandah scrape against the track.

Sneaking out, eh? Well, two could play that game.

On my way to intercept Iris, I passed Rose, who started to say something, but clammed up when I pointed a "don't get in my way" finger at her with a glare.

I stepped out of my shoes, then tiptoed through the library to slip out the door to the opposite side of the verandah. At the front corner of the house, I peeked around and saw Iris doing the same thing at the end of that section, her back to me as she watched the sliding door into Cissy's room.

I crept up on her, waiting till I was close to grab her arm, which sent her half out of her skin. "Aaagghh!"

She tried to pull away, but I drew her close. "Oh, did I scare you?" The words dripped with sarcasm. "So sorry. Of course, it's nothing like making you think I'd *drowned*."

Iris was anything but contrite. "If you had any idea what it was like for me, you'd never have asked me to go under that dock." Her eyes narrowed in contempt. "I wouldn't be this way if you hadn't spent my entire childhood throwing spiders on me. You've never been afraid of anything. You have *no idea* what that did to me."

I wasn't buying it this time. "Stop trying to blame *me* for everything that's wrong with you. We grew up in the same family, with the same parents. As Dr. Phil says, 'Get over it!'"

Rose and Vi came out, probably to referee if I got physical, but they needn't have worried. Despite my threats, I had no intention of sinking to Iris's childish level.

Iris's jaw jutted forward. "Dr. Phil didn't spend his entire life thinking he was worthless because he had *you* for a big sister!" she fired back at me. "Did you ever once try to comfort or defend me? No."

"I tried all the time," I told her, "but you were always so busy playing the victim you wouldn't listen, so I gave up."

She straightened to all five feet of her height. "*That* is a bald-faced lie. You never!"

"I absolutely did. You've just erased it. Ask Mama. Dog dammit, Iris, you have no idea what *my* life has been like, and you never have."

"Blame yourself for that, not me," she defended. "You never confided in me about anything that really mattered. Not once. All because I was the only one with the guts to stand up to you."

"I did confide in you, but whenever I did, you *told*. And when we were older, you just threw it back in my face, as if my troubles couldn't hold a candle to yours. I was only trying to keep my grades up and dance, not hurt you."

"Oh, right. Meanwhile, the rest of us were wearing hand-me-downs and secondhand *shoes* so you could take your precious dance lessons, then go to New York while we collected coat hangers and bottles to buy a Coke."

"At least you got to drink one. My budget was so tight, I lived on water and canned tuna the whole time I was gone," I shot back.

Mortally frustrated, I took a deep breath, trying to calm myself, then peered at Iris. "Would you rather I hadn't tried to reach my dream?" She remained defiant. "Did you ever even have a dream of your own? Or were you too busy resenting me? And what in God's good green earth makes you think I've never been afraid of anything? Everybody has fears. And problems, including me."

Her expression went dark. "Well, you wouldn't be having the ones you've got if you hadn't been such a know-it-all, Miss Perfect shopaholic all the time. Did you ever think how much pressure your spending and your constant criticism put on Harrison? No wonder he and Junior left! They were probably sick of living with a pathological perfectionist who couldn't see past the end of her own nose!"

Iris's accusation struck me like a tractor-trailer, and my hand flew free of her arm, as if my body didn't want to remain in contact with such cruel energy.

"Iris!" Rose gasped out.

Vi hauled off and slapped Iris, demanding, "How dare you say something like that to Dahlia?"

Iris slapped her right back, then turned to me, unrepentant. "The truth hurts, doesn't it?"

Seeing her smug satisfaction, I finally understood the depth of her jealousy, an emotion I didn't own. Ambition, yes, but I'd never blamed anybody else for what happened to me. Nor had I ever taken pleasure in seeing anyone else suffer, even when they deserved it.

Okay, well maybe just a teeny bit with Iris, but only when the circumstances were minor.

But Iris's eyes told me she really, truly hated me in a way I'd never hated anybody, even Harrison. Why else would she have said what she did?

"Well?" Iris goaded.

"You're always accusing me of being self-centered, but I would never even think about doing to you what you just did to me." My words came out hoarse. "When I said I loved you, I meant it."

"Oh, please," Iris said. "You want to see a martyr, look in the mirror."

Rose stepped between us. "This has already gone too far. Neither of you say another word."

"Rose," Iris challenged, "You know I'm right."

"I don't know who said those cruel things," Rose replied, "but it's not the loving sister you've been to me. Dahlia's been through hell in the past few years, and the only one at fault was Harrison, not her. She's been a better wife and mother than any of the rest of us. I can't believe you attacked her like that." She searched Iris's sullen expression. "The worst is, you're not even sorry. You're glad you did it, aren't you?"

Vi struck a pugilist's pose at Iris. "Put 'em up. I don't care if you are short, you deserve whippin' for that, and I'm the one to do it. C'mon. Let's settle this once and for all." She shoved Iris's shoulder. "C'mon!"

Iris returned a halfhearted shove of her own. "Oh, shut up, Vi. This is between me and Dahlia. We're grown women, not six-year-old boys on the playground."

"What you just said to Dahlia is as cruel and spiteful as any mean little boy I've ever met." She poked Iris's shoulder again. "Let's see how you like bein' attacked by somebody who's supposed to love you."

I shook my head. "Stop it, both of you. This is stupid." I was queasy, not even angry anymore. And I didn't understand what horrible crime I'd committed that Iris should hate me so.

"Okay then," Vi said, her chin raised in defiance. "Plan B." She grabbed Iris and threw her into a fireman's hold, then started for the door.

"Violet Waycaster Barrett," Iris protested, the veins bulging in her neck and face as she pummeled Vi's back and tried without success to escape. "Put me down!"

Before we knew it, Vi was on the verandah and down the stairs, headed for Mama's dock. She carried Iris as if she were just a rolled-up quilt instead of a plump, wriggling human.

Rose and I followed, but neither of us intervened. I was too empty, and Rose was too curious.

"Where are you taking me?" Iris demanded. Her voice shifted to apprehension. "Vi, what are you doing? If you put me in that hole in Mama's porch, I'll never speak to you again."

"You'd be doing me a favor," Vi snapped.

The closer Vi got to Cardinal Cottage, the higher Iris's protests went. "Stop! Put me down! I mean it. I will never forgive you!" A threat that only she, of all of us, was equipped to follow through.

To Iris's visible relief, Vi carried her past the house to the dock, then down the ramp to the platform. Standing like the Colossus at the edge of the dock, Vi finally spoke. "You deserve a lot worse than this, but if you ever so much as hint at anything mean about Dahlia again, you're going to end up here, regardless of what you're doin'. If you're in the tub, I'll take your bare ass down in broad daylight for everybody to see." Then she promptly heaved Iris into the lake.

Rose waited till Iris came up, sputtering, to applaud what Vi had done. "Brava, sweetie. Brava."

"Rose," Iris scolded, paddling toward the swim ladder.

Vi beat her to it and blocked her exit with a long foot. "Oh, no, Iris. No ladders for you. Gooshy bottom exits, only. With snakes in the wisteria. And spiders. Try to get out anywhere else, and I'll just throw you back in again, and I can do it."

Finally giving in, Iris complained her way across the icky bottom to the sand, but she didn't do any blaming. She just headed back up to the house, her spine rigid.

Rose watched her for a while, then followed. Judging from the look on Rose's face, Iris hadn't heard the last of this.

I appreciated Vi's and Rose's loyalty, but took no satisfaction from it. Normally, I'd have been the first to laugh and get past things, but this wound went far too deep.

I sat at the far side of the dock, numb.

Vi came up behind me. "Do you want me to stay?" she asked quietly, knowing better than to touch me.

I shook my head, so she left.

A few minutes later, she returned to drop a float and life vest beside me. "Don't go out too far. If anything happened to you, there'd be a huge hole in the world nobody else could fill." She started back, then paused. "Iris can be petty and hateful sometimes, but she really does love you underneath. What she said is pure crap. She just needs a good ass-whippin'."

I dropped my head, tears blurring my vision, and nodded.

There's something to be said for numbness. Once Vi was gone, I waited till all the lights at Hilltop went out. Then, with only a tiny crescent of moon and the stars as witness, I slowly stripped out of my suit and stood straight at the edge of the platform, my life vest left behind, and dove, shallow, into the warm water's embrace. Then I started to swim toward the point, my stroke restored, strong and effortless.

I didn't think, I just swam the way I used to dance, my tears lost in the lake.

When I got to the little beach at the point, I walked ashore, glad for the acres that gave me privacy and darkness. I sat at the water's edge, my back braced against a weather-beaten log, my arms extended to my raised knees, and cried.

God, I missed Daddy. He would have made sure Iris's grudge box got emptied on a regular basis, instead of getting so full it became lethal.

We always want what we can't have, don't we?

I wanted Iris to love me, but she didn't. Probably never had, really. I would forgive her, because resentment poisons the one who harbors it, and my faith commanded forgiveness. Already, I could feel sorry for her. She'd poisoned herself for a long, long time over the thousand cuts I'd never known I was inflicting. But if I'd known, would I have done differently? For the life of me, I couldn't think how. Still, I owned my part in that, then prayed God's forgiveness. Maybe I could ask Iris's, but not right away. She'd hurt me too deeply, said the things that never should be uttered.

When the rough sand and pebbles worked their way through to my bony ass, I sat atop the log, not even praying, just letting the silence and the darkness do their work.

Then from the other side of the narrow point, I heard the sound of a strong, even stroke and a sleek-moving craft. Canoe. Somebody was coming.

I slipped back into the water just in time to see Clete round the point, scanning the water as he paddled.

A mighty big coincidence.

"Looking for someone?" I asked loudly when he shipped his paddle to search the shore.

He jumped, flustered, turning toward my voice. "Dahlia?"

I made a long, low underwater passage to the canoe, then pulled my head above the side, grateful that it concealed my nakedness. "I asked you a question. Who were you looking for?"

My eyes had adjusted to the darkness, so I was able to make out the mixture of relief and embarrassment on his face. He didn't hesitate. "You."

"Really? Why?"

"Are you always this direct?" he deflected.

"Always. Especially when I want answers."

He nodded. "I was worried about you."

"And why was that?"

"I was sitting outside after Ernest dropped me off, trying to settle down after what he did, when I heard y'all calling for Iris. I could tell you were scared. I decided to come over and help look for her when I heard Vi say she was okay, so I sat back to finish my tea." His mouth went wry. "Then I heard the argument. Sound really carries on still nights like these, and you two have quite a set of pipes. I couldn't resist hearing the latest installment." He looked at me without wavering. "It's not like you were trying to keep it private."

I sensed he was being honest. Not that I approved, but at least he was forthcoming. He could have made up some lame story, pretended he didn't know I was there.

When I didn't respond, he said, "Cissy told me what happened with your ex. She was really worried about you."

Not enough to send money, I thought, then had the good grace to be ashamed of myself.

"What Iris said to you," he went on, "nobody deserves that. Frankly, I was hoping Vi would clean her clock. But throwing her into the lake was pretty good. Then I saw you sitting there. Just a silhouette, but . . ." His brows drew together in concern, his dark eyes sympathetic. "I looked away, then looked back just as you dove in and swam off. Without the life vest."

Or a bathing suit. "Naked," I said, teed off by his omission of that very important little detail.

He looked at me afresh, noting my bare shoulders. "Really?"

"As if you didn't know," I accused.

"I didn't." Instead of getting defensive, he merely lifted a brow. "If I had, I might have paddled faster."

I probably should have been afraid, naked and alone there with a man I hardly knew who'd been eavesdropping and watching us from across the cove, but I wasn't. Why, I couldn't tell you. Maybe it was because he sat there so still and guiltless, inside and out.

"And exactly what do you intend to do next?" The minute the words were out of my mouth, I realized they could be interpreted as a come-on, which was the opposite of my intention.

"That's up to you," he said, then apparently experienced the same reaction I had. He looked down, then into the middle distance. "What do you want me to do?"

Whoops. Did it again.

Dueling double entendres. I fought the urge to smile, even though my heart still throbbed with a dull ache over what Iris had done. "Turn around and go home. And stop eavesdropping on me and my sisters, even when we're yelling. People yell sometimes. It doesn't mean they want what they're saying to be public. It means they're mad. Iris and I will work it out."

He nodded. "Okay, I'll leave, but only if you'll take this vest and wear it home. Otherwise, I'll have to follow you." Keeping the paddle across his lap, he tossed the vest into the water just behind me.

I didn't like ultimatums, especially when I was naked. "What business is it of yours whether I make it home or not?"

"Cissy asked me to look after you," he said evenly, "and I promised I would."

"And why would she ask you?"

"Because she knew she could trust me not to take advantage of the situation."

So much for Vi's theory that he lusted after me. Silly though it was, I felt disappointed.

At least he wasn't a voyeur. Maybe.

"As to the rest," he said, "I'll mind my own business, but it won't be easy if y'all keep hollering the way you were tonight, especially when you're at my house. You've got to admit, it's not every day a lady college professor calls out a lady CPA who just happens to be her sister, then throws her into the lake."

He had a point. "We cleared the air," I told him. "Now it's over."

"If you say so." He averted his gaze. "Casting off now. Stand clear."

I grabbed the cord of the vest and went deep again, shrugging into it just before I surfaced a safe distance away.

Careful not to look in my direction, Clete turned the canoe around, then retraced his course, disappearing around the point.

Watching him, I came, dad-gum it.

Not that I had any intention of doing anything about it. My life was complicated enough.

One thing was to be said for him, though: When I swam home, I wasn't thinking about Iris anymore.

The only trouble with being a houseguest is that you might like it too much.
—MAMA LOU

....

*T*HERE'S NOTHING LIKE a long cry to make you sleep like a rock, even if you're mosquito-bitten from sitting near the water at night without your Deet.

Vi woke me up at ten the next morning, offering coffee, along with her Bible from which she read the Lord's Prayer, Saint Paul's description of true love, then his account of the gifts of the spirit, stressing the necessity of forgiveness in all of them.

Groggy and depressed, I told her, "I've prayed to forgive her, but I can't feel it. Not yet. What she said . . ." I let out a sigh that hurt down deep in my chest. I looked at Vi. "Why does she hate me so? Did I make her feel that way? Did Rose resent me, too?"

"Of course not," Vi retorted. "Rose loves you almost as much as I do." She gave me a sidelong hug. "We both thought you hung the moon. I *knew* you did, and still think so. But Iris came so close behind you . . ." Vi struggled to find some justification for Iris's blaming me, instead of God, for all life's shortcomings, but there weren't any, and we both knew it. "Well, she's just jealous of you," she said flatly. "Always was, and after all these years, there's not much chance she'll up and change. But that's not all she is. It just comes with the package. She's still our sister."

A sister who wanted to hurt me. A nuclear-grade emotional booby trap, poised to spring shut on my soul. Forgiving Iris didn't mean that I had to trust her. The whole thing left me feeling sick and weary. "Well, God knows, she doesn't have any reason to be jealous of me now," I told her.

Vi exhaled sharply. "When it comes to you, I don't think she knows how to be anything else. All we can do is choose to overlook it. Not throw the baby out with the bathwater." She hugged me again, tight this time. "Oh, honey, I'm so sorry this happened. You don't deserve it."

My mind knew I didn't, but my heart was laden with guilt anyway. And I was stuck in the same house with Iris till the end of the summer. Now that I knew the truth, I'd have to accept her as she was, without judgment, but it wasn't going to be easy. Frankly, I questioned whether I could.

As if she'd read my thoughts, Vi told me, "Don't worry about Iris going after you anymore. If she so much as looks at you crossways, she's back in the lake, and that's a promise."

"Good," I said with conviction, hugging her back, hard. "That makes me feel better." It shouldn't have, but it did. After I'd soaked up enough of Vi's hug to steal a little peace, I pulled back. "But I don't want to get up. I want to sleep." My eyes still felt swollen.

"Oh, no, missy." She stood and pulled back the covers. "No way am I letting you hole up under the covers for a pity-party today. It's pure-D gorgeous out there, and the two of us are going on a day trip. I'm taking you to the Smith House in Dahlonega for lunch, then the outlets in Dawsonville. Just the two of us. And I'm going to buy you something pretty. So there."

Appealing as that was, I felt obliged to ask, "What about Rose and Iris?"

"They left at the crack of dawn to do the garage sales and flea markets in the area."

So Vi and I were free. The prospect evicted a lot of my inertia and took my mind off obsessing on all the woulda-coulda-shouldas about Iris. "Great." I got up and started to change, completely unselfconscious in Vi's presence.

She stepped forward to help me fasten my bra in back. "We are gonna have fun today. Just fun."

"Without you and Rose to buffer me from Iris—and vice versa—who knows what might have happened last night?"

"You'd have worked it out," Vi assured me. "You pretend to be a lioness, but I know you're a softie at heart."

I pulled on my tee. "I wasn't talking about me hurting Iris. I was talking about me and me. What she said . . . it was almost more than I could take."

Vi sobered. "What do you mean?"

I picked up my brush, then started the process of French-braiding my hair. "I have a confession to make," I confided, knowing we had the house to ourselves. "After y'all went to bed, I swam to the point. Without anything."

Alarm erased the humor from Vi's expression. "No ski vest? Dahlia, that's suicidal. What in God's green earth—"

"I wasn't suicidal; I just wanted to feel better. Without *anything* pressing on me," I emphasized. "Even a bathing suit. And who should show up at the point in a canoe with no lights, but Clete?"

Vi tucked her chin. "That's some coincidence."

"My thoughts exactly. I confronted him, and he said he saw me dive in without the life jacket and swim off, so he came after me, pretending he was worried because he'd promised Cissy he'd look after us. But if he could see that jacket on the dock, he could see that I was nekkid."

She smiled, pointing at me. "You said *nekkid*."

As my favorite down-home radio talk show host Ludlow Porch always says, *naked* means you don't have any clothes on, but *nekkid* means you don't have any clothes on and you're up to no good.

"Could we please stick to the subject?" I asked, then compulsively justified, "I thought the whole lake was in bed. How in the world was I supposed to know Clete was up there in the dark watching? There wasn't a single light on in his house."

She tried to look concerned, but an impish spark betrayed her. "Umhmm. So what happened after you saw him—or he saw you, as the case may be?"

"He didn't see me. I heard him coming and got back into the water," I told her as I continued French-braiding my hair. "Then I asked him what he was doing there."

"Aha." Mischief danced in her eyes. "So that's when he said he was worried about you."

"Yes. Then I swam underwater to the canoe and pulled my head above the side, where he couldn't see the rest of me."

Clearly, Vi wasn't taking it seriously. What was it about Clete that made the others trust him?

"So you swam *to* him," she said. "I see. And what happened then?"

I flushed, even though I hadn't done anything wrong. "He claimed he hadn't known I was nekkid."

"Ha!" She pointed. "You said it again."

I shot her a brief glare. "Do you want to know what happened, or not?"

"I'm all ears," she said. "What happened then?"

"We exchanged some equally embarrassing accidental double enten-dres," I said, "but the gist of it was, I asked him to go back where he came from and leave me alone. And quit eavesdropping on our fights."

"In his defense," she offered, "we weren't exactly whispering, you know."

My lips compressed. "That's what he said, but I reminded him that we were in the throes of an argument, and mad people yell. It doesn't mean we want to be eavesdropped on."

She handed me the covered rubber band for the bottom of my braid. "Did he take sides?" she asked, way too comfortable with the fact that he'd been listening.

I shrugged. "He said Cissy had told him what happened with Harri-son, and nobody deserved what Iris had said to me." I couldn't help tak-ing some satisfaction in relating, "Then he said he wanted you to clean Iris's clock, but throwing her in was good."

"He really likes you," she singsonged like Sandra Bullock in *Miss Congeniality*. "He's your Prince Charming. He wants to date you—"

"Vi, the last thing in this world I need is a man. Especially a sneaky one who's keeping something important from me."

She chortled. "But you're not keeping anything important from *him*. Oh, no." She grinned. "Nothing like *two dead bodies*."

"Violet, that isn't fair," I whispered back, reflexively worrying that somebody might have overheard her. "I've thought about it, and I'm deeply sorry I dragged y'all into that. If anybody realizes the truth, I'm taking all the blame, and that's that."

"Oh, no you don't. Regardless of what Iris said, you're not powerful enough to make us do anything against our wills. She chose to do that, and so did we. Our reasons were our own, and nobody else needs to know them."

As she followed me into the bathroom, I felt the weight inside me get heavier. "I don't want to talk about this," I told her through foaming toothpaste, then rinsed and spat. "I don't want to talk about anything bad for the rest of the day."

"Excellent idea," Vi said, "and flog me with a wet noodle for making you feel bad again. Let's go get some serious diner breakfast, compliments of the kitty, then try on clothes at the outlet."

Which would be harmless enough on my budget, since most things were cut way too short for either of us, and made in Third World countries that were clueless about anything bigger than a B cup. "You're on." I picked up the Kate Spade rip-off purse Vi had given me to go with my flats.

"Then we'll do lady lunch. And after we get back," she chirped while we were going down the stairs, "we can take a nap so we'll be fresh for the dance tonight."

Oh, no, no, no. "Speak for yourself. I'm not going to any dance."

"Oh, yes you are," she said as we headed for my car.

"Oh, no I'm not," I said cheerfully, setting off our usual ritual for such situations.

"Are, too," she retorted, just as cheerful.

"Not."

"Too."

"Not."

She always outlasted me. Halfway to the main road, I knuckled. "Okay, I'll go. But I'm not dancing with Clete, and that's final."

Grinning, she raised her brows in challenge. "Oh, yes you are."

"Oh, no I'm not." And on it went.

That argument, I had no intention of losing. After calling our contest a draw, which unofficially tabled the topic till later, we headed for Dahlonega and the Smith House. The food was good and plentiful as always, but afterward we'd hardly gotten halfway to Dawsonville before I was surreptitiously scratching at my clothes, particularly my back. Violet prescribed an antihistamine, so after a stop at a drugstore, we headed for the discount mall. The antihistamine helped a little, but by the time we made it to the Saks outlet, I was suffering the tortures of the damned. Not wanting to cut Vi's excursion short, I surreptitiously scratched till I found a great-looking red washable linen dress with a circle skirt and big white polka dots. Trying it on over my clothes, I was delighted to see that the waist was long enough, but I needed to make sure the deep vee neckline was modest with just my underwear. So I found Vi with an armful of prospects, and we headed for the mass dressing room.

Fortunately, there were only two other women in there, at the far bank of mirrors.

When I pulled off my tee to slip on the dress, I heard Vi gasp, and the two other women peered at me via their mirrors.

I could tell from their expressions that I was about to get bad news. Turning to look over my shoulder at the mirror, I saw that my back was covered by bites. Hundreds of them. As were my sides, and part of my front. "Oh . . . my . . . gosh," I said with a mixture of dread and embarrassment. "I must have been in the middle of a swarm of mosquitoes last night, but I didn't hear anything or feel them bite me."

Vi's mouth had dropped open in pity. "Dahlia, where did you sit when you got to the point?"

"On a big piece of driftwood. More of a log, actually. Then I sat on the sand and leaned against it. Why?"

"Honey, I hate to tell you, but I think those are chigger bites. My girls got them sitting on a log when we were camping once."

The one time I'd gone out without my Deet, and I sit on a nest of chiggers. Stupid, stupid, stupid.

Watching us in the mirror, the other two women winced, then resumed whispering behind their hands.

Vi's expression clouded. "Maybe you ought to quit trying things on," she whispered. "I don't know if that can spread them."

I leaned in, horrified. "You mean, like *lice*?" I whispered.

"No, not that awful," she whispered back. "I just don't know if they hop off on clothes."

Suddenly, the itching magnified exponentially. "So what can I do about them?" I pleaded. "They're driving me nuts."

"The drugstores carry expensive stuff to paint over them, but it's basically nail polish. It seals them off, so they suffocate."

"They?"

Her face cranked awry. "The chiggers," she murmured after a sidelong glance to the other women. "They burrow into your skin."

Live bugs were eating me in every one of those bites? "Shit!"

She shushed me with, "Don't panic. Do you have any nail polish back at the house?"

"I haven't had the time or the energy to do my nails for months," I snapped.

"Well, Rose has plenty. I'm sure she won't mind letting you use some of hers." She took the dress out of my hand. "The dress is yours. My treat."

I'd have argued, but it had been reduced six times, from two hundred thirty-five to eighteen dollars, probably because the waist was so long, and altering a circle skirt was almost impossible. "Thanks."

"Let's get another antihistamine into you," she said. "I'll charge the dress, then take you home and help you put on the polish."

That was far too intimate an indignity for me to bear. "I can do it myself."

Vi didn't cross me. "Okay, but if you need help, all you have to do is ask."

Why was I taking it out on her? "Sorry. It's not your fault," I said, trying not to claw my back. "The one I'm really mad at is me. It's my own fault." I pulled my tee back on, the increased heat and friction setting the bites alive.

While we had cell phone signal, Vi called Rose and asked if I could have some of her nail polish. Maybe a lot. But she spared my feelings by not telling Rose why. Rose, of course, said I could have it all. Then, since it was just the two of us in the car, Vi wasn't above speeding between towns to get us back to Hilltop more quickly, stopping only to buy two huge boxes of baking soda. "This'll help with the itch. We can put a box into the sunken tub and fill it with cool water for you to soak. By the time the others get back, you'll be feeling a lot better."

She was right. I felt much better after a long soak, then I rinsed off and returned to my room to put Rose's polish to good use.

There was something cathartic about smothering each little beast, and—thanks to my flexibility—I was able to reach every single bite, including the ones on my fanny and other unmentionable places. After standing like a scarecrow in front of the fan to dry, I bolted my door against nosy Iris, then lay spread-eagled on the bed with the fan blowing over me, thinking cool thoughts.

I sure could have used some of Clete's air-conditioning. If I could make it for the rest of the day and the next, I'd have it. Drugged by the antihistamine, I fell into a deep sleep and didn't wake till dusk, when I heard Vi going into her room. Pulling up my floral sheet to spare her the gory details, I was waiting when she came through the sleeping porch with a big glass of artificially sweetened decaf tea and a bacon and tomato wrap.

"Thanks," I said, the words hoarse. "What would I do without you?" But I didn't sit up. The idea of moving against the sheets kept me immobile.

"How are you feeling?" she asked, her blond brows drawn together with worry.

"The itching's flared up again."

"That's because the antihistamine's worn off. With your asthma, that's not the best thing to take, but I didn't want to give you anything else till they wore off." She knew my infirmities as well as she knew the rest of me. She fished a blister pack of cortisone pills out of her jeans pocket and laid it beside my hand. "I always carry one of these with me when I travel. Start with the dose of seven. But don't take them till you've eaten."

"Thanks," I croaked out.

"You're hoarse," she said, crossing to my purse to retrieve my inhaler. "Better take a hit."

I did, and the faint itching in my throat and bronchial tree eased.

"The others are going to the dance, but I'd be glad to stay, if you're at all uneasy."

"No, go." Alone time, at last. Only I wasn't able to enjoy it fully. "I'll be fine with the cortisone."

She cocked her head. "You're sure?"

"Positive."

She nodded. "Good, 'cause Martin and Taylor and Wilson are coming."

Their husbands. "And you weren't going to tell me?" I fussed.

"Not if you had gotten worse. It wouldn't kill Taylor to come back up another time." She waggled her eyebrows. "Maybe for a quickie at that new motel in town."

I didn't even envy her. The chiggers had put my libido on dry ice. "Just be home before dawn," I teased, "or I'll have to tell Mr. Johnson."

"Actually," she said, "this is gonna be pretty interesting. Feels like when we were dating."

"Good. Enjoy." As she started out, I had one more question. "What did you tell Iris and Rose about me not going?"

"That you started feeling bad on the way down to the outlets, so I took you home and put you to bed."

"And Iris left it at that?"

Vi smiled. "Of course not. She badgered me for particulars all through supper, but I just kept repeating what I said. Rose finally had to tell her to drop it and back off."

"Don't tell Clete," I said, knowing perfectly well she wouldn't, but asking anyway, just to be safe. "He'd probably laugh his head off."

"He doesn't impress me as the kind of person who would ever take pleasure in anybody else's misfortune," she said, "but this can stay between the two of us for as long as you want."

"Try forever," I told her.

She gingerly patted my arm where there weren't any bites. "Don't worry about tomorrow. If you're still under the weather, I'll pack for you. I've got a flowered muumuu that doesn't touch anywhere but the yoke. You can wear that over to Clete's. Then you can hole up in the air-conditioning for as long as it takes to get better. I'll run interference for you. It took several days for the girls to get back to normal."

"God bless you, darlin'." I closed my eyes.

She rose. "Just rest. Everything will be okay, I promise."

"Not if it keeps up the way it's been going."

"If the cortisone jazzes you up, help yourself to one of my sleeping pills in the bedside table."

The only time I ever took them. "Thanks. Now go see that husband of yours, and give him a kiss from me."

"Will do. But if you feel at all weird, call 911 and ask them to find us at the dance. There's a phone at the boathouse store, and it stays open till ten."

"You're starting to sound like Iris," I warned.

"Sorry. Leaving now." She unlocked the bolt, closed the door behind her when she left, then went downstairs.

I waited till everything was quiet to eat my wrap and savor the cold sweetness of the tea. After taking the first seven cortisone tablets, I walked like Frankenstein to the shower so nothing would touch the scarlet bites all over my torso. Turning away from my image in the medicine-cabinet mirror, I pinned my hair up in a messy coil at the crown, then started my shower with tepid, gradually easing off the hot till the cold water ran over my skin.

Grateful for the numbing flow and my solitude, I thanked God for them both. But not for the chiggers.

Then I took a sleeping pill and went back to bed, looking forward to the day when the garish evidence of my stupidity finally disappeared.

Only me, I thought as it finally took hold. Only me.

If I'd known what was coming, though, I'd have thanked God for even the chiggers.

· 18 ·

When it comes to love, give me a good dose of illusion every time.
When truth moves in, I move out.
—CISSY

. . . .

I SLEPT ONLY fitfully, in spite of the sleeping pill, then woke up long before Boat Church, so miserable I didn't care what Rose and Iris thought. There was no way I could pretend to be anything but what I was: the newest high-rise condo for chiggers at the lake. A bra was out of the question, but I did manage to tolerate a pair of white cotton bikini underpants beneath Vi's muumuu. I headed downstairs, still walking like Frankenstein, for canned chicken with mayo and something cold to drink.

Rose and Iris were both at the table, bright and cheerful—probably because they'd gotten some after the dance—but when they saw me, their smiles disappeared.

"Dahlia, what's the matter?" Rose asked.

Iris acted as if our big blowup had never happened. "Why are you walking like that, honey?"

Honey, indeed.

I stood in the doorway to the breakfast area, elbows out and feet planted wide. Might as well tell the truth. They'd find out, anyway. "I've got chiggers. Bad. I was so embarrassed, I didn't want to tell y'all, but it's miserable. There's no way I can pack."

"I can do that for you," Iris said, eager to do penance. (As long as she didn't have to apologize.)

"Oh, honey," Rose said to me, "you don't ever have to be embarrassed with us."

I shot Iris a pointed look. "I sat on a log. It was stupid, but I couldn't handle getting judged or teased about it."

Rose offered a sympathetic smile. "We wouldn't do that, sweetie." She turned to Iris. "Would we?"

Iris shook her head, earnest. "Absolutely not." She was trying, at least. I gave her credit, but still felt like I was in the room with a cobra.

"That's why I needed the nail polish," I told Rose. "Vi told me it would help."

Iris might have repented, but she was still nosy to the bone. "Would it be okay if we saw them?"

Rose nodded, just as eager. For her, I agreed. "May as well." I lifted the muumuu up to my neck, grateful for the cool air.

"Ohmygod!" Rose blanched.

Iris shot to her feet in horror. "Just wait here. I'm calling 911."

"Why?" I looked down, then back at them.

"Because they're—" Rose leaned forward, focusing on the bites, then broke out laughing.

"Rose," Iris scolded.

Rose pointed at my torso. "You're supposed to use clear polish, not red."

Iris looked closer and sagged with relief. "Lord, you scared me to death."

I dropped my muumuu and tried to salvage my dignity. "Nobody said anything about using clear. How was I supposed to know?"

"You couldn't," Rose acknowledged. "Nobody's blaming or judging, least of all me."

"Would you please just do me one favor, though?" Iris asked.

I tucked my chin. "That depends. What is it?"

Iris smiled. "Would you show that to Vi the same way you showed us? I can't wait to see the look on her face."

If Iris could lighten up, so could I. "Okay."

"Oh, goody." She clasped her hands like a little kid on Christmas morning. "I'll go get her."

As I stepped aside for Iris, Rose waggled her hand toward Iris and whispered, "Tell her you're really worried about Dahlia. That'll get her up."

"Y'all are cruel," I said with a smile.

Both of them sobered. "We won't do it unless you want to."

"It's okay," I answered. "Vi will get a big laugh out of it later."

And boy, did she.

So in spite of my condition, the morning went well. Vi and Rose went to Boat Church by car, and Iris stayed home to play backgammon with me on the verandah, where wind from a distant hurricane made it feel like fall.

I didn't relish the idea of being alone with her, but the game gave me something to focus on besides my bug bites, and in backgammon, at least, we were evenly matched. Game by game, the palpable tension between us began to ease, if only a little.

We were setting up the board for another match when Iris paused, her features twisting, and dropped her focus, unable to look at me. "Dahlia, I'm sorry. I . . . wish I could take it all back."

An apology! Pack my bags for glory. But she hadn't recanted, only apologized for saying it.

Still, I gave her credit. "Thank you, Iris. I appreciate your apology."

After a strained silence, she frowned. "There you go. You never fight back."

I threw my dice. "In case you've forgotten, I was ready to beat your ass after you let us think you'd drowned." I took my move, doubling up my stones for safety.

"Yeah," she said, "but you didn't. Vi did it for you. Even Rose." She unconsciously rubbed the cheek Rose had slapped. "You always clam up and close up—*bam*—with those big, wounded eyes, and I end up being the villain."

So now it was my fault, again.

My guard went up. "Iris, I do not have it in me to go for the jugular. When somebody blindsides me, I don't want to hurt them back. I want to protect myself and escape." And I didn't want to keep talking about it, when there was obviously no reason to keep doing so. "You are who you are, and I am who I am. I've always accepted our differences. I don't own a grudge box, and neither does Rose or Vi. Yours is big enough for the whole family."

Iris bristled. "You have no idea whether Rose does or not. She's never trusted you enough to confide in you, but she knows I'm safe. You blab everything."

"I never blabbed a damned thing about Rose," I clipped out, keeping my tone even despite the heat that rose in my chest, "because she never told me anything, thanks to you. You're the one who convinced her I couldn't keep a secret. It wasn't anything I ever did."

It struck me afresh how little I really knew about what made Rose tick. "Does Rose have a grudge box, too?" I challenged. "Does she blame me for ruining her life the way you do?"

Iris's nostrils flared. "You know she doesn't. She never blames anybody for anything. She's a saint."

No she wasn't. Rose was human just like the rest of us, repressed and emotionally guarded to the extreme, but I knew Iris would go ballistic if I pointed that out.

Iris took her move on the board. "You can try to turn her against me all you want," she said as conversationally as if she were announcing the time of day. "But it won't get you anywhere. Rose loves me just like I am, and she doesn't trust you."

"Hell, Iris," I said. "Why in God's good, green earth would you think I'm trying to turn her against you? This isn't a competition."

Iris shoved her dice into the throwing box, her chin lifted to a stubborn set. "Rose is mine, and she always has been. You can't have her."

I stared at Iris, incredulous. "Have her? Damn, Iris, I'm not trying to steal anything from you, and I never did. Rose is my sister. I just want to get to know her better. Grow up, for God's sake." So much for staying calm and polite.

This wasn't getting either of us anywhere.

"Damn, Iris," I told her, rolling double sixes, which just made her madder. "I'm trying to bury the hatchet, here. Why can't you just focus on the good things? I'm a decent person, doing the best I can, and I'm way too old and too tired to get stuck in what happened fifty years ago." Even though I knew it was probably useless to try to reason with her, I had to try. "I don't *have* ulterior motives," I said, believing it. "Could you just try to focus on the positives, here, for a change? Please. We have to spend the whole summer together. I just want it to be as pleasant as possible for all of us, you included."

"Just, just, just," she muttered as I took a huge advantage on the board, sly resentment coloring her closed expression. "I do focus on the positives," she stated. "I just don't put on a fake façade and *always* focus on the positives, in complete denial of reality, the way some people do." Meaning me. "I'm honest about my feelings, and I have a right to have them."

And I'm just the middle child, echoed from our childhood. I resisted the urge to roll my eyes and focused on the game. "It's your move."

She sniffed, doing that little pursed-mouth thing. "So it is." She took it, then I rolled doubles again to win the game.

Without comment, I started resetting the stones.

Something had to change between me and Iris, or I'd end up in the loony bin long before September. Surely, there was something I could do. Some way to make me less of a threat to her. Then I had an idea. "Can I ask a favor of you?"

"That depends," she responded, every bit as wary of me as I was of her. "What is it?"

"Could we play a few games of backgammon every day, you pick when, just the two of us? We could talk, or not, whatever you want. I just want to spend some time with you."

Her eyes narrowed. "As long as you promise not to poor-mouth about money. It drives me crazy."

Ah. If there were going to be conditions, I could think of a few, myself. "Deal," I said, "as long as you don't keep trying to get me to give up red meat. That makes me crazy."

"Deal." Her posture eased a little . "As long as you don't whine about your weight. That makes me crazy. You're a bone compared to me, and it makes me feel like a cow."

"Deal." I'd saved the thing that got under my skin the worst for last. "As long as you don't keep insinuating I'm some kind of prescription junkie because of all the meds I have to take."

She straightened slightly, brows rising, but agreed. "Deal."

I waited for a counter, but there wasn't one. "Okay, then," I said. "The daily backgammon boundaries have been set."

"Speaking of meds," she said, glancing down and to the right. "Rose made me promise yesterday to see her therapist and try some of those antidepressants." Hallelujah! "And maybe some hormones." She risked a brief, defensive glance at me. "I mean, why should I be the last middle-aged woman in America without them?"

That was a big concession, telling me, probably as close to a real olive branch as I was going to get. "I hope they work as well for you as they have for me," I said. For all our sakes. "Those give me back myself."

"Forget that." She focused on the board, rolling a single die to determine the first move. "I want to be somebody a lot happier than me." A six.

I rolled a five, so Iris won the toss. Five and six combined for a good move, taking one of her stones halfway home in safety. "You go first."

It was a start.

After a few more games, I had to get out of my clothes for a cool shower, then bed, with nothing touching me except the sheet. When Vi and Rose got back from church, the two of them fussed over me like Nurse Jane Fuzzy-wuzzy, bringing me cold drinks and packing up my things for the move to Clete's.

Since the divorce, I'd been working so hard for so long that I'd almost forgotten how good it felt to be cared for.

Meanwhile, the wind blew cool through the screens, making it easier to sleep.

The next morning, I woke up—still scratching, but only occasionally—at ten till seven, to crisp Canadian air. After a huge yawn and stretch, I put on my flats and the muumuu, then headed down for my first cup of hot coffee in days. The nippy morning kept me from having a kickback of itching, and I savored the caffeine. I didn't even mind my good-morning hugs from Rose and Vi.

By the time the four of us had eaten in peaceful silence, swapping sections of the Sunday paper from the day before, we were all among the living and in decent spirits. While the others went to finish packing and loading the cars, paranoia about the bodies drew me to the basement for a final look-see before the fumigators arrived. Once there, I opened the

French doors to a cool gust of dry air, then went to the back corner to stand, nursing my coffee and staring at our handiwork.

Did it really look as good as I thought it did? Or was I only kidding myself?

Only Clete had been to Hilltop enough to remember how it had been. Even though he'd probably sprayed the basement for years, logic told me that he wouldn't linger there, much less pay attention to the root cellar doorway, which I doubted he'd ever seen unobstructed.

But Clete was no ordinary bug man. His intelligent gaze was always inspecting, analyzing, evaluating.

Speak of the devil, there was a polite knock on the doorjamb across the basement, and I turned to find him standing there, way too attractive in khaki pants, good shoes, and a brown linen vest over a white pinpoint oxford shirt with rolled sleeves. Not exactly work clothes.

And there I was, in a muumuu. I had actually let a man see me in a muumuu. How far I had fallen.

I headed toward him, hoping he hadn't caught me staring at the foundation.

"Good morning." He was clearly glad to see me, even in a muumuu.

"Clete." A combination of fear, embarrassment, fashion-shame, and sexual self-consciousness set my chiggers to itching, so I gripped my cup to keep from scratching. "You're early." I hadn't meant for it to sound like a reprimand, but that's how it came out.

He didn't take offense. "I thought y'all might need a little help loading up, so I came on over. How are you feeling?"

The others had sworn not to blab about my chiggers! I went aloof. "Why do you ask?"

"Your sisters said you were under the weather," he said. "At the dance." Then, as if he'd read my mind, he added, "They didn't go into detail."

I felt myself flush even deeper, and looked down. "Sorry to snap. It's kind of you to ask." After a little time to collect myself, I met his gaze. "I'm feeling better. A few more days, and I'll be myself. But don't worry. I'm not contagious."

"The thought never crossed my mind." He scanned the basement. "Y'all have done a remarkable job down here." He looked toward the back corner, then headed that way, zeroed in on the cellar door. "Especially back here. Amazing work."

My pulse skipped a beat. Did he know? But how could he?

I desperately tried to come up with some quip to distract him, but my brain went blank.

Blessedly, Clete turned toward Poppy Jack's shop. "If it's okay with y'all, I'll bring over a crew from the plant this morning to take Poppy Jack's equipment and that pile of scrap metal anywhere you'd like."

"That would be wonderful." An itch flared right between my legs. Do not scratch! "Is the scrap metal salvage yard open today?"

"If it's not, it will be," he said with confidence. "I have connections." He turned back to the root cellar door. "Amazing work, and all by yourselves. That huge pile of metal and junk, gone." His gaze shifted to me, an ironic gleam in his eyes. "It feels a lot better once you've gotten rid of all the awkward stuff, isn't it?"

I peered at him through narrowed eyes. What exactly did he mean by that?

But before I could respond, the others came down the stairs en masse.

"Clete." Vi strode over and gave him a big hug, which didn't seem to embarrass him.

He had all those brothers and sisters, of course.

"I came to see if I could help y'all load up," he said as if they were old friends.

"Very nice of you," Iris said, "but we finished ten minutes ago. May we offer you some breakfast?"

Clete grinned. "Very nice of you, but I finished mine two hours ago." He scanned the basement, lingering just a little longer on the root-cellar quadrant. "I'm very impressed by what y'all have accomplished down here."

"We worked really hard," Vi told him. "But the mold was awful. So we had to pour a ton of bleach over the whole place and let it all air out before we could finish. Sorry for the delay."

Part of the truth, at least.

He nodded, a slight twist to his smile. "I figured out the reason."

"So, what's the timetable for today?" Iris asked.

"My house is yours, anytime," Clete answered. "Eileen has everything ready for y'all. I'll be over here supervising till lunch. Katie's got a nice one planned." He looked to me and said without a hint of sarcasm, "No bread, no milk, no mushrooms, no cheese, and no vinegar in the salad dressing." He turned to Iris. "All organic, and ovo-lacto compliant for you."

Iris brightened, clearly flattered. "How did you know about that?"

"Cissy left Katie strict dietary instructions about how to feed y'all."

Iris was surprised. "I had no idea Cissy gave anybody but Dahlia a thought."

I could have sworn Clete tensed slightly at her catty comment. Or maybe it was just my imagination. "She was always talking about all of you," he said. "So proud of what the four of you had accomplished." He looked to Iris. "Especially how you worked your way through school with two small children, then earned your CPA and built a thriving business."

"Me?" Iris had to chew on that one. "I never imagined."

"And Rose's preschool work, and Violet's basketball career."

"I guess that puts us at a disadvantage," Vi said. "Apparently, you know all about us, but we hardly know anything about you."

A truck rumbled down into the pasture. Clete glanced at his watch. "Why don't we talk about that at lunch? If it's all right for me to join you."

"Join, join," Vi told him. "It's your house."

He smiled. "Now, if you'll excuse me, I need to get these guys started." He headed for the approaching workers, most of them local-looking, plus a few Hispanics.

I followed my sisters to the stairs, looking back to see Clete speaking rapid Spanish with one of the workers. Odd, but I didn't want to leave him, even though we were going to his house, where he would be at lunch.

Rose grinned back down at me from the hallway. "C'mon, you. You'll get to see him plenty when we're at his house."

I hated being so transparent. "Who says he's going to get to see me?" I said, haughty, as I marched up after her.

When I closed the door behind me, the others signaled *perfect*, then pointed down toward the root cellar door, but said nothing, lest we be overheard.

At least they were confident. I wasn't so sure.

. . . .

"WELCOME TO THE ridge," a plump fortyish-looking woman greeted us in a thick mountain accent, opening wide two of the glass sliders that made up the entire front of Clete's house. She turned to me, maybe because I was the oldest. "I'm Eileen. If any of y'all need anythang, big 'r small, just let me know, and I'll see you git it. And don't worry about your stuff. Hoke'll brang it all in for ya."

Stepping into the great room, I took a subtle sniff and was amazed to find not a hint of mold in the air, even though the house was bermed on the back and sides. The décor was classic essential: comfortable, but not cluttered, all in tones that echoed the mountains. The focal point was a huge fireplace whose clean lines were made from a glassy fusion of cut quartz, like giant jewels, in every color I'd ever found nearby—deep purples to soft rose to amber to almost white.

The fireplace's raised hearth extended the length of the left-side wall, providing plenty of long, leather-covered cushions that matched the bleached muslin slipcovers on the classic chairs and sofas. One of the covers' hems was awry, revealing a glimpse of distressed golden-chestnut leather underneath. Just enough throw pillows took the tones of the fireplace into the room.

I turned to the back wall. Above waist-high built-in bookcases filled with classics and popular fiction, lighted glass cases with glass shelves offered a glimpse of the hallway behind while displaying a select but impressive collection of local-themed art. An excellent original watercolor re-created a busy day at the old Clare's Boathouse. Cherokee beading and bags rested safely where they could be appreciated. Folk dolls sat in little hand-carved and caned chairs. Super-real carved birds perched on pine and dogwood: a little white-faced barn owl, a cheerful thrasher, a cardinal, an indigo bunting in flight, and others I couldn't name. They were interspersed with beautifully carved rhododendron and mountain laurel, even a branch of ripe huckleberries that looked ready to pick and eat. Beyond the open casement to the hallway was a museum-quality collection of large Moulthrop wooden bowls, almost identical to the ones that had been stolen from Hilltop while I was on tour, when Cissy leased a room to a local who turned out to be a druggie.

Eileen's voice cut into my daydreaming. "Would you ladies like to come into the breakfast area for a snack and some coffee before I show you your rooms? Katie's mighty proud of herself today. She found a great recipe for sugar-free gingerbread on the Internet." She laughed. "Both of us could stand to lose a few."

The four of us looked at each other.

"If it's all the same to y'all," I said, "I'd like to rest a little."

They opted to look around a bit before lunch.

"Okay," Eileen said. "Clete told me to tell you ladies the house is yours." She leaned out the door and hollered, "Hoke! I need ya to brang in Miss Dahlia's thangs."

"Please," I said. "It's just plain Dahlia."

Eileen responded with approval. "Thanks, Dahlia." This time, she didn't bother sticking her head outside to call, "Hoke!"

Then she turned back to us and confided, "You know, don'tcha, that Clete built this place fer your granny."

All four of us did a double take.

"Yep," Eileen went on. "He was always so proud of what-all yer granny taught him. Always said, if it wasn't fer her, he'd still be sprayin' houses. When he finally sold the pest-control business and went on a consultin' basis, he worked out every little detail of this place with yer granny so she could come here and let us all look after her in her final years." She looked to me. "You come by yer mold trouble honest. Miss Cissy had it, too, and that old place kept her sick as a cat. So there ain't a scrap of mold or mildew in this place, and never will be."

She shook her head. "But you know Miss Cissy. Proud, proud, proud. Even after all that plannin'. We tried everthang but kidnappin' her, but she still wouldn't leave Hilltop. Maddest I ever saw her at Clete. She said they'd have to take her out of that house feetfirst." She shook her head. "Clete couldn't tell how much of that was real and how much was slippage." She tapped her temple. "But he didn't want to upset her, so he had his crews fix whatever she'd let 'em, which was precious little."

How Eileen knew so much about Clete, I didn't know, but I decided the two of us were about to become *very* good friends.

A tall, rangy man about Eileen's age came from the back of the house, ball cap in hand, eyeing us openly. "I'm Hoke. Good to meetcha." He extended a long-boned workman's hand to me, and I took it. "Hey," he said with a slight nod of acknowledgment.

"Hi." How many servants did Clete have?

Next he moved to Iris for a shake. "Hey."

"Hi. I'm Iris. Could you please bring in the black suitcases with the butterflies stenciled on them first?" She motioned to me. "My sister wants to lie down. She hasn't been feeling well."

Hoke nodded.

"All the bedding and the air mattresses stay in the cars," she added.

Hoke nodded again, his every move slow and deliberate. I got the impression he did everything at his own pace, not unlike old Mr. Slocum.

While he shook with Rose and Vi, I turned my attention back to the great room. More books covered the rest of the walls, even over the doorways and under the high clerestory windows that brought in unfiltered light from above the covered patio.

I couldn't remember when I'd come into a place that made me feel as happy to be there. Of course, the no-mold part was a major plus.

"You don't need to be standin' here on this hard floor, Dahlia," Eileen said. "Let me show you to yer room."

"Thanks. That's very thoughtful." All through my many travels, I'd been to so many generic places, but when I came to one as unique, yet elegant, as this, I loved to soak up every vignette and detail. So when I followed Eileen back into the house, I made a mental floor plan as I caught glimpses of the kitchen, an impressive mirrored workout room with equipment, a study filled with all kinds of reference books—many of them relating to chemistry and biology—and three spacious bedroom suites before mine at the end of the hall.

Like the other bedrooms, mine looked like a five-star hotel suite, simply yet elegantly appointed, with a king-sized bed and windows overlooking the lush gardens that cascaded in terraces down the back side of the ridge, flowers and vegetables mingled in fertile splendor. I went to the window and saw a long, low wing that stretched out from the far side of the house. "How many bedrooms are there here?"

"Eight," Eileen said, turning down the duvet, "but we only open the east wing when the whole family comes to spend the night, like at Christmas and Thanksgiving."

She opened the bathroom door to reveal a gorgeous soaking tub and curtainless shower below a high bank of windows. She flicked a switch, and warm light bathed the room. "Everything in the house is handicapped accessible. The floors are all heated." She pointed. "Switch is there. And take all the hot baths you want. We recycle the water fer the gardens."

If it wasn't for my chiggers, I'd have turned on the hot water right then.

Leading me back into the bedroom, she pointed to two switches just outside the bathroom door. "The blue switches here are for the UV lights in the bathroom. Just make sure you're not in here when you run 'em, and keep the door closed. They're strictly fer sterilizin' the tile."

"Wow." Heated floors. All those lights. All that glass. "I hate to think what your power bill runs."

Turning down the covers, Eileen laughed like a girl. "Not one dad-blamed penny. Fact of business bein', the power company pays us. Clete's got this whole place on solar and wind and geo-whatsis. Hot water comes from a bunch of tanks that git the best sun, with solar backup. The air-conditionin' steals the cool sixty feet down and pulls the air up here. Works the opposite when it gits below fifty-five outside."

She motioned to various features. "The TV remote's in the bedside table. Screen's behind that paintin', there. Just push the button. It's satel-lite." She pointed to the desk. "And that laptop works anywhere in the house, high-speed from the satellite, too. Phones are free long distance. Help yerself." She looked around, plump arms akimbo on either side of a gingham apron just like the one Beaver Cleaver's mother wore. "I think that does it. How soon before lunch do ya want me to git ya up?"

"If you have to go through all this with my sisters," I said, "it might be lunchtime already."

She smiled.

I sat on the side of the bed.

"Oh, and everthang's hypoallergenic, so no feathers to worry about. Ye got that from yer grandmamma, too."

And how would she know?

I heard suitcase wheels and heavy footsteps, then Hoke appeared at the hallway. "Is it okay fer me to brang these in?"

I straightened, self-conscious. "Perfect. Just put them anywhere."

When he started to park them at the door, Eileen glared at him, point-ing to a low dresser on the bedroom wall. "You know where they go, mister."

"I wasn't gonna leave 'em hyere," Hoke protested. "I was just goin' back fer another load."

Poor Hoke. "Sorry. I don't know how to pack light."

He nodded, restricting his annoyance to Eileen. "Don't you worry, Dahlia. That's just all right."

After he left, I slipped out of my shoes, then lay back on the bed, pulling up the softest sheet I'd ever felt. "Whoa. This is heaven."

"Those sheets're made from kudzu fibers. We're testin' em fer a friend of Clete's," Eileen said.

I closed my eyes, savoring the lack of humidity and mold in the air. "Well, whoever he is, tell him they pass."

The sound of the door closing behind her was the last thing I remembered till I woke up to find it was getting dark. I jumped to my feet and headed for the next room, but found nobody till I got to the front of the house and looked through the wall of glass to see my sisters talking and laughing on the patio.

Fortunately, Clete wasn't there, so I didn't need to go back to my room and clean up.

I slid open one of the doors and said through the screen, "How come y'all didn't wake me up for lunch?" Taking the cue, my stomach growled loudly.

"I tried," Vi said, "but you were too far gone. You've missed a lot of sleep since Friday, so I figured you needed to catch up."

"But Clete was there." I couldn't conceal the disappointment in my voice. I'd planned to ask a lot of questions.

The others misunderstood my motive and teased me about liking him.

Ignoring their taunts, I stretched, yawning dragon-mouth through the screen. "But he'll be at supper," I said.

The others exchanged glances. "Well, actually, no," Vi said. "He's staying with his brother down the hill while we're here. Not Hoke. One of the others."

I halted. "Hoke's his brother?"

They nodded.

"The next younger one," Iris clarified, checking the names off with her fingers. "Then there's Eileen, then Ted, then Hank, then Larry, then

Willette who drowned on a school field trip to the Nantahala when she was twelve, so sad. Then Katie. She's the baby, and one heck of a cook."

And I'd thought they were servants. Not cool.

"We saved your plate of grape chicken salad, no vinegar in the mayo," Vi said.

Rose got up and headed my way. "I'll get it for you."

"No, I can do it," I said. "I just have chiggers. I'm not an invalid."

Rose ignored my protest, giving me a brief hug as she came inside. "It's time we heated up the dinner Katie left us, anyway. If you'd rather, you can have that." I followed her while the others started gathering up their glasses.

Like everything else in Clete's house, the kitchen looked deceptively simple, but it was definitely a cook's kitchen. I followed Rose to the big refrigerator concealed behind perfect slabs of knotless old-growth pine that matched all the other cabinets. The space and light in the kitchen kept the wood from looking dark or cramped.

She pulled a covered roaster out of the well-stocked refrigerator, but I zeroed in on the gorgeous lunch plate with a huge mound of chicken salad in the middle.

I took it out and lifted off the plastic wrap. "That looks seriously yummy."

"It is," Rose said, placing the pot on the gas cooktop and turning the flame to medium.

I took a fork from the already-set table and tasted the salad. Fabulous. Minced celery, toasted almonds, and bits of fresh orange. "So Clete's not coming to dinner."

Rose grabbed a fork and stole a tiny bite from the other side of my plate. "He's such a gentleman, Dahlia. Really. When we said it was silly for him to go, he said he didn't want anybody to get the wrong impression. That it wouldn't be proper for him to stay."

Perfect. Just when I was seriously considering getting a bit improper. My chiggers were good insurance that I wouldn't let things go too far. The thought of kissing him, though . . . For the first time since the divorce, the idea of kissing somebody seemed appealing.

"I sure hope he doesn't have bad breath," I mused, focusing on my plate. "Or sleep with his teeth in a jar."

Rose observed my expression with a knowing one of her own. "We could ask him on a picnic somewhere."

"Anyplace but Bold Creek Park," I quipped.

"I'll ask Katie what he likes." She closed the lid. "We could cook it ourselves."

"I haven't really cooked in so long, I'm not sure I can still do it."

"Don't worry about that," Rose reassured me. "You can make the deviled eggs. I never met a man who doesn't like deviled eggs."

"I was looking forward to finding out more about him at lunch. But wouldn't he be less guarded on his own turf?"

Rose shook her head. "Guarded people usually have good reason to be that way. Take it from me, Dahlia, some secrets are best left buried."

The others arrived with all their empty drink glasses and copies of the Franklin paper.

"Guess what?" Rose chirped. "We're taking Clete on a picnic, as soon as it's convenient for him." She shot me a pointed glance. "And one of us just might take a nice long walk in the woods with him, all by herself."

"Me, of course," Iris joked.

"No, me," from Vi.

They both turned to me. "What about you?"

"Maybe," I said. "We'll see."

· 19 ·

Plan all you want, but God has a sense of humor.
—MAMA LOU

....

ROSE ASKED CLETE to our picnic, but he wasn't free till Friday, so
we had three whole days to nap, read, play bridge and backgammon, swim, and soak our weary bones. And, in Iris's case, snoop through
Clete's things.

I walked by his study on Thursday morning and caught a glimpse of
her at his big partners' desk. When I backed up to see what she was doing, she'd disappeared.

Odd. I could have sworn I'd seen her there. I stepped inside. "Iris?"

Tar baby, he don't say nothin'.

There was no other way out of the room. Lord, had I started hallucinating?

Just when I began to doubt my sanity, somebody passed gas under
the far side of the desk.

"Iris?" What in the world?

I came around to find her tucked into the back of the kneehole, behind the chair, but the smell gave her away.

I pulled out the chair and bent over, waving my hand to dispel the evidence. "It was the cabbage last night, wasn't it?"

"Dog dammit," she said. "It would be you."

"Careful," I warned her. "If Vi hears you talking to me that way, you might end up in the lake."

She glared at me. It took a while for her to wriggle out, during which she grumbled the whole way, her criticism directed at the desk, not me. When she finally stood up, she straightened regally to her diminutive height, then blew the hair out of her eyes with an explosive puff. (From her mouth, not the other end.)

I retreated to the doorway, subtly blocking her escape.

Iris tugged her clothes back into place. "Oh, all right. You caught me."

I nodded, waiting for her to elaborate.

She shot a wistful glance toward the hall beyond me, then said, "I just . . . Did you take a close look at those Moulthrop bowls on display in the great room?"

"No. Why?"

"Because," she said, "I did, and they're Cissy's. Her name is burned into the bottoms, right above Ed Moulthrop's mark."

I shrugged. Now that the suspicion was on the other foot, I found myself defending the man. "There must be an explanation. If Clete didn't come by them honestly, he'd be a fool to leave them out where we could see them."

Iris wasn't convinced. "It's been a long time. And criminals always slip up eventually. Or maybe he's arrogant under that polite exterior."

Rose came by, and seeing us, nudged me into the room to stand beside me. "Hey. What's up?"

"See for yourself." Iris crossed dramatically to the polished-mahogany wall of concealed storage and opened a set of double doors on the far right. On the deep shelves inside sat Poppy Jack's sterling silver punch bowl with vermeil lining, the one the bank had given him when he retired in 1920. And the genuine Ming bowls and figures and vases Great-grandmother's father had brought home from a diplomatic mission to China after the War Between the States. On the two shelves below that, dark brown silver-cloth bags filled almost all the space.

I crossed to the cabinet and opened a few of the brown bags to find Great-grandmother's good flatware and all of her sterling platters and bowls and serving pieces. The tarnish trapped in the silver-impregnated flannel bags smelled so bitter I could taste it, and it made me cough.

Damn. What was Clete doing with all this? Cissy had sworn her druggie roomer had stolen it all.

Just when I'd decided to trust Clete enough to kiss him.

"Why are y'all snooping around in Clete's cabinets, in the first place?" Rose asked with a frown. "That's very rude. A complete breach of our host's trust."

Staring at the Ming figurines, I asked anybody and nobody, "Why didn't he tell us about all this?"

"About what?" Rose asked. "It's also rude to talk about things your sister doesn't understand in front of her."

I'd forgotten how young she'd been when we stopped coming up to the lake—only seven. Of course, she wouldn't recognize anything. "These are all of Great-grandmother's most precious possessions. Cissy told us they were stolen by a boarder she took in during the seventies, but the police never found them. And now, here they are. This looks bad. Very bad."

"Maybe she gave them to Clete," Rose said. "Then lied about it so we wouldn't be jealous. He was already helping her then. You know how proud Cissy was."

I shook my head. "I talked to the police at the time. They sent the guy to prison for dealing drugs, but he wouldn't ever admit to taking her things, and they didn't have any evidence, since he lived there." Another thought occurred to me. "Maybe Cissy was delusional, even then. She was so adamant that the guy stole everything, but . . . I don't know. Even then, she'd started to hide things. Maybe she put them somewhere for safekeeping, and only thought they were stolen." Which still begged the question of why Clete had them. "I'm not sure we can trust anything Cissy told us."

"Except Sergei," Rose reminded me.

"And Ernest Hemingway," Iris added. "Those letters looked authentic, and he and Cissy *were* in Paris right before Mama was born."

Staring at the familiar objects, I waved a hand in dismissal, then pinched my lip, pondering.

Rose was uncommonly brisk. "We should at least give Clete a chance to explain."

"Oh, really? And how do you propose we do that?" Iris said. "We'd have to admit we were snooping."

"*We* weren't snooping," Rose corrected. "*You* were snooping. Dahlia and I just happened to come along."

"And what makes you so sure Dahlia wasn't in on it, too?" Iris challenged.

"Because I know Dahlia," Rose said, "and I know you." For once, she stood up to Iris. "We are all adults, and as adults, we must be willing to accept the consequences of our choices. Which means, you need to fess up to Clete. Then we'll ask him what's going on."

Iris rolled her eyes.

Passing by, Vi did the same double take Rose and I had. "What's up?" She came in, then saw what was on the shelves and pointed to Poppy Jack's punch bowl. "Is that what I think it is?"

"It is," Iris said gravely.

"Cool." She moved in for a closer look. "I thought the junkie roomer stole all that stuff."

"That's what Cissy said," I told her, hoping there could be an honest reason why they were now in Clete's possession, but I sure couldn't think of one.

"Lunch is ready," Eileen's voice announced from behind Vi, and we all jumped like we'd been caught with our hands in the till, but it was the other way around. Eileen cocked a curious expression, then saw what we were looking at. She turned sharp eyes on us and clearly realized what we must be thinking.

She threw her hands up. "Oh, Lord, dear Lord, I was supposed to tell y'all, and I clean forgot."

Hope sprang anew. "Tell us what?"

"Well," she began, her signal that a long story was coming. "Clete was still in the navy when that sorry-ass Luther Bettis stole all those things from yer granny. She'd already helped Clete so much with his—" Eileen caught herself. "Well, Luther didn't get far afore the cops caught up to him, empty-handed, but the DEA took over, and after Luther agreed to testify against his drug supplier for a lesser sentence, he clammed up and wouldn't say a word about robbin' yer granny. Probly so he wouldn't git time for the robbery, too. A shame. Like to broke yer granny's heart, losin' all this stuff."

She paused for breath, leaving us teetering on the edges of our imaginations. "First thang after Clete comes home from Vietnam," she resumed, "he starts visitin' Luther in jail, and the next thang ya know, he promises to git Luther a job with the bug people once he gits out, long as he kicks the drugs. So Luther tells him where he sold the loot. It took Clete half a lifetime to finally git it all back. He gave it to yer granny fer her eightieth birthday, and she was so proud. Laughed and cried all over him. But she wouldn't take 'em. Asked him to store it all hyere, so's it'd be safe, fer y'all."

Eileen was a simple woman, transparent as a mountain spring, and the explanation was far too complex to be made of whole cloth, on the spot. Surely she couldn't be lying.

All four of us let out a huge sigh of relief.

"Thank you, Eileen," Iris and Vi said at the same time.

What an amazing thing for Clete to do for Cissy. I hugged his sister. "We thought—"

"You don't have to tell me," Eileen told me. "I could see it, clear as day. But I could see you didn't want it to be true, too." She exhaled long and slow. "I'm *so* sorry I didn't do what I was supposed to. Clete'll spit briars when he finds out."

"I see no reason to tell him," I said, scanning the others. "Do y'all?"

"Heck, no," said Violet as Iris seconded her with a sideways waggle of her head.

"That's sweet of y'all, but no," Eileen said. "We had to do a lot of lyin' when we was kids, till Clete and Hoke got big enough to keep Daddy from . . . Well, once the boys got big enough to keep thangs right, Clete set us all down, and we took a blood oath never to lie to each other again, no matter what." She grinned. "Sooner's better than later when it comes to admittin' mistakes. Clete'll be mad, but he'll git over it quick. Always does. It's a whole sight better'n nursin' grudges."

Amen to that!

"What ever happened to Luther?" I asked about the junkie/thief.

"He went to AA and kicked the drugs," she said proudly. "Been clean and sober these thirty years. Worked fer Clete till the pest control company sold. Now Luther's district manager fer the new folks."

She rubbed her hands together. "Enough about all that. Y'all wash up.

Lunch is gettin' hot." She left chuckling at her own little joke about Katie's wonderful salads. Vi and Rose followed right behind her.

I sank into the office chair as Iris closed the cabinets. Then I flashed on what she'd been doing when I first passed her, and reached for the desk drawer.

Iris stopped me with a firm hand. "Dahlia, don't go there. Trust me, you don't want to know."

Oh, for crying out loud. "Have I waked up in the middle of a soap opera, here? Because that's what you sound like."

You don't want to know, indeed. Spare me.

"First you make me think Clete's a thief," I told her. "Now you're protecting him. Could we have a little consistency?"

"It could be nothing, just like Cissy's things," she said.

"Then why are you being so dramatic?"

She made a face at me. "Maybe it's contagious, drama queen."

"Vi!" I hollered toward the kitchen. "Iris called me a drama queen!"

"You are," Vi called back, "so that's not a dunking offense!"

Iris stuck out the tip of her tongue at me in satisfaction. "C'mon," she coaxed. "Forget what's in there. Let Clete tell you himself. I promise, you'll be glad you did."

The desk drawer beckoned, but the last time I ignored *you don't want to know,* I'd made felons of my poor, innocent sisters.

"Come on," Iris pleaded. "We'll eat, then plan what to fix for the picnic."

Experience said I should probably do as she advised, but curiosity is a powerful thing, particularly when it involved a sexy man who was attracted to me, and vice versa. "You go on," I said. "I'll be there in a minute."

She blew out an exasperated breath. "You'll be sorry, but this is the only time you'll hear me say it."

She marched away, leaving me to reconsider, which I did for all of half a second. Then I opened the drawer and found an enormous scrapbook that filled the whole space. My name was embossed into the cracked leather cover that had probably once been white. When I lifted it out to see what was inside, a few recital announcements and dance programs fell out, along with a clutch of photos.

I picked them up and saw that they were photos of a smiling Cissy beneath the marquees for many of my American starring roles. In some, she pointed to my name, in others, she just stood there, proud and smiling. In the more recent ones, she braced with her walking stick or used it to point out my name.

New York. Chicago. Seattle. San Francisco. Houston. Denver. L.A. Boston. New Orleans. Spoleto in Charleston. D.C. Lots of Atlantas.

Why hadn't she told me? She could have come backstage, and I'd have shown her off to the company, proud to prove she really was my grandmother.

Shaken, I opened the first pages of the scrapbook to find pictures of me from infancy, the earlier ones in Great-grandmother's lap and Mama's. My heart did a gallop to see Great-grandmother so young and strong.

Then I was older, kneading brown bread in the kitchen at Hilltop. Picking blueberries. Holding the Captain's hand as I stood on Billy Goat's Gruff. Then working in Cissy's studio on the lion statue she'd taught me how to make from cylinders and spheres.

Cissy was gorgeous. The dramatic white streak in her hair made her look exotic, not old. As I processed the photos, so many things came back to me, in a rush.

Why hadn't Iris wanted me to see this?

Scanning through the pages, I found copies of all the pictures Mama had taken at my recitals, from age five on, each one carefully dated and annotated with words of praise from Cissy.

I started briefly scanning pages. There would be time later to look them over more thoroughly. Halfway through, I came to pictures of Clete and Cissy: Clete, probably nineteen, all knees and elbows in a sailor suit, bearing a strong resemblance to Howdy Doody. Then Clete, older and more solid in an officer's uniform. Scrambled eggs on his visor. He must have done well.

Clete, his expression intense, mouth open, as he read to Cissy from the chair beside her bed. Clete and all his brothers and sisters with Christmas presents, caroling beside her bed. A grinning Clete kneeling in Great-grandmother's garden, his eyes shaded by his uplifted trowel. Cissy at tables full of Slocums, Easter, Thanksgiving, and birthdays.

Clete lost in reading on the verandah.

Cissy and Clete at the Fourth of July barbecue. An older Clete driving his restored Chris-Craft festooned with flag banners, Cissy in her big straw hat beside him, waving her handkerchief.

Proof positive that Clete had been telling the truth, one Cissy had kept from all of us. But why had she kept him a secret?

I flipped to the back of the album and found pictures of Clete and Cissy and a young Katie under the Fox marquee at the last gala benefit I'd danced in Atlanta. Then a shot of Eileen and Cissy and Katie. Clete must have taken it.

But the most telling were the ones taken inside during the performance, the flashless photos sometimes grainy. In the first, Cissy sat erect with a subtle smile, and beyond her Clete leaned forward in profile, lost in what he was seeing. Then a few shots of a tiny me dancing the finale of *Anna Karenina*.

Then there was another shot, closer, of Clete in profile, watching me, his face rapt and hungry. More of the same. And more. There was no mistaking that look: the word *obsession* came to mind.

I didn't know whether to be flattered or frightened.

That was more than fifteen years ago. I was happily married. Harrison might not have been, but I was.

"Dahlia!" Vi summoned from the distant kitchen. "If you don't get in here, now, we're coming after you!"

I tucked the loose photos roughly where they'd come from, then closed the scrapbook and put it back in the drawer. "Coming!"

Clete and I had a lot to talk about if I got him alone on the picnic.

Before I kissed him, or after?

I'd have to wait and see.

. . . .

IRIS HAD BEEN about to pop with curiosity since I'd come to lunch, acting as if nothing had happened. To her credit, she didn't pester me about the scrapbook. Didn't even follow me when I went back into the office and closed the door so I could go through the scrapbook with a fine-tooth comb to make sure I hadn't missed anything. But beyond the discovery of Clete's presence in Cissy's life and his fixation on me, I found only memories I thought I'd forgotten, memories that flooded my thoughts for the rest of the afternoon, even through supper.

Then I pondered my way through a long, hot soak, peeling off the last of my garish nail polish spots for tallying. Later in Clete's divine bed, I thought and thought about Cissy, trying to figure out why she hadn't told me about Clete or seeing me dance or the fact that his whole family had adopted her.

Of course, Cissy never had done what was proper or expected. Unless Clete knew and told me, the reason she'd kept him a secret had died in the lake when she did.

So much to process. Weary of wondering, my thoughts turned to all that had happened.

Could it only have been weeks since we got there? It seemed like a lifetime. I'd been so worried about losing my house when I came, as worried as Cissy had been about Hilltop. But now, that didn't seem nearly as important as it had. Buckhead seemed very, very far away, almost as far as the married woman I had once been, a woman who'd loved what I had without question, simply because it was there. Loved doing what I did, simply because it was what women like me did. Never looking beneath the surface. Never letting myself slow down enough to see how wrong Harrison and I were for each other.

Not that I would have done things differently. Regret was a waste of time and effort. But, for the first time since I'd left the stage, I considered other choices, other places, other people.

Slowly, I felt my anchor shifting.

. . . .

GETTING READY FOR the picnic the next morning proved therapeutic for all of us, giving us something safe to focus on, with each of our responsibilities clearly defined. Rose and Vi pan-fried the chicken (with lots of drumsticks for Clete), while I set out to make the best deviled eggs in the Western world. Iris did the potato salad, leaving out the onions—possibly because her body had betrayed her in Clete's office, though I doubted she meant to play hide-and-seek anymore.

"Dahlia," she said from the sink where she was pulling the skins off the boiled potatoes. "Could you please do me four hard-boiled eggs for the potato salad. No, six."

"Aye, aye, cap'n." I liked potato salad with lots of eggs. Just not too much mustard.

"Here you go." Rose handed me another carton. "All these eggs are from Katie's henhouse. She just uses the store-bought cartons to keep them from breaking."

I paused. "Please tell me I'm not going to start peeling one of these and find a boiled baby chicken."

"They're organic," Rose said, "not fertile." She shot an impish glance at Iris. "At least, I don't think they're fertile."

"Gross," Iris protested. "You could have gone a long time without saying that. It might put me off eggs forever."

"Fine," I said. "That'll leave more for the rest of us." I added six to the dozen in the Dutch oven on the stove. When Vi passed me on her way to the pantry for more flour, I asked, "How long do you think it'll take to cook eighteen eggs?"

She opened a drawer and pulled out an egg-shaped clear plastic thingy with a flat bottom and a layer of red halfway down marked with *soft* near the edge, then *medium,* then *hard* near the center. "Put this in the middle of the pot. It gradually turns dark red from the edges. When it gets to *hard,* they're done." She continued her mission.

"What won't they think of next?" I lowered it into the center of the pot. "How did you know where to find it?"

"I brought it from home," she said, flour in hand, then went back to dredging the chicken.

So I wasn't the only one who didn't pack light.

I looked at the near-mountain of chicken they'd already fried. "Is anybody coming that I don't know about? Say, the Rotary Club?"

Rose shot me a smile. "Iris and I thought it would be nice to do enough for Katie's family, too, while we were at it, so we gave her the day off."

"Good idea. Should I devil more eggs?"

Rose peered into the pot. "Better use another pan. Things take longer to cook at this altitude."

"Okeydokey." I opened the wide cabinet under the cooktop and pulled out a shallow drawer stacked with clad-bottomed stainless steel cookware. There were three more Dutch ovens just like the one I was using. "I guess with a family as big as Clete's, he needs all these pots and pans."

"Katie said they all have potluck here almost every Sunday after church," Iris told me. "Then the younger kids take naps and the grown-ups sing shape notes together, whatever that is. Katie said they wanted their children to learn, so that was the best way to do it. The kids all want to get big enough to skip their naps." She got out two bunches of celery. "Katie's husband John plays the fiddle, and Larry plays the mandolin."

"Who plays bass?" Vi asked, handing a cookie sheet of floured chicken to Rose.

"Guess." Iris waited.

"Ted," I guessed.

Iris shook her head, smug.

"Hank," said Rose.

Same reaction.

Vi held up a vee for victory with both hands. "Eileen," she crowed.

Iris pointed to her with a celery stalk. "And we have a winner."

"I cheated," Vi confessed, unrepentant. "She told me."

"That's a lot of togetherness for a lot of people," I mused aloud. "I wonder how they all get along."

Iris started stringing the celery, then rinsing it. "Katie says they argue sometimes, but never for long. It's that truth pact. Their daddy was an alcoholic, but she said never to mention him around Hoke."

Yet another question to ask Clete, but it was last in a long list.

"And what are Katie's hopes and aspirations?" I asked as I got out the pickle relish and mustard. "And her favorite color and song?"

For once, Iris didn't get defensive. "She wants to send her daughter to nursing school at Northeast Medical in Gainesville. Or was it Brenau? One of those. And she wants her two sons to finish college. And her favorite color's pink. Song's 'Ahab the Arab.'"

"Those aren't her aspirations," I said. "They're her hopes for her kids."

Iris didn't miss a beat. "Well, actually, she's always wanted to be a belly dancer," she said, dead serious, "and her favorite color is camouflage, and her favorite song is 'Lonesome Whippoorwill.' That's why it's on the jukebox at the Boat Church."

I tucked my chin. "You are makin' that up."

She smiled at me over her shoulder. "Well, I told you what she told me, but you didn't like it."

"Iris, my girl, you are definitely lightening up, and I like it. Good for you."

She nodded like a duchess acknowledging her vassals. "Thenk yew. Thenk yew verra much." A duchess, as Elvis. Very good.

Many hands make light work, so by the time noon rolled around, everything was ready. We'd found sturdy checkered tablecloths and matching napkins in a special linen closet, and Rose discovered several picnic baskets and coolers in the utility room.

By the time Clete arrived at quarter after twelve, we were good and hungry.

Iris held the vat of potato salad, which left me with the decaf tea, a gallon in each hand.

"Wow," Clete said as he came in from the garage. "Something smells awful good."

Vi wasted no time handing him the heaviest picnic basket. "We made enough for Katie's family, too. Gave her the day off."

Clete cocked his head in approval. "That was nice of you."

"We're nice people," Rose said, handing him the other basket. "Now. Where did you decide to take us?"

He smiled. "All that news made me think of Bold Creek Park . . ."

The four of us froze in mid-heartbeat.

No, no, no, no, no!

"It's really nice," he went on, oblivious to the fact that we'd all stopped breathing. "Unspoiled. Off the beaten path."

Breathe! I ordered myself. How would I explain it if I passed out?

He shook his head. "But, considering what they found there, I ruled it out." A basket in each elbow, he picked up the cooler as if it were empty instead of full of ice and sodas. "So we're going to Blackrock, instead. Great view of Clayton. You can even see some of Lake Clare from the overlook on the far side."

Anywhere but Bold Creek.

Thank You, thank You, thank You, Lord.

I opened the door to the garage for him, then flared my nostrils at my wide-eyed sisters as they filed out after him.

"Dry as it is," Clete said as he started loading the food in the back of his SUV, "we probably won't see any bears at the park. They're sticking close to the water. Still, it wouldn't be a bad idea to keep an eye peeled while we're there."

Bring on the bears. Just not at Bold Creek Park.

Once everything was onboard, the others piled into the backseat, leaving me to sit up front by Clete.

Still rattled by the Bold Creek scare, I waited till we started down his long, gravel drive to blurt out, "Eileen says y'all like to sing shape note."

"She did, did she?" He smiled, eyes on the road. "We do." As we passed the tidy drives to his family's homes, he pointed out each one and gave us a thumbnail sketch of when and how it had been built (always by family), then a brief bio of his respective siblings and their families.

Larry, who had worked his way through college as a finish carpenter, was principal at a private boarding school in nearby Tallulah Falls, married to Angie, with three girls.

Eileen's husband was Frank, a plumber and distant cousin of the same last name. They had three girls and two boys.

"That's Hank's house," Clete pointed out. "He makes cabinets in the barn out back. He and Lila have two boys and six grandkids." He indicated the brick ranch half an acre away. "That's Ted's. He's the pastor of Cold Hollow Baptist. Married his high school sweetheart, Carlene, and they're still lovebirds. They have three boys and two girls. Ted keeps us all on the straight and narrow."

We jolted over a pothole. "That next one down is Katie and John's. He's a civil engineer, graduated Tech. Supervises most of the county's projects. They have a son and daughter. No grandkids yet."

All of them sounded like good, productive people. I gave Clete a lot of credit for the pride in his voice when he spoke of them.

We came to the last house on the hillside, a small, rustic cabin. "That's Hoke's. He's our bachelor."

Not much of a bio. And we weren't supposed to mention their daddy around Hoke. I logged that onto my list of questions.

As for our picnic, I have just one thing to say: Whenever the devil gets out his weird-stick and starts hunting for somebody to beat on, he always ends up clobbering me.

· 20 ·

Careful, or you'll get a bite instead of a kiss.
—MAMA LOU

. . . .

*E*VERYTHING WAS FINE during lunch. Clete relaxed and started telling funny stories about his family, scraps he and his brothers had
gotten into, crazy things they'd done to his sisters.

Then his face went soft and he told about Great-grandmother and the
quarters and seeing me when I was only five, dancing even then. And
about the other nice things Great-grandmother had done for his brothers
and sisters and mother. The list was long, and I heard the love in his
voice when he spoke of her.

Then, to keep things from getting too serious, he went back to family
lore.

By three, the shadows were beginning to lengthen, and the heat of the
afternoon set in. "We can clean all this up, Dahlia," Rose said. "Clete,
why don't you take Dahlia to that overlook on the other side? She needs
some exercise."

Perfect. How would I know whether he wanted to or not? Rose left him no choice. Embarrassed, I got up, closing the egg-taker. "You don't have to. I can—"

"I want to." He took the eggs from my hand and gave them to Vi. "If we're not back in an hour, call 911." Then he placed his hand to the small of my back and guided me toward the forest path, where a low sign and arrow said WEST OVERLOOK.

Iris pulled out her cell phone and said, "Ooooo. I've got great signal up here." That would keep her happy for a while.

Once we entered the woods, I deliberately slowed our pace, suddenly self-conscious. I definitely wanted to kiss this man, but I couldn't just grab hold of him and plant one on him. I wouldn't want someone to do that to me.

Unless it was Clete.

When I was young, I had to fight men off. That, I knew how to do. This was a whole lot more complicated.

Clete seemed at sixes and sevens, too. He started pointing out local wildflowers, ferns, and the "monkey pods," as Great-grandmother had called them. I bent low to gently push aside the dead leaves, and there they were at the base of the stalk: little brown pitchers with hairy insides for catching little bugs.

Clete pointed out the herbs and roots his mother had used to treat their ills, and before long, I forgot why I'd come, fascinated by his knowledge of the old ways of the mountains, and the new.

Then, when we could just see the overlook beyond the trees, he simply drew me into his arms and kissed me.

It was tender, at first, a chance to test my willingness, but the moment I responded, he was ardent, his arms enfolding me and lifting me off my feet.

Holy smoke.

Kissing Harrison had never been that good. Kissing *anybody*, man or boy, had never been that good.

Even my dreams of Clete hadn't been that good.

Suddenly hungry as a teenager in heat, I kissed him back with the same desperate passion as his, and both of us disappeared into a place apart from time and circumstance.

By the time he dragged his lips from mine, I was getting dizzy. He pressed the side of his face into my hair and gently swung me side to side, all my weight in his strong arms. "I've dreamed of doing that since I was seventeen."

And?

I didn't think "Was it as good for you as it was for me?" would be appropriate, but I sure wanted to know.

"It's okay to put me down," I said softly. "I promise I won't run away."

His hand stroked my hair. "I'm afraid to let go. That if I do, it won't be real."

"It was real, all right," I murmured. "But maybe we ought to do it again, just to make sure."

It was only a kiss, I told myself. How much trouble could that get us into?

Still holding me, he drew back only far enough to focus on my face, his gaze searching mine with as many questions as I'd stored up for him. But questions could wait. I just wanted to kiss him till we both were senseless. So I closed my eyes and planted one on him. By the time that one ended, I wasn't sure I could stand up on my own.

"Why didn't you tell me about the scrapbook?" my voice asked quietly. "And Cissy's things?"

No! I did not say that! Erase, erase, erase!

His body tensed.

Fool! Idiot! I swore inside. What were you thinking?

I wasn't; that was the trouble. Safe and comfortable in his arms, I'd let down my guard and spoken my mistrust, ruining everything before it really got started.

He lowered me to the ground. "You found the scrapbook." A flat statement, not a question.

"Iris did," I answered, ashamed of myself even as I said it. I tried to make up for it with, "She asked me not to look at it, but I knew there was something important you weren't telling me, so I did anyway."

He nodded, looking to the treetops. "Right after Iris found Cissy's long-lost treasures, and y'all thought I'd stolen them."

"I didn't think you'd stolen them," I said. "Not at first, anyway."

He turned his back to me, his shoulders quaking slightly.

Surely he wasn't crying. No, no, no. He couldn't be crying. I was the one who was supposed to do the crying.

He wasn't, as it turned out. He was laughing.

He pivoted, catching me up with a grin, and swung me around. "I was afraid to tell you about the scrapbook," he confessed, "afraid you'd think I was some kind of stalker when you found out how long I'd been in love with you."

In love with me?

Back up, Jack!

Kissing. All I wanted was the kissing.

He kept on with, "Afraid nobody could live up to my dream of who you were. But none of that matters now. You're better than I dreamed." He lowered me to my feet, then cupped my face in his hands, this time looking at me in wonder. "Stronger, funnier, smarter. Braver. More beautiful. Even after what happened with Harrison and your son. Even though you were afraid to trust me."

I raised a pointer finger. "Clete, that was the best kiss of my life, bar none. And I sure would like to do it again sometime. But you've only known me for a month. The rest . . . you, of all people, know how Cissy exaggerated, embellished everything. There are things about me, if you knew . . ."

He drew my waist in close, way too close to think straight when faced with the evidence of just how much he'd liked kissing me. No Viagra in that medicine cabinet. "Everybody has secrets," he said, sobering. "For good reason. The truth can hurt people." He searched for words. "I don't care about your past. What matters is now, and what future we both have left. Dahlia, we're not children. There's been a lot of water over the dam for both of us. But what you see is what you get with me, the same as it is with you."

Not with me. I couldn't ever tell him about the bodies, how I'd dragged my sisters into it for my own personal gain. If he knew . . .

"I only care about what affects us," he said.

Like having the cops take me away in handcuffs?

"Here. Now. We don't have to spill our guts to each other," he told me. "Probably shouldn't. All I'm asking for is a *chance* for something permanent, on whatever timetable you want."

"I'm . . . I just . . ." I'd always been so sure of myself. What I wanted. How to get it. "Clete, your life is here. Your family. My life is back in Atlanta, my home. My sisters. We'd only be making ourselves miserable to pretend that's not the way things are."

He wasn't going to let me get away with that. Grasping my upper arms, he bent his knees to put his eyes level with mine. "How long has it been since you felt joy, Dahlia? Not after the divorce, but before?"

"My faith gives me that," I said. "I've had a good life. A blessed life, and privileges far beyond what I deserved."

He shook his head no. "We share that faith. But I'm talking about something tangible." He turned away, arms akimbo, then left me space when he came back, not touching me. "I've been blessed, and I've been cursed, but until I kissed you just now, I've never felt that joy."

Whoa. Way too much responsibility.

Seeing my expression, he backed off a bit, smiling that wry smile. "Cissy set us up, you know. Why else would she have insisted y'all stay for the summer? And arranged for me to fumigate the house after y'all got here, and put you up at my place? It makes perfect sense to me now."

I could see the truth dawning on him as he put the pieces together, and Gary Cooper changed to Tyrone Power, speaking his thoughts as they came. "Years ago, she made me swear a solemn oath to look after you when she was gone. Then she left her treasures with me, not Mr. Johnson, so you'd see how much she trusted me." One eyebrow lifted. "*That* one sure backfired, didn't it?"

He looked to me. "She knew us both to the bone. Knew we'd be good together."

Not that Cissy was a good judge of relationships.

"And my house . . ." A light went on, and he started pacing. "From the minute I started planning it, she insisted I make sure it was mold-free. I thought that was her subtle way of asking to move in, and I was glad to do it. It's why I built so close, so we could all take care of her."

He shook his head. "The crafty old thing. When she refused, I thought it was senility. Fear of change. But she never intended to move in." He stilled, meeting my gaze. "Now I know why. She was thinking about you, not herself. She wanted it to be safe for you."

Whoa. It had only been a few kisses.

So why did half of me want to throw off my clothes and have at it, on the spot, let the chips fall where they may?

But I had never given in to that reckless urging, and didn't intend to start. I was sixty, not the idiot girl who'd fallen for idiot *Richard* in high school, for heaven's sake. I'd thought he was great then, too, but this was reality. I knew better than to let my hormones get the best of me.

The other half of me wanted to run, far and fast, to somewhere I could sort this whole thing out.

Iris had found out from Katie that Clete was divorced. "Why did you get divorced?" my idiot voice asked.

Shit. I did *not* just ask that!

Clete drew in a sharp breath, then held it briefly before answering. "I married someone I didn't love because it was time to get married, and Lila wanted to. You were the toast of ballet, reigning over another world, and Lila was, *is*, a good friend." He sighed, looking to the ground. "I figured it would help me move on, that things would get better if I married her. She figured the same, but it didn't work out that way. I buried myself in work, always gone, always at the plant, even late at night. She got lonely. And angry." He looked me in the eye. "It was all my fault. I can't blame her for finding somebody else. Hank had always had a case on her."

"Hank, as in your *brother* Hank?" Was the whole world a soap opera, only I just didn't know it?

He nodded. "She wanted to hurt me, but it ended up being the best thing for everybody. Hank really loves her. They have a good, solid marriage. You'll meet her Sunday."

This definitely wasn't going the way I'd thought it would. Actually, I'd never thought past the kissing, but even if I had, I'd never have dreamed up anything like this.

"Dahlia, I've never talked to anybody about that. Only you, because I want you to see me for who I am. What you see is what you get. I know that's hard to believe after what Harrison did to you, but I'm not Harrison. I've waited a long time for you. I can wait a while longer."

I took a step back, palm toward him. "Well, now, there you go again. I really appreciate your honesty, but it's . . . this is moving way too fast. Talkin' about how long you've waited for me . . ." I clasped my hands, fingers interlocking, then briefly pressed them, hard, against my lips. "My life is complicated. Really, really . . . complicated right now." How could I convince him without driving him away? "I just need some time, here. Kissing is fine. Kissing is *great*, but I need to get to know you. I have questions—lots and lots of questions—before this goes any further."

He listened, stoic.

"I know a lot *about* you, Clete, but I don't know *you* yet, and even though you think you know me, you don't. You only know what Cissy told you."

If Vi were there she'd probably clobber me with a picnic basket for taking everything so seriously, but how else could I take it? Clete was serious enough for both of us, and then some.

"I saw you dance," he said as if it were a prayer. "And I knew what you'd sacrificed to do it. That was real." He took a step toward me. "I held you in my arms and danced with you. That was real. Our kiss was real."

I started backing up, slowly at first. Clete read my expression with a look that hurt my heart to see.

"I know I said I wouldn't run away, but I think I'm gonna," I warned him. "Just till I can figure this out. Please don't take it personally. It's me, not you."

For some reason, though, I couldn't turn my back on him.

Clete's features abruptly congealed. "Dahlia, stop. Do not move." His expression gave me the creeps.

I took another careful step backward. "We'll talk about this tomorrow, okay?"

"Stop," he choked out. "God, just stop." He was looking past me to the forest slope.

I turned and saw a raccoon wavering a few feet uphill from the path, its back arched. "Oh, look. A raccoon."

The moment I spoke, it bared its fangs and came at me like it was shot out of a cannon, making a sound like a huge dogfight and catfight and train wreck rolled into one, so loud, I couldn't believe it was coming from just one animal. Demons. It sounded like demons.

"Whoa!" I took off running, not scared, just trying to avoid it.

Damn! Damn, damn, damn!

It was gaining on me even as I heard Clete's long strides pounding right behind it.

I wasn't afraid, just did *not* need any more complications in my life.

A weight attached to my left ankle, and I looked down to see it was on me, biting, biting, biting, his fangs punching bloody little punctures through my slacks, still making that hideous sound, slobber flying everywhere.

Shit! *I was gonna have to take the bleemin'* rabies *shots!*

I don't mind telling you, that seriously ticked me off.

Then Clete was there, a blur of sandy hair and pinpoint oxford, his hand extended toward the crazed raccoon.

"Clete, no!"

He grabbed it by the scruff of its neck and jerked it off me. It bit him once on the arm before he dispatched it with a twist of its neck, and it went limp. He dropped it on the ground, shaking his injured hand as blood mingled with the deadly saliva, staining his slacks.

Me, Tarzan, you Jane, in real life, but the whole thing was so bizarre, it didn't seem real.

"Oh, no," I said. "Now you'll have to take the shots, too."

Totally in rescue mode, Clete tore off his shirt and wiped the blood from his hand. "Just let me make sure Animal Control finds it before somebody else does," he said, grim. After wrapping the dead animal in his bloody shirt, he left it on the path and scooped me up into his arms. "Don't worry. I'll get you to help."

"Clete! I can walk!" I protested, but his arms were tight around me, and he was already bounding down the gentle slope to the car.

"We'll have you to the hospital in no time."

"Please. I can walk just fine. You don't have to run. We have plenty of time."

He didn't listen. He was too into being my knight in shining armor, which was really nice, except I didn't want it to give him a heart attack. But never underestimate adrenaline. The guy was past sixty, yet he carried me at a lope for more than a city block.

"Call 911," he shouted as we broke clear of the trees.

"Clete, really. Put me down!" I ordered him, alarmed by the bulging veins in his neck and face. "You're gonna scare my sisters to death."

He totally ignored me, shouting to the others, "She got bitten by a rabid raccoon!"

Iris whipped out her phone and dialed while Rose and Violet ran around like ants, haphazardly heaving the picnic leftovers into the back of the SUV.

Clete put me into the front seat, then pulled a roll of paper towels, a plastic bag, and some hand sanitizer from the glove compartment. "We're okay," he said as he cleaned the blood from his injured hand, the arteries in his neck throbbing.

"Clete, you're scaring me. Your carotid arteries are hammering a mile a minute. I can see them. Please take some deep breaths. We have time." I wasn't sure how much, but seemed to remember that several hours were fine. "Hours and hours."

"Ummm." He twisted a paper towel around his hand to put pressure on the bite, then bent and gently lifted the left leg of my linen slacks. He closed his eyes. "Damn."

With visible effort, he kept his voice even. "There are at least half a dozen puncture wounds. Thanks to your pants, I don't think any of them are too deep, but it drew blood." He was taking it a lot harder than I was.

"But it's a hundred percent treatable," I reassured him, stroking back his hair before I caught myself. "We'll be okay. We just have to take the shots. They're not so bad," I said as if I knew what I was talking about, which I didn't. "They don't give them in the stomach anymore."

He nodded, not meeting my gaze. A siren cranked up in the town below.

Iris thrust her cell phone at him. "It's 911. I told them y'all had been bitten, and the paramedics are on the way."

Clete took the phone and paced away from the car. "This is Clete Slocum. Clete. C-l-e-t-e, S-l-o-c-u-m. I'm in Rabun County, Georgia, at Blackrock State Park. Near Clayton. No, *Georgia*. My . . . a friend of mine was attacked and bitten by a rabid raccoon. She has some immune problems, so she needs to be treated as soon as possible." He kept pacing, in profile, phone pressed to his ear with one hand, the other fisted against his waist. "It bit me, too, when I pulled it off her, but I'm not worried about that, I . . . on my hand, but she's the one who needs . . ." He scowled. "Yes. I'll hold."

I still could hardly believe what had just happened.

I should have been upset. I should have been afraid. Why I wasn't, I could not tell you.

Instead, I found myself noting perversely how taut and muscular Clete's upper body was, and tanned.

Iris scrambled into the middle of the backseat, then leaned out the open door behind me to scold, "Y'all, hurry up! Come *on*!"

Vi went around to the driver's side and got in, leaning forward to whisper at me, "Put your eyes back into your head, Dahlia. This is an emergency. Leering is not appropriate." I was glad to see that she didn't seem afraid, either.

Rose got into the seat behind mine. "Lord, honey," she said softly, admiring Clete without his shirt. "That man must have had a body transplant."

"Nope." I admired him right along with her. "Those battle scars are real. I like 'em."

Then he turned his back and bent forward a bit. All three of us gasped. Long, straight white scars crisscrossed the entire lower portion of his back.

"I've seen marks like that," Rose said. "Child abuse. Probably a belt. See how thin they are, and how they extend farther to the left? They probably wrapped his rib cage when he got them."

My heart went out to him. "Clete said he'd been cursed," I told them. "It had to be their father."

He turned our way again, still focused on the phone. "There's no question that it was rabid," he told the operator, still pacing. "It's dead. I pulled it off her and broke its neck." He stopped, staring sightlessly over the gorgeous vista. "We left it on the path to the west overlook, tied in my shirt. Yes." He nodded. "No. I didn't damage the skull. Not that I need to see any test results to know it was rabid. Take my word for it, it was rabid." His eyes moved rapidly. "Yes." He nodded. "Punctures, on her calf and ankle, I don't know how deep . . . Yes, she can." He frowned. *"Northeast General?* That's an hour and a half away, even by ambulance! Franklin's a lot closer." He bobbed a spasmodic nod of frustration, then took a deep breath. "Well, if that's it, then that's it. I'll try to get a chopper. Tell Northeast General we're on our way."

He got in and handed the phone to Iris. "Thanks." After buckling up, he pulled a much heavier phone with a thick, flexible antenna from the console and turned it on. He dialed a few numbers, then launched us toward the road with a screech of tires, gravel flying.

All four of us grimaced and hung on for dear life.

I don't know why it is, but I'd never been able to bring myself to yell at anybody for driving too fast, no matter how scared I was. When Harrison had gotten behind the wheel, he turned into a maniac—with good reflexes, but no sense of mortality. Junior had driven the same way. After all that had just happened, though, I considered screaming at Clete to slow down, but was afraid it might cause a wreck.

"This is base," a scratchy voice said through static on his phone.

Clete pressed a button. "This is Clete. Dahlia and I had a set-to with a rabid raccoon, and it won. Till I killed it. We're on our way to Northeast General to get our shots. Don't worry. We're both fine."

Not if he didn't slow down!

I recognized Eileen's voice when she responded. "Clete Slocum, you'd better be tellin' me the truth about bein' okay! If you turn up dead, I'll never let you hear the end of it."

He shot me a grin. "That's what Mama always used to say when any of us got hurt. Eileen's just like her. Always fusses when she's scared or worried." He pushed the button to reply. "Tell the others, but don't make a huge thing out of it. We have to go to Gainesville to get the shots, but it'll be fine. See you tomorrow. Don't wait up. I'll call from the ER."

As we careened down the mountain, I closed my eyes and hung on, trying not to think about where we were when centrifugal force slid me against the door in the switchbacks.

Then the sound of Clete rummaging in the console made me look.

"Ha." His eyes still on the road, he pulled out a regular cell phone, then handed it to me as he braked before the next hairpin turn. "Could you please turn that on and dial pound twenty-six for me?"

I took the phone and mustered up the brass to say, "Only if you'll slow down. You're scaring the wits out of me. I'm not bleeding to death. We have plenty of time."

He slowed a little, but not much.

A glance in the rearview mirror showed my sisters bolt erect, eyes closed, Vi with a death grip on the handle above the door, and Rose and Iris white-knuckled as they held each other's hands.

"Slower, or I'm not dialing." I threatened, finally bringing him to a saner speed. "Thank you."

I opened the phone, did as instructed, then handed it back at the first ring.

Clete waited, then said, "Zack, you sorry son of a bitch. I sure am glad you're home."

The distant siren was getting louder.

"I've got a little situation, here. Can I borrow the chopper?"

"Borrow?" My eyes shot open, and I turned to him. "Borrow?"

There was that wry smile. "Just to Gainesville," he said into the phone. "I'll have it back tomorrow morning, if not before." He glanced my way. "Let's just say, I'm taking a pretty lady to dinner." He frowned in consternation. "How in the world did you find out? It just happened."

He rolled his eyes, exhaling. "Yes, but I'm also taking her to dinner. Okay. Gas 'er up and start the preflight checklist. See you in a few minutes. Great." He flipped the phone closed. "I'm a licensed pilot with over a thousand hours in a chopper, several hundred of them in Zack's. Trust me, you'll be safe."

"Do I have a choice?" I asked.

"Nope."

I heard Iris inhale to speak and looked into the rearview mirror to see Rose grab her pointed finger and shake her head *no.*

"Maybe the State Patrol could take us down there," I suggested.

"At this time of day, on a Friday?" Clete shook his head. "Half of Atlanta is on its way up here, and southbound traffic isn't any better. There's a Braves game tonight."

Clete followed my line of vision and said into the mirror, "You ladies sure are quiet back there. Don't you have anything to say about this?"

After a brief pause, Rose shot forward between our seats with a ferocious growl, fingers clawed like the rabid raccoon.

After my initial shock passed, I couldn't help but laugh. Clete did, too.

He shook his head. "God, I love your sisters. Even nosy Iris."

"I beg your pardon," she said, defensive.

"You heard me, and both of us know it's true," Clete said back.

She glared at my reflection in the mirror. "I cannot believe you told him!"

"She didn't," he said. "Eileen did."

I turned to him, skeptical, and he nodded to confirm it.

"But it's okay," he said to Iris. "There's nothing to hide in my house. So you might as well stop looking for any birth control or Viagra. You won't find any."

Iris went scarlet, clearly guilty. "What?" she accused. "Do you have hidden cameras everywhere? Have you been watching us?"

Clete wasn't intimidated. "Don't need any cameras. Eileen knows exactly where every single thing in that house is supposed to be. Me, I wouldn't have any idea if things had been moved around, unless we're talking about a bed or a sofa. But Eileen's got a photographic memory. It really helped her in law school."

Iris's mouth dropped open. "Law school? I thought she was your maid!"

So did I.

The siren got louder.

Clete chuckled, clearly enjoying shattering our stereotypes. "First in her class at UGA. She was one hell of a trial lawyer for fifteen years, but it got to her eventually. She couldn't stand representing clients she knew were guilty. Now she just does wills and deeds and adoptions from home. She helps me out at the house because she wants to, and I let her because I need it. Same with Katie, only she usually just sends the food up with one of the kids. She's only coming in every day because y'all are there."

The siren got really loud.

We turned a corner into a straightaway and saw the Fire Department ambulance approaching in the opposite lane.

Clete slowed, lowering his window to flag them down. The driver pulled even with Clete and rolled down his window. Beyond him, his partner was a tall drink of water.

"Hey, Miles," Clete acknowledged.

The fireman nodded. "Clete. Y'all okay?"

"Will be, soon as we get to the ER at Northeast General and start the rabies shots. Zack's gassin' up the chopper."

Both the driver and his partner craned to see me past Clete. "Anything we can do fer ya?"

"Yeah. We left the coon on the path, tied in my shirt. You could pick it up for me, but be careful. Wouldn't want y'all to have to take the shots, too. There's some blood on the ground, too. Might want to bleach the path down good, so it can't hurt anybody else. Is Animal Control on its way?"

"Shoot, Clete," the driver said. "It's Friday afternoon. They're supposed to work till five, but it takes dynamite to git 'em out on a call this late. We'll make sure that coon gits to the state lab."

"Thanks."

"Yo, Clete," the other fireman said, extending a dark blue paramedic's shirt past his partner and out the window. "Take this. Git it back when you can. No rush."

"Thanks, Alvie."

Alvie saluted Clete with two fingers to the forehead. "Good thing I picked up my laundry after our last run."

"I'll have it cleaned before I return it." Suddenly self-conscious, Clete hurried to put it on and button up. "Sorry, ladies. In all the excitement, I forgot I was half naked."

At least he hadn't said *nekkid*.

"Want an escort?" Fireman Miles asked as he put the ambulance back into gear.

"Not necessary," Clete told him. "But you might call in and ask Louise to tell the county mounties I'm comin' that way. Probably ought to notify the papers and radio stations to alert the public, too. And the *AJC*. Wouldn't want some kid to get bitten next."

The fireman shot his thumb and pointer finger like a gun. "You got it." They pulled away to retrieve the raccoon.

"Y'all sure seem casual about all this," Vi said as we resumed progress down what was left of the mountain. "Do people get attacked by rabid animals all the time up here?" She shivered just saying it.

"Not that I know of." Clete relaxed. "Dogs, yes, all the time. Especially since the coyotes started comin' in. Some folks have been bitten by strays that got away, so they had to take the shots, just to be on the safe side. We've had a lot of rabies in the foxes, too. But as far as I can remember, Dahlia's the only human who actually got bitten by a rabid animal in a while."

"Perfect." I could see it now, Clete with a little nephew on his knee. "Well, the first time I kissed your aunt, we both had to take rabies shots."

A most unladylike chortle escaped through my nose.

Lord. Now he had *me* thinking about our future together.

When we reached U.S. 441, Clete sped all the way through town. To my amazement, county police and state troopers had posted themselves at the three main intersections, waving us through as my sisters and I watched in awe.

Clete answered my question before I got it out. "It doesn't hurt bein' the largest employer in the county for thirty years."

Apparently not. "And beloved," I added.

Clete liked that. "Absolutely." He took a fast right, zoomed for another mile, then took a left down a gravel road flanked by level fields and pastures. Then the road ended at a rundown farmhouse with a huge corrugated metal barn out back. "Here we are," Clete said as the gravel turned to dirt driveway.

The four of us eyed each other in mute trepidation as we bumped past the house, then alongside the barn—which wasn't a barn, but a hangar, its rear doors open wide—and there was the helicopter, motor running on its impressive concrete pad.

Not a new helicopter, mind you, but one of those that looked like a big dragonfly, with a clear globe for a cockpit. I tried to think where I'd seen one like it. Not for a long, long time.

A man in a grease-stained jumpsuit and cap appeared from behind the cockpit, carrying a big wrench and an oily rag. He motioned us over with the wrench. "Y'all better git on in while the engine's still runnin'."

I almost threw up.

"It's okay, Dahlia," Clete assured me. "He loves to say stuff like that to scare people, but I'll take that chopper over any of the new ones with solid-state boards and computer components. That's his baby, there. Both of us could take 'er apart and put her back together in our sleep."

"Let's just hope you don't need to," I said.

Clete left the keys in the car and came around to help me out, which wasn't necessary. He leaned in and said to the others, "Take the car. Do what you'd like with it. I'll call the house when we get there, and keep you updated."

Iris lifted a finger. "I don't care if you are Prince Charming. If you don't get my sister there and back in one piece, I'll go through every drawer and every cabinet in every house on that mountain, then publish the embarrassing stuff in a full-page ad in the *AJC*."

Clete grinned. "You and my ex, Lila, are really going to like each other."

Zack got in the cockpit and revved the motor up, blades spinning with a downwash so strong I couldn't have stood up straight if I'd wanted to.

Clete seated me, then he and Zack swapped places. While Clete was getting himself and the headset all hooked up, Zack made sure I was safely in my harness. He leaned in close to help put on my protective headphones, but before he put the right earpiece in place, he leaned over and said, "Clete's the finest man I've ever known. Don't hurt him." Then he lowered the earpiece and whacked the plastic beside me with a thumbs-up to Clete.

Clete returned the signal, and Zack ran for the hangar.

My sisters, standing by the pad with hands above their eyes against the late afternoon sun, watched us lift off and waved, then headed for the car.

I leaned over to get Clete's attention with a poke. "How old is this thing?" I hollered.

Clete smiled and hollered back, "You don't want to know."

That, again. Good thing I wasn't superstitious.

I risked a glance to my right and saw that we were getting pretty high. My stomach did a flip.

What was the worst thing that could happen? We could crash, and I'd wake up in heaven, beyond the cares of mortals. I leaned over and poked Clete again. "If this thing goes down," I shouted, "just make sure it kills me. I'm not afraid to die, but I really don't want to be maimed. Okay?"

He shook his head, amused, then started talking with somebody about our flight plan. I made out *medical emergency* and the name of the hospital.

The next fifteen minutes were the longest of my life.

· 21 ·

Whatever you do, Dahlia, just don't be ordinary.
—CISSY

....

𝓗EART IN MY throat, I did my best to strangle the life out of my safety harness, trying not to look down at the traffic moving north on Route 365.

Whirlybirds, on black-and-white TV! That was where I'd seen one of these. Our screen hadn't been wider than ten inches, with a radio and storage underneath. The show starred that blond guy from *Terry and the Pirates*. I couldn't have been more than eight.

I subtracted 1950 from the present, then added eight. Zack's chopper could be . . . only seven years younger than I was! That definitely didn't help.

Suddenly, I felt queasy. Very queasy.

Clete glanced over, then reached under the seat and offered me an airsick bag. "Use it if you need it," he shouted.

Just having it made me feel better, as did looking ahead to see we'd finally reached I-985. Clete hung a right over the northernmost exit, and within seconds, we were over the hospital. After a perfect landing (during which I slammed my eyes shut and didn't breathe), we were greeted by two stretchers and a passel of nurses and orderlies.

We motioned them away. "Thanks, but we can walk."

This time, he let me, tucking the chopper keys into his jeans.

"Okay, let's get you to admissions," one of the nurses said. "Right this way."

"I thought there were two of them. When did you get the call?" she asked Clete as we went.

He frowned, then looked down at his shirt. "Oh, I'm not a paramedic. He just loaned me a spare shirt. I got blood all over mine."

"Hmmm," she said. "And where's the raccoon?"

"Back where it happened," he told her. "They'll test it, but there was no doubt it was rabid." He aimed a thumb at me. "Came at her like it was shot out of a cannon. Sounded like a hundred demons." My exact thoughts. "I couldn't believe how loud it was."

We passed through double doors, then a long hallway, before arriving at the crammed waiting room for the ER. The nurse escorting us said loudly to the check-in clerk, "Cathy, these two are the rabies cases from Rabun County."

She made it sound like we were rabid instead of the raccoon.

Conversation halted immediately, and all eyes turned our way. I wished I had the courage to pounce at them the way Rose had in the car, but I didn't.

The clerk asked us to sign in, so I wrote Clete's name first and was about to put down mine when he told the woman, "She needs to go first. She has immune issues. There are some complicating factors."

"No, take him first," I insisted. "He carried me a quarter mile at a run. I want to make sure his heart's okay. I thought he was going to stroke out, then and there."

She pressed a button on her phone, then pointed to Clete as two nurses materialized and descended on him, one with a wheelchair that she almost ran into the backs of his knees. "Are you having any chest pain"—she glanced at the sign-in sheet—"Mr. Slocum?"

"No!" Clete glared at me, then the wheelchair.

"Please, sir, we need you to sit down." She looked to me. "Did you notice any other symptoms? Any gray cast to his face or lips? Any shortness of breath?"

"Definite shortness of breath, but only after he carried me a city block," I said. "His pulse was a mile a minute. I could see it in his neck."

"Any heartburn?" the other nurse asked him, pushing him down into the wheelchair. "Numbness or pain in your arm? Crushing sensation?"

"No!" Clete tried to get up, but both nurses held down his shoulders.

"Nugene," one called to a huge human throwback in an orderly's outfit. "Could you please help us get Mr. Slocum back to Cardiac?"

Only then did I become aware of the CHEST PAIN CENTER banner across the far wall.

Uh-oh.

Clete looked at me in pure-D frustration.

Apparently, I'd said the magic words. "Sorry, Clete," I called after him as they whisked him through the double doors. Better safe than sorry, though.

I turned back to the clerk. "What are they going to do? Where will they take him?"

"Don't worry . . ." She glanced at the sign-in sheet. "Mrs. Slocum. Your husband's in good hands. Let's take care of you, now. Could I please see your Medicare card and any secondary insurance?"

"He's not my husband," I snapped, annoyed by her assumptions, "and I do not have a Medicare card, and won't for years and years." Not so many, really.

"My mistake," she said, clearly not sorry one bit. "Proof of insurance, then, please, and a driver's license, passport, or official Georgia photo ID card." I pulled my license and insurance card out of my wallet.

"Thank you, ma'am. If you'll take a seat, please, the triage nurse will be right with you."

I sat down in a vacant chair, and the people on both sides of me promptly got up and went to the other end of the waiting room, acting like I had the plague.

A woman in a white coat stepped out of one of the tiny offices behind the desk, then looked at the clipboard in her hand. "Cooper?" she called. "D. Cooper?"

"Here." I got up and headed toward her.

The clerk offered me back my ID and insurance card as I passed. "You're all set."

Watched by every person in the waiting room, I took them, then went into the triage room. The nurse twisted the blinds closed.

I sagged. "Thank you. I could use some privacy. This hasn't been the best day."

She glanced at my chart. "And you are Day-*lee*-ah Cooper?"

"It's Dăl'-yuh," I corrected. "Yes, I am."

She put my hospital ID band on my wrist, then snipped off the excess. "Okay. First, I'm just going to check your blood pressure." She snugged the cuff around my upper arm. "Just try to relax. I know you're probably upset about your husband, but he's getting excellent care."

I closed my eyes as it inflated. "He is not my husband," I clipped out, nearing the end of my patience. The cuff slowly let off pressure. "My husband hocked my house in Buckhead, then absconded to the South Pacific with his secretary. And my ungrateful son."

No! No! Stop! Brakes, please. Do not air your dirty laundry before a total stranger who'll probably repeat it over coffee in the staff lounge.

But my mouth kept right on going. "*And,* for the first time since the divorce, I finally wanted to kiss a man and did it, and then I get attacked by this insane raccoon, which bites him, too. And then I have to let him fly me down here in a helicopter as old as *Whirlybirds,* and now they've taken him away, when all I said was that I wanted to be sure he was okay after carrying me to the car, at a run."

The nurse stared at me. "That's awful. No wonder your blood pressure's one-sixty over one-forty."

"It's usually ninety over sixty," I snapped.

"Would you mind repeating what you just told me to an associate of mine? I think she—"

"Not on your life. I'm no psycho; I need my rabies vaccine. And if you give me antibiotics, I have to take two hundred milligrams of fluconazole a day during the entire course of treatment, and for a full week afterward, or the yeast in my body will eat me alive." I reached into my purse and produced the medical history I always carried with me. "Here's my history. All the meds are current."

Clearly unimpressed, she didn't even look at it, just unfolded it and put it under the sheet she'd been filling out.

I stood. "Where's the doctor? Let's get this show on the road."

"Are you always this belligerent?" she asked as if she were merely offering me a drink of water.

Belligerent? She didn't *know* from belligerent, but I kept my voice down. "Only when I've been bitten by a rabid raccoon."

"Do you happen to remember when you had your last tetanus shot?" she asked.

"Ages ago. At least ten years."

"Okay. That's all I need." She rose. "Let's get you into an examining room."

"What about my friend? It bit him, too, but they took him to Cardiac. He needs his rabies shot."

She patted my arm. "They're just checking him over to make sure he's well enough to take the shot."

"Considering the fact that death is the alternative, I'm pretty sure he wants the shot, regardless."

"Then he'll just have to sign a release."

A *release*? That was all she cared about?

She opened the back door into a corridor, then led me down a long, windowless hall to a cubicle six feet square with no windows. "The doctor will be with you shortly." She started to close the door.

"No, no, no, no," I minced out as politely as I could, already feeling like I'd been stuffed into a coffee can and lidded. "Could we please keep that open? I'm not good in small spaces with no windows."

"Sure." She left it open, but it wasn't much comfort, since it faced a dead wall.

In the quiet that followed, my bladder and my thirst both woke with a vengeance.

At least the air was moving. I sat on the examining table, antsy as a two-year-old.

The doctor came in a few minutes later. At least, I thought it was a few minutes. The room had no clock. He listened to my heart, looked at my throat, felt my glands, then said, "Try to get as comfortable as you can. We're thawing the vaccine for you and your friend now. Don't worry if it takes a while. You're well within the range of safety."

I nodded. "Thanks. Is it okay if I go to the bathroom?"

He nodded, pointing with his pen. "It's right down the hall to the left."

I felt much better minus all the iced tea I'd guzzled at the picnic, and returned to wait in my cubicle.

Then the oddest thing happened. One by one, staff members started showing up outside the door to stare at me, mostly one at a time, but occasionally, two.

None of them said a word, just stared.

By the fifth one, I couldn't help but ask, "Excuse me, but why are you staring at me?"

She smiled. "Sorry. I've never seen anybody who's been bitten by a rabid animal before."

For heaven's sake. What did they expect, foaming at the mouth? The *raccoon* hadn't even foamed at the mouth.

These people were medical personnel. Surely they knew the incubation period for rabies was at least two weeks.

Just when I was about to lie down and go to sleep, Clete came in, clutching a hospital gown closed behind him with one hand and carrying his clothes in a plastic bag with the other. His white socks were pulled up high on his muscular calves, and EKG terminals had been stuck all over his neck, upper arms, and chest.

He pointed to me. "You owe me for this. Major."

I laughed before I could catch myself, pointing back at him. "I'm sorry, but you make a pretty funny picture. Assuming you're okay."

"I'm okay." He sat in the lone chair, which wasn't close to big enough for a man of his stature. "Just waiting for the test results to make it official."

"Good. I was worried about you."

"Please." He lifted his palm toward me, fingers splayed, and looked out to make sure nobody had overheard me. "That's what started the whole thing in the first place."

I mimed zipping my lips.

Lord, he was cute, sitting there in that ridiculous gown, his long legs crossed at the ankle as he leaned back against the wall.

"Does anybody know you're here?" I asked, then kicked myself for mothering him.

He nodded.

I looked out the door to find another starer, a man, this time.

Clete scowled at him, and he went away. "What was that all about?"

"They've never seen anybody who's been bitten by a rabid animal before," I told him. "They never say anything. Just look. I guess they want us on their résumé."

"That's ridiculous." He stood and moved toward the door, flashing just a glimpse of the short white boxers beneath his gown. Call it a quirk, but I could never get serious about a man who wore briefs for anything but sports. "I'll close the door."

"Please. No." I grabbed the edge of the door. "I don't do so well without any windows."

"Sorry." He sat back down. "Did they say how long it would be? I want to take you to Poor Richard's for supper. Our first date. No pressure."

Despite all I'd eaten at the picnic, a nice steak and salad sounded awfully good. "The doctor just said they were thawing the vaccine, and not to worry if it took a while."

Shoot! I jumped up. "I forgot to call the others and tell them we were here!"

Clete waved me back down. "I called on my way from Cardiac. I think Eileen's more upset than they are."

That was a relief. I gripped the edge of the exam table and started to swing my legs. "My friends Maggie and Charlie live here, and say Poor Richard's is great. Fabulous steaks, and a great spinach salad with hot bacon dressing."

Clete ignored the small talk, cocking his head. "You're really not worried," he said as if it were a compliment.

I shrugged. "Don't get me wrong; I love this life. But if they were selling bus tickets to heaven, I'd buy the next one."

"Don't say that," he bit out.

I stretched. "Dying's scary, but not death."

Before he could respond, a cute girl in a white pantsuit with a yellow STUDENT PARAMEDIC tag bopped into the room. "Hi," she said to me. "Do you mind if I see your wounds and ask you a few questions?"

It was a teaching hospital. "No. That's fine," I told her. "Fire away."

She inspected our bites, then asked about the attack. I told her what happened, complete with sound effects, which clearly impressed her. Then, when she was about to leave, she asked one more question: "What were you doing right before the raccoon attacked you?"

Clete sat bolt upright in his chair and choked, then had a coughing fit.

Ignoring him, I focused on the student. "That question's rather personal," I confided to her.

She colored and hastened to say, "Oh. Sorry. I only meant . . . I mean, like, was there anything you did that might have set it off?"

"Better." I nodded in approval. "No. It went crazy, all by itself."

Red-faced, she thanked me and left us alone at last.

When she was gone, I bent my face into my hands in mock despair. "I cannot believe this. We're the local entertainment for this whole darn place."

"In that case," Clete said, "I think I'd better get dressed." He stood. "Please close your eyes. And don't look till I tell you to."

I heard him push the door almost shut, then the rustle of the plastic bag holding his clothes.

Followed by several short ripping sounds. I started counting. Four, five, six times.

I peeked through my fingers and caught Clete in his plain boxers, wincing as he rubbed a red bald spot on his chest where one of the EKG stickers had been.

That had to hurt. He had just enough body hair—not too little, not too much.

Then he turned around and bent to put on his jeans, giving me a very nice view of his boxers strained across a tight, tidy ass. And the scars above them, but the rear end won my attention.

I shut my eyes. Men his age weren't supposed to be built like that. But then again, women my age weren't supposed to be built like I was, either. Shows what hard work and lots of exercise can do. Maybe sixty really was the new forty. Boy, I hoped so.

I couldn't resist one more glimpse.

What was I thinking? Never in my life had I ever peeked at a man, even Harrison. Or imagined one without his clothes. Thank goodness I hadn't sunk that low.

Yet.

I heard Clete shrug on his borrowed shirt, tuck it in, then zip his jeans. Opening the door sent a nice wash of air my way. "Okay," he said. "You can look now."

He was slipping his feet into his Topsiders when I did.

"I'm getting fanny fatigue," I ventured, to fill the silence.

Clete sat down, clearly antsy himself. "I find that pacing helps."

"I'm not a pacer." I looked at the tattered *Golf Digest* by the sink. "I don't suppose they have any cards or games here."

"If they did," he said dryly, "I can guarantee you wouldn't want what came with them."

Germs. Of course. The magazines were probably rife with them, too.

I saw Clete look up toward the corridor, then suppress a smile. Following his line of sight, I found our student paramedic standing beside six other baby paramedics, still badgeless in their dark blue uniforms.

Trying not to laugh, I looked back at Clete, who was staring toward the ceiling.

Even the girl in the white uniform remained mute.

I shook my head with a quiet, "What I wouldn't give for a can of Reddi-wip right this moment."

Clete chortled in amusement.

"Monkeys in the zoo," I singsonged with the same inflection Drew Barrymore used when she studied E.T. in the closet.

Without looking down, Clete quoted what she'd really said, in the same inflection. "'Alligators in the sewer.'"

Ohmygoodness! My head pivoted faster than Linda Blair's in *The Exorcist*. Clete spoke movie!

I tested him with John Belushi from *1941*, dragging out, "'The radio's wrong.'"

He looked at me with the same serendipity I was feeling. "'Lemme hear yer guns. Nya, nya, nya, nya, nya, nya, nya, nya.'" He even did the hand motions.

"Agggh!" I crowed. "You speak movie?"

"'It just doesn't matter,'" he chanted, deadpan, from *Animal House*. "'It just doesn't matter.'"

Be still, my heart. "'*Double* secret probation,'" I quoted the dean from the same movie.

This could not be. "You really *do* speak movie."

He nodded. "Only the good ones. With a minor in fifties TV and Dick Van Dyke. Drives my family nuts."

"Mine, too." I might have to marry him, after all.

Marry? Was I crazy?

But a coincidence like that wasn't just a coincidence. It was a sign. "This is serious," I said, unable to look at him.

"I know."

Of all the crazy things, and all the people in this world . . .

I glanced into the hall and found the baby paramedics gone.

We sat there in awkward silence till the student paramedic breezed back in and plopped her purse on the counter. "I'm off, but I'm gonna stay and watch you get that shot," she announced.

Before I could think of a response, brisk footsteps preceded two nurses clad in cheerful print smocks, both holding up a formidable syringe in each hand, for a total of four.

"Who wants to go first?"

Clete pointed to me at the same time I raised my hand.

"Very good, Mrs. Cooper," the younger one said. "These are your injections. Two go into your upper arms. That's your rabies and the tetanus. Would you mind removing your little overshirt? Very cute, by the way."

"Thanks." I slipped it off, exposing my arms. The older one nodded to the student paramedic, who swabbed both my upper arms with alcohol, then stood back. Using eye contact only, the two nurses each gave me their injections at the exact same instant, emptying, then pulling them out at the same time, too.

"Boy. Y'all are good." I could barely see where they'd been.

"Sorry," the younger one said. "I know that was painful, but it seems to work best if we do it that way."

"Didn't even feel it." I was a career ballerina. Pain was relative, and those shots didn't even make it into the category.

"The next two, we have to give in the hip." A polite euphemism for the ass. "That'll be your rabies immune globulin and antibiotics."

"Will you give me the fluconazole by injection, too? Because I really get a serious kickback with candidiasis when I have to take strong antibiotics, and I'm violently allergic to any kind of fungus."

"We'll check with the doctor on that as soon as we finish." She probably thought I was just talking about the usual female rebound. I'd have to educate her later. And the doctor, if necessary.

Clete stood to leave. "I'll be back when you're done."

"Don't go far," the nurse cautioned. "You're next."

His only response was retreating footsteps.

When I turned to lie on my stomach, I saw that the baby paramedics were back, solemnly lined up in the hall.

The older nurse leaned close. "Would you like me to close the door?"

I shot her an evil grin, unzipping and unbuttoning my slacks as inconspicuously as possible. "No," I whispered. "If they want to see me get that shot, they're gonna have to look at my wrinkly old ass."

Both nurses chuckled. "I like you," the younger one said.

"Ditto," from the other.

Without further ado, I pulled up the back of my camisole, then shoved my pants down well past my fanny, giving it a wiggle as I did.

The baby paramedics gasped and snorted in shock, then fled, the boys laughing and the girls buzzing.

"Mission accomplished," I said into the paper under my face, and both shots went in at the exact same moment. After I pulled my pants back on and sat up to fasten them, both nurses gave me the thumbs-up.

"Mrs. Cooper," the older one said, "I do believe you have just entered this emergency department's Patient Hall of Fame. And not because of the bite that brought you here."

I tucked in my tank top. "I am humbled, and will do my best to live up to this great honor."

I'd just put my overshirt back on when Clete appeared. "The other room they had me in is now occupied by somebody who really seems to need it," he said. "But I found the doctor, and it's official: My heart is fine."

The older nurse changed the paper on the exam table. "Glad to hear it. If you'll just sit right here and roll up those sleeves, we'll be right back."

"Would you like me to close the door?" I asked when they were gone. "From the outside?"

"Not till they come back." He sat on the table. "What happened to the baby paramedics?"

Proud of myself, I said, "I mooned them, and they ran away. The boys thought it was funny, but the girls were horrified."

He shook his head, that wry expression on his face. "Only you."

"You could do it, too," I offered, deadpan. "I'll get them, if you want."

He shook his head no. "Might be too much for 'em, two ripe rear ends in a day."

Not old. Ripe. I liked it—except for the connotation of odor in one of its meanings, which definitely didn't apply.

"If you'll excuse me, then," I said, picking up my purse, "I'm going to call Mama and tell her all about what happened."

He looked up sharply.

"Just about the raccoon," I clarified. I waggled my fingers good-bye, then left.

Mama wasn't going to believe this.

Heck, I couldn't really believe it.

And all I'd wanted was a kiss or two.

No telling what the next few would end up causing.

· 22 ·

Quit overcomplicating everything. Sometimes things really
are what they seem to be. Enjoy.
—CISSY TO DAHLIA (AGE NINETEEN),
WHEN ASKED WHETHER OR NOT
TO ACCEPT THE RASNIKOV BALLET'S OFFER

. . . .

*A*FTER A BRIEF hop from the hospital to the deserted parking lot of a Hispanic grocery store across from Poor Richard's, supper proved my friend Maggie right. The steaks were great, as were the salads, but neither were as good as the company. Clete didn't talk about what had happened. Instead, we spent the evening categorizing and comparing our favorite movies, then our siblings', and had a ball. He didn't bat an eye at my aversion to anything occult, but we both agreed that *The Changeling* was really more of a psychothriller, and a great movie.

You can tell a lot about people by the movies they like. Iris hated *Braveheart* because of the violence and the ending. I loved it, because I closed my eyes in the gross parts and already knew from reading historical novels what was going to happen.

Clete said Hoke only liked comedies, particularly Mel Brooks's, but also the *Elf* guy's and all those Ben Stiller spoofs. Then we argued about *Blazing Saddles*, which Clete loved, but I considered stupid and childish.

We settled on picking *Young Frankenstein* as best black comedy/spoof, tied with *Dr. Strangelove*. *Grosse Point Blank* rated a close second.

I confessed that edge-of-your-seat thrillers had been way too intense for me since the divorce, as had anything about cheating, which included one of my perennial favorites, *Moonstruck*.

Clete confessed that after piloting medevac choppers to the hospital ships in Vietnam, blood and guts gave him flashbacks, so he'd shut his eyes in the gross parts of *Braveheart*, too.

By the time we moved on to books, the restaurant was closing.

The trip back wasn't nearly as scary as the one down. Maybe it was the fact that I couldn't see exactly how high we were in the darkness. Ted was waiting for us when we landed back at the hangar, but didn't attack us with questions. I liked him immediately, maybe because he was so laid-back. On the way home, he and Clete argued good-naturedly about Ted's taste in movies, some of which Clete had gotten way wrong.

When we drove up to Clete's front door, I briefly wondered if he'd kiss me good night in front of his minister brother, part of me wanting it, and part of me embarrassed at the prospect of Ted's seeing us smooch.

As it turns out, Clete did kiss me—on the forehead—followed by a murmured, "Time, it is."

The wanting part of me like to had a fit, but Ted's presence kept me from doing anything about it.

Unlike Ted, my sisters were all waiting inside to bombard me with questions after Clete and his brother headed back down the mountain.

Suddenly exhausted, I rubbed and flexed the sore arm where I'd gotten my tetanus shot, then asked them for a rain check.

Rose herded Iris away, while Vi took me to my room. Clete's room.

His bed felt like heaven. "Whew," I said, going boneless. "I had no idea how tired I was."

"No wonder," Vi said. "Here. Let me help you get those things off." She pulled off my flats, then tossed me my favorite Spoleto sleep-shirt, and I sat back up with effort.

After disappearing for a minute, she came back with a tall tumbler of ice water cradled in a paper towel. She looked at my ankle. "They didn't even bandage them."

I looked down, too sleepy to worry about it. "Nope." She handed me the water, and I sucked down half of it before my thirst was satisfied.

"Perfect." I put the tumbler onto the crystal wine coaster on the bedside table, then plopped back down on the pillows. "I don't think I've got the energy to brush my teeth," I confessed.

"That's okay." Vi pulled up the covers, then stroked my hair. "Nothing will rot out before tomorrow morning, I promise."

"Mmmm."

The light went out, then she stopped, silhouetted in the doorway. "Sleep as long as you want."

"Wonderful." Semiconscious, I rolled onto my side, pulling a pillow under my top knee, then hugged the one under my head like it was my mama's waist, burrowing into its softness.

I knew no more till the next afternoon, when Vi woke me with a soft knock. "Dahlia?"

I reared up in the dusky room to find the curtains drawn. "I'm up."

She paled when she saw me. "We were getting worried. You stopped snoring an hour ago, and Iris was afraid you'd up and died on us."

"Don't worry; I'm fine." I yawned hugely, then stretched, only to waken every aching muscle in my body. "Sore, but fine."

"You sure don't look fine," she said.

Boy, did I need to tinkle. "I'm okay," I said as I stood up. Then the Mack truck hit me.

Vi raced over and helped me into the bathroom. "Easy. Take it slow."

"They said I might be sore or have flulike symptoms, but I didn't know they meant *real* flu symptoms. I am seriously achy."

Vi made sure I didn't pass out while I took care of business, then she helped me back to bed.

"How's your stomach?" she asked as she arranged the covers.

"Fine. Empty."

"I'll get you something to eat, and your meds to take afterward." She started toward the door.

"Vi, you don't have to wait on me like this," I fussed halfheartedly, feeling guilty. "Y'all go out and have some fun. I'm fine."

She turned my way, frowning. "I looked at the hospital paperwork you left on the chair, to make sure you weren't missing any essential meds while we let you sleep. They gave you enough antibiotics yesterday to put you in bed for a month from the kickback, plus sixteen hundred milligrams a day for a week. Not to mention the rabies vaccine and gamma globulin. And you've still got four more vaccines to go. That spells Hiroshima for your weird immune system. You need to stay in that bed and rest and let us take care of you." Seeing my discomfort with the idea, she exhaled heavily. "Put the shoe on the other foot. How much fun could you have if I had your immune system and went through the same thing you just did?"

"Okay, okay." I surrendered. "I hereby promise to rest. Except for my stretches. If I skip those for even a few days, I'll draw up like a wet leather shoelace in an oven." I wasn't asking permission, just explaining.

"Fine. Do them," she said. "Just make sure one of us is there to help out if you get dizzy." She left.

Wondering if Clete was having the same side effects, I found his cell number on my pocket calendar, then dialed it.

Eileen answered. "Clete's cell phone."

"Oh. Hey, Eileen,"

"Dahlia!" She sounded really glad to hear from me. "How are you doin', girl?"

"Not so bad, considering. My sisters have ordered me to bed and are waiting on me hand and foot, but I'm just sore and tired. How's Clete doing?"

"*Sir Lancelot* hasn't complained. Never does. Got up early and went to look at some property he bought near town. Then he spent a few hours at the plant. Then, for the first time in history, he came home and took a nap." So he was tired, too. "I stole his cell phone so he could sleep." She paused, but I didn't have anything else to ask. "He's been down for quite a while. You want to talk to him?"

"No, please don't wake him." Guilt hit me in the heart. "But could you do me a favor, woman to woman?"

Eileen didn't hesitate. "It's yours, honey. Just ask."

"Could you call me and let me know how he's doing?"

"How many times a day?" she asked, her tone brisk. "Three? Five?"

I laughed. "Once will be fine. Unless something changes."

"You got it, sugar."

I looked at his beautiful room. "And if he gets sick, would you bring him home to his own bed? Men don't deal with sickness very well. I can bunk in with Vi. I hate to think of him being sick away from home."

"What about you?" she asked. "You're pretty far from home, yourself."

"Funny," I confessed. "I don't feel that way here." What Clete had said about the house came back to me, good reason for my feeling so at home there.

"Don't you worry," Eileen said. "If he gets sick, I'll do just that, even if I have to hog-tie him. Y'all can keep each other company on the patio. I told him from the beginning that yer sisters were chaperones enough, but once Clete gits somethin' in his mind, it ain't easy to change it. I'll call back this evenin' and give you an update."

"Thanks." I hung up, then lay back down, hoping Clete felt better than I did.

By Sunday night, I was feeling much better, but still pretty tired. My problem was the cure, not the cause. All those antibiotics and antifungals, on top of everything else.

According to Eileen, Clete bounced right back to normal after that one nap.

I'd just settled down in bed at eight when the phone rang. Usually, Iris picked up immediately, but this time it rang and rang, so I got it, instead.

Unknown on the caller ID. "Hello?"

"Dahlia," Clete's voice said, clearly glad it was me who answered. "How are you?"

"Much better, thanks," I said. "How are you?"

"Absolutely fine." After a brief pause, he confessed, "Actually, I already knew how you are. Iris has been giving me updates. I was really worried about you at first, and so was she."

"I have a confession to make, too," I reciprocated. "Eileen's been updating me."

"I know. She told me." The truth pact in action, again.

I didn't mind her telling him; I hadn't asked her not to.

"That's not the reason I called," he said. "I called to ask you out for a rabies shot and dinner at Poor Richard's tomorrow."

That was day three, time for another vaccine. Followed by day seven, fourteen, and twenty-eight, exactly, no leeway. The people at Northeast General had scheduled us to take them in one of their smaller facilities ten miles north of town.

"It's short notice, I know," Clete said, "but I had a feeling you might be heading that way, yourself."

I chuckled, then balanced my fatigue against having to get in that helicopter again. "Do you feel up to driving, this time, instead of taking the helicopter?" I asked him. "I'd like to keep my blood pressure down in normal range."

"Sure." I could hear the smile in his voice. "We can leave early enough in the afternoon to get our shots, then have supper."

"Sounds great to me. As long as you don't make it a high-speed chase. I'm still jumpy from that trip down the mountain."

"Scout's honor, we will take the slow road and absolutely amble."

I could get used to the whole boundaries thing.

"Then it's a date."

And a lovely date it was. We stopped at several shops and galleries on the way down, checking out the local artists. When we got to the smaller emergency room, there were only two other people in the waiting area, and we barely caused a stir.

At supper afterward, we had the same secluded booth and the same waitress we'd had on Friday. We talked about books and politics and Cissy, laughing a lot. Clete was one of the most well-read men I'd ever met.

And when he brought me home, we shared several more of those very great kisses in the shadow of the sheltered doorway, this time without any major revelations or talk of the future.

It felt so good to have a man's arms around me. The touch and smell and feel of him were so clean and steady, it made me forget everything else—including the dead bodies from the root cellar.

By the time I hit the hay, though, I was beyond ready.

The next morning, I popped up at my first whiff of coffee, expecting to feel even better, but there was that Mack truck again. It knocked me clean into Thursday.

Right after supper Thursday night, Clete called and asked me out again, saying he'd like to take me to a place called Luna this time.

It surprised me, how glad I was to be invited. Though the trip loomed long and daunting, I still didn't want to take the helicopter. So I told him that would be fine, but I might have to lie down in the backseat with my pillow on the way home, so we called it a date.

Our shots were uneventful, and the food at Luna was great, but by the time we finished, Clete looked worried, and I was *so* glad to stretch out in the backseat with my pillow.

Standing beside the open car door above my head, he leaned down and kissed my forehead. "Have you talked to the doctor about how tired you are?" he asked.

"The ER nurse," I said, shifting my pillow. "The doctor on duty said fatigue wasn't one of the listed side effects. So I called my friend at the CDC, and she talked to one of their rabies specialists, who also said fatigue wasn't one of the side effects. She probably just looked it up on their medical network, same as the ER doctor. Then she told me to talk to my primary."

"And?"

"And, my primary moved away three months ago because her husband got a residency at Johns Hopkins, so I haven't had a chance to break in a new one."

Clete looked down into my face. "Dahlia, it's totally out of character for you to be this exhausted," he worried aloud. "We've got a week till the next shot. Let me take you to Mayo, or someplace where they understand your condition."

"That's the sweetest thing anybody's ever offered to do for me," I said, truly touched. "But I'll be okay. It's probably just from the antibiotics. They always throw me for a loop. I'll sic Iris on the Internet to see what she can find out. She loves to do things like that, and thanks to your satellite hookup, she can."

He wasn't convinced. "If you're not better after the next shot, I might just have to kidnap you."

I reached up and drew his head down alongside mine. "My Sir Galahad. But I promise, I'm not a damsel in distress." Well, maybe I was, but I refused to admit it.

He nestled his face against me, inhaling my hair, then straightened and closed the door.

We hadn't gone but a few miles before I fell sound asleep. He must have carried me in when we got home, because I don't remember anything till I woke up late the next morning.

That time, it was *two* Mack trucks. On my way to the bathroom, my heart beat so fast I couldn't seem to catch my breath, but I didn't tell my sisters.

Large doses of antibiotics can cause anemia. That was probably it. At least I was through taking those. I just needed more red meat and broccoli to build my blood back up, but I was so tired, I didn't even want to eat.

Eileen called regularly to report that Clete was fine, but he worried about me. Then she always made me laugh with one dry take or another on life in their big, bumptious family. I was beginning to like her a lot. She and Vi were definitely cut from the same bolt, straightforward and no-nonsense, with hearts of gold.

Rose and Iris and Vi came in often on any pretext, but I just slept, or pretended to so I wouldn't have to talk. I didn't even feel like bridge or backgammon.

I heard them whispering outside my door, but didn't even care. I just wanted to sleep, and thanked God that I was in a place that wouldn't make me sicker.

Tuesday afternoon, Iris came in with half a truckload of e-mails and Web site info from jillions of hits about my yeast. "It isn't easy sifting through all the junk and wonder-cure-claims info," she said, "but I finally came across some legitimate doctors and researchers who seem credible, so I contacted them all, and got differing responses. There's one at the Mayo Clinic who said he'd be glad to call your primary for a phone consult, but when I told him yours had just moved away, he looked through his files and came up with a Dr. Farkum in Asheville who's doing a study about the effects of antibiotic therapies on people with chronic fungal infections that weren't caused by AIDS or chemo. So I called and talked to *him*."

Clearly, she was trying to make amends, and I was grateful, but the hurt she'd caused me still lingered heavy between us. Unlike her, I couldn't just pretend it had never happened.

But Iris could get through to the president if she had a mind to, and she'd found an expert to help me. "He can't put you in the current study because of the rabies shots," she explained, "but he said he could help you get through this and get things under control. He got really excited when I told him about the rabies, though. Said it would make a perfect basis for another study, specific to that. He called me back in person with the appointment, and told me he'd already contacted the CDC and NIH about referring rabies-bite victims with chronic fungal infections." She handed me his e-mail. "You, my dear, are going to advance the base of scientific knowledge."

"Glad to be of service." At least that could benefit other people like me, but I doubted there were more people out there like me. Chronic yeast sufferers who'd been bitten by rabid animals? Probably three in the whole world. I had to laugh.

"What?" Iris asked when I did.

She wouldn't get it. "You are amazing, that's what." It was the best I could do.

She nodded, pleased. "Your appointment with Dr. Farkum is at eleven. Clete's picking you up at eight tomorrow morning. I'll bring you breakfast at seven, with plenty of protein, then we'll all help you get ready."

Another peace offering—breakfast in bed—but that only made things wonderful in TV commercials.

"So Clete knows about this." Not that I minded, but I was turning out to be a full-time job.

"He's the reason I got through to that guy at Mayo," Iris said. "And Dr. Farkum. I swear, Clete's more connected than any politician I ever met."

"Hmm." That sounded suspiciously Harrisonesque. At least Clete wasn't a developer, God forbid.

An awful lot of men headed for the hills when confronted by anybody else's chronic health problems, even their wives'. Harrison hadn't wanted to hear a word about mine—it was too inconvenient and embarrassing that I couldn't eat what everybody else ate or drink what everybody else drank—so I'd dealt with it alone for the past twenty years. But Clete didn't seem the slightest bit put off or embarrassed about it, just accepted me as I was, weirdnesses and all.

Which was more than great, another strong tug in his direction. If a person like me married somebody like that, she'd be blessed.

Not that I could ever marry anybody this late in the game. I snored like a yard blower, had to wear a bite guard to bed, and would either have to blindfold my husband every night, or sleep in makeup for the rest of my life. I'm serious. Without makeup, I really did look like one of the aliens in *Close Encounters of the Third Kind*: featureless, except for my nostrils and irises. The effect is jarring.

Then again, I'd read that people could have eyebrows and eyeliner tattooed on . . . and lipstick. But the thought of it gave me the willies.

As for my appointment in Asheville the next day, let me just say one thing: It sure was nice finally to be taken seriously by a doctor who knew I wasn't a hypochondriac and offered me hope of improvement.

Well, maybe two things: It sure was nice to get all those tests for free.

Okay, three: Four emergency rooms across America had already responded to Dr. Farkum's request for referrals.

Imagine that. Maybe I wasn't quite as weird as I thought, but I was still too weird for somebody as normal as Clete.

· 23 ·

There can be no joy for the gifted unless they exercise those gifts.
Then, even when they're miserable, they're happy.
—CISSY

....

*W*HILE I WAS lolling around in Clete's bed, Hilltop was declared borer-free, then unwrapped and, thanks to Clete, cleaned within an inch of its life. Vi was helping me pack to move back there Thursday morning when the doorbell rang. I took advantage of her answering it by sitting down to rest. Then she hurried back and closed the door behind her. "It's Clete," she said, grabbing my brush, then pulling the covered stretchy from my haphazard ponytail. "He wants to talk to us all, together."

I looked in the mirror and Casper—with dark circles under his eyes—looked back.

"Makeup!" I said in a stage whisper.

"Wait. Hair, first." She brushed through my long hair, then deftly sectioned just above my ears and drew the top back into a tight little braid. "I always liked your hair this way." Satisfied with the results, she put down my brush and stood. "Now, makeup. I'll go tell Iris and Rose."

By the time I put on my eyes, then covered the deep circles beneath them and brushed a little instant tan onto my cheeks and forehead, you almost couldn't tell I'd been under a rock for the past two weeks.

To counteract my sallowness, I threw on a pink knit top with slim, three-quarter sleeves and a sweetheart neckline, then got into a pair of gray capris—just barely.

Shoot! Lying around like a yam was starting to make me look like one.

I slipped on some comfy dark gray canvas flats with pink polka dots (Marshall's, $15.99), then, breathless, sat down and took several long, slow, deep breaths to make sure I remained conscious all the way to the great room. To paraphrase the Three Stooges, slowly I rose. Inch by inch, step by step . . .

I found Clete sitting on the sofa like a guest in his own house. He stood the minute he saw me, his expression relieved. Thank goodness for bronzer and concealer. Actually, it felt good to be up and dressed.

Stopping well short of him, I left plenty of room between us. "Hi."

"Hi."

I lowered myself into one of two facing pairs of club chairs at each end of the sofa.

He took one at the opposite end, leaving the sofa for the others, and looked across the long coffee table at me, the seconds stretching to a minute of strained silence.

Why did it feel so awkward? I was a woman well past my prime, not afraid of anything, but when we saw each other, I felt like a dateless sixteen-year-old.

And he acted like a knob-kneed, junior varsity cross-country runner at a cotillion, totally out of his element.

"I hate this part," he said quietly, his gaze on the hand-hooked rug.

I relaxed a bit. "Me, too. We're friends now. Why does this always happen when we first see each other?"

He peered out the window. "Probably because I'd rather we were doing something else."

Like stretching out with my head in his lap, watching a good movie on the big TV. I sighed. "Me, too."

His expression brightened. Obviously, he'd been thinking of something more intimate.

My neck and ears shot up to a hundred and five degrees in embarrassment.

"Well, in that case," he said, "can I interest you in a rabies shot and dinner tomorrow?"

"No." That took care of his smug expression. "But you can interest me in a rabies shot and *lunch*."

He chuckled. "Done."

After another lapse in conversation, he peered at me, earnest. "There's something else I'd like to ask you."

I prayed it wasn't anything serious. I wasn't up to serious. "Ask away."

"Will you be my date for the Fourth of July barbecue and parade? You and Rose and Vi and Iris can ride in my boat for the parade." The traditional restored and decorated Chris-Craft promenade. "My nieces and nephews have great plans for the decorations. We're thinking a win, this time."

On the surface, a most appealing prospect—as long as I could sit down. I was beginning to get cabin fever. But if things at Lake Clare still worked the way they used to, I wasn't so sure. "I don't know," I said. "Wouldn't that send a signal . . . I mean, if you took me, people might get the wrong idea."

"What wrong idea?" he asked, all innocence. Now he was having fun with me.

"You know perfectly well. That we're exclusive . . . or something. It's the *something* that worries me." Call me Pollyanna if you want to, but for me, sex meant marriage, and I didn't want people thinking otherwise.

He nodded, then peered my way. "Have you been out with anybody since your divorce?"

"Lord, no. My life is complicated enough without . . . *dating*." So why did it sound so stupid, saying it?

"So you haven't been out with anybody else." Clete remained calm and objective, simply stating facts. "How many times have we been out together?"

I counted our shots: day one, day three, day seven. Then Dr. Farkum. "Four." Friday would be five.

"And how was it for you?"

A big smile escaped before I could edit it out. "It was fun. Very fun. Except the helicopter part."

That clearly made him happy. "Have you gone out with anybody else during that time?"

"You know I haven't." I wished he'd get to the point.

He leaned back, a droll cast to his expression. "That's it, then. It's official."

Alarm bells went off. "What's official?"

My sisters chose just that moment to come in, betraying the fact they'd been eavesdropping with "What's official?" from Iris.

Clete rose, smiling. "Your sister and I are going steady."

I laughed, partly from relief, and partly because of embarrassment. Going steady, indeed.

He came over and granted me a stiff little bow. "Would you prefer my ID bracelet, or my senior ring? All you have to do to break us up is give it back, and I'll honor your decision."

He wasn't making it easy to say no.

It was just a joke, anyway, nothing serious.

At summer's end, I was going back to Atlanta, where I belonged, and he was staying at the lake, where he belonged. We both knew it, but that didn't mean we couldn't have a little fun till then. Except for the shots, my "dates" with Clete were the first fun I'd had in eons.

My sisters peered at me, brows sky-high in anticipation as I considered.

I let eenie-meenie-miney-moe decide. "The ID bracelet, I think."

The girls exploded with cheers and clapping and hugs all around, making *way* too big a deal out of it.

Clete knelt before my chair, then drew from his pocket a slim, gold ID bracelet that was far too small for him, but just right for my wrist. His name was carved in a no-nonsense font into the slightly curved plate. All caps, but not too large. As he fastened it on, he glanced at me with mischief in his eyes. "Lighten up, Dahlia," he said quietly. "All this means is that you won't date anybody else while we're seeing each other. If you want to break up, you don't even have to tell me. Just send it back."

My sisters crowded around to see it, chattering up a storm. "Eighteen carat," Vi whispered in my ear, as if it made a difference, which it didn't. The bracelet was his, not mine.

When they'd had their fill of inspecting it, I extended my wrist to see how it looked on me. "It's beautiful, Clete. How did you know I'd say yes? And that I'd pick the bracelet?"

"I didn't know you'd say yes. I just hoped you would. As for the choice . . ." His smile spread when he pulled from the other pocket a heavy senior ring sized down with wax, then extended it toward me on his open palm. " 'Be prepared' doesn't just apply to Girl Scouts."

I picked up the ring and studied the inscription. On one side, *1966*, on the other, *Rabun County High*.

I handed it back. "What if I'd said no?"

Those brown eyes danced. "You didn't."

"I could have."

He looked at me with "that look" I'd been missing for so long. "But you didn't. I'll accept that as my miracle of the day."

"Okay, then," I said. "Now that we're going steady, could we dispense with the initial awkwardness when we first see each other?"

"Works for me," he said, his eyes alive. "What do you suggest we do instead?"

Boy, was it hard not to love that man. "How about hugging?"

"An excellent suggestion."

But when I opened my arms, he'd already stood and turned to the others, who laughed and pointed at me. Good natured, but laughter nonetheless.

"I have an invitation for all of you," he told them, "but first, there's the matter of the house to be settled."

Talk about throwing a bucket of cold water on everything.

All our expressions clouded, and the others subsided onto the sofa like see no evil, hear no evil, speak no evil. "I thought Cissy already paid for that," Iris said, defensive.

"She did," Clete hastened to clarify. "No, I'm talking about *this* house."

We all frowned.

Clete sat in the chair beside me and propped his elbows on the upholstered arms, his fingers intertwined. "I know I said you could stay here till Hilltop was aired out, but it's ready now, and I don't think you should go back."

My sense of relief surprised me. But we had to go back to meet the terms of the will.

"The mildew went rampant after we wrapped the place and let it sit in the heat for more than a week. I've had a top-notch cleaning crew and a mildew-abatement team in there, but the mildew guys said anything they do, short of setting out huge pans of formaldehyde and sealing everything back up for a month—which came with no guarantees—is like trying to put out a forest fire with a candle snuffer."

His sandy brows furrowed. "So I'm asking you to stay here, if that's okay with you. Work over there if you need to, using the respirators, but it's not healthy for any of you to sleep there, especially Dahlia. Under the circumstances, the judge said that wouldn't break the condition, because the will provides an out if Hilltop isn't safe to occupy, which it isn't." He cocked a thumb toward the far slope of the ridge. "I've got seven houses down the ridge to choose from."

"We accept," the others said in unison, grinning like they all had oversized false teeth.

"But Clete," I told him. "We've already kept you away from home so long. Don't you miss your room? Your things? Your solitude?"

He was pleased by my concern. "Dahlia, in the last twenty years I've had enough solitude for three lifetimes. I just want to be sure you and your sisters are safe for the rest of the summer. Mr. Johnson agrees with me."

The mention of Mr. Johnson made me remember bumping into Clete there, and how clearly Clete hadn't wanted to be seen there. And those plats he was hiding. I made a mental note to ask him about it when we were alone. "So I guess we'll stay, then," I conceded.

"Good." He relaxed.

"Only if you let us cook for ourselves," Iris told him. "We've imposed on Katie long enough."

The others agreed, albeit a bit wistfully.

"That's Katie's call to make, not mine," he said. "Why don't you ask her about that?"

His brows lowered a bit at me, then he got up. "I'm glad to see you feeling better, Dahlia, but I don't want to wear you out. If it's all right with you, I'd like to leave early for our shots and take you by some property I just bought before we head for Gainesville. There's somebody there who's dying to meet you. I promise, it won't take long."

Sounded like a big day, but after all Clete had done for me, I couldn't refuse. "Great. What time should I be ready?"

"Nine-thirty?"

"It's a date." I made up my mind to be ready and able.

When I started to escort him to the door, the others took a powder, leaving us alone in the foyer.

Clete grasped my wrist with his big, work-worn hand as if to seal the bracelet beneath it to my skin. Then he guided my hand to his side and kissed me, not as urgently as before, but more with wonder and relief.

For me, it felt like coming home, drowning out any doubts or questions.

Afterward, we stood there hugging for a while. It felt so sweet, tears welled in my eyes. So much of me wanted to take Clete at face value and give it a rip, but Harrison had left me far too wounded and wary for that. Caution, I told myself. Caution. If you let yourself care, it will hurt too much to leave. "I guess you'd better go," I whispered at last. "Wouldn't want to make you late to Mr. Johnson's."

A subtle tightening of Clete's muscles surprised me, shattering the safe, happy bubble we'd been in. "Dahlia, I . . ."

I waited, but nothing followed for long seconds. Then he gave me a good squeeze before he broke away. "See you tomorrow." He didn't meet my eyes.

What was it he was afraid to tell me? Something big. Something bad. I could feel it.

And then he was gone.

As I watched him leave, my doubts returned, but by then Rose and Iris and Vi were too busy inundating me with questions about what had happened before they got there, so I gladly shifted my attention to that.

Everybody has secrets, he had told me, and I had a feeling I didn't want to know the one that had stolen the comfort from our embrace.

"Y'all," I told my sisters, "you are making way too much out of this whole going-steady thing."

. . . .

AT NINE-THIRTY SHARP the next morning, Clete drove up with coffee for both of us. I surprised myself with how glad I was to see him, and how satisfying I found his welcome hug. Then I climbed into his SUV and buckled up, and we were off into the unseasonably cool and comfortable morning.

"So, what's the deal with this property you want to show me, and how do I figure into it?" I asked.

"You'll see," he said, his smile smug.

"Clete, I don't like mysteries." It sure was nice feeling free to speak my mind. "What's the scoop?"

"It used to be old Wayman Boggs's farm," he said, "two hundred acres of great bottomland on the river, halfway to Clayton, with a sturdy farmhouse and huge barn on high ground, overlooking it. He left it to the county, but they don't want to maintain it, so they've offered to sell it to the Arts Council for a dollar and other valuable considerations, in exchange for honoring Wayman's wishes for the property. As chairman of the Arts Council board, I got delegated to make the final decision. I figured you could check out the facilities and give me some expert input."

An arts council in Rabun County. Who'da thunk it?

I liked being considered an expert, having my opinion valued. "Sure. What were his wishes?"

"That," he said, "will have to wait till we get there."

About three miles past Alley's Store in Lakemont—which hadn't changed a whit since I was a kid—we turned down a well-graveled road that made a shallow ford across the crystal-clear river, then skirted acres and acres of bottomland sown in healthy corn. Up the hill ahead, a sturdy white two-story farmhouse with wide verandahs presided over the little valley, and behind it, three-foot-tall white letters blazoned BARN DANCE across the front of a huge, old-fashioned red barn. In smaller letters below that, MUBBIE GROGAN SCHOOL OF DANCE was followed by a local phone number.

Mubbie. Never heard of that name before.

"Who's Mubbie?" I asked.

"A friend from high school." Clete pulled into the graveled parking area behind the house, passing a small Honda, a faded pickup that had seen better days, and several bicycles parked near the barn, to pull into the shade of a towering hemlock by the house. "She moved to Atlanta, then came back up here to teach dancing. She's on the board of the Arts Council, too."

A committee of two? I got out, reveling in a wafting breeze.

Clete guided me toward the verandah. "We've had an awful lot of really talented people retire here over the past decade."

Close up, I saw that the house had clearly been well maintained, its paint fresh white against the dark green foliage of blooming hydrangeas around its base. Native species prospered everywhere, in shade and sun.

"Wayman must have been some gardener," I said, appreciating the subtle texture and order of his yards.

Clete nodded. "Between him for the crops and his wife Miz Bonnelle for the flowers, they taught me most of what I know about growing things. I was probably about nine when I started catching a lift across the lake when the Captain went for the milk. Cissy gave me her old bike so I could ride over here and crop a share with Waylan." Yet another intersection between the Slocums' needs and Cissy's generosity. "We sold some to the tourists, and Miz Bonnelle canned or froze the rest for us. She even let Mama keep it here. We didn't even have power then, much less a freezer."

It still baffled me how Cissy could be so perceptive and caring to Clete and his family, yet so thoughtless and aloof with Mama and my sisters.

I reverted to our previous topic of conversation. "How many people do you have on the Arts Council board?"

"Twenty-six. We've got oil painters and authors and singers," Clete enumerated, "and musicians and wood-carvers and sculptors." Our footsteps met with solid support on the gray-green-painted porch boards. He pointed toward town. "A world-class metal sculptor just finished a house and studio on the river about a mile up. And we have a thriving handmade-pottery co-op. People come from all over the country to the three-week summer camp they have at the conference center in Tiger."

He sounded just a bit too much like a chamber of commerce promotional blurb trying to entice new businesses to the area.

We arrived at four white rockers on the front and sat. Looking out over the upland cove of corn, I soaked in the timeless sense of nature's rhythms. "This is beautiful. What did Waylan want the county to do with it?"

Clete's expression was filled with happy ghosts from the past. "To keep the bottomland for farming. It's about a hundred fifty acres. The Arts Council kicked the idea around and came up with a plan to make it a handicapped-accessible organic community garden, available to any county resident, with paved paths to every quarter-acre plot. The county's agreed to put up and maintain a nine-foot fence around the fields, to protect the crops from deer and rabbits, plus plow every spring." He pointed to the far end of the road frontage, masked by a dense stand of trees. "And they'll donate free mulch from the three-acre recycling site we're giving them just past those trees."

The project sprang vivid in my mind.

"From May through August," he went on, "we'll provide advisors on-site four days a week from nine to four—mostly local volunteers, a lot of them master gardeners and farm experts—to answer questions for any-body who commits to a plot." He pointed to the center of the field. "We'll offer home-composting equipment to the participants, and there'll be a gazebo-style pavilion in the center with air-conditioned bathrooms and covered porches with ceiling fans and rockers. A good place to connect and talk to other gardeners."

It sounded wonderful. "You thought of all that, didn't you?"

He reddened, smiling as he nodded. "I told them I wouldn't be on the board unless they included gardening as an art. Too many kids today have no idea how to grow things, especially how to do it in harmony with nature."

Clete's dream was contagious. I turned to the house, looking through its sparkling windows into the tall-ceilinged parlor crammed with gen-erations of furniture styles, complete with a huge grand piano. "And what about the house?"

"We want to use it as a music conservatory: instrument classes, recit-als, practice rooms. We'll have to gut it, replumb, insulate, rewire, and put in new windows and central heat and air, but the floors are gorgeous, and the bones are strong. We've already had lots of local craftspeople volunteer to help with the renovation, training apprentices from the lo-cal high school as they do the work."

Again, I saw Clete's imprint. Apprentices would learn, experienced craftspeople would teach, and a wonderful facility would be born. "And the barn?"

He stood, his smile telling me that we'd finally gotten to the point of this trip. "A performing arts center. Come on. Tell me what you think of it."

We crossed the wide, graveled parking area, then stepped through an access door into a masterpiece of peg-and-beam construction. "It's huge." The floor was narrow tongue-and-groove, softened by age—just like they used to have at the Kress's on Peachtree at Tenth in Atlanta. I heard clump-ing and taps from a closed area above the wide stage, and saw the dance school's logo on a door beside the platform.

Clete brought me a folding chair from the perimeter of the dance floor. "Here. You just sit tight. I'll be right back with Nell Welch. She's been hounding me mercilessly to let her meet you. So has Mubbie." Once I was seated, he crossed to the door and opened it to reveal a wide stairway, then closed it behind him.

After just a minute or so, I heard a clatter of footsteps down the stairs, and the door burst open to reveal a young ballerina of indeterminate adolescence in toe shoes. She literally danced across the thirty yards between us, and I saw my young self in her joy and energy. Obviously, an amazing raw talent, but not well trained.

Mubbie and Clete came grinning behind her.

Nell ended up bowing dramatically at my feet. "I can't believe you're really here," she panted out. "The real Dahlia Barrett. This is *such* an honor, Miz Barrett."

I lifted her chin and saw the same fire that had raged in me when I was her age. "It's Dahlia Cooper, now, but you can call me Dahlia."

She rose, stepping back to a respectful distance. "I'm Nell." She regarded me as if I were the Second Coming. "I've prayed and prayed that God would send somebody, and He did. He sent you."

I wasn't comfortable being idolized, and realized Clete had set me up for this . . . whatever it was.

Clete and Mubbie finally got there. "Dahlia," Clete introduced, "this is my good friend Mubbie Grogan."

Mubbie all but shook my arm off. "This is such an honor, Miz Barrett. *Such* an honor. I was so hoping you'd get a chance to meet Nell and see her dance while you're here. She's the most talented dancer I've ever had, but I was never much on ballet, and I thought maybe . . . if you saw her dance, you might know of somebody who could tutor her."

Clete had a definite "gotcha" look in his eyes. "Nell's mother has MS," he said, "so Nell needs to stay close to home, but I was hoping you might agree to teach her for the rest of the summer. Whatever time you could spare."

Nell and Mubbie hugged each other in desperate anticipation.

"For free, of course," he clarified, the amusement in his face deepening.

I would have agreed anyway, but it annoyed me that Clete had made it impossible for me to say no without looking like a cruel, heartless monster.

"I'd be delighted to," I said. "But I haven't been feeling very good lately, so would it be all right if we worked at Clete's to begin with?"

Mubbie jumped in with, "Oh, that wretched raccoon. Of course that'll be all right. I'll bring her. Anytime before four on a weekday would be fine."

"Aaagggh! Thank you, thank you, thank you!" Nell started bouncing and leaping and hooting for joy, then streaked back to the stairs, probably to tell her friends. I thought of the audition scene from *Flashdance*, and couldn't help laughing.

"God bless you," Mubbie said. "That girl's had so much heartache in her life. Dancin's the one thing that sets her free. Tell me the truth. Do you think she's got a chance?"

I considered the energy in her leaps and the suppleness in her movements, assessing her bone structure and the lean muscle of her body. "Absolutely. She just needs training."

"I knew it!" Mubbie crushed me against her, clapping my back so hard I almost lost my breath. "I knew it!"

Clete laughed out loud, circling Mubbie's waist from behind and literally lifting her off me. "Down, girl. Don't want to squeeze the life out of her before she even has a chance to help Nell."

After an embarrassing profusion of thanks and *see you soon*s, we got back to the SUV. I waited till we were well out of sight to turn on Clete with an emphatic, "Shame on you, Clete Slocum. I would gladly have taught that girl while I'm here, *for free,* but I certainly don't appreciate being set up like that. Now she'll never know if I did it of my own free will, or because you left me no choice."

Slowing for the stream, Clete refused to be intimidated. "Number one, you perfectly well could have said no. Those rabies shots are a plenty good excuse. And number two, Nell doesn't care if I put a gun to your head. All she cares about is that you agreed to teach her. You ballet girls tend to be a bit focused when it comes to dancing."

"That's putting it mildly. But she really does remind me of me at that age. Of course, I'd been taking ballet at a good school since I was four." At the expense of my sisters. I let out a long sigh, suddenly very tired and deflated. I stared, sightless, out the windshield.

Clete frowned, capturing my cheek with his right hand and gently turning my face back toward him. "You are up to it, aren't you? 'Cause if you're not, we could postpone this a few weeks."

"I'm fine. Nell just needs some retraining on the basics, then lots of practice. Most of my input will be verbal, so I could do it lying down."

"I'll have Hoke and Jack move one of the chaises into the workout room and put up a barre. You can show them where it needs to go." He still looked worried. "You're sure you're well enough?"

I nodded. "I'm okay." I reclined my seat. "But I think I'll take a nap till we get to lunch." Something I'd never done before the rabies shots.

When I woke, Clete was leaning over me with the softest look in his eyes. "Ready to eat?"

Logy, I stretched, arching my torso, and Clete couldn't resist the chance to smooth his palm down my ribs, then bend close for a slow kiss that turned to fire.

Wow. Now, *that* was my kind of wake-up call, and boy, did I ever wake up, especially the parts I'd put to sleep since my marriage.

After that, even the excellent home cooking at the Longstreet Café was an anticlimax. Everything was anticlimax, including the shots.

Worn out after we left the emergency room, I fell asleep again on the way home, waking only when the car stopped somewhere in between.

I opened my eyes to find Clete watching over me just as before, with the same conclusion, but this time, he drew me to my feet before kissing stars into my peripheral vision.

After he tore himself away, he let out a long, slow exhale, then said, "I made dinner plans for us. Or I could take you back home to bed."

The "back home to bed" sounded seriously tempting, sending a wrench of desire through me.

"We're close to home," he said. "But I'll be happy to do what you want."

What I wanted was for him to come home and go to bed with me, but that wasn't in my "personal value set," as they called it in our politically correct era. So I settled for food. "Let's eat."

I finally focused on my surroundings and realized that we were at the base of Eileen's driveway. "Oh."

Clete looked sheepish. "Honesty compels me to tell you it's an ambush. Most of the family's here. They've been badgering me to let them all meet you. But you don't have to go if you don't want to."

"Of course I want to." We were going steady, after all. "As long as they're clear that there's no long-term significance to this."

He cocked a wry half-frown. "I already told them. Maybe you'll have better luck convincing them than I have."

I chuckled. "Bring 'em on."

I went inside and met way too many people to figure out exactly who went with who, but I had a ball and ate way too much fabulous food. Clete stuck close, helping me with names and connections. I counted thirty-four people, give or take a few—because none of the little ones stayed in one place long enough for me to be sure I hadn't already counted them. As for Clete's seven siblings, the ghosts of their childhoods seemed to have made them even closer and more appreciative of the lighter side of life. Even usually dour Hoke took turns holding all the babies and making them laugh, his own smile transforming his face.

I wasn't so naïve that I thought they were without problems. With that many people, I knew there were bound to be the usual traumas and challenges of life, but nobody focused on those. Sullen teenagers were ignored. Screaming babies were whisked from the room. Cousins played with cousins, the boys deviling the girls till a nearby grown-up broke it up. But mostly, there was happy chatter about the mundane happenings of life.

None of Clete's brothers or sisters or their spouses sat me down and grilled me. They just subtly observed me as I interacted with the family, then held my own at a rousing game of Spoon after the babies and grandbabies had been put down in a room full of porta-cribs.

If I had to sum it up in two words, they'd be *life* and *love*—rare things in this crazy world.

When it came time to leave, I found myself wishing I didn't have to. Wishing I didn't have to leave Clete at summer's end. But those were just childish wishes. My life was elsewhere.

Not that I'd mind teaching ballet at the new arts farm. I could always do a special summer ballet camp. Maybe that was just a childish dream, too, but it didn't feel like one. It felt like peace.

Yet home was far away, along with everything I did and everything I was.

And if I wasn't careful, Clete could end up ruining it all, including my heart.

· 24 ·

....

*N*ELL STARTED COMING to Clete's exercise room for tutoring sessions on Saturdays and Sundays after church. All it took was encouragement and proper instruction, and she burst into bloom as a dancer—far better than I'd have been in her place.

All the frustrations of dealing with Buckhead stage mothers evaporated, and I was caught up in the joy of what the dance had been for me, and now her. Nell was so gifted and so grateful and so teachable, I could hardly wait for our lessons.

Since my sisters insisted I rest till I'd finished my shots and gotten back my energy, Clete and I began doing more and more things together when I wasn't teaching, many of them mundane, yet always enjoyable. Slowly, I came to know his family and his work through the countless ordinary errands that connected them. He made it so easy, so comfortable, to fall into depending on his wry, quiet presence. Not that he infringed on my independence. He always asked for and respected my decisions, something totally new for me.

I liked it, and him, more and more, even though I knew that the more I cared, the bigger piece of myself I'd have to leave behind at summer's end. But because of all the shots I'd taken, I didn't have the energy to worry about that.

Before I knew it, I settled into a routine of rest and tutoring and spending time with Clete and playing bridge or backgammon with my sisters when they weren't working at Hilltop.

Then the bishop called and said he'd had a wedding cancellation the following Saturday, so we notified the caterer, then put up flyers inviting the county to come to Cissy's memorial service at eleven in the morning, expecting a small crowd. To our surprise, the Lake Clare Association canceled the dance for that night out of respect for Cissy. Even more surprising, several hundred people crowded the orchard for the service, each of them conveying their condolences to Clete, then to us, making it clear they'd come more for him than for any other reason. Despite the strain between me and Iris, we presented a united front and thanked everyone for coming.

During the brief rite, Clete stood apart, his features etched with profound grief that showed just how much he'd loved Cissy—maybe even more than I had. When our eyes met across the crowd, it became a tangible bond between us. Because of that, I talked my sisters into letting him join us, after everyone left, for the illegal but satisfying disposition of her ashes. Once it was done, his voice caught as he thanked us for allowing him to participate, then he strode away before his emotions got the best of him.

As I watched him go, my heart went with him in spite of my intentions to insulate myself.

I didn't see him for several days, then we resumed our laid-back routine as if nothing had happened. But it had, binding us closer, soul to soul.

Though things remained dicey between me and Iris, that didn't ruin the good time we all had at the Fourth of July Volunteer Fire Department rummage sale and barbecue. Clete's boat won the grand prize—thanks, in part, to our presence dressed as mermaids in homemade costumes Katie had fitted to us. And every single item we'd donated from Cissy's estate sold, probably as talismans of the weird old lady of the lake, but for a good cause, nonetheless.

After Clete and I finished our rabies shots, we continued our dinners at restaurants from Highlands to Buford to Asheville, but he never ventured into my turf in Atlanta. I'd suggested it, but Clete had quickly put the kibosh on that, making it clear he felt like a fish out of water in my world.

But every Saturday night, we danced ourselves into happy exhaustion at the Boat Church.

And every time Clete kissed me good-night, pulling away got just a little harder.

I kept telling myself it was just a summer romance, nothing more, which made it safe enough to let myself love him just a little. The trouble was, I'd never been able to stop with just a little of anything I'd ever wanted, and I found myself wanting him more and more.

So I gradually forgot about all the questions I'd once had about the scrapbook, and Eileen's convenient explanation about why Clete had Cissy's things. And the suspicion that there was some connection between Clete, our sale, and Mr. Johnson.

It was so much easier letting him adore me, even though I knew the real me could never live up to the idealized Dahlia he'd constructed over the years. The real me was no saint. I was impulsive. Picky and temperamental. Besieged by boring health problems that weren't going to go away. Snoring like a chain saw. Sleeping with a bite guard. And I'd developed vile personal habits living alone, like blissfully belching and passing gas in the solitude of my bedroom.

Yet something in me couldn't bear to kill Clete's illusions. I liked his version of me so much more than the real one, and seeing her in his eyes almost made me believe I could be that woman.

So I fell in love with being loved and took each day as a gift, knowing it was selfish, but doing it anyway. But the joke was on me, because I was falling in love with Clete, too, even though I couldn't admit it.

Clete took me to the next meeting of the Arts Council, where they agreed to take on the farm. I was really surprised by the level of talent represented there. There were five painters whose work I had long admired. As many expert potters and woodcrafters. Two renowned sculptors. A host of retired musicians—from concert pianists and violinists, to bluegrass banjo pickers and fiddlers. Four best-selling authors. And at least a hundred arts supporters, many of them wealthy retirees. And every one of them treated me like a national treasure.

Several of the older members suggested I abandon crass Atlanta immediately and move there, where I'd be properly appreciated. I suspected Clete of putting them up to it, but he denied saying a word to *anybody* about me, including his family.

And when I was alone in Clete's wonderful house, resting in the security of his bed, I did a lot of thinking and slowly began to see the truth of my past. All my life, I'd been striving toward one goal or another: to be the best dancer, the best daughter, the best wife, the best mother, the best volunteer, the best person. For the past two years, that had meant working fourteen hours, seven days a week, to keep from losing my sole remaining shred of security: my house.

It wasn't till Cissy had posthumously coerced me into leaving all that crisis and busy-ness behind to be there at Lake Clare, and the rabid raccoon had stopped me dead in my tracks for a month, that I realized what a harsh master my search for perfection had always been—not just to me, but to those I loved. There in the peace of Clete's house, I was finally able to see my life clearly—without the lies I'd made myself believe to avoid the pain and make the unacceptable acceptable. Only then did it hit me like a ton of bricks how politely miserable Harrison and I and my son had been beneath that taskmaster.

From that, I learned firsthand why truth is both a blessing and a curse. Once you see it, there's no going back to the lie. But the good news was, I no longer wanted to. Letting go of the lies I'd told myself got so much easier, yet, oh, how it grieved me.

I cried myself to sleep a lot after that, more for the loss of my own illusions than for the things I'd only pretended to have: the happy marriage that had never been; the relationship I'd wanted with my son and Iris; Lake Clare, and all it meant to me; and last, but not least, the powerful wish that things would work out if I threw caution to the wind and jumped in love with Clete, consequences be damned.

But none of those things could ever be, any more than Iris and I would ever be anything but oil and water. I'd tried to make peace with her, but her resentment had slowly reemerged after the raccoon attack, and she was back to all her old tricks.

Still, seeing the truth made me determined not to re-create the same mistakes that had already cost me so dearly. I didn't need, or want, to be rescued by any man, even Clete. I cried about that, too.

For everybody's sake, I needed to be whole and safe and happy on my own.

Yet each time I went through my private little devotional of grief, I woke a little less angry—at God, at myself, at Harrison, at my son.

Slowly, I began to heal.

So I decided that when September rolled around and I finally had to take my new-and-improved self and my inheritance home, I meant to start over with Junior. Though he hadn't grown up to be as kind and gracious as I had wanted him to be, he was mine, and I would find a way, somehow, to let him know how much I loved him, as he was, without judgment.

But with boundaries, this time. Junior might not like that part of it, but thanks be to God, there was time to rebuild something stronger, more accepting, and much healthier than before. The important thing was to try.

I couldn't give that up, not even for Clete.

But in the meantime, his steady, loving presence showed me the simple pleasure of just being. I watched and learned as he savored each day as a simple gift of time, open to every good and decent possibility, not chased by the past or gobbled up by useless what-ifs.

Fortunately, it was contagious.

Knowing I had to leave made every moment we had precious and alive. Accepting that and savoring each day as it came, I gradually began to lighten up without even trying.

For that, and for the way it felt to see the love and desire in Clete's eyes, I would be eternally grateful. And for the peace I found in his presence. The Dahlia who went back to Atlanta would be a better woman, by far, than the one who'd come there.

Assuming I wasn't arrested for moving the bodies, in which case I might end up in the pokey, but a better woman, nonetheless.

By the end of July, I was so happy, it scared me. And the happier I got, the more Iris seemed to resent it.

"Vi," I said as the two of us were cleaning up after supper one night when Rose and Iris had gone to Clayton for a matinee and dinner. "Do you think there's anything I can do to keep Iris from being jealous of me?"

Vi exhaled heavily. "As long as you're you, I doubt it. Something inside her makes her think that everything you have comes at her expense. Even Clete."

Baffling. "Why? She's happy with Wilson, isn't she? And she's successful."

Vi paused with a dish in her hand. "Sometimes I wonder if she even knows what happy feels like." She stuck it into the dishwasher drawer. "Personally, I think we should have been putting Prozac into her orange juice since Day One, but she's promised to see Rose's therapist when we get home, so maybe that'll help."

She grinned. "Since you and Clete have been joined at the hip, you've mellowed out like nobody's business. I like it."

"I like it, too." I wiped the granite countertop. "Makes me want the summer to last forever, but it can't."

She leaned in close, nudging me with her elbow. "Have you and Clete 'done it' yet?"

"Violet," I scolded, flushing with embarrassment. "Shame on you."

"Does that mean yes?"

"You know me better than that," I defended. "And anyway, the way things are is better than yes."

She eyed me askance. "And what, pray tell, could be better than yes?"

"*No* at the end of the evening makes all the little *yesses* getting there mighty fine, madam." My choice not to have sex outside of marriage had given every kiss, every touch from Clete crystalline clarity and intensity. Just thinking about those kisses made my precious parts do an electrified double flip, and I shivered with desire sharper than a paper cut. "You ought to try it with Taylor sometime. Take a mutual oath that you won't consummate, then go parking."

I heard the front door open.

"Go parking with Taylor?" Vi shook her head.

"Hey!" Iris called. "We're back. The projector at the theater broke, which was okay, because the movie wasn't nearly as good as the critics said it was."

Rose trailed her into the kitchen, looking flushed and bubbly and coy. "Hey."

"So," Iris said, unusually cheerful. "What's this I hear about parking?"

Vi shot me a mischievous glance. "Dahlia said Taylor and I should try going parking with the agreement we wouldn't make love. It seems celibacy has really hiked the hubba-hubba factor with her and Clete."

"Vi!" I glared at her. What in God's good green earth had possessed her to wave that red flag in Iris's face? She knew better.

Sure enough, Iris jumped on me like a duck on a June bug. "Oh, please. The Virgin Queen speaks. I swear, Dahlia, are you *ever* going to stop being Miss Goody Toe-shoes and sitting in judgment of all the normal people in the world?"

Worn out with her snide remarks, I shot back, "Are *you* ever going to stop being so judgmental of *my* beliefs?" She could dish it out, but she couldn't take it, and I'd had enough. "Apparently, nobody is entitled to have old-fashioned standards anymore? God's explicit opinions aside, which of course, they aren't, I'm convinced that if Clete and I just up and 'did it,' we'd turn something that's supposed to be *sacred* into something that's just another 'it'—something other people do all the time, like scratching an itch or wolfing down a burger on the fly at dinnertime." Why was I justifying myself? "Just because you're politically correct and I'm not, doesn't give you the right to criticize me, Iris. I have as much right to the way I feel about things as you do, so lay off about it! I don't impose those feelings on anybody else, including you."

Vi shot Rose a flat-mouthed look of regret for starting the whole thing.

"Temper, temper," Iris said to me, her expression sly. "Obviously, I struck a nerve."

I was overreacting, and I knew it, but all the old baggage between us landed right on top of me. "No, Iris," I snapped. "You've gotten *on* my last nerve. I've had it with your sly comments and your resentments. If you can't say anything kind, just don't say anything to me. Ever."

Flustered by the confrontation, Rose intervened with, "Come on, y'all. Can we just rachet it down, here, and call a time-out?"

"This is between Iris and me," I told Rose, then turned back to Iris. "I've endured your resentment, tacit or otherwise, from the first day we got here, and I'm tired of it. I mean it, Iris. I've done my best to be kind and accepting of you, but it hasn't done a bit of good. So lay off. Leave me alone. Don't mutter, don't grumble, don't sneer, don't stare at me. If you can't be kind, zip it."

"Oh," Iris shot back. "Now that we all went along with your scheme about the bodies, you don't want to hear the truth from me? Okay. *You* won't hear a word from me. I have plenty of other people who want to talk to me, and I'll talk to *them* about whatever I want."

"Was that a threat?" I challenged. "Are you threatening to tell?" Lord, we sounded like ten-year-olds.

"Whoa! Truce." Vi got between us and took my upper arms as my hands fisted.

"Dammit, Iris," Rose said with unprecedented pique as she steered her toward the bedrooms. "That's dirty pool, and you know it. We have to talk."

Vi urged me into a chair at the long trestle table. "Dahlia, I love you more than life, but you can't let Iris get to you that way. She's who she is, and you're who you are, and never the twain shall meet."

"So why do I always have to be the one who overlooks everything?" I griped.

"Because you can," she said, "and Iris can't. That's the long and short of it."

Not what I wanted to hear, but still, the wind went out of my sails. I hated being the grown-up all the time. "We've got another month under the same roof. How in God's good green earth am I supposed to make it without choking her?"

"Focus on Clete," Vi said. "Leave Iris to heaven. Who knows? Maybe there'll be some miracle, and she'll finally forgive you. You never can tell."

"I'm not so sure I believe in miracles anymore."

Vi shook her head. "How soon they forget. Cissy left us her land. If that ain't a Red Sea miracle, I never saw one."

She had a point. "Okay. That qualifies. But that may be our allotment for life."

Smiling, she shook her head in disagreement. "I don't think so. Come on. Let's hit the hay. Things'll feel better in the morning. They always do."

She was right. For a while, anyway. Till it really hit the fan.

· 25 ·

Money: An article which may be used as a universal passport
to everywhere except heaven, and as a universal provider
of everything except happiness.
—THE WALL STREET JOURNAL

The present, second Wednesday in August. Hilltop Lodge, Lake Clare

THANKS TO OUR latest set-to, Iris wasn't speaking to me, which simplified matters immensely as we finished the final clean-out at Hilltop. Our estrangement was my one regret for the summer—well, maybe the thing about the bodies, too, but the verdict was still out about that one—but I'd finally quit going to the hardware store for milk, and accepted that we couldn't be friends.

Before I knew it, we were done. By noon, the last boxes had been marked, sealed, and sorted into each of our stacks against the log wall where the honky old piano had once been. The four of us stood in the living room, letting the fact sink in.

The house, now sparsely furnished with just the few things the others wanted, gleamed the way it had when Great-grandmother was alive. Even stripped of decoration, it showed off the strong and ageless bones Poppy Jack had designed.

Iris had claimed and packed away the family flags the Captain had made, so the high windows in the living room washed the space with good north light. All the moldy books from the shelves had been shipped away for freeze-drying, a process Rose swore would make them safe for even me, but since I had a house full of books in Buckhead, I let the others have them all. Same with the furniture, except for the little slipper chair Poppy Jack had carved. The others had boxed up all Cissy's mementos for me and sent them off with the books. As for the rest, I'd only wanted the portrait of our brown-eyed lady ancestor and the little sterling cake compote that first Great-grandmother, then Cissy, had used to serve me little cucumber sandwiches when we had "tea." Those were talismans enough.

Below us, the basement stood empty, the Captain's war memorabilia now with his grandchildren in Virginia, and Poppy Jack's rusted safe and machinery sold for quite a tidy sum to the scrap dealer. For the first time in memory, the library stood vacant, its homemade "couches" and platforms gone to the dump along with all the other decaying mattresses, and the Raj desk off to Sotheby's.

The "library" that had never held any books looked so much bigger empty, its floor now agleam.

There in the living room with the others, I shook my head. Amazing—considering the blizzard of *stuff* Cissy had clung to—how little of any value, sentimental or otherwise, remained. Just four compact stacks of boxes against a wall and Poppy Jack's hand-carved furniture. My heart tightened in my chest.

It put a fresh perspective on all the *stuff* I'd accumulated back home. What would my child or grandchildren want from the carefully orchestrated clutter in my house? Very little, I realized, and it hurt to admit it.

Vi scanned the room to make sure we hadn't missed anything. "I can't believe we're finally done," she said in reverent tones usually reserved for church.

"I can," Rose chirped. "That leaves us three whole weeks to sit back, play bridge, swim, eat, and sleep."

"Bridge," I seconded, glad for that happy prospect. "I vote for at least once a day." As long as Vi and I were partners, Iris didn't have to speak to me.

Iris lifted an eyebrow and frowned my way, but didn't refuse.

"What about Clete?" Vi asked me, having taken up Iris's place as official nagger on that subject.

"Clete can't play bridge," I responded, determined not to encourage her. The last couple of weeks, my working at the lodge had provided a perfect weaning period. We still saw each other a few times a week and danced every Saturday night, but Clete seemed to be getting the message. He couldn't transplant, and I wouldn't. That was that. "Anyway, I asked you not to bring him up anymore."

Rose smoothed things over with, "Once-a-day bridge sounds good to me. I'll bet we can get a book about the new bidding methods at Wal-Mart."

"Or online at he-who-shall-be-nameless's," Vi said.

"Maybe it is time we brought our games out of the Dark Ages," Rose commented.

The phone rang in Cissy's room, and Iris leapt to answer it. She was, after all, still Iris.

"Great!" we heard her say after a thumping run down the hall. "What time?" Pause. "Just a minute." Her voice escalated. "Hey, y'all! How soon can you be ready to go to town? We got a cash offer!"

Hallelujah!

Excited, we looked at each other, then said in unison, "Not for at least thirty minutes." We were a mess, dusty and sticky.

"Okay!"

Moments later, she came in, so excited she forgot to be aloof with me. "I told him we'd be there in two hours, so we'd have time to eat and clean up."

"Did he say how much the offer was?" Vi asked.

She shook her head no. "He wanted to discuss the terms with us first, which makes me think it's not for full asking price, but he said there were other factors involved."

"C'mon. Let's get this show on the road," I said, heading for the boat.

Two hours later, fortified by bacon and tomato sandwiches (wraps for me), we all collected in Lawyer Johnson's office, giving me a sense of déjà vu about that day back in April when we'd heard the news about Cissy's estate.

"Good afternoon, ladies," he said, his florid face beaming. "So glad you could be here this afternoon for this happy occasion." He made it sound like a done deal.

Vi cut to the chase, as usual. "So, how much is the cash offer?"

His good humor congealed, but only a little. "We'll get to that, but first, there are some very good stipulations we need to discuss." I could feel all our guards go up as he continued with, "The buyers are a consortium of investors, both local and those who have vacation homes at the lake, and as such, they have a vested interest in preserving the environment and residential character of the property."

That was good news.

"They're also proposing a 'green' development." He went on to outline an impressive set of environmentally friendly restrictions for a low-density development that had the capacity to function completely off the grid in emergencies, with wide frontages and native plantings.

We looked to each other in approval.

But all that would cost big bucks. I prayed we weren't about to be lowballed.

Mr. Johnson went on. "All roads and driveways will be a mesh of hollow pavers with a sturdy ground cover to minimize runoff and visual impact."

Even better.

"And, conditional to the developers' honoring these restrictions—which I can assure you they will—the county has agreed to add a recycling center and an additional Dumpster at the current location below the dam to accommodate the increased demand."

"How can you be so sure the developers will comply?" I asked him.

"I know most of them personally," he told us, "and I can vouch for them."

Vi spoke what I was thinking. "That sounds like a conflict of interest, to me. How can we be sure you're looking out for our best interests in this?"

Iris, Rose, and I nodded gravely.

Mr. Johnson let out a heavy sigh, but remained undaunted. "In this day and age, a man's word means less than nothing, but to me, it's everything. I can only offer you my solemn word that I have your best interests, and those of the lake, as you instructed me, at heart. And tell you that if you accept this offer, you will not regret it."

Clearly, he knew more than he was saying. "Who are these investors, then?" I asked.

His upper lip inflated briefly. "I'm afraid I can't tell you at this time. It's one of the stipulations of the offer. But the funds are in escrow. I have hard proof of that."

"Speaking of which," Iris zeroed in, "how much is the offer?"

"Even Lake Clare isn't bulletproof in this real estate market," Mr. Johnson replied. "Due to current conditions, several of the offers contingent on financing have been withdrawn. The best remaining offer contingent on financing, for ten million, won't close till the first of next year, if then. This offer is for cash on the barrelhead for nine million, take it or leave it, to close September first, as you requested."

Nine million! Cash! I didn't think there was that much money left in the world anymore.

"But there is a condition," he added.

Uh-oh. Here came the deal breaker.

"They want all the property for that price, including Cardinal Cottage."

My heart wrenched. Our last tie to our childhoods . . . my last to Cissy.

I could see why they wanted it. It was the choicest lot of them all. But . . .

I looked to the others for their reactions. Eyes narrowed in thought, Rose was clearly considering it but, as always, waited to see what the rest of us thought. Finger rubbing across her upper lip, Vi stared unseeing at the law books behind Mr. Johnson, her expression definitely not negative, but not positive, either. Iris had fallen into her old scowl.

It was Iris who spoke first, looking to us. "We need to talk this over." She turned to the lawyer. "Mr. Johnson, could we please have some privacy to discuss this?"

He jumped up as if somebody had sent a current through his chair. "Of course. Please. Don't get up." He left and closed the door behind him.

Iris leaned in and said in confidential tones, "Even though I've never wanted to come back up here, this summer has changed things. Without the bugs, the lake's a pretty nice place. I was thinking maybe we could use some of the money to fix up the cottage. Put in air-conditioning. Heat."

The rest of us eyed each other to see who might volunteer to head up that particular brainstorm, but none of us was willing, and it showed.

"Honey," Vi said, "the only way to fix up the cabin is to tear it down and start over. And the septic system is on Cissy's land. With no easement."

Without even polling me and Rose, Iris shrugged. "I don't want to be the one to rebuild it, any more than y'all do. It was just a thought. It might have been nice to have a weekend getaway."

Besides her condo in Panama City Beach, a snide thought tacked on, but I banished it immediately. No more of that. To make up for it, I phrased my own reaction in Iris's own language. "The money and the environmental considerations are really tempting, but it feels weird to think that my last tie to the lake would be gone."

Normally, Rose had to poll everybody's feelings before she expressed her own, but she surprised us by stating firmly, "We didn't even know Mama still owned Cardinal Cottage till Cissy died." She directed the next to me. "And you're the one who said we should sell. It was a good decision for all of us. Considering the state of things, the money will be a godsend. I vote we take the money and run."

Vi smiled at her in approval. "Why, Rosie. You sound like me."

"Good," Rose said. "I consider that a compliment. I think this is one case where it would be a mistake to let vague feelings interfere with a decision we already made. We asked for a green offer, and we got one, cash on the barrelhead, to close exactly when we asked, from people who care what happens up here, whether we know their names or not." She lowered her tone to an adamant whisper. "I don't even care if Mr. Johnson is one of them, himself."

"That would be illegal," Iris said, as if she knew what she was talking about, which she didn't. "A clear conflict of interest. He'd have to declare it, in writing, or the offer would be void."

I wasn't so sure about that, but it would definitely be unethical. I caught myself looking at the light coming under the door to see if anybody was outside listening. No sign of shadows.

"As long as we get our money," Violet said, "and the lake gets a nice development, I don't care what the offer is."

I surprised myself by saying, "This is one case where we don't need to make a quick decision. We can take it home and talk things over for as long as we need to."

Iris raised a finger. "We could, but who knows how long this offer will be on the table? Unless we have a contract, one or more of the investors might need their money back, and there goes the deal."

She had a point.

I could see the CPA financial wheels turning in her head before she announced, "I think we should take it, contingent only on receiving a higher cash offer with comparable environmental restrictions."

Brilliant, but totally out of character. "Am I hallucinating?" I asked anybody and nobody. "Did you just make a major decision, off the cuff?"

"I've always been able to make financial decisions," Iris retorted, "and make them fast when necessary. It's my work, and I'm very good at it."

Rose's brows lifted as she nodded. "Better than good. She's great."

Iris looked to me without accusation. "You've just never seen that side of me. Whenever I mentioned helping you with your finances, you ran the other way as far and as fast as you could."

"That was because I couldn't face them," I said in a moment of clarity. "And I knew you disapproved of my decisions in that department."

Rather than take offense, she proposed, "I'll make you a deal. Let me help you with only ten percent of whatever you have left after paying off all your debts—strictly on a professional basis—for six months. If you're not happy with the results, I'm off the case, no questions asked. What do you say?"

Rose and Vi swiveled from Iris to me in expectation.

Maybe that could be the bridge between us. Either that, or we'd never speak to each other again, but I was willing to try it. Still, I couldn't resist giving her a little dose of her own medicine. "I'll have to think about it and let you know."

Iris came right back with, "Good idea. How much time will you need? Twenty-four hours or forty-eight?" She was closing me! Dithering Iris was going for the deal, cut-and-dried, on the spot.

It was a good sign. "None. It's a deal."

"Which leaves us with the offer," Vi reminded.

After all my coercion to make this happen, including the Dancing Santa Caper, I could hardly be the lone holdout. I took a deep breath and said good-bye to Lake Clare forever, part of me dying in the process. "I'm in. If y'all want to take the deal, I'm in."

A visual consult was the only confirmation we needed. It was unanimous.

Vi picked up the offer from the desk. "Okay. Time to read the fine print."

"We might have questions," Iris said, then went to the door. "Mr. Johnson," she trilled toward the conference room. "We need you."

Then we all sat and waited, deadpan, for him to return.

"We'd like to take a close look at the offer," I said when he came in. "And we might have questions."

"I am at your disposal." Smelling a deal, he subsided into his chair with just a hint of hope showing.

Blessedly, the contract was written in clear, concise language. The four of us read slowly and carefully through every jot and stipulation. The only technical terms concerned building codes, EPA standards, and specifics about the various community water treatment, cable, compost, backup power, and solar facilities.

By force of will, I made myself digest every word and wait quietly while the others finished each page.

It took us forty-five minutes, but at the end, each of us confirmed the decision with a simple nod.

Vi laid the offer on the desk between us and the lawyer.

"With one condition, we have a deal."

His expression solidified. "And what would that condition be?"

"We accept this offer as stated, conditional only upon receiving a higher cash offer with comparable ecological considerations that can close on September first."

"Shrewd," he complimented. "I think that's a perfectly reasonable condition. I'll notify the buyers, then call you as soon as I hear anything." He rose. "Do you have other business in town, or will you be going back to Clete's?"

"Let's celebrate," Vi suggested. "What's the nicest restaurant in the area?"

"The Verandah," Mr. Johnson answered without hesitation. "It's on the Burton road, four blocks west of Main. Opens for dinner at five. With your permission, I'll call and tell them you're coming."

"Thanks." Suddenly feeling buoyant, I realized this was really going to happen. Hard as it was to leave the past—and Clete—behind, we were going to close on time. Come September, I'd have my life back. For the first time in a long, long time, I let myself hope.

We'd scarcely walked into the Wal-Mart when Iris's cell phone rang. She flipped open her phone, answered, then said, "Thank you." She snapped it shut with a beaming smile.

"That's the shortest phone conversation you've had in your entire life," Rose commented. "What's up?"

Iris dragged out a dramatic pause, then erupted into unadulterated glee. "They accepted!" She grabbed Rose and Vi, and they grabbed me for an unabashed group hug that I didn't mind one bit.

Iris broke free to open her cell phone. "I'm calling Wilson."

Violet grabbed it before she could finish dialing and whispered, "Not here. It'll be all over the county before sunset, down to the penny and conditions. Wait till we get home."

Rose nodded. "She has a point."

"Okay," Iris relented, "but dibs on the phone, first." She hooked Rose's elbow with her arm. "C'mon." She headed for cosmetics. "Let's all highlight each other's hair tomorrow. My treat."

"Forget highlights," Vi told her. "I want to go home a redhead. A *rich* redhead."

"Intervention!" I ruled as they made their way toward the hair care aisle. "I love you too much to let you do that. My friend Cassie dyed hers red on a whim, and she said the only way to get it out was with Drano. Trust me, she tried everything else."

Violet laughed. "This from the woman who hasn't seen the inside of a salon since nineteen seventy-six."

I smiled. "Just think of all the money I've saved."

Rose and Vi started kidding around about what outrageous colors they might try, and Iris enlisted their opinions regarding her highlights. Watching them, I realized it was all over but the shoutin', and my sisters were really, truly happy. Knowing that made it a little easier to let go of Lake Clare and all it meant to me. I'd do my crying back home, in private, where I always had, but this time without the wolf at the door.

I could take the whole month of September off. Sleep late in my big, cozy bed, until I finally caught up. Then I'd plant my bulbs—tons of red tulips and purple hyacinths for the spring. And more daffodils. There could never be too many daffodils.

I could go to Spa Sydell for the works, erase the effects of hard work and sickness from my skin and hands. Get a manicure every week, if I wanted to. I had once taken such pampering for granted. Now, it was precious and extravagant.

I could get two season tickets to the ballet and the symphony and the Alliance Theater. Savor every step, every note, and every play with somebody I liked. Go to all the museums.

Free from the deadly reek of financial desperation, I could take back up with my friends. I still had friends. I'd just been working too hard to invest any time in them.

Once they'd picked their hair colors and supplies, we browsed the rest of the departments to kill time till the restaurant opened, ending up in the produce section, where we splurged on artichokes and pomegranates and fresh apricots and bing cherries and freestone peaches.

When we finally arrived at the restaurant, the proprietress greeted us with a suspiciously broad smile. "Well, if it isn't our ladies of the lake. Come in. Come in. We have a little surprise waiting in our private dining room."

"Maybe Mr. Johnson sent champagne," Iris hoped aloud.

That, and then some. There, standing behind every other seat at a roomy table for eight were Martin, Taylor, Wilson . . . and Clete.

What were they doing there? What was *he* doing there?

"Congratulations!" they called to us.

Mr. Johnson was the only one who'd known we were coming. Who had set this up? I glanced at my sisters, but they seemed as surprised as I was.

Somebody must have spilled the beans. If it wasn't my sisters . . .

Either our lawyer had broken client privilege, something I doubted, or Clete was in on the deal, a prospect that called into question his motives about our relationship from the beginning.

Ignoring Clete, I strode over to Martin and tried to keep my voice calm and even. "Congratulations for what?"

He grinned, giving Rose a sidelong hug. "I called the house and got Clete. He said y'all had finished clearing out your grandmother's, then gone to see the lawyer. We figured y'all might like to celebrate a job well done."

"That's all? A job well done?"

He studied me with concern. "That's what he said. Why?"

I took a leveling breath, deliberately not looking Clete's way. Maybe I'd just jumped to the worst possible conclusion, as usual. But when I did look at him, his usual candor was missing, replaced by a guarded calculation I'd seen only when I'd asked him why he loved Cissy so much.

He could tell I knew. I saw that in his face, too.

Proffering a bubbly flute like an offering, he came my way, leaving the others to share the news. "It's sparkling cider," he assured me. "Compliments of Horatio, along with the champagne, from his private stock, and the dinner."

"And what prompted this party?" I asked with more of an edge than I intended.

"I came by the law office right after y'all left and heard him calling the restaurant," he answered. "When I asked if y'all would mind my horning in, he beamed and suggested we make it a party, invite your brothers-in-law. Said the whole thing was on him."

"And how did they get here?" I clipped out.

"Taylor drove up. I picked up the others with the chopper. We just made it back in time."

"How did you know how to contact them?"

He frowned. "Iris posted their numbers in my kitchen in case of emergency."

That she had, but I still smelled a rat. It was all just a little too convenient.

He drew me farther from the others. "What's wrong? You're acting like I committed a crime. It's just a party."

I asked the question I should have asked in the beginning. "Do you have any kind of financial interest in the deal we just signed? Is that how you knew where we would be, and why?"

His eyes shuttered. "Dahlia, as much as I want to answer that question, I cannot. You'll have to trust me on this. I know that doesn't come easy after what Harrison did to you, but I'm not Harrison. I'm not a crook, and I would never do anything to hurt you."

My sisters flicked worried glances my way, but none of them interfered. "Then tell me the truth," I told Clete. "About you and Cissy. About your brother Hoke. About this offer. About why you're here."

He glared right back at me. "Are you trying to tell me you never lied to me about anything that matters?"

Only the bodies, but I couldn't tell him about that. It would make him part of it if he didn't turn me in, and I knew he'd never do that, any more than he would have turned in his brother. "Yes," I lied. "That's exactly what I mean."

Pain and shame flashed in his expression. "Not here." He looked to the others. "Y'all excuse us for a minute." Then he drew me out onto the verandah, then down to a path in the back garden that led to a sheltered bench, safely out of earshot. I sat, but he remained standing.

I'd never seen him so torn.

"You want the truth about Hoke, well, here it is: My brother killed my father for beating our mother to death while we were out plowing. The wind was up, so we couldn't hear her call for help. When we came in for supper, she was lying there in the kitchen, and Daddy was drunk as hell, shoveling in the stew she'd made, and cussin' a blue streak, like it was all her fault. Hoke didn't say a word, just walked up behind Daddy and twisted his head one, hard jerk. Snapped his neck, just like that." The more he told, the more his accent ebbed back into a mountain twang. "And I was glad. I went over and hit Daddy so hard he fell out of the chair, then started kickin' him as hard as I could, but Hoke stopped me." The horror of that long-ago afternoon radiated through his grim control. "Then he picked Mama up and carried her out onto the porch and rocked her, cryin' like a kid. Wouldn't let us touch her all night."

"That's enough," I said softly, wishing I hadn't asked, wishing he didn't look that way, staring, wounded, into the past.

"You wanted the truth," he said, bitter. "This is it. The rest of us got together and tried to make it look like Daddy hung himself after he killed her, but the forensics didn't back it up. Sheriff said he hated to punish Hoke for doing what somebody should have a long time ago, but he arrested him anyway." The pain ebbed from his voice, along with his twang. "Hoke never said a single word. Didn't for another four years. Horatio did his best to get him off on temporary insanity, but those days, an awful lot of men blamed the victims of domestic violence for not leaving their menfolk. As if she had someplace to go, with all of us. Half the deputies bought their weed and shine from Daddy, so Mama knew going to law would only get her in worse trouble. Thank God for the four women on Hoke's jury. They held out for second-degree manslaughter, so Hoke only served three years. He was home another two before he started talkin' again."

"Clete, I—"

He raised a staying hand. "You asked about why I loved your grandmother. I didn't tell you, because I knew you looked down on me already. I was afraid if I told you the truth, I'd kill whatever chance I might have with you. But here it is: I was functionally illiterate when she met me. It didn't take her long to find out, and she never made a big thing about it. Instead, she said she could see how intelligent I was, and she'd learned to help people with reading problems when she worked in New York."

This time, his stare into the middle distance was marked by wonder. "She was the first person who'd ever told me I was intelligent. I knew I was good with chemicals and machines, picked things up easy as long as reading wasn't involved, but she was the first one to believe in me."

He glanced at the ground with a small smile. "It seemed to take forever, but she was always patient, always encouraging. At the end of every lesson, my reward was listening to her read a chapter from the great classics in her library. I came as much for those as for the lessons. For those other worlds and adventures. For all the noble characters who triumphed over evil. And every time she closed the book, she said I was one lesson closer to being able to read those books for myself."

He faced me squarely. "That was why I loved her. Not because she encouraged my ambitions and helped me get started with my business, but because she gave me the privilege of reading, then taught me about all the great books and minds in literature. And music. And dancing."

Tears welling, I felt humbled to the marrow and guilty for demanding he expose his greatest insecurity, yet felt bound to him stronger than ever. "She gave me dancing and music, too." I said. "And all the books, besides."

"Hey, y'all." Vi's voice carried across the garden. "Quit smoochin' and come order. We're getting' plastered and hungry."

I stood.

"There was one more question," he said, his voice hard. "I told you, I'd like to answer, but I can't. Not that I won't. I can't. Can you live with that?"

If the answer brought either of us as much pain as I had just caused him, I didn't want to know. Not then. Then, all I wanted to do was hold him and cry, so I did.

Clete clung to me as if I might evaporate any minute. "God, Dahlia, please don't leave me. I loved who I thought you were for so long, but knowing who you really are, I love you even more." He searched my face. "Not with a kid's crush, but fierce and real and open-eyed. Just as you are, with all your infirmities. Marry me. Stay."

My heart started breaking, but he wouldn't give up. "You can do so much good here. I'll make you happy, I swear on my life. Marry me, Dahlia." His embrace tightened, his kiss harsh with desperation.

I pulled away. "Please, Clete, let me go," I pleaded.

He stilled, his arms falling to his sides as he closed his eyes the way he must have that awful afternoon so long ago.

I sagged against him. "If you love me, let me go."

"Go, then," he said, the words wrenched from him as he turned his back. After a deep breath, he said, "Give me a minute."

"I'm sorry," I said, wishing with every atom of me that things were different, but they weren't. I had to go back and try to make things right with my son. I headed inside.

Thanks to my nonpoker face, my solo return to the party threw a definite wet blanket on the festivities. Awkward, the others ordered, leaving me and Clete to last. When the waitress got to me, Iris got up and started for the verandah, but I stopped her as she passed. "He may not be there," I said, unwanted tears welling.

"Oh." There was no satisfaction in her expression as she sat back down.

I managed to regain my composure and lifted my glass of no-longer-bubbling cider. "Here's to Cissy. God bless her, for this summer together and for the money." And for Clete, a sad inner voice chimed in. "May she rest in peace, and may we be good stewards of all she's given us, especially each other."

"Hear, hear," the others toasted.

We all tried to regain the excitement of the afternoon, and the food was superb, but the empty chair beside me made it the loneliest dinner I'd ever eaten.

Back at Clete's, we found Cissy's scrapbook on the kitchen table with a note addressed to me. The others quietly left me alone to read it. I opened the envelope and took out a note in Clete's strong hand.

Dahlia—
Cissy gave this to me before she died. I kept it so I would have something to remember you by if things didn't work out between us, but I think you should have it. She was so proud of you.
Eileen and I will be touring our suppliers for the rest of the month. If anything comes up, Ted or Larry can handle it. Enjoy the house as your own. I'll see you to say good-bye before you leave.
I won't make things harder for us both, but if you ever change your mind, I love you.

Clete

I didn't wait till I got back to Buckhead to do my crying. I did a lot of it that night, alone in Clete's bed, in his perfect house, in the magic place I was giving up forever so I could start over where I really belonged.

When people want to do something, they grab a tool. When God wants
to do something, He usually grabs a person.
—QUOTED BY WADE ASH, BLACKSHEAR PLACE BAPTIST CHURCH

The present, first Monday in September. Hilltop Lodge, Lake Clare

J'M NO GOOD at leaving. Or at letting go.
       But there it was, the morning of the closing.
Everything had gone according to schedule. No hiccups. No last-
minute crises.

The night before at Clete's, Iris had totaled, cross-referenced, and cal-
culated our meal units to the fraction of a cent, rounding things off only
at the bitter end. "Just to be fair."

Checks for odd amounts had been exchanged, and we were square.

Mama and David had called and wished us mazel tov, with instructions to spend some of the money on plane tickets to come see them. (You
couldn't blast them out of Florida anymore.)

Well rested, tanned, and bridged to smithereens after three weeks of
R & R at Clete's, we'd packed up our cars and driven to Hilltop for one
last walk-through before we headed to Clayton to sign away our heritage.

No surgical exits for me, this time. I was glad when Rose and Iris dithered through their list of endless leaving rituals. But now the dithering was done.

I should have been happy. I was going home, back to my privacy and the house I loved. Back to reclaim the life I'd lost through Harrison's betrayal. I was getting everything I'd prayed for, except for Junior's love. But even though God's power might be limited when it comes to a spoiled teenager, I still had hope for that.

Everything would be ready and waiting back in Atlanta. Once our offer had been accepted, I'd instructed Cathy, my assistant at the ballet school, to hire a crew to clean my house till it sparkled and a lawn service to groom the grounds. And thanks to her organizational skills, the ballet school had the healthiest bottom line we'd ever earned, even with the expenses for replacing the leaky roof.

And I was about to become a millionaire, twice over.

So why did I feel like I was on my way to my mother's funeral?

The four of us stood silent in Cissy's living room for one last, long good-bye, not to each other, but to Hilltop and the lake. For me, it seemed more like a dream than real.

But endings come.

The room, now clean at last and bare, no longer spoke to me in happy childhood whispers. Suddenly, the whole house seemed merely empty.

This was so much harder than I'd thought.

We lingered there in silence, each one making peace with all that we'd learned and done and were about to do. We'd worked so hard to get there, and I'd gained so much along the way.

We should have planned some sort of transitional ceremony, with lofty resolutions for the future and a reunion fund, even though we knew we probably wouldn't ever come back to Lake Clare.

Cissy's Boot Camp for Sisters, I thought with a smile, despite the obstacle course Iris had provided.

Then I thought of Clete, how lonely the past three weeks at his house had been without him, and felt a fresh stab of grief.

I told myself for yet another time I shouldn't focus on what I was losing, but all I'd gained. I'd been loved and I'd loved, though not in equal measure. And yet again, I tried my best to be grateful for the wonderful months he and I had shared.

I tried my best.

Standing with the others there, I closed my eyes and turned my open hands to God, imagining my loss as feathers drifting up, away. Clete. My hopes and illusions about my son and my marriage. And only then did stillness settle in my soul, the way it had so long ago with Daddy holding me at dawn as all the silent clouds lifted, revealing all.

I breathed out long and deep, as if I could exhale my grief, but when I opened up my eyes again, it was to face reality, not what I wished could be.

Ironically, it was Iris who finally declared the official Time of Death. She glanced at her watch. "I guess that's it, then. It's ten-thirty. Don't want to be late to the closing." Ironic, coming from her. She headed for the door. "Time to go close the deal."

Vi circled my waist. "Come on, sweetie. You'll feel better once you're home."

God, how I loved her.

I took a bracing breath. Then I smiled and hugged her and Rose briefly. "Come on, y'all. Let's go get rich."

I didn't look back, just went straight to my car and drove to Mr. Johnson's office, trying not to look left or right at the familiar milestones I was passing. The springhouse. The blueberry patch. The old road to Clayton. The spot where we'd picked up the license plate. (There was no murder. That redneck was just jerking us around.) The Arts Farm.

Relax, I told myself. Pretty soon it'll be a month from now, and you'll be back home and in the swing of things, and all this will be behind you, the jagged edges worn away.

When I got to the law office, the parking lot was almost full of trucks and SUVs, but four spaces in front had been reserved for us with tidy signs. My mortgage representative, an attractive young woman in a tight suit and very expensive heels, introduced herself when I got out, then followed along as Mr. Johnson's secretary escorted us into his crowded little office.

I had a vague feeling that something was a bit odd, but didn't realize till later it was because the secretary nervously blocked the conference room door as she showed us to the office, then made sure to keep us sequestered inside.

One by one, my sisters arrived, until the four of us were seated in front of the lawyer's desk, with my lender wedged in behind me.

Arrayed across the desk were eight copies of the closing documents. I pulled one over to check the buyers' signatures, but didn't recognize the name designated as power of attorney for Green Cove Limited Liability Corporation.

As I replaced it, my mortgage lender, Miss Ellison, leaned in close and handed me my new mortgage documents. "As soon as y'all close, your attorney will wire the funds you specified into your mortgage account, which—as you can see on page three of the documents—we have adjusted to current fair market value determined by recent sales in your neighborhood, including short sales and foreclosures, as you stipulated."

As *Iris* had stipulated behind the scenes, God bless her, pointing out the lender's potential liability in allowing Harrison to fraudulently leverage the house that was in my name. I'd had no intention of suing, but they didn't know that, and Iris had shrewdly worked that to my advantage.

At last, I'd be "right side up" again, which was still a long way from paid for, but Iris had convinced me not to pay the balance in full, opting to take advantage of the interest deduction instead and keep more of my assets liquid.

Assets. I'd never thought I'd have assets again. Thank you, Cissy. Thank you, God.

Even thank you, Iris.

Miss Ellison pointed out the nitty-gritty portion of the agreement. "The remaining balance will roll over without fee into a four-point-six percent fixed-rate, fifteen-year loan with no prepayment penalty. You can sign these as soon as y'all close."

I placed the loan papers in my lap and turned toward the door as it opened. Mr. Johnson entered, somewhat red and flustered, with a stack of bulging accordion files under his arms. I thought I heard a low rumble of conversation, but his secretary whisked the door closed behind him. "Forgive me, ladies. There were a few last-minute details to be attended to." He sat with a plop.

Last-minute details? My chest tightened as my sisters went alert. "We're still closing on time, aren't we?"

"Of course. Of course," he reassured us. "One of the principals had a little hiccup with his funds, but we're all set, now."

Now? He'd told us when we'd accepted the deal that the funds were already in escrow!

My soul, my soul. Vi and I exchanged dubious glances.

Mr. Johnson nodded to my lender. "Nice to see you again, Miss Ellison." He started handing out the documents. "I have personally inspected these to make sure the terms are in accordance with those of the sales contract, and they are. We've flagged each place that needs a timedate initial or full signature with colored tags. Blue for initials, green for signatures."

I accepted a copy.

"Please don't forget to date, time each one," he went on. "I suggest we do a circle-sign till all of them have all your signatures and initials. My secretary will make sure we didn't miss any, then we'll give the buyers their copies, and that will be that."

I put two and two together and realized who must be in the conference room. Then I focused on my copy of the closing papers. There were an awful lot of flags, considering there had been no changes from the sales contracts. But they turned out to be acknowledgments of disclosures or the specific payment terms Iris had gotten Mr. Johnson to negotiate.

Mr. Johnson rubbed his hands together. "After everything's finished, there will be a small celebration in the conference room."

Pen poised, I tried to sign, but suddenly my hand refused to cooperate.

For crying out loud!

Despite my mixed emotions, the die had been cast. The Rubicon had been crossed. The writing was on the wall. The fat lady had sung.

When I ran out of trite metaphors, I realized I was balking like Iris, who was taking her own sweet time reading every word, which made sense to me instead of getting on my nerves, a fact I found disturbing.

Vi and Rose glanced at her indulgently, then began initialing.

Reminding myself that I was only a few signatures away from being a millionaire—twice over with an extra quarter million for good measure— I forced the pen to paper and marked the date, time, and initialed. Then found the next flag and did it again. And again. And again. I got to the final page and signed my full name above where it was typed, all three times, finishing almost at the same moment as Vi and Rose.

Then the three of us waited for Iris to finish before swapping for the next round. Fortunately, she only felt the need to read the first copy, and kept up nicely after that.

And then it was done.

One by one, we handed the contracts to Mr. Johnson, who thanked us, then left with them.

On Iris's advice, we'd each set up several fully insured accounts in different credit unions she'd researched and selected for their solvency. The buyers had agreed to wire our funds into those accounts in fully insured increments, so our money would be safe and immediately available.

Iris sure knew money, but she was still nosy. While the rest of us waited with anticipation thick as smoke from fresh-cut hickory, she started plying Miss Ellison with questions about her personal life.

We all jumped when the door flew open, but it was just the secretary with a tray. "Coffee, anyone? Port?"

Vi was the only taker, opting for coffee, so the secretary left the tray and exited. My stomach was in knots, and from the look of her, so was Rose's. Iris was busy asking Miss Ellison progressively nosier questions, which was pretty entertaining to watch, actually, though the woman had my sympathies. But instead of being embarrassed, as I would have been in June, I realized it wasn't my responsibility to rescue Miss Ellison or apologize for my sister. Miss Ellison was an adult, and it was up to her to handle Iris.

As the minutes lengthened into ten, then fifteen, then twenty, I was about to decide that maybe the signers were somewhere else. Then I heard the conference room door open and close.

We all froze, eyes turned toward the door to the reception area, and Iris stopped talking in mid-sentence.

We heard Mr. Johnson say something to his secretary, who responded too low for me to make out the words, then things fell silent again.

After a few tense minutes of clock-watching, the entertainment resumed as Iris started back in on poor Miss Ellison, this time asking why she wasn't married.

Just as Miss Ellison's interrogation was getting interesting, the door opened abruptly, all but sending us out of our skins, and in walked a beaming Mr. Johnson and his secretary with our four fully signed, notarized copies, each topped by the wire-transfer confirmations for our funds. "Ladies," he announced, "it is my honor and privilege to *show you the money.*"

After making sure all the account numbers matched, I showed Miss Ellison the confirmation for my quarter-million loan payment, then signed the new mortgage.

She handed me a receipt, shook my hand and thanked me, then escaped with the secretary before Iris could ask her if she'd ever had a social disease.

Rose flopped back in her chair and lifted her hands to heaven. "We're rich," she said as if she couldn't believe it. "We're really rich."

"Ah-ah-ah!" Iris corrected, waggling a cautionary finger. "You go thinking that, and you'll end up broke in two years."

"We're out from under," Rose substituted in the same amazed tone. "We're finally out from under."

And my ordeal was over. I closed my eyes and let it sink in, feeling the financial burden inside me lift for the first time since the divorce. "I'm gonna buy myself a new Prius on the way home, and give Queenie to Nell Welch."

Rose and Vi laughed, but Iris groaned. "Two years," she predicted sadly, "and you'll be hard up again."

"No, ma'am," I shot back, feeling magnanimous. "I've got a very good financial advisor, who happens to be my sister, to help me with my investments."

That made her smile.

"But only when I ask her," I qualified. No way was she getting her nose into my other finances.

Iris nodded. "Works for me."

An elegant idea popped into my head, prompting an evil little chortle.

"That's a mighty smug little snort, there," Vi noted.

Deliciously elegant. "I was just considering buying a condo right next door to Junior in Paridalla."

Vi hooted. "Oh, Harrison will *love* that," she said with glee.

"The *South Pacific*?" Iris protested. "Do you have any idea what airfare costs to get there?" She sighed, eyes toward heaven. "Two years."

Mr. Johnson took advantage of the pause that followed to announce, "And now, ladies, if you will all please join me in the conference room, we have a little surprise prepared for you."

First in is last out, so I couldn't see past the others till we were all inside the conference room, where more than twenty well-dressed men and women were crammed around three sides of the table, with champagne glasses lifted, Clete among them, and a scale model of the proposed development atop the mahogany surface.

At the sight of him, a stab of adrenaline-laced desire shot through me, but when he saw me, his grim expression reminded me that I'd burned that bridge. Stricken, I looked back down at the model. Every building site was marked SOLD with a name, except four cove lots facing Clete's compound that said RESERVED.

A distinguished-looking man stepped forward. "Welcome, ladies. Please come in," he said, then motioned for quiet. "I'm Rob Thomason. As chief operations officer of Green Forest Developers, I'd like to propose a toast." He lifted his flute to us, and the others followed. "To our wonderful ladies of the lake."

We nodded in acknowledgment as they drank, even though we weren't ladies of the lake anymore.

He went on, "For accepting our contract and generously ceding the Cardinal Cottage property to us, we'd like to reciprocate with a gift for each of you." He looked to Clete. "I think it would be most appropriate if the man who put this whole deal together told you, himself. Our chief executive officer, Clete Slocum."

After a brief leveling breath, Clete pinned me with a solemn gaze and said, "Dahlia, you asked if I had an interest in this deal. I did, but I had signed a confidentiality agreement with the other investors. I hope you can understand why I couldn't tell you."

He didn't say it as a rebuke, or even a justification. Just an honest accounting of why he hadn't told me the thing that I'd made a condition of my trust.

I felt lower than a grub.

He turned to my sisters. "In gratitude for your shared vision for Cissy's legacy and the concession of Cardinal Cottage, Green Forest Developers hereby grants each of you a fifty-year, one-acre renewable lease, transferrable only by inheritance, for the lot of your choice from those marked reserved, in exchange for one dollar per year, prepaid. With no vacancy clause."

We stared at him, stunned, then looked at the model and the four lots they'd reserved for us. They were steep, granted, but they were there, right across the cove from his place.

My sisters exploded, laughing and hugging and shaking hands with the other property owners.

Forgetting to breathe, I stared at the model, then back to Clete.

His expression remained closed, but we connected, wordless, in a bubble of silence amid the laughing and thanking and congratulating.

He'd gotten us the money *and* the lake!

And all along, I'd thought he was trying to cheat us somehow, when he was only trying to help us. Wrong! How could I have been so wrong, wrong, wrong?

Oh, God. The exterminator really had been Mr. Right, and I'd blown it. Totally blown it.

Eyes welling, I forced air into my lungs. "Thank you," I said, from the bottom of my heart.

He'd been right that night at the restaurant. He was the one who'd ended up being used, not me.

Only when my sisters mobbed him for a group hug did he wave them off, grinning. "Wait. There's more." The room fell quiet. "We are also providing free labor for our crews to build each of you a house and boathouse, with gazebo."

Iris and Rose and Vi went teeny-bopper crazy, but I felt too guilty to move. I'd been so wrong about him. Even when it had cost him our relationship, he'd kept his word.

The COO approached me with a wry chuckle. "Clete drives a hard bargain. He made your lots a condition of our participation from the get-go."

No wonder it had taken him so long to put together the deal. I scanned the faces and realized many of them had been at long-ago boathouse dances in my childhood. Oldies but goodies, these investors.

Not only did I have my home in Buckhead back, but I would have a new one at the lake.

If I could bear to go there.

I shook Rob's hand and croaked out a hoarse, "Thank you. Thank you so much. All of you."

He sobered. "Thank Clete."

Speak of the devil, Clete chose just that moment to walk up, and the COO discreetly stepped away. I saw a tiny shard of question in Clete's solemn expression, but I couldn't give him what he wanted, even after all he'd done.

Looking down, I told him, "I have to go home now." I couldn't bear his scrutiny another instant, afraid I'd shatter completely. "I have to go home." Clutching my papers and my purse, I turned and fled.

My sisters sent worried glances my way as I passed them, but I managed to escape to my car without having to explain. Half blinded by the tears I finally allowed, I put the car in gear and started back to Atlanta.

Just get away, I told myself. Get through the next few weeks without him. I could do it. I was a rational woman, not some teenager driven by hormones and emotions. Time would take away the pain, put our summer romance in perspective. Meanwhile, I'd concentrate on my son.

I'd made the right decision.

In time, the feelings would fall in line with what I knew I had to do. Concentrate on Junior. I could afford to go see him now. Try to talk some sense into him.

In time, I'd accept the wisdom of my decision about Clete.

But I still cried all the way to Clarkesville.

My eyes red and swollen, I stopped at Jaemore Farms and bought six hot dried-peach pies and three cold Coke Zeros, then ate and drank my way back to Buckhead, arriving at the Lenox Road exit stuffed and belching from all that fat. I got off the expressway and started for home, but decided at the last minute to go by the ballet school first. I needed to reenter my life where I'd be welcome, with plenty of people around me.

The lot was full of SUVs and hybrids. I had to park almost a block away on Buckhead Avenue, then walk back to our building and climb the exterior rear stairs to the office.

My key didn't work in the door!

Confused and more than a little insulted, I went back down and circled to the front, then took the stairway between the tailor's and the lamp repair shop to the second floor, the sound of dancing loud in my ears.

When I walked into the studio, I did a double take. Gone was the aging brick above the mirrors. Somebody had painted it *pink*! I hardly recognized the place. Everything but the trusty mirrors had been shifted around or replaced. The effect was fresh, but garish.

And everywhere, there were students and instructors, more than we'd ever had. I recognized several of my best girls teaching the little ones. Two of them spotted me and waved in delight.

An unfamiliar, officious young woman in leotards approached me with a clipboard. "Excuse me, ma'am, but could you please sign in and fill out this visitor's tag? It's for security purposes, something we started this summer, just to make sure all our little tutus are safe and accounted for."

I stared at her in indignation, then remembered what Mama Lou had always told us: *If you ever think you're irreplaceable, just stick your finger in a bucket of water, then pull it out and see what kind of hole you leave.*

No holes, here.

When I didn't respond, the girl poised her pen over the clipboard and asked a haughty, "Name, please?"

I went into duchess mode. "Dahlia Barrett Cooper, the owner of this establishment."

The girl had the good grace to be embarrassed. "Oh, Ms. Barrett, I mean, Ms. Cooper, please forgive me. I thought you moved to the mountains, and you don't, I mean . . ." She shot a glance at one of my old prima ballerina posters on the now-pink walls above the mirrors. In the reflection below, my outraged expression confirmed that my swollen eyes, sans makeup, and my red nose indeed did not resemble my former, glorious self.

I let out an exasperated sigh, then headed for the office. I opened the door and stepped in, took one look, then backed up to make sure I was in the right place. Everything had been rearranged, cleaned to within an inch of its life, stowed away, and painted white, including the heart pine floors.

An ice-cream set with colorful chair cushions stood in the alcove where broken equipment had been, brightened by light from a now-clean, curtained window. And a new microwave sat atop a new studio-sized refrigerator.

I heard a flush from our private bathroom, then Cathy emerged to find me glaring at her.

"Dahlia!" she said with a guilty expression. "I wasn't expecting to see you today." She collected her courage, chin rising. "How do you like the changes?"

Words failed me.

She arched her brows. "You said I could take care of anything that needed it, and this place had gotten really rundown looking, so when we had the leaks, I decided to organize and bring everything up to date. Frank and I cleaned and painted every chance we got for a month. And I had the dance floor refinished. Thanks to the extra money we're bringing in, I was able to have my son put in decent lighting and a new sound system, and still show a profit."

Seeing how proud she was and hearing how hard she'd worked, I relented with a sigh. "It looks just like you: clean and cheerful and vibrant." Unlike the arrogantly shabby, warm, classic New York loft look I'd loved. But what was done was done.

"I came to the back door first," I heard myself say with far more of an edge than I'd intended. "Why didn't my key work?"

She colored. "I'm so sorry. I left you a new key at the house, and a note explaining. I never dreamed you wouldn't go there first." She leaned in for a confidential, "I had to change the locks. After I inventoried everything and started tracking our supplies, I realized somebody had been stealing bottled water and snacks from back here, plus toner cartridges and a lot of other things. So I had the doors rekeyed and put up notices that we had discovered some thefts and put in a new alarm system. Haven't missed a thing, since."

"What kind of alarm system?"

She laughed and pointed to her eyes, then mine. "These, instead of those. But they don't know that."

Feeling totally inadequate and displaced, I nodded.

Her expression crumpled. "You're not happy," she said. "I was afraid you might not like it." Then hope reemerged. "But our enrollment has soared, and our costs have gone down. Thanks to bartering free lessons for our best senior girls if they teach the little ones, we're handling twice the students we were in May, and our junior instructors can put that on their résumés." She was so excited. "One of the senior girls is a whiz with computers, so she set us up with a whole new accounting system that makes payroll and expenses and taxes a breeze. We can e-pay everything but the insurance now, too."

Not me. I didn't know a thing about computer accounting. My few attempts had always ended in frustration when the program had asked me to go somewhere or fill out some document I had no idea how to find.

Seeing my bewildered expression, she turned big, kicked-puppy eyes my way. "Don't you like any of it?"

She'd meant well, I reminded myself. And she'd done a far better job than I ever had with the business.

It dawned on me that I wasn't needed there anymore, and I surprised myself by feeling as if a great weight had been lifted from me. I'd always left the stage before the applause died away, and I realized it was time to take my final bow.

"You did a great job, really," I reassured her. "As a matter of fact, I was wondering if you'd be interested in taking over the business." Her happy surprise took some of the sting out of becoming a has-been.

"I'd love to," Cathy said. "You know I would. But I don't have much money on hand, and credit is really tight—"

"No money up front," I heard myself say. What? "We'll work out reasonable payments, maybe a small percentage of your gross. Beyond that, all I ask is that you scholarship up to three girls of my choosing to train here." Nell Welch could be the first. She and her mother could stay at my house. Maybe I could get her mother in with some better doctors, too.

For once, my impulsiveness made perfect sense. "I'm seriously considering getting a vacation place close to my son, and I have no idea when I'll be back." This felt better and better. "And I'm buying a Prius. New. Tomorrow."

So there!

Cathy, bless her heart, burst into tears and hugged me within an inch of my life, alternating between gratitude and premature declarations of sadness that I was leaving.

I realized she might actually miss me, especially since we'd no longer be butting heads. "Could I still use the space for some special sessions?" I asked her.

"Of course," she cried. "We wouldn't be the same without you."

After extracting myself and making a stop at Henri's bakery for some chocolate éclairs and a roast-beef-on-onion-roll, I hitched up my get-along and headed home, down West Andrews and over to Habersham.

At the far end of the cul-de-sac beyond the shady, canopied streets of my neighborhood, there at last stood my house in all its Georgian splendor, nestled in immaculate grounds.

Too immaculate.

I looked closer as I drove up. Shoot! The lawn crew had pruned my double knockout roses into round mounds! And the gardenias! And my heritage roses.

Oh, no. My gorgeously spiked forsythias now looked like salmon croquetes!

What kind of idiot masquerading as a gardener had done *that*?

Fuming, I drove around back to the garage, past the sparkling pool surrounded with mounds of blooming red geraniums. Unloading could wait. I wanted to take a swim, then sit by the pool in a warm terry robe and eat my Henri's treats, even though I had barely digested all those fried pies.

I got out my key at the kitchen door and said a brief arrow prayer that it would work.

Happily, it did.

The house smelled of pine and freshness. Every window and surface sparkled. Cathy had stocked my refrigerator with the essentials and left the new key to the studio and her note next to a vase of dark red alstroemeria.

I took my swim, noting with surprise how loud the sound of traffic seemed. Then I sat in the late afternoon sun and savored every bite of my sandwich and dessert till the last piece of éclair, when the fried pies caught up with me and bloat rolled over me like the Blob. "Uuuhhh-hlllll."

I'd expected the others to call and make sure I'd gotten home okay, but they didn't, and I realized they were probably celebrating with their families.

Three months of looking forward to my solitude, and now all I felt was lonely.

You can't please some people.

Time for a warm shower, then bed.

I would not think of Clete. I would think of what lay ahead.

I washed my hair and shaved my legs, then put a towel over my head, closed the shutters, and climbed into my very own bed with the air-conditioning going strong against the city's heat.

Calling Junior could wait.

Maybe I wouldn't call—just surprise him, instead, when I got there. For that night, I curled between fresh sheets and finally breathed easy in the safety of my home, alone.

But even so, I dreamed of loss and loneliness, chasing some elusive goal through elaborate obstacles, then waking empty.

. . . .

FOR THE NEXT week, I rested and went to Divorce Anonymous meetings every chance I got, chasing some serenity about Clete. Rose and Vi and I exchanged calls only briefly, our conversations suddenly awkward. I didn't even talk to Vi about Clete, and she knew better than to ask. Whining would only make things worse.

I didn't hear from Iris at all, despite the brief thaw between us for the closing. She was probably swamped catching up with work, which suited me. I couldn't handle any pressure from her. We could go into my investments when I was ready.

Between meetings, I busied myself by planning my trip for the last two weeks in September, then finding a local realtor to help me research the condos where Junior lived in Paridalla. (Iris was right. The plane tickets cost a fortune.) Turned out, the condos where he and Harrison lived weren't condos at all, but rentals, which suddenly made the arrangement seem a lot less permanent, and I couldn't help wondering if Harrison had told him. To my surprise, I wasn't sure how I felt about that.

I wasn't sure about anything but trying to get over Clete.

I reserved the furnished penthouse for a month (dirt cheap) then shopped—very carefully and economically—for tropical clothes, deciding to wait till I got back to get the Prius.

Next I had a well-recommended business attorney draw up the agreement to sell my share of the business to Cathy. I kept the building as an income—assuming it made more than it cost, which was anybody's guess from year to year.

That kept me busy for a while, but the more I tried to distract myself, the more the truth kept nipping at my heels. My house seemed bigger and emptier by the day.

I called up all my friends and invited them out for lunch, but most of them demurred, saying they were too busy getting the kids ready for college, or looking after the grandchildren, or doing charity work. The few who accepted acted like polite strangers, and I began to realize that I was even less welcome in their tight, insular couples' world now that I was unattached with money.

A few men asked me out at the prodding of their sisters who knew me, but none of them held a candle to Clete. They were either culturally backward or heavy drinkers, and all of them looking for a mother, a meal ticket, or both.

As far as I could tell, the good ones were already taken. Along with all the marginal ones.

My newfound fortune hadn't changed any of that.

By the time I went to Paridalla, I was more than ready to get away from the noise and dirt and congestion of the city. And the growing loneliness inside my house.

I was already worn out by the time I landed in Hawaii, but the flight was late getting in, so I barely had time to stretch my legs before boarding a smaller plane to the Marshalls, then taking what looked like an ancient seaplane (!) to Paridalla Bay. When the captain/flight attendant/landing crew opened the door to let us board the waiting tender, heat and humidity slammed me like a Mack truck. Sore, dazed, and sleep deprived, I looked out to see a string of high-rises crammed tighter than Miami along dark beaches so crowded with people (mostly Japanese and Australians, as it turned out) that you could barely see the sand. Beyond Mondo Condo, a few garbage-heaped pockets of abject poverty clung to the base of the jungled mountains that marched inland to a roiling *volcano!*

No wonder the place was cheap.

My only son was living in Pompeii!

I clung to the tender's side as we bounced through the waves to a ramshackle dock that smelled of fish and gasoline. Then I climbed out and watched the driver complain bitterly in his native tongue as he unloaded my bags. Meanwhile, the other passengers left in all the waiting pedicabs and weird little half-truck-half-motorcycle taxis.

I tipped the driver generously and tried not to think about all the mold I was inhaling. Then I asked about a taxi.

He looked at my luggage, laughed, and took off in his boat.

Shit.

Left alone, I started moving one bag at a time to the road. I checked my international cell phone. No signal, even if I'd known who to call, which I didn't. I didn't even know their number for directory assistance—assuming they had one.

I scoped out the bar-slash-store across the street that emitted clouds of pot smoke and the sound of rough men's voices, and decided I might end up in the hands of slavers if I risked going in, so I started walking and sweating and moving my bags toward Mondo Condo, then walking and sweating and moving my bags a little more. Fortunately, I hadn't been doing it more than ten minutes when a battered motorcycle-slash-truck-slash-cab arrived in a gust of BO. "Hello, pretty lady," the plump driver said. "Where I take you?"

"Shangri La Apartments," I said, grateful for the chance to rest in the shade its canvas canopy provided.

The driver brightened. "Ah, velly good! At other end of island." He picked up my first bag and let out a grunt. "You got rocks in here, pretty lady?" He heaved it with dismaying force into the small load bed behind my seat, but I was too worn out to ask him to be gentler with my things.

Instead, I closed my eyes and imagined taking a long, cold shower in my "luxury" penthouse apartment, then sleeping for a few days before I surprised Junior.

"All full," the driver announced as he shoved my thirty-pound carry-on into my lap, almost knocking the wind out of me. "You carry."

Coughing and heaving, I barely managed to hold on as he took off like a bat out of hell, weaving between potholes, people, an assortment of domestic animals, and fruit stands as the buildings got closer together and nicer.

The driver merrily provided a running travelogue over his shoulder, completely ignoring the traffic signs when we finally got to some, and almost running down half a dozen hapless tourists.

Heart in my throat, I made a note not to get within a mile of any motorized vehicles.

By the time we arrived in front of the Shangri La, I didn't know whether to tip him or perform a citizen's arrest. Since it was such a small place, I opted for discretion and gave him a twenty after he filled the slightly rusted luggage cart from the unattended lobby.

Big mistake. Instead of helping me get my things to the apartment, he thanked me profusely, then took off with me calling after him.

I returned to no sign of anybody, wishing Junior would exit the elevator when I pushed the button and watched the floor indicator slowly drop to the lobby, accompanied by an alarming assortment of creaks and groans before it finally opened, empty.

At long last, I made it to Penthouse A, and sure enough, the keys were on the bar between the tiny kitchen and living room, all furnished in ersatz Polynesian, with terrazzo floors.

A hot, humid sea breeze blew in the open sliders to the balcony, and I stepped out to scan the crowded beach, but couldn't tell if Junior was there or not.

I didn't even know what apartment he was in.

After ransacking the apartment for a directory, I gave up and took a tepid shower. (The cold wasn't even cold.) Then I put on my briefest shortie gown and went to bed.

It took me three days to get over my jet lag and find out which two apartments Junior and Harrison lived in, then another before Junior called the number I'd left in the note I'd put under his door.

"Mom?" he said, clearly none too pleased.

"Thank goodness. I'm so glad to hear your voice, honey. I was afraid I'd come halfway around the world for nothing."

"Where exactly are you?" he asked, guarded.

"Here," I said. "Like I told you in the note. I came to see you."

"I thought you were broke." I might as well have been a debt collector.

Taken aback, I decided to go into that later. "Honey, I miss you. You're my son. I love you. I want to see you. Hug you." When that got no response, I tried a different tack. "Let me take you to dinner. Where's your favorite place? Sky's the limit."

"Too expensive for you. Dad won't even take me there anymore," he complained.

Aha. So even Dear Old Dad had his limits. Or maybe Barbie-doll had gotten tired of Junior's freeloading and laid down some limits. Welcome to my world.

"Meet me in the lobby, and I'll take you. Just name the time."

"People don't eat till late here," he said, still clearly suspicious. "Make it nine."

"Nine it is," I said cheerfully, resolving to snack beforehand.

"We're at the north end of the beach," he said, "at—"

I sprang my surprise. "I know, honey. I'm right upstairs."

"Upstairs!"

"Mmm-hmm. Penthouse A."

"In the same building?" he choked out, his voice breaking. "Does Dad know?"

"Of course not," I said, enjoying myself immensely. "I didn't come to see him, I came to see you. And I'd appreciate it if you didn't tell him, either. We both have our own lives now. I wouldn't dream of disturbing him."

"Whatever." Pregnant pause. "Did you win the lottery or something?" Junior asked with hope in his voice.

At last, I'd gotten through his sullen veneer. "You'll have to have dinner with me to find out."

"Damn, Mama. You don't even sound the same."

"Good, because I'm not. See you at nine."

I hung up and got a cold drink from the tiny refrigerator, then sat on the shady balcony watching the sea. But I soon got up, antsy. With hours to kill, I reconsidered my decision not to tell Harrison I was there, and decided to pay him a call instead. Then I got dressed to kill and went down to his apartment on the second floor, praying that he'd be home and answer the door.

My prayers were answered. Harrison's voice approached from the other side of the door. "I *told* you, I'm not giving you any more money this week, and that's that. If you choose to smoke up your whole allowance by Tuesday, it's no—" The door jerked open and Harrison took one look at me, then stopped in mid-word, slack-jawed.

"Tell him there won't be any allowance next week if he keeps bugging us," Barbie-doll hollered from the apartment.

"Dahlia," Harrison choked out as if I'd come back from the dead.

I couldn't resist. "Hi, honey. I'm now a U.S. Marshal, and you're under arrest."

His eyes and nostrils went wide.

"Just kidding," I told him with a grin. "Aren't you going to ask me in?"

Hearing a woman's voice, Barbie-doll appeared in the entryway. "Well, if it isn't the Saint of Buckhead." Claiming him, she took Harrison's arm and demanded, "What the hell is *she* doing here?"

I waggled my fingers her way with a smile. "I'm not deaf," I said cheerfully. "You may speak to me directly. I came to see our son, but decided it would be polite to drop by and say hello."

Barbie-doll stepped between me and my ex-husband to block the way. "Well, say good-bye. You are not welcome here."

Harrison bristled, taking her upper arms and drawing her back. "That's the mother of my son you're talking to."

"All the more reason to kick her out," Brandi retorted, then turned to me. "That son of yours has been soaking us dry since he got here."

I smiled sweetly. "Welcome to my world."

"This is my house, Dahlia," Harrison snapped at her, then corrected, "I mean Brandi, and I'll ask any-damn-body in I want to."

Outraged, she stomped away with a clatter of sandals.

Ah. Trouble in Paradise—or Paridalla, as the case may be. I surprised myself by not feeling smug. By not feeling anything.

"Please excuse Brandi," he clipped out. "She doesn't understand teenagers."

Considering Junior's behavior, I couldn't blame her.

"Come in." He motioned me toward the living room.

I entered to the sound and percussion of Brandi's slamming the bedroom door.

"Can I get you anything?" Harrison offered. "I'm afraid I don't have any sodas, just beer and wine on hand, but there's water."

"Nothing, thanks. I'm fine." And I was, in more ways than that. Funny, how alien this man who had been my husband seemed, as if we'd never shared a bed and a life for all those years. Looking at him, I saw a hassled, middle-aged stranger who looked at me with more than a smidgen of regret.

He sat, clasping his hands between his knees and staring down at the floor. "Dahlia, I'm sorry for what happened." Not what he did; what *happened*, like the changing of the seasons. "You didn't deserve it. But I was desperate. I kept thinking I could make back the money, but things just got worse and worse, and I didn't know what else to do."

Seeing him there—clearly, like the lake after the mist had risen—I wondered why I'd ever held on so tight in the first place. God bless them. He and Barbie Brandi would be penance enough for each other.

I actually felt pity that he'd ruined his whole life for money. And I grieved that our son had learned that lesson from him so well.

"That's all past," I said. "I'm not mad at you anymore, Harrison. I'm fine now."

"But the money," he argued, "you don't—"

"I'm fine. Really." I stood to leave, finally freed from his power to hurt me. "I really did come to see Junior, not you." I extended my hand and shook his when he stood. "No hard feelings. I'll let myself out. Tell Brandi I won't be coming again."

"You don't have to do that. Forget Brandi; she's as spoiled as Junior. Drop by anytime you want to." He searched my face. "Actually, it's good to see you."

I shook my head no. It would only hurt him to say that I was finally whole without him, so I didn't. "Good-bye, Harrison. Thanks for the good times. Try to think of those. I do."

Back in my penthouse, I sat back on the balcony and sucked down a cold iced tea, not even feeling the heat. All I felt was peace, and relief.

Then dinner rolled around, ruining everything.

By the time our entrées arrived, Junior had pestered me so much about how I was paying for everything that I weakened and told him Cissy had left me some money.

Dollar signs immediately appeared in his eyes. "How much?"

"Enough to get back on my feet."

"A lot then," he said, the wheels turning behind his eyes. He waved to the waiter. "Double Scotch, Inverness Black Label, neat." Then he turned back to me as if I were a prospect and he was a door-to-door salesman.

"Junior," I scolded mildly.

He shrugged, granting me a slick smile. "There is no minimum drinking age here."

The waiter set down his drink, from which Junior promptly took a long draw, without so much as a shudder afterward. "Did she leave any money to me? Is that why you came? I am her great-grandson."

I hated the mercenary gleam in his expression. "No. She left it to me and your aunts."

He frowned. "What about Mimi? Nothing for her own daughter? That's cold."

"Mama chose to let us have the money. She said she and David had enough."

A harsh laugh escaped him. "There's no such thing as enough money. You, of all people, should know that, working night and day, eating no-name crap from the grocery store, leaving the air-conditioning at eighty-damn-five and the heat at sixty."

I could tell he was talking about his own inconveniences, not mine.

"Never mind all that. I have enough now, that's all that matters, besides you." I took out the plane tickets I'd bought for him and laid them on the table. "I'm going home at the end of the month, and I was hoping maybe I could talk you into coming back with me."

He stiffened.

"Not forever," I qualified. "Just for a visit, if you want. I miss you so much, honey. You can come back here whenever you choose, but I was hoping you might want to give college another try. I can afford it, now. Whatever school you can get into. Your choice."

His eyes narrowed. "It must have been a *lot* of money."

"Honey, don't you want to get a degree so you'll have something to fall back on?"

"I don't want to go back to school," he clipped out. "I hate school, and I always have, and you know it. I want you to share some of that money with me because I'm your son and I need it. And I want you to accept me for who I am, not who you want me to be."

Scalded by his tone, I straightened and managed to keep my voice even. "I do accept you for who you are. I won't give you money, but I will gladly give you a future."

"Mom, I need the money," he wheedled. "That bitch Brandi wants all Dad's for herself, so she's poisoning him against me. He hardly gives me enough for food anymore."

"I know you might not understand this right now, but I care about you too much to give you money to spend on dope and booze."

"You don't care about me," he lashed out, turning mean so fast it took my breath away. "You're just embarrassed because your *sisters* and all my brainwashed cousins will know you have a dropout for a son."

"I don't give a rat's ass what anybody else thinks," I shot back. "But I refuse to bankroll a meaningless life of drugs and booze. What will you do when the money runs out? And it will run out. Even if I gave you all I had, it would eventually run out." I struggled to get a grip on my emotions, lowering my tone. "Isn't there anything you want to do, to be?"

"Yes," he snapped, "exactly what I'm doing and being, exactly where I'm doing it."

"Harrison," I pleaded, using his name for the first time in years. "Please. I only want what's best for you. I love you, but that doesn't mean I'll let you manipulate me. That's over."

Glaring, my only-begotten son slugged his Scotch, then took out a tightly rolled joint and lit up, sending a strong cloud of marijuana straight into my face.

Coughing, I gasped out, "Stop that this instant. Get high if you must, but do not inflict that on me."

"You need to get high. Maybe it would loosen you up," he said, his voice harsh and void of respect. "No wonder Dad left you. He couldn't stand living with a rigid, frigid bitch like you who never thought he was good enough, and I couldn't, either."

The accusation ricocheted through me like shrapnel, a deadly echo of what Iris had said. I bent almost double from the shock of it. My son, my only son, had said this thing, and he'd meant every word.

"Oh, right." He sneered. "Here comes the hypochondriac. Well, I'm not buying it, any more than Dad did." He stood, snatching up the plane ticket. "This might come in handy someday, but I'm not promising I'll use it to see you. You've made it perfectly clear that money means more than I do. If you want a relationship with me, send a check. Then we'll talk."

He strode past the waiter who was carrying our entrées. The man paused before setting them down. "Is Madame all right?"

What did he think?

"I'm . . ." Words failed me. I took a drink of bottled water, then managed a shaky, "I'm all right."

My son, my son. He was so lost—so cruel, so *wrong*—and he didn't even care. I loved him, but hated what he'd become, and my heart shattered all over again.

"The gentleman's food?" the waiter prodded politely.

It wasn't the poor guy's fault. Suddenly queasy, I scanned the nearby tables and saw a young couple being seated. "Send the food to them, all of it, with my compliments, and bring me the check. Quickly, please."

I couldn't get out of there fast enough.

Back in the penthouse, I threw up, then took two sleeping pills and retreated into dreamless oblivion. The next afternoon when I woke up hot and logy, it was to the same bitter reality I'd tried to escape.

For the next few days, I tried to call Junior a million times, but he blocked my number and hung up when I used a pay phone. So I ordered in and wore my knees out praying before I finally admitted there was no point in staying. Then I wrote a long letter to my son, explaining that I loved him exactly as he was, but I could no longer accept unacceptable behavior. If and when he wanted to reconcile, it would be with the understanding that he treat me with the same respect and kindness I would give to him.

Then I changed my tickets to the next flight. Not up to telling anybody but Vi about it, I tried to call her to say I was coming home early, but got her recording and had to leave a message. After slipping the letter under Junior's door on my way out, I mourned my way home across the vast Pacific and an entire continent.

Driving back from the Atlanta airport, I tried Vi for the fiftieth time and again got the message. I'd just plopped back down on the pity pot when my cell rang.

Vi. Thank God. "Hey."

"Hey, honey. Where are you?"

"On the Connector, stuck in gridlock after three days in an airplane."

"Uh-oh. Must not have gone well. How are you?"

"Awful," I confessed. "Junior was awful. And I hated that place. Just the ultrarich and the desperately poor, nothing between. Not that Junior would notice. He was too wrapped up in his own pleasures, which consist of smoking pot, drinking, partying all night, and sleeping all day."

A zigzagging idiot on his cell phone in a red sports car almost ran me off the expressway.

I shook mine at him and yelled, "Hang up and drive!"

"Maybe *you* ought to hang up and drive," Vi suggested, knowing how distractible I was when I was upset, much less upset and driving while on the phone. "Call me back after you get home in one piece."

"No," I hastened. "Please don't hang up. I don't do well alone anymore."

"Okay," she said. "Tell me what happened when you saw Junior."

I eased over to the right lane so I could take I-75 to the Northside Drive exit. "I told him I loved him and invited him to come home and give college another try, but all he wanted was money." I'd relived it so many times that repeating the words no longer had the power to pierce me, but hung like a stone in my soul. "When I refused, he blew weed in my face and went for the jugular. Called me a rigid, frigid bitch, then said his dad had left me because he was sick of never measuring up, and so was he."

Violet gasped. "That little bastard! I've half a mind to fly over there and take him to the woodshed. That boy needs a beatin'!"

"I don't know what he needs, but I know it's not money."

"Oh, honey. I'm so sorry. God knows, he didn't learn to act that way from you."

"Vi, I hardly knew Junior when he turned on me. He was so cruel, so hateful." I told her what he'd said about my loving money more than him.

"Dahlia," she responded evenly, "that wasn't him talking, it was his habits. He's hooked, and people like that say anything for money. But you know enabling will only make things worse, and you can't help him till he's ready to be helped. He'll hit bottom and want to get better."

My throat tightened. "That's what I've told myself for the past four days, but I don't think I believe me." Weary tears escaped along with the confession I'd been denying. "I told him I loved him just the way he was, but I'm not sure I can anymore."

"Oh, sweetie, you don't have to. But God can. Junior's still young and very stupid, and Harrison is hardly what you'd call a good role model. If anything, his father's responsible, either by nature or lack of nurture. With God's help, the boy'll grow up eventually."

"Harrison didn't."

"We'll just pray a hedge of thorns around Junior, then. And God can restore the love to your heart, even when he's acting like an idiot."

I started to change lanes and almost ran somebody else off the road. "Oh, sorry! Didn't see you there!" I waved in apology. "Sorry."

"You need to get off that phone before you kill yourself and somebody else," she said. "Do you need me to come? I don't like the idea of you holed up all alone in that big old house."

"You don't have to. I just want to go home and sleep for a few days. I'll be okay."

"You really don't want me to come?" she asked, skeptical. "Or do you want me to insist? Because I'd be more than happy to come. I'm coming."

"No, really, don't," I said, not up to the sympathy she'd bring. Solitude sounded more manageable.

"Okay, but call me if you change your mind, any hour of the day or night."

"I will." Suddenly, I needed very much to stop talking and be home. "Bye."

Remembering how I'd felt in the face of my son's rejection, I flashed on Clete's expression when I'd told him I couldn't marry him, and felt worse than ever. Had I hurt him as badly as my child had hurt me? God, I hoped not. And God, how I needed him now.

But that would be using him, wouldn't it? As selfishly as how Junior had tried to use me. Or would it?

Guilt and better judgment cried "No!" and "Yes!" at the same time, and I had no idea who'd said which.

When I let myself into the back door and disarmed the alarm, I waited for that familiar sense of belonging to bring me some comfort, but it didn't. Instead, the house felt huge and lonely and totally disconnected, just like Hilltop on that last day.

The clouds in my mind began to rise, and I realized my house was just a house. Perfect, sterile, and empty.

Suddenly I hated my furniture, my careful décor, hated all the useless trifles I'd accumulated. Hated my friends who weren't friends at all. Hated the shallowness that absorbed so many around me. Hated the shallowness of my own life with Harrison. Hated my *child,* God help me. Hated the financial security I'd sacrificed so much to win.

Hated the person I'd been.

And the gaping abyss opened by that hatred threatened to swallow me completely.

I'd been so blind, so stupid.

Clutching my suitcase, I sank, sobbing, to the middle of my heart pine floors in the kitchen. "Clete, help! I can't do this. Cleeete."

The thought of him burned like a faraway beacon in that abyss. But I'd ruined everything between us. Somehow, I had to find the strength to face my life alone. But how could I?

My cell phone rang, and I was too blinded by tears to see who it was. A soggy "Hello?" was all I could manage.

"Dahlia?" Iris's voice radiated concern. "Are you okay?"

Not her. Not then. "What do you want, Iris?"

"Vi told me what happened. I called to say I'm sorry. Not just about that, but for a lot of things. I've been going to counseling, and it's helped me see how unfair I've been to you. Dahlia, I'm so sorry. Please forgive me."

She'd had time to think. She was sorry. She wanted forgiveness. Absolution.

But I didn't have anything left to give. I was too empty. "I can't talk about this, Iris," I told her, tears sheeting down my cheeks. "I can't talk about anything. I just want to go to sleep and not wake up. It's too hard. Everything's too hard."

I hung up and lay down on the floor, not feeling anything but despair. My cell phone rang again and again, but I didn't answer. I didn't care. The house phone rang, too, but I stumbled to my room and turned it off, then lay across the bed.

I don't know how long I cried there before I fell asleep. It was dark when the sound of the back door unlocking woke me. Too worn out to be frightened, I didn't even react when I heard someone hurry in. "Dahlia?" Iris called from the kitchen, bald panic in her voice. "Are you okay? Dahlia!"

Who gave *her* a key? I didn't.

Go away. Leave me alone.

I closed my eyes tighter, trying to retreat into sleep, but she wouldn't let me. She came into my room and rolled me onto my back, her face limned in fear. "Dahlia."

"Please," I begged her, my voice sounding flat even to me. "Just leave me alone. I'm okay. Just go."

"Dog dammit," she lashed out. "You scared the bejeezus out of me! I was afraid you might do something to yourself. It took forever for me to find Rose and get the alarm code and find out where you hide the key. Shit!" She burst into tears, shaking me. "Let me help you. I'm your sister."

I turned away from her. "I'm miserable, not suicidal. You don't have to be jealous of me anymore. I royally screwed up my marriage and my son and my life. I hope that gives you some sense of satisfaction. Get out of my house, Iris. Leave me alone."

Still crying, she snatched me up to cradle my head against her shoulder. "No. I won't. I know I've been an awful sister to you, but that's over. I am helping you. I'm getting you what you really need. Dahlia, you deserve to be happy. I want you to be happy. I swear to God, I do."

I wrenched from her embrace and turned my back, curling on my side. "Leave me alone." Why wouldn't she go?

"No. I'm staying. I won't bother you, but I'm staying."

Again, time went fuzzy, till the sound of a car racing up the driveway pulled me from my fog. Brakes halted it with a screech, then doors opened.

Iris stood. "It's going to be all right, Dahlia." Then she left, at last.

As I curled back into a tight ball, I heard pounding footsteps and Iris say, "She's in there."

The footsteps pounded close. I didn't have to open my eyes to recognize the feel of Clete's arms around me when he scooped me up off the bed and held me tight, swaying back and forth. "I'm here, honey. Iris called me, and I'm here. It's all right." Shaking, he sank to sit on the bed with me in his arms. "It's all right."

The back door closed, and outside I heard Iris say I was okay, then Rose reply "Thank God" in relief. Then a car drove away, leaving just the two of us there.

Clinging to Clete, I sobbed out, "I can't do it by myself anymore. I need you." Just saying the words released the torrent of love and hunger I'd denied. "Can you forgive me for hurting you? I'm so sorry."

"God, yes," he choked out, kissing my temple, then both my eyes.

If he could forgive me, I could forgive Iris, and Junior. Just thinking it made me know it was already true. "Thank you," I breathed into the clean, comforting scent of him. "Thank God."

My hand slid up to cup his head, making sure he was really there and not a dream.

He gasped, then tightened his hold and started to rock me gently, his cheek against my hair.

"I love you," I told him, surprised at how easily it came and how deeply true it was.

He nodded, barely breathing.

I opened my eyes to see that his head was thrown back, eyes closed as if in pain, and I was suddenly afraid the truth had come too late.

No, no, no. I tried to sit up. "I'm sorry. I shouldn't have—"

Holding fast, he bent and stopped me with a tender kiss, then cupped my head against his chest. "Thank God." It rumbled through his bones to mine. "Thank God you did." He shifted to search my face, stroking my cheek with one of his big, work-worn hands. "I don't know if I could have stood another day without you."

Comforted at last, I whispered, "I don't belong here anymore. Please take me home." My heart still ached, but I knew I was finally safe.

His eyes welled, lips compressed and nostrils flaring as he nodded. "Only if you marry me."

"Of course."

At last, he smiled. "Tonight?" he hoped aloud.

Taking our families into consideration, I said, "Saturday." That gave us time to get the license. "Can Ted do the service?"

The lines around his eyes relaxed. "Absolutely. Where?"

That was easy. "Boat Church. Our house, if it rains."

Clete's eyes began to dance. "What time?"

I considered. "Two." That would give everybody plenty of time to get there.

"Perfect. I'll have the east wing ready for your family to stay over."

I pulled back. "Thanks, but no thanks. I do not want our wedding night to be a family affair. After the ceremony, we can have an early reception, then everybody can go home. I want you, and our house, to ourselves."

"Sounds like a plan." He rose as if I weighed nothing in his arms. "Come on, then. I'm putting you to bed."

Not *taking* me to bed. *Putting* me to bed.

"But I want to go home with you."

Clete's brows knit in pained frustration. He laid me onto the bed, then faced me and stroked my eyebrow with his thumb. "Dahlia, my love, if I

don't get out of here, and get out fast, we're both going to end up doing
something we know better than to do."

My libido cried *No!* but my conscience said *Thank God for an old-
fashioned Christian man.* I sighed and admitted, "You're right."

"You're sure you're okay here alone, now?" he asked.

"Yes." I hugged him, tight. "I'm not alone, really. Not anymore." We
were part of each other, at last.

He'd waited for me for a lifetime. I could wait for him till Saturday.

I lay back down. "Where are you going?" I hadn't even asked how he'd
gotten there so quickly, but surmised he must have choppered in after
Iris's SOS.

He cocked that wry smile of his. "To the nearest hotel with a treadmill,
where I plan to run myself into the ground."

The hunger in his face made my insides flip. "Do I need to call you a
cab?"

"No. Rose said she'd leave me her car and ride home with Iris."

"You're not going back to the lake?"

He shook his head. "Not till I take you for the wedding. I don't want
to let you get away, so plan to spend the rest of the week with me." He
kissed my hands, then let them go. "How about breakfast at the Original
Pancake House in the morning?"

I nodded, suppressing a yawn as peace suffused me. "Not too early."

"I'll call."

"I'll answer."

He backed toward the kitchen. "I'll lock the door on my way out."

"I'll walk you there." I followed, hoping for another of those exqui-
sitely tortuous nothing-but-a-kisses.

I got my kiss, and a few more besides, till Clete tore himself away and
jogged to Rose's car.

Too aroused to sleep, I went back inside and called Mama to tell her,
then invited my sisters to my wedding.

· 27 ·

The only people who ought to get married are the ones who absolutely,
positively, can't help it.
—CISSY, CIRCA 1923

. . . .

*Y*OU LOOK SO perfect," Iris said that Saturday in the bathroom at
Hanson's as she adjusted one of the full-blooming pink roses
that flanked my chignon. "This color is perfect."

Mama would have done it, but David had come down with the flu, so
they couldn't make it. She'd said it was probably better luck that way,
since she'd been to my first one, and we both knew how that had turned
out. I smiled remembering the happiness in her voice when I'd told her
about the wedding.

Rose handed me my little bouquet that matched my simple pink wrap
dress. "Looks like it's time."

"How many flower girls did we end up with?" Vi asked through the
open door.

"Four," Iris told her. "And three ring bearers." All of them Clete's great-
nieces and -nephews.

For a simple wedding, this one sure had gotten out of hand, but I

didn't mind. I wanted everybody to have a good time and feel important, so four flower girls and three ring bearers it was. And all of Clete's
siblings and in-laws were groomsmen and bridesmaids along with my
sisters, with Hoke as the best man and Vi as my matron of honor, all in
their Sunday best.

Clete's family had laid out a spread you wouldn't believe back at the
house.

A decidedly bluegrass version of Handel wafted our way.

"It's time," Vi told me. When I joined her, she asked quietly, "Any res-
ervations?"

"Not a one."

She smiled. "Good, because if there were, we all agreed to make you
go through with it anyway."

I grinned. "I can't tell you what that means to me."

"What?" she shot back from our childhood repartee. "Tell."

"I told you, I can't tell you," I finished, and we laughed like we had
when I was twelve and she was eight and thought that was the funniest
thing she'd ever heard.

When our line of sight got above the stairs to the road, I stopped in
shock. There had to be at least three hundred people there, spilling out
of the Boat Church onto the lawn. When the rest of the wedding party
waiting at the rear saw us coming, a buzz and a shuffle rippled through
the crowd from back to front, and everyone parted down the middle, smiling as they watched us approach.

"Where did they all come from?" I asked through a fixed smile as I
started toward Clete at the other end with his brothers.

"Beats me," Violet answered. "Maybe Ted drummed them up with
the pontoon boat and the megaphone."

I couldn't help but laugh as we joined the rest of the wedding party.

Then the bluegrass band struck up with the processional, and the
flower girls preceded the ring bearers (two of whom shared one pillow,
which led to a subtle but insistent tug-of-war down the aisle).

Next came Clete's sisters-in-law, then his sisters, then mine, which
barely left room in front of Ted for the bride and groom.

All the while, Clete kept his eyes on me as if I'd disappear if he looked
away.

Everything went fine till I got halfway to the pavilion and I saw the sheriff standing just ahead of me with a warrant in his hand, a frown on his face, and his eyes boring in on me.

He knew about the bodies. I could see it, clear as day.

Please, God, don't let me get arrested at my own wedding!

I halted, eyes wide, not knowing what to do.

Then I took a step backward.

Clete took a lurch toward me, clearly thinking I was about to bolt. "Dahlia, don't!"

I took another step back, prompting my sisters to hiss alarmed instructions to stop, and an even louder murmur from so great a cloud of witnesses.

That did it. Clete said to the guests, "Please sit tight and excuse us for a moment. I need to have a word with my bride." Then he strode after me as I turned tail, hyperventilating, and made for the bathroom.

Hot on my heels as I went inside, he caught the frame of the door and filled the space, blocking out the sunny afternoon. "What?"

"I can't marry you without telling you . . . There's something bad," I blurted out. "Clete, those bodies, the Dancing Santa ones . . . they were in the root cellar at Hilltop. We found them by accident. Rose wanted the chairs. My sisters wanted to call the police, but I was afraid it would delay the closing, so I bagged them up and moved them, then phoned in the tip. I'm a criminal. The sheriff's out there, and he knows."

Instead of getting upset, Clete burst out laughing and grabbed me, then pulled me outside. "I know all about it!" He picked me up and spun around, his head laid back as he guffawed. "Chuck's not going to arrest you. I told him all about it." He frowned. "I'll have to have a few words with him about scaring you like that. Some wedding present."

I stiffened in his arms. "You told him? How did *you* know?"

"Cissy told me about those mummies a long time ago."

"Cissy!" And she hadn't warned us! "Do you know who the mummies were?"

Nodding, Clete did his best not to smile. "Your great-grandmother's brother and his aide from World War One. They got gassed in the trenches, and after the war, they took to making moonshine. Since it kept him busy, your great-grandparents looked the other way. But one day when your great-grandmother went into Clayton, she found the whole town up in arms about seven deaths attributed to bad moonshine, from the mayor to the Methodist minister to the town drunk. She hurried home to tell her brother, but when he didn't turn up by the next morning, she sent your great-granddaddy to the still to look. He found them, all right, dead from their own bad hooch.

"Your great-grandmother was so mortified by the shame of it that she salted them down, then buried them in the root cellar and told everybody he'd moved to Florida for his health."

I saw red. "And you didn't warn us?"

He winced. "Actually, I'd forgotten all about it till I saw the changes in the root cellar door. I was trying to make you like me; I was afraid you'd get mad at me for not warning you, so I didn't say anything. But when the bodies turned up—those bags had to be Rose, right?—I figured out what had happened and told Chuck." The sheriff. "He got quite a kick out of it, but let the publicity go on for a while. It was good for business."

I heard a scrape of gravel, then kid-steps retreating from the top of the stairs. "Hey, y'all!" a boyish voice hollered toward the wedding guests. "Guess what!"

I was too mad at Clete to care that the cat was out of the bag. Inflated in outrage, I pulled free of him, my feet planted wide in combat-ready posture. "And you didn't tell *me*? All this time, you let me think I'd committed a crime?" I swatted his arm with my bouquet, petals flying.

"Ow!" he exaggerated.

"Do you have any idea how many nights I lay awake and worried that I might have talked my sisters into committing a *felony*?" I blurted out, then realized I'd just implicated them. Shit!

"Well, if you'll recall," he responded evenly, "I wasn't exactly at the top of your list at the time. But I took care of it."

The buzz of conversation from the Boat Church pavilion rose to a roar punctuated by laughter.

I pointed toward the top of the stairs. "Now everybody in town knows! I'll be a laughingstock."

Clete took my face into his hands and kissed me, hard and quick. "No you won't. You'll be a legend," he said with pride, then hustled me back up the steps with a firm arm around my waist. "Come on. You can be mad at me all you want, but we're getting married now."

372   Haywood Smith

As we came into view, the entire crowd burst into cheers and applause.

I couldn't very well stay mad at him in front of everybody, so I let out a sigh of resignation and walked beside him with as much dignity as I could muster. Grinning despite Clete's poisonous glance as we approached him, Sheriff Chuck tore up the bogus warrant.

Then, just as we reached Ted and the crowd fell silent, the giant hawk swooped into view and circled to land on the railing just to his right.

Everybody froze in awe.

The hawk blinked and sat right where he was, as if he'd come to give his benediction.

Even a stir among the children didn't faze him.

Then Ted began. "'Dearly beloved, we are gathered in the sight of God and this company—'"

The rite was simple and to the point, the vows traditional, and then we were saying, "I do."

The hawk waited until Ted introduced us to the congregation as Mr. and Mrs. Clete Slocum to soar away amid a welcoming roar of applause and good wishes. It was the last time I ever saw him.

Halfway down the aisle, I halted again. "Oh, good Lord."

Clete looked at me in mild exasperation. "What is it now?"

I pulled a face. "I just realized my last name is *Slocum!*"

For the second time that day, he let loose laughing, and once again, the joke was on me. "I *know!*"

Take my word for it. By the next morning, I did not mind a bit. Trust me, he was worth it.

Everything in that whole awful, wonderful summer was worth it, and the long years leading up to it, because I'd found my bug man, and I was living and loving with my eyes wide open at last. Thanks be to God—and Cissy—amen.

Turn the page for a sneak peek at
Haywood Smith's new novel

Waking Up in Dixie

AVAILABLE FALL 2010

The present: Whittington, Georgia

THE SUNDAY AFTER CHRISTMAS, ELIZABETH knelt in the pew beside Howe and prayed for help to forgive him for his greed and lack of love, then went through the motions of the service by his side, as she had for more than a quarter of a century.

When it came time for the sermon, Elizabeth settled back and tried to look interested, though she knew the message would be anything but. Father Jim's sermons had been dry as melba toast lately.

Men of the Whittington family had been falling asleep—sitting up—in the second pew of St. Andrew's Episcopal Church since their ancestors had built the place in 1793, and Howe was no exception. So Elizabeth took little notice when he went rigidly still beside her while their aged minister made a thready connection between the daily Epistle reading and the topic of global warming.

Her mind wandering, Elizabeth tuned out the priest's monotonous delivery, suppressing a sigh. Normally, she accepted the humdrum of her weekly routines with gratitude—she'd had enough drama the night of the party to last her for quite a while—but on this particular Sunday, the minister got on her last nerve.

She looked across the aisle to see her mother-in-law focused on the priest as if he were delivering the Word of Heaven straight from God Almighty, which only annoyed Elizabeth more.

Father Jim was a kind man, but wholly ineffectual, and clearly out of ideas for his homilies. The man needed to retire, and that was all there was to it. Unless St. Andrew's got somebody livelier, the Baptists would end up with all the young people.

The Baptists might just end up with *her*—a thought that made Elizabeth smile, even though she knew she'd never dare. Her mother-in-law would disown her for sure, and there was already no love lost, no matter how hard Elizabeth had tried to win the woman's approval.

As the sermon meandered on, Elizabeth discreetly opened her purse and glanced down at her pocket calendar to review the upcoming week: Women's Club tomorrow; bring her strawberry flan.

Errands and shopping in Atlanta on Tuesday, as usual, and lunch with P.J. They hadn't seen each other since before the party, so she was looking forward to it even more than usual. Her ego really needed a boost. She wanted to tell P.J. what had happened at the party.

Nobody knew Elizabeth had been seeing P.J., and nobody needed to.

It was all innocent enough. She'd bumped into him a couple of times back in September on her regular Tuesday shopping trips to Phipps Plaza, and they'd chatted about their old high school days over lunch at Maggiano's, hitting it off immediately. P.J. lived and worked nearby, and they both loved the restaurant, so they'd fallen into splitting the huge servings every week, but lunch was all it was. Elizabeth wasn't about to risk her reputation with anything more.

Even so, people might not understand that the relationship was strictly platonic. On her part, anyway.

As the minister droned on, she focused back on her calendar. Sewing Circle Tuesday night—or "whine and cheese" as some of the husbands called it, where she offered sympathy, but never breathed a word about her own sterile marriage or friendship with P.J.

Altar Guild Wednesday; remember to pick up the altar cloths from the cleaners on the way.

Teeth cleaned and whitened on Thursday.

And her regular hairdresser's appointment on Friday; not so dark with the color this time.

Respectable. Predictable. A decent life, all in all.

She and Howe would see each other in passing, always pleasant, always polite.

Even though Howe had helped her friends, he'd only done it under duress. So she'd given him the cold shoulder all week. Now, though, guilt told her she should be happy that Howe had relented about the Harrises. She ought to be happy enough with her life.

She focused on the blessings God had given her. Their son Charles was such a darling, and even spoiled Patricia would eventually come to appreciate her as a mother one day, if only when she had children of her own.

Speaking of mothers, Howe's mother was mortal and past her mid-eighties; that was big on Elizabeth's gratitude list. Augusta Whittington would croak one day, and Elizabeth would be the one who could rest in peace. No longer would she be Princess Di under her mother-in-law's critical eye. The thought relaxed her.

Maybe next weekend Elizabeth would slip away and take a drive up into the mountains. She was free. Charles and Patricia wouldn't be coming home from college for another month— unless Patricia ran out of money again, in which case, she'd show up at the bank and wheedle it out of Howe before going back to Athens. If the weather was bad, she could read. She loved to read, as long as the books had happy endings.

Something ought to have happy endings.

The pipe organ signaled the end of the sermon and her daydreams, so she stood and opened to the hymn she'd marked with her order of service. She got through the first line before realizing Howe hadn't risen beside her. Mortified that he hadn't woken up, she gave his foot a firm poke with her own, but he remained seated, eyes closed.

Everybody in the rows behind her could see, so she tipped slightly toward him and said out of the corner of her mouth, "Howell, wake up."

Usually, the use of his name was enough to get his attention, but he didn't respond.

Elizabeth bent to whisper an adamant, "Howell, wake up!" in his ear, but when she did, he started to tilt toward her, his eyes still closed.

A bolt of alarm shot through her as she sat and pushed him back erect. "Howell?" she whispered, gripping his arm.

Dear God, he was pale as paste, and stiff.

But his chest was moving. He was breathing.

Elizabeth turned to see Mitt Wallace from the club on the row just behind them. She grasped his forearm and drew him toward her. "Mitt," she whispered as the choir started recessing down the aisle, "something's the matter with Howell. Help me get him out."

Her husband would be humiliated if anybody realized the state he was in. God forbid he should have a seizure in public, or worse. His battle-axe of a mother had made it clear from the beginning that appearances must be maintained at all costs, and Elizabeth had spent the past quarter of a century seeing that they were.

So far, the recessional had distracted everyone enough to keep them from realizing what had happened. By some miracle, Howe's mother was busy mouthing for Catherine Wilkerson to meet her in the vestibule as the choir passed, so she didn't barge in and take over.

Mitt came around and helped Elizabeth lift Howell. At six one, Mitt was as tall as Howe, but even with adrenaline working in their favor, they struggled to get Howe up and out into the side aisle, then into the minister's study as inconspicuously as possible, his feet dragging across the polished stone floors.

Once in the study, they heaved him onto the velvet three-cushion sofa.

Mitt grabbed the desk phone and called 911, while a panicked

Elizabeth rubbed her husband's hand and demanded, "Howell, can you hear me? Howell!"

"My friend is unconscious," Mitt told the 911 operator. "He's breathing, but unconscious. We're in the minister's study at St. Andrew's Episcopal in Whittington." Pause. "He just closed his eyes in church and didn't open them again." Pause. "No. He never drinks too much." Mitt turned to ask Elizabeth, "What medications does he take?"

"None. He's healthy as a horse." At least, he had been, till this happened.

"None," Mitt repeated, along with the rest. He scowled. "How should I know?" He immediately reconsidered. "No. No drug use. No pot, no cocaine, no nothing." Pause. "Trust me, I'd know."

Everybody who knew Howell knew he'd never indulge in anything that might interfere with his iron control of his life. The sole exception to that was his doting affection for their daughter. He'd been wrapped around Patricia's little finger from the moment she was born. But that was his only weakness. Except for the floozies, but they were just nameless sex objects, a fact that made the situation bearable.

"All right," Mitt said. "I'll be waiting for them out front. But please, ask them to cut the siren before they get here. Church is just letting out, and he wouldn't want a scene." Mitt hung up. "They're on their way. Ten minutes, tops. What can I do?"

Elizabeth shook her head. "I don't know. He's breathing. His heart's beating. He's just not responding." She laid her head to his chest, the most intimate contact they'd had in years. "It's kind of fast, but it's beating."

There had been many times when she'd dreamed about the compensations of genteel widowhood, especially since she'd been seeing P.J. She'd imagined what it would be like not to cater to Howe's rigid habits; not to have his private peccadilloes hang over her, threatening her precious respectability. But now that she faced the possibility, panic pounced on her. "Howe," she said, maintaining a calm exterior by sheer act of will. "You're going to be all right. The paramedics are on the way. Hang on. Don't leave me." She shocked herself at how frightened she felt.

Then her husband did something he hadn't done in years: he laughed—a sharp, disjointed guffaw. One, loud, bizarre laugh, then silence.

I died laughing shot through Elizabeth's mind, and the panic tightened, but Howe kept right on breathing, his eyes closed to tiny slits, with no movement beneath his lids. She shook him. "Howe?"

Why would he laugh?

He couldn't be playing possum. Howe never, ever joked.

The door to the study opened, but it was only the priest. "Sorry," he said, hesitating. "I didn't know anyone was—" Father Jim registered what was going on and became grave. "What's happened? Heart attack? Have you called 911?"

"Don't know what's the matter," Mitt said. "I already called for an ambulance. They're on their way."

The priest hastened over. "I know CPR. When did this happen?" he asked Elizabeth.

"He just closed his eyes during the sermon and didn't open

them again," she explained. "Out cold, sitting up. But I don't think he needs resuscitating."

"Good Lord," the priest said. "I should have listened when my wife told me that sermon was lethal." He wrung his hands. "Not that I wouldn't be in good company. Saint Paul bored a man to death with his preaching once—guy fell out the window—but he was able to resurrect him."

What?

Appalled, Elizabeth stared at him in consternation. "Joking? Are you joking?"

Mitt made things worse by letting out a shocked chortle, then said, "It's like the one about the Episcopalian who died sitting up during the sermon, and the paramedics had to haul out fifteen people before they found the right one."

"Kindly do not talk about dying," Elizabeth snapped. "Howell is right here, and we don't know what's the matter yet."

"Please forgive me," the priest asked.

Penitent, the two men exchanged rueful glances, then Mitt headed for the door. "I'll go wait for the paramedics," he volunteered.

It seemed like eons, during which Elizabeth gauged every breath her husband took, but only ten minutes passed before the metallic rattle of a stretcher on the flagstones preceded the paramedics. They came in and immediately started hooking up leads and an IV as they relayed symptoms into their radiophones. After overhearing that Howe's blood pressure was elevated and his heart regular, but fast, Elizabeth tapped one of the paramedic's shoulders. "What is it?"

"We can't be sure, but my guess is, Mr. Whittington may have had a stroke," he told her. "We've administered medications to lower his pressure, but the sooner we can get him to the hospital, the better his chances for recovery."

His *chances* for a recovery. Elizabeth's heart sank. The nearest hospital was forty minutes away, and its emergency services were notoriously inadequate.

Suddenly, the sound of a helicopter grew louder and louder outside, then she heard a vehicle zoom up, then halt with a screech of brakes.

The paramedics raised the stretcher and started for the door with Elizabeth close behind, but before they got there, the side door of the church burst open and Howell's mother stormed in with four uniformed medical attendants hot on her heels, bearing a sleek, plastic patient transport. A force of nature at eighty-five, Augusta Whittington clipped out, "I heard on the scanner. We're airlifting him to Piedmont. My neurologist and neurosurgeon will be there waiting. And the best cardiologist in town."

For once, Elizabeth was grateful for her mother-in-law's interference. "Thank God. Bless you, Mother Whittington."

The woman glared at Elizabeth as if what had happened was all her fault. "This is my only son. I'll move heaven and earth to get him the best care possible." She motioned for the attendants to transfer him to their stretcher.

Clearly insulted to have their patient usurped, the local paramedics nevertheless stepped aside without comment, because nobody in Whittington—or the state of Georgia, for that matter—dared cross Augusta Whittington. But the whole scene would be grist for the gossip mill within minutes.

"I'm grateful for the medevac," Elizabeth told her mother-in-law. "I'll call your cell as soon as we find out anything."

"Call, nothing," her mother-in-law said. "I'm going with him."

The lead attendant raised a staying palm. "I'm sorry, Mrs. Whittington, but we only have room for one extra person besides the patient, and for legal reasons, it should be his wife."

Mrs. Whittington shot him a look that would shatter granite, but he didn't relent, and as Elizabeth followed the stretcher out, her mother-in-law flipped open her cell phone and dialed, then barked out, "Eddie Spruill"—the local sheriff—"this is Augusta Whittington. I'm at St. Andrew's. Howell has been stricken ill, and they're choppering him to Piedmont. Come get me this instant and take me to the hospital." She scowled in outrage. "I don't care if you're eating. The Golden Corral will be there when you get back, but if you're not here in five minutes, you'll be going home without that badge, and you know I can do it." She snapped the phone shut as Elizabeth followed the stretcher past her toward the waiting chopper.

"Don't you let anything happen to him before I get there," Augusta called after her. "I'm holding you responsible if it does, Elizabeth."

Of course.

As the chopper took off, Elizabeth watched her world grow smaller and smaller, and wondered if she would still be the wife of the richest, most powerful man in the county when she came home.

> "A veritable gold mine of Southern homespun homilies and hospitality, where the Ya-Ya Sisterhood would feel right at home."
> —*Booklist*

Lin tries to navigate her way through the second act of her life with nothing more than a broken heart and plenty of Prozac....

Five longtime friends plot revenge against one of their cheating husbands in a story that serves up laughter, plenty of wine, and the power of friendship.

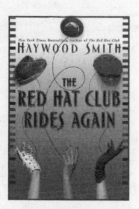

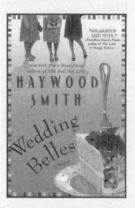

After one of their friends falls off the wagon, The Red Hat Club stage a hilarious kidnapping to Vegas to prove that when all else fails, they will see you through.

The Red Hat story continues when one of their daughters gets engaged and the intended groom is a man *they* went to high school and college with....